喚醒你的英文語感！

Get a Feel for English !

TOEIC® Master
英語認證測驗國際標準版

New TOEIC® Reading

新多益大師指引

閱讀滿分關鍵

2018
題型
更新版

作者／多益滿分專家 **文喬**

命題 **David Katz**

貝塔語言出版
Beta Multimedia Publishing

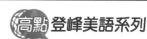
高點登峰美語系列

作 者 序

　　在英文的 Listening、Speaking、Reading、Writing（聽／說／讀／寫）四個技巧當中，Listening（聽）和 Reading（讀）是屬於接收訊息 (input) 的能力，在取得資訊、瞭解內容、消化並融會貫通之後，也才有可能做 Speaking（說）和 Writing（寫）以表達意見 (output) 的動作。因此，透過 Reading 閱讀來吸收新知、增加單字量，並進而訓練理解能力的重要性可見一斑。

　　2018 年在台灣實施題型更新的新多益測驗中，針對 Reading 閱讀部分的改變頗多，不但增加生活中的手機訊息等題材、新增插入句題，還將題組類的文章篇數由雙篇增加到三篇，新型態的多益測驗對閱讀理解與文章處理的重視自然不在話下。新制多益在閱讀部分的變革，包括將文章長度拉長，原本九篇單篇增為十篇單篇文章，題組的部分則是有兩組雙篇和三組三篇的文章，如此加總起來亦即多達二十三篇文章要處理。尤其經過聽力與文法的作答後，考到最後一部分閱讀題時，精神體力都消耗得差不多了，在最後四十分鐘的時間內，不單單要閱讀二十三篇文章，並找出上下篇的關連性，還要找答案回答問題，回答問題之前可能還要做同義字的轉換，其挑戰性其實是相當高的。

　　筆者最常聽到應試者的考後心得就是「時間太趕，文章看不完！」的確，僅七十五分鐘可處理文法題目和多篇的閱讀文章，時間是相當緊迫沒有錯。那麼，考試單位為何如此設計？何不給考生兩個小時慢慢欣賞文章再答題？其中原因便是，希望考生不要逐字地閱讀，而是要具備「可分辨主要資訊和次要資訊」的能力；將專注力全部集中到僅處理「主要資訊」──「足以回答問題的關鍵點」上即可，而非將注意力發散到無關緊要的訊息上。再者，要能判斷「主要關鍵點」之處，就要靠技巧的運用了。考生應試時，務必心無旁鶩，非常明白哪些是問題所問之重要資訊、哪些細節其實是不用花時間看的、該如何精準地鎖定題目之解答，而非陷入一堆密密麻麻的英文字當中而迷失了方向。有鑑於此，本書將討論針對新題型的閱讀策略、應試技巧，再搭配模擬試題，期望讓同學不僅可以在規定時間內抓到文章大意，還能準確地回答題目，取得高分。

另外，除了為了考試取得理想分數，建議讀者還要思考一件事——您想從準備新多益當中獲得什麼不一樣的英文學習體驗？這個問題的重要程度絕對不亞於考取高分這個目標！新多益考試內容聚焦於辦公環境、行銷業務、出差旅遊、客戶服務等情境，也就是說，只要是可能發生在日常生活或職場的狀況，如 email 或信函，都有機會出現在新多益的考題中。既然都是生活與工作上無可避免一定會遇到的狀況了，那麼不如就趁此準備的契機，也好好地將閱讀能力建立起來。藉由準備新多益的閱讀考題，來瞭解日常辦公情境中會接觸到的電子郵件溝通、新聞報導、廣告文案和商業報告等，並熟悉這些商務書信的格式、內容和用字，如此對自己整體的閱讀能力之提升與日後在職場上的應用，亦都助益匪淺！

於當今網路發達、資訊爆炸的時代，在網路上找到的許多資料皆以英文呈現：學生在學校得讀英文原文書，上班族在公司裡須以英文寫報告、打 email、看英文企劃書等，這意味著英文閱讀在您我的日常生活當中是無法避免的。現在起就讓我們開始以新多益 Reading 為跳板，一起來領略英文閱讀與洞悉文意的美妙之處吧！

文喬

CONTENTS 目錄

Part 3　模擬試題解析

Part 4　實用商務字彙補給（同義字 600 組）

Part 1

閱讀攻略

閱讀奪分技總透視

在深入討論英文閱讀策略之前，請讀者先回想一下傳統的英文閱讀方式。一般都是拿到原文書之後，便自第一行開始逐字地看，中間遇到生字就停下來翻查字典，在將中文意思寫上去後，再看下一個句子；看到下一句又遇到生字，於是只好又停下來查字典。就這樣，從打開書本起，光看前面兩句外加查字典和寫中譯的時間就花了數十分鐘，再繼續看個三五句就心生厭倦了，心想不如將書本闔起來，去書局買本中譯本來看還比較有效率！這種情形對大部分讀者而言是否很熟悉？

的確，我們從小時候學看書開始，就是逐字在「處理意思」的，那是因為小孩學習閱讀另一重要的目的是為了學認字，而且孩童所閱讀的資訊還不是很多，所以逐字地看文章似乎不會發生什麼問題。但是當我們長大了之後，要看的文章變長了、種類變多了、內容變深入了，若仍使用「逐字閱讀法」（再加上還要在心裡英翻中）閱讀文章，便會導致速度慢、理解不足、有看沒有懂……等問題接踵而來！換句話說，面對生活中與職場上篇幅長、種類繁、內容艱深的文章，靠「逐字閱讀加遇到生字就翻閱字典」這一招是行不通的；一定要採取更有效率的閱讀方法，才有可能應付公司或日常生活中排山倒海而來的文章與資訊。

那麼，面對一篇長篇的英文文章時，在不能逐字看、不能查字典、不能頻頻英翻中的前提下，要怎麼做才能增加效率進而提升整體閱讀能力？在接下來的討論中，筆者將從六個角度來窺探一篇文章的究竟，這六個關鍵分別是：**掌握文章架構、掃瞄要點主旨、找尋細節資訊、推論言下之意、替換同義字彙與基本數字演算**等，而 New TOEIC 閱讀部分的考題也正是由此六個面向出題的。請看以下範例文章。（此篇範文取材自網路文章 May, 2017 / www.inc.com）

3 Scientific Ways to Recover From a Setback

We all make mistakes. It's what we do after we stumble that determines our success.

To paraphrase Mark Twain, good judgment comes from experience, but experience comes from bad judgment. Mistakes enable growth. Do you let the problem paralyze you, or do you use it as learning experience? There are coping mechanisms and mental approaches that are scientifically proven to help you better handle missteps. Here are three tips that will help you bounce back from setbacks and even use them to your advantage.

1. Be an optimist.

If you weren't born one, fear not: optimism can be taught. Dr. Jacinta Jiménez, a Stanford-trained psychologist, says that research shows that if we can adjust our "explanatory style"--the way in which we explain to ourselves why we experienced a particular event--we can learn to stay positive in the face of adversity. Next time you are eye-to-eye with a setback, Dr. Jimenez suggests thinking about Seligman's 3 Ps: permanence (how permanent is the setback?), pervasiveness (will the setback affect your whole life or just part of it?), and personalization (is the setback really something you caused?). Optimistic people do a good job of recognizing bad events as temporary, compartmentalizing them so they don't seep into other aspects of their lives, and externalizing them rather than completely blaming themselves for what happened.

2. Use healthy coping mechanisms.

Active coping, in which you use your resources to manage negative emotions and improve your situation requires more effort but will help you feel better in the long run. Active coping methods include engaging in social activities and exercising, which releases endorphins, the chemicals in our brain that make us feel good. People who take part in a creative activity they enjoy have higher levels of well-being. Especially after a disappointment, engaging in a creative activity can restore your sense of self-control and broaden your perspective.

3. Learn from your mistakes.

Another healthy thing to do in the wake of a setback is to reflect. Try growth-oriented thinking, in which you focus on what you have learned and how this knowledge can help you advance your career, rather than fixating on the perceived failure. Your mistakes can even help those around you. Ash Norton, a chemical engineer, says she's made lots of mistakes throughout her career, but she never let them hold her back. In fact, she made a conscious effort to share them with those around her, which helped her whole organization improve.

There probably is not an entrepreneur among us who hasn't faced a setback. It is how we handle those challenges that determine our success. Luckily, we have science on our side.

現在，我們以看懂「文章架構」的角度出發，在不逐字看完全文的情況之下，須先將文章的「架構」(organization) 釐清。就好比蓋房子，在灌水泥之前，要先規劃設計圖，再架鋼筋讓整體架構呈現出來，才可能做後續的其他步驟。處理長篇閱讀也不例外。我們首先需要掃瞄整體文章的段落組成。如此約略瞭解架構的好處是，在心裡對全文有個大概的認知，瞭解段落的分配，之後對要點細節的搜尋，比較容易看清楚哪個要點出現在哪個段落上，而非要找什麼資訊都得從首段開始找起。

以上頁約 450 字的範文為例，雖說看似一篇頗長的文章，但大致掃瞄整體結構後，也可看出此篇文章有五個段落，除了首段 opening 之外，當中有三個 body paragraphs，最後有一結尾段落 conclusion。

範文架構解析

主標題 **3 Scientific Ways to Recover From a Setback**

次標題 We all make mistakes. It's what we do after we stumble that determines our success.

開場段落 To paraphrase Mark Twain, good judgment comes from experience, but experience comes from bad judgment. Mistakes enable growth. Do you let the problem paralyze you, or do you use it as learning experience? There are coping mechanisms and mental approaches that are scientifically proven to help you better handle missteps. Here are three tips that will help you bounce back from setbacks and even use them to your advantage.

第一要點 **1. Be an optimist.**
If you weren't born one, fear not: optimism can be taught. Dr. Jacinta Jiménez, a Stanford-trained psychologist, says that research shows that if we can adjust our "explanatory style"--the way in which we explain to ourselves why we experienced a particular event--we can learn to stay

positive in the face of adversity. Next time you are eye-to-eye with a setback, Dr. Jimenez suggests thinking about Seligman's 3 Ps: permanence (how permanent is the setback?), pervasiveness (will the setback affect your whole life or just part of it?), and personalization (is the setback really something you caused?). Optimistic people do a good job of recognizing bad events as temporary, compartmentalizing them so they don't seep into other aspects of their lives, and externalizing them rather than completely blaming themselves for what happened.

第二要點 2. Use healthy coping mechanisms.
Active coping, in which you use your resources to manage negative emotions and improve your situation requires more effort but will help you feel better in the long run. Active coping methods include engaging in social activities and exercising, which releases endorphins, the chemicals in our brain that make us feel good. People who take part in a creative activity they enjoy have higher levels of well-being. Especially after a disappointment, engaging in a creative activity can restore your sense of self-control and broaden your perspective.

第三要點 3. Learn from your mistakes.
Another healthy thing to do in the wake of a setback is to reflect. Try growth-oriented thinking, in which you focus on what you have learned and how this knowledge can help you advance your career, rather than fixating on the perceived failure. Your mistakes can even help those around you. Ash Norton, a chemical engineer, says she's made lots of mistakes throughout her career, but she never let them hold her back. In fact, she made a conscious effort to share them with those around her, which helped her whole organization improve.

結論段落 There probably is not an entrepreneur among us who hasn't faced a setback. It is how we handle those challenges that determine our success. Luckily, we have science on our side.

在掃瞄完文章大概的結構，瞭解段落的組成之後，下一步就是要掃瞄各段落的要點主旨了。在掃瞄時，先試著不要第一時間就想將段落內所有細節都看到，而是先看出每段「要旨」為何，對文章每段落的大意有個全面性的瞭解。要培養這樣的能力，就是要能夠判斷文章內容中各組成元素的重要性，我們要將重要性高的「主要資訊」元素和重要性低的「次要資訊」元素分開，然後將精簡的重要元素，也就是「主要資訊」的重點概念，優先消化。

重要性高的「主要資訊」通常是包括作者所提出要討論的議題，每段落的主題句 (topic sentence) 和結論等。若能抓到這幾個要點，應該就可以瞭解六七成的大概內容了。以下再度以此文章為例來說明。

範文解析

3 Scientific Ways to Recover From a Setback
We all make mistakes. It's what we do after we stumble that determines our success.

To paraphrase Mark Twain, good judgment comes from experience, but experience comes from bad judgment. Mistakes enable growth. Do you let the problem paralyze you, or do you use it as learning experience? **There are coping mechanisms and mental approaches that are scientifically proven to help you better handle missteps. Here are three tips that will help you bounce back from setbacks and even use them to your advantage.**

1. Be an optimist.
If you weren't born one, fear not: optimism can be taught. Dr. Jacinta Jiménez, a Stanford-trained psychologist, says that research shows that if we can adjust our "explanatory style"--the way in which we explain to ourselves why we experienced a particular event--we can learn to stay positive in the face of adversity. Next time you are eye-to-eye with a setback, Dr. Jimenez suggests thinking about Seligman's 3 Ps: permanence (how

permanent is the setback?), pervasiveness (will the setback affect your whole life or just part of it?), and personalization (is the setback really something you caused?). Optimistic people do a good job of recognizing bad events as temporary, compartmentalizing them so they don't seep into other aspects of their lives, and externalizing them rather than completely blaming themselves for what happened.

2. Use healthy coping mechanisms.
Active coping, in which you use your resources to manage negative emotions and improve your situation requires more effort but will help you feel better in the long run. Active coping methods include engaging in social activities and exercising, which releases endorphins, the chemicals in our brain that make us feel good. People who take part in a creative activity they enjoy have higher levels of well-being. Especially after a disappointment, engaging in a creative activity can restore your sense of self-control and broaden your perspective.

3. Learn from your mistakes.
Another healthy thing to do in the wake of a setback is to reflect. Try growth-oriented thinking, in which you focus on what you have learned and how this knowledge can help you advance your career, rather than fixating on the perceived failure. Your mistakes can even help those around you. Ash Norton, a chemical engineer, says she's made lots of mistakes throughout her career, but she never let them hold her back. In fact, she made a conscious effort to share them with those around her, which helped her whole organization improve.

There probably is not an entrepreneur among us who hasn't faced a setback. It is how we handle those challenges that determine our success. Luckily, we have science on our side.

　　在掃瞄完此文的議題、每段的主題句與結論之後,便可約略歸納出文章的主旨,包括:

一、文章旨在討論遇到挫折時，如何恢復與修正情緒，並指出有三個參考策略。

二、這三個策略分別是：

    a. 保持樂觀正面的心態

    b. 做些對身心有益的活動

    c. 從錯誤中學習

三、最後，作者再度重申，失敗之後的反省才是致勝的關鍵。

    由以上「掃瞄要點主旨」的例子說明可看出，要瞭解全文在討論些什麼，並不需要將所有文字都看完，只要抓住全文的要點、每段落的主題句，以及結論內重申的要點句，便可理解文章六七成要表達的內容了。要具備「快速看出要點」的能力，多練習自然是不二法門。更重要的是，須先擺脫「想逐字看完全文，還一邊在心中翻譯成中文」的傳統閱讀習慣，改由將注意力集中於「抓大方向」的關鍵上，才有可能練就「一眼看出要旨」的功夫。

找尋細節資訊

在瞭解了「架構」的重要性之後，我們接下來要討論的是「細節」。如同蓋房子一般，當決定了風格（主題），搭好了架構（段落要點）後，當然就是要進行灌漿或裝潢等細部作業。換言之，亦即找尋文章中的一些細節了。細節的描述提供更多的資訊讓整篇文章更具體與生動，也同時讓讀者瞭解更多所需資訊。若缺少細節，一篇文章可能變得無意義亦無趣味。

那麼，該如何找出細節資訊？商業界經理人常使用的「80/20 法則」正可套用於閱讀技巧。商業界的 80/20 係指一間公司 80% 的業績是由 20% 的客戶所貢獻的。此處我們可以這麼說：「將 80% 的時間精神放在看 20% 最重要的關鍵字詞。」練習時，可藉由幾個問題方向來協助自己找到正確的細節內容，比方說：

Who ——此篇文章主要針對的讀者是哪類族群的人？是學生？（那可能要使用較淺顯易懂的字彙）還是商務人士？（便可能出現商業行話或相關說法）亦或是文中是否提及某人的特殊經驗？

What ——此篇文章中所提及之概念或行動相關的細節。例如：遇到困難該以什麼樣的心態面對？或該採取什麼行動以解決等。

When ——文章中是否討論到時間或階段性？

Where ——文章中是否討論到地點？是在學校？還是公司裡？

Why ——文章中是否有提到行動背後的原理？欲採取某行動的理由？

接下來，讓我們使用同樣的範文來練習，找出 20% 的關鍵字詞以協助理解細節梗概。

範文解析

3 Scientific Ways to Recover From a Setback
We all make mistakes. It's what we do after we stumble that determines our success.

To paraphrase Mark Twain, good judgment comes from experience, but experience comes from bad judgment. **Mistakes enable growth.** Do you let the problem paralyze you, or do you use it as learning experience? There are coping mechanisms and mental approaches that are scientifically proven to help you better handle missteps. **Here are three tips that will help you bounce back from setbacks and even use them to your advantage.**

1. Be an optimist.

If you weren't born one, fear not: optimism can be taught. **Dr. Jacinta Jiménez, a Stanford-trained psychologist, says that research shows that if we can adjust our "explanatory style"**--the way in which we explain to ourselves why we experienced a particular event--**we can learn to stay positive in the face of adversity.** Next time you are eye-to-eye with a setback, **Dr. Jimenez suggests thinking about Seligman's 3 Ps: permanence** (how permanent is the setback?), **pervasiveness** (will the setback affect your whole life or just part of it?), **and personalization** (is the setback really something you caused?). **Optimistic people do a good job of recognizing bad events as temporary, compartmentalizing them** so they don't seep into other aspects of their lives, **and externalizing them** rather than completely blaming themselves for what happened.

2. Use healthy coping mechanisms.

Active coping, in which you use your resources to manage negative emotions and improve your situation requires more effort but **will help you feel better in the long run**. Active coping **methods include engaging in social activities and exercising**, which releases endorphins, the chemicals in our brain that make us feel good. **People who take part in a creative activity they enjoy have higher levels of well-being.** Especially after a disappointment, **engaging in a creative activity can restore your sense of self-control and broaden your perspective.**

3. Learn from your mistakes.

Another healthy thing to do in the wake of a setback is to reflect. **Try growth-oriented thinking**, in which you focus on **what you have learned and how this knowledge can help you advance your career**, rather than fixating on the perceived failure. **Your mistakes can even help those around you. Ash Norton, a chemical engineer, says she's made lots of mistakes** throughout her career, but she never let them hold her back. In fact, **she made a conscious effort to share them with those around her**, which helped her whole organization improve.

There probably is not an entrepreneur among us who hasn't faced a setback. **It is how we handle those challenges that determine our success.** Luckily, we have science on our side.

　　在進一步掃瞄文章之後，可瞭解此文主要在討論從錯誤中學習，從挫折中恢復的方式。針對文中提及三個策略，也有更進一步的細節。包括：

a. 保持樂觀正面的心態
　　✓ Permanence
　　✓ Pervasiveness
　　✓ Personalization
b. 做些對身心有益的活動
　　✓ Engage in social activities
　　✓ Exercise
c. 從錯誤中學習
　　✓ Learn from mistakes
　　✓ Share experience with others

　　至此，我們對這篇文章大架構下的細節已有進一步的認識。

4 推論言下之意

　　任何英文能力檢定的文章閱讀皆包括 "inference questions" 推論型的題目，新多益也不例外。這類題目的特性是：題目所問的答案，在文章段落內應有相關線索資訊，但並不會明確地或直接地點出，而是要請應試者根據文中的線索資訊來推論出句子的言下之意 (connotations)。因此，應試者不僅必須看懂文章中字句的表面意思，更要能 "read between the lines"，也就是將句子的「弦外之音」看出來，以選出正確答案。下列再度以上篇文章中的幾個句子為例。

1. Active coping, in which you use your resources to manage negative emotions and improve your situation requires more effort but will help you feel better in the long run.

原義　採取積極的方式來面對困難，是比較花精力，但就長遠來看是有益的。

推論　若遇到問題卻展現出消極的態度，等著他人來相救，看似一時之間不用花什麼精神沒錯，但終究自己也不會有所長進。

↑ 即便文中並未確切地以文字描述出來，但其實可由原句中的意思推論出來！

2. Active coping methods include engaging in social activities and exercising, which releases endorphins, the chemicals in our brain that make us feel good. People who take part in a creative activity they enjoy have higher levels of well-being.

原義　做運動＝身體釋出 endorphins（腦內啡）＝讓人感到快樂

推論　做運動本身對心情好壞可能影響不大，但運動時所釋放的腦內啡正是讓心情愉悅的關鍵。

　　我們再以下列其他句子來瞭解 "connotation" 的含意：

1. Contrary to what the supervisor might think, Jerry works really hard.

推論　老闆認為傑瑞不是很努力工作。

2. Unlike her mother, Linda has little business sense.

推論 琳達的媽媽很有商業概念。

3. Only senior managers are invited to attend the conference.

推論 其他一般職員都沒受邀參加研討會。

4. Tablets outsell laptop computers.

推論 筆電銷售比平板差。

5. Bill came in wet, because he didn't bring an umbrella.

推論 外面正下著雨。

　　由以上例子可以看出，要在閱讀測驗取得理想分數，必須眞正對文句有深入瞭解，而非僅停留在文字表面的意思，更要透視文句背後的「言下之意」。這也就是爲什麼推理能力如此重要，且各類英檢考試一定都會納入推論理解類的題目了。

5 替換同義字彙

　　字彙是聽、說、讀、寫四項英文能力的基礎，若連基本的字彙能力都不具備，怎麼有辦法吸收資訊、理解消化，進而跟外國人溝通意見？因此，擴充字彙量是非常重要的！所幸，New TOEIC 考的單字範圍有限，並不會天馬行空地考一些冷僻、不實用的字，而考的都是日常生活、辦公環境、商業情境或出差商旅中常用到的單字。

　　一般而言，一篇文章若能看懂大約 70% 的字彙，就能瞭解其大意了，剩下 30% 不懂的字就算跳過去不看，也不會影響到對文章的理解能力！建議讀者平時就應該多記單字，以期在考試時有所幫助，如此不但能提高對文意的瞭解程度，更可有效地縮短答題的時間。

　　背單字時，光知道中文意思與默背拼法是不夠的，最好可以進一步瞭解同義字／反義字，或是否有其他相關片語，行有餘力的話再深入瞭解單字的應用，比方說搭配字、應用情境或造句等。（事實上，New TOEIC Reading 的單字考題停留在考「同義字」的層面上，若加試 Writing 才會有要使用搭配字或造句的機會。）

　　以下我們就以同一範文為例，列出幾個對多數人來說可能是「生字」的字彙，並將這些字的意思、同義字、反義字列在其後的表格中。

範文解析

3 Scientific Ways to Recover From a Setback
We all make mistakes. It's what we do after we stumble that determines our success.

To paraphrase Mark Twain, good judgment comes from experience, but experience comes from bad judgment. Mistakes enable growth. Do you let the problem paralyze you, or do you use it as learning experience? There are coping mechanisms and mental approaches that are scientifically proven to help you better handle missteps. Here are three tips that will help you bounce back from setbacks and even use them to your advantage.

1. Be an optimist.

If you weren't born one, fear not: optimism can be taught. Dr. Jacinta Jiménez, a Stanford-trained psychologist, says that research shows that if we can adjust our "explanatory style"--the way in which we explain to ourselves why we experienced a particular event--we can learn to stay positive in the face of adversity. Next time you are eye-to-eye with a setback, Dr. Jimenez suggests thinking about Seligman's 3 Ps: permanence (how permanent is the setback?), pervasiveness (will the setback affect your whole life or just part of it?), and personalization (is the setback really something you caused?). Optimistic people do a good job of recognizing bad events as temporary, compartmentalizing them so they don't seep into other aspects of their lives, and externalizing them rather than completely blaming themselves for what happened.

2. Use healthy coping mechanisms.

Active coping, in which you use your resources to manage negative emotions and improve your situation requires more effort but will help you feel better in the long run. Active coping methods include engaging in social activities and exercising, which releases endorphins, the chemicals in our brain that make us feel good. People who take part in a creative activity they enjoy have higher levels of well-being. Especially after a disappointment, engaging in a creative activity can restore your sense of self-control and broaden your perspective.

3. Learn from your mistakes.

Another healthy thing to do in the wake of a setback is to reflect. Try growth-oriented thinking, in which you focus on what you have learned and how this knowledge can help you advance your career, rather than fixating on the perceived failure. Your mistakes can even help those around you. Ash Norton, a chemical engineer, says she's made lots of mistakes throughout her career, but she never let them hold her back. In fact, she made a conscious effort to share them with those around her, which helped her whole organization improve.

There probably is not an entrepreneur among us who hasn't faced a setback. It is how we handle those challenges that determine our success. Luckily, we have science on our side.

單字	詞性	中文意思	同義字	反義字
stumble	v.	絆倒、失足	**fall down**	continue
judgment	n.	裁決、判斷力	**acumen**	ignorance
paralyze	v.	使癱瘓、使停頓	**immobilize**	strengthen
optimist	n.	樂觀主義者	**positive thinker**	pessimist
adversity	n.	逆境、厄運	**disaster**	advantage
engage	v.	從事、參加	**involve**	neglect
perspective	n.	看法、洞察力	**viewpoint**	---
perceive	v.	察覺、感知	**identify**	overlook
conscious	adj.	清醒的、有知覺的	**attentive**	unaware

　　這些單字的「同義字」即 New TOEIC 頻出考點。因此讀者平時在準備時，除了瞭解單字的中文意思之外，也應多找幾個同義單字來練習換字喔！

6 基本數字演算

　　New TOEIC 為商務類的考試，在商務環境中說要不接觸到「數字」，那是不可能的。而既然是職場上必然會遇到的，自然便會出現於 New TOEIC 題目當中。不過，閱讀理解測驗裡的「數字類」考題，僅限於基本的「加、減、乘、除」範圍，對應試者而言應不成問題。

　　舉例來說，某篇文章內容提及 "Over the past two years the company has spent $2 million, about half per year, on improving manufacturing process ..."，而數字類的問題問 "How much did the company spend on the manufacturing process last year?"。根據文中提到的關鍵點，過去兩年 "$2 million"（兩百萬）的花費是 "about half per year"（大約一年一半），而 $2 million ÷ 2 = $1 million，答案就是 "$1 million"。

　　除了基本的數字「加、減、乘、除」，應試者若能對以下「數字」相關的要點加以熟悉，在考試時更可以加快判斷語意與作答的速度！

一、數字單位

百	a hundred	100
千	a thousand	1k
萬	ten thousand	10k
十萬	a hundred thousand	100k
百萬	a million	1m
千萬	ten million	10m
億	a hundred million	100m
十億	a billion	1b

二、分數

　　New TOEIC 文章中也常會寫到以分數來代表的量，以 "Customers had taken their business to Company B where costs were a sixth what they were in Company A." 為例，其中 "a sixth" 即 1/6 之意。另請看其他分數表示：

a half	$\frac{1}{2}$
a third	$\frac{1}{3}$
a quarter	$\frac{1}{4}$
a fifth	$\frac{1}{5}$

three-quarters	$\frac{3}{4}$
four-fifths	$\frac{4}{5}$
seven and a half	$7\frac{1}{2}$
eight and two-fifths	$8\frac{2}{5}$

三、倍數

New TOEIC 的文章也可能提及「倍數」，比方說 "The company profits have doubled to more than \$4 million."（公司的盈利已成長了兩倍至四百多萬。）以下請看「倍數」的表示方法：

twice	兩倍	Jenny's office is **twice** as large as mine.
three times	三倍	The production this week is **three times** the amount of last week.
twenty times	二十倍	〔數字 + times〕以此類推
double	變成兩倍	My company's profits have **doubled** this year.
triple	變成三倍	Jack wants to **triple** his investment through stock trading, but he is inexperienced and doesn't know what to do.
quadruple	變成四倍	The boss is thinking about how to double or even **quadruple** the number of new sales leads for each month.

雖然說「數字類」的題目僅須做基本的運算處理即可，但還是建議應試者在準備考試時，亦應從各種不同的「文章背景」和「數字」來瞭解兩者間的關係。

比方說，在一篇「求職信」內所提到的數字可能與「薪資」(salary / wages) 有關；在一篇「銀行廣告」中提到的數字可能跟「利息」(interest rates) 有關；在一篇「企業經營」類的文章中所提到的數字則可能跟「業績」(revenues / profits) 相關。

事前的瞭解與準備，對在考試當中加速理解能力有很大的幫助喔！

單篇／多篇文章閱讀策略

✎ 文章與題目之數量分配

　　2018 年在台灣最新改版的 New TOEIC 考試之最後一部分「文章閱讀理解」共有 54 道題目。單篇文章十篇、雙篇文章兩組，另新增三篇文章三組。單篇文章出 2 ～ 4 題不等，雙篇與三篇文章每組固定問 5 題（見下表），而問題的順序通常會依照文章的順序，因此建議應試者就順著文章與題目順序作答，不要以跳躍式的方式漫無目標地尋找答案。

Part 7 文章閱讀理解		
單篇文章	10 篇	每篇 2 ～ 4 題不等
雙篇文章	2 組（共 4 篇文章）	每組 5 題
三篇文章	3 組（共 9 篇文章）	每組 5 題

　　單篇文章題長度由短篇增長為中等與較長的篇幅，內容大致上偏生活化，多取材自日常溝通或辦公場合內會用到之短文，並不會出現特別冗長或須具備某種特殊商業背景知識才可回答的內容。雙篇文章題之間會有關連性，可能是「招募廣告」搭配「應徵信件」，「客戶詢問報價」搭配「廠商回覆報價單」，或「客戶抱怨信件」搭配「客服經理善意回應」等類型。而新增的三篇文章題的關係則再稍微複雜一點，可能是「新聞稿」、「客戶意見函」再搭配「公司回應」，或「研討會邀請函」、「報名表單」再搭配「主辦單位報名費繳交提醒函」等組合。當然，新題型三篇文章題之複雜度可謂不低，要搜尋出正解須發揮更高的理解力，且應保留更充裕的答題時間，否則很可能陷入因時間一分一秒流失卻找不到答案而心生焦慮的惡性循環。

✎ 時間掌握的策略

　　New TOEIC 閱讀測驗的時間為 75 分鐘，在很快地做完文法選擇題與克漏字題後，時間的分配上最好預留 40 ～ 45 分鐘來完成單／多篇文章理解題，否則極有可能寫不完。多數應試者之所以對文章閱讀心生恐懼、作答速度過慢，絕大部分癥結在於字彙量不足：導致對題目用字感到陌生，當某單字在文章中換個字表達就看不出意思了。若是如此，建議應試者在準備考試時，應盡力增加單字與其「同義字」的量，方可加速看文章的速度，並節省下理解題目與文意的時間。

另一方面，若單就「考試技巧」而言，其實文章中並非每一個字的重要性都一樣，有的單字是可以用來回答題目的關鍵字，有的單字則否，不懂其意思也不會影響理解的字，看不懂也沒關係。因此為了節省時間，應試者應將焦點放在「足以回答題目的關鍵字」即可，而非試圖費時處理所有的單字與資訊。

多篇文章的關連性以及答題線索分佈

針對處理「雙篇文章題」與新增的「三篇文章題」，首先第一步就是要將文章之間的「關連性」看出來。在釐清文章之間的關係後，再著眼於各篇文章欲傳遞的要點主旨。接下來的技巧便是要一邊先看題目，一邊回顧文章尋找可回答題目的關鍵字。雙篇／三篇文章題的題目通常比單篇的題目變化較多，也就是說，答案線索可能出現在兩篇／三篇文章之間兩三個不同的地方，故覓得正解可能較耗時。因此建議最好多預留點時間（約 15～20 分鐘）來處理多篇文章題組。

為了在有限的時間內迅速地找到答案，與其想要達成「將文章看完並看懂再來作答」之不可能任務，倒不如運用一些簡單且有效的「答題技巧」，其報酬率還比較高。（許多應試者都想要將文章一字不落地看完，還一邊在心裡翻譯中文意思，然後才去看題目，再來來回回找答案。但這些考試文章、信件等都是虛構的，想要完全看懂的意義何在？）回答長篇文章閱讀理解題，最重要的是：在茫茫字海中判斷出文章最精要的主旨，當題目問到細節時應「立即聚焦至相對應的資訊」上，其他不相關的訊息便無須多花時間去處理。接下來筆者將針對掃瞄文章之訣竅，並依問題類型討論各種不同的實戰答題策略。

1 文章類型

A. 單篇文章：

　　單篇文章閱讀理解固定考十篇，文章內容雖然範圍頗廣，但其實都是日常生活中或辦公環境內會遇到的溝通狀況與信件往來。可能出現的文章包括以下類型：

- Charts and graphs（圖示、圖表）
- Schedules and calendars（會議時間表／議程、火車／飛機時刻表）
- Advertisements（商品廣告、事求人分類廣告）
- Announcements and notices（辦公室公告）
- Newspaper and magazine articles（報章雜誌文章）
- Forms（表格）
- Indexes and tables（索引）
- Reports（企業財務報告書）
- Labels（商品保證書）
- Letters, faxes（商業書信／傳真）
- Memos（留言訊息）
- Bulletins（公佈欄告示）
- Others（其他）

B. 多篇文章：

　　2018 年在台灣實施的 New TOEIC 改制，其中最大的變動應屬多篇文章閱讀了。本來四組雙篇文章，改為兩組雙篇，另新增三組三篇文章的新題型。而雙篇／三篇文章之間是彼此相關的，應試者須將文章全都大致掃瞄過，並瞭解其中之關連性後，才有辦法回答五道問題。

雙篇文章可能之組合
- 企業求人廣告 + 申請人應徵信函
- 客戶抱怨信 + 廠商善意回覆
- 新產品上市消息報導 + 客戶詢問相關細節

- 客戶寫信詢問產品及要求報價 + 廠商回覆產品說明與價格
- 公司寫信給客戶介紹產品 + 附上產品功能列表
- 邀請學校教授演講的電郵 + 教授回覆電郵婉拒

三篇文章可能之組合

- 工程師寫信詢問技術細節 + 公司提供解決方案和訓練課程 + 工程師回覆課程報名表
- 部門發出開會通知 + 員工回應詢問細節 + 主管發電郵提醒會前應準備之報告
- 雜誌刊出食譜 + 讀者建議事項 + 食譜廠商回應感謝
- 研討會訊息 + 報名表 + 主辦單位提醒繳交報名費之信件
- 客戶申請信用卡之信函 + 申請表格 + 銀行回絕信用卡申請信函
- 公司產品介紹 + 附上客戶評論 + 新客戶寫信邀約討論報價

2018 年改版的 New TOEIC，除了既有的六大題型之外，還新增了亦出現於 TOEFL iBT 的 "Insert Text"「插入句題」，這些題目類型詳列如下：

1. Main Idea（主旨題）

- What is the purpose of this passage?
- Why was this letter written?
- The main idea/topic/point/purpose of the article is ...?

★★★ 解題技巧 ★★★

無論單篇或多篇，多數文章所搭配的第一題極有可能就是「主旨題」。想當然爾，「主旨題」即詢問「該文章主要內容」為何，而應試者應將注意力放在掃瞄文章的首句或標題，通常是字體加大、加黑、加粗之處，藉由這些重點來瞭解整篇文章之主旨。

再來就要注意每篇文章的第一段、第一句、第一行。英美人士寫文章或談話通常是比較直接的，不會以迂迴的方式表達，故通常一篇文章之重點在「文章最開頭」的地方就會被提及。而且文章作者要傳達給讀者的「主要訊息」大都簡短明瞭。因此，為了節省時間，請應試者不用將整篇文章都看完才回答題目，而應該在大約掃瞄到標題，閱讀了第一段首句內的關鍵點而掌握主旨之後，就試著回答第一題。

2. Positive Factual（正向問細節題）

- Who? (Who wrote the memo?)
- What? (What is one problem with the management?)
- When? (When can visitors see the exhibit?)
- Where? (Where will the meeting be held?)
- Which? (Which of the following would be included?)
- Why? (Why was the call made?)
- How? (How do people to raise money?)

除了首句可能是主旨之外，文章的其他部分則可能是一些「細節」資訊，目的在於更深入說明並延伸文章的內容。為了在極有限的時間內掃瞄完文章並回答完為數不少的問題，接下來便應該一邊看題目，一邊以「快速掃瞄」的方式搜尋出可回答問題之「關鍵字」。

例如，看到問題：Who is in charge of Marketing?，心中就大概有個底了，既然題目是以 Who 開頭的問句，那麼便可判斷須找到與「人名」、「職稱」等相關的資訊方可答題，於是回去文章內容搜尋類似：Mr. Smith 或 VP of Marketing 等可以回答 "Who" 問句的關鍵字。另外請記得，文章中並不是每一個字的重要性都一樣，若看到「轉折語氣」字所引導出的句子時應特別注意。比方說，"She was a good manager, but ...!" 此句中有「轉折語氣」的用字 but 出現，則須注意其後所提到的內容。因此，有時先看題目找到文章中對應的關鍵字後，也有可能當句非正解，正確答案係出現於 but、however 等轉折詞之後。

3. Negative Factual（反向問細節題）

- EXCEPT for Sundays, the stores are open ...?
- Which of the following is NOT true?
- All of the following are true BESIDES ...?
- Employees are the LEAST likely to ...?
- Which of the following payment methods is NOT mentioned?

除了上述問「文章中真的有提及」的細節之外，細節型的題目還有可能是以「反向的方式」來提問的，而此類型的題目中通常會包括 "NOT" 字眼；也就是必須找出「在文章當中並沒有被提及的資訊」。以 "Which of the following payment methods is NOT mentioned in the article?" 為例，應試者就要快速地在文章中搜尋出「提到三種付款方式」之處，再排除掉「未被提及」的付款方式選項，以回答問題。

4. Inference（推論題）

- It can be inferred from the article that ...?
- Where is this advertisement likely to be found?
- It can be assumed that ...?

New TOEIC 閱讀測驗的問題大都可以在文章中找到解答，但是推論題旨在考「理解能力」，自然便不會被設計成一眼就看出正解的型態，而需要應試者善加利用文中線索來推測出可能之答案。這種類型題目的答案並非顯而易見，必須經過理解、思考後才會浮現，相當具有挑戰性；要正確回答這種題目與「反應力」和「理解速度」有關，因此建議讀者，平時多練習批判思考的能力，以便應試時能加快破題。

5. Computation（計算題）

• How much does the total package cost?
• How much more does it cost for five than two?

筆者一再強調，New TOEIC 考試內容大都採納與日常、工作相關之題材，因此考題除了英文本身之外，對「數字的處理能力」也頗為重視。（試想我們在生活中、職場上，不正也要常常計算數字或閱覽業務報表？）所幸這類數字處理的問題，也只是簡單的「加 / 減 / 乘 / 除」而已。計算類題目最有可能出現在問報價單、業績表格等情境之文章，也有可能出現在求職書信中的薪資計算等，但通常都不會超過基本的四則運算，故一般而言應可應付自如。

6. Vocabulary（同義字題）

• The word "complimentary" in paragraph 2, line 1, is closest in meaning to

如前所述，所有閱讀的基礎皆在於單字量，且 New TOEIC 也十分偏好與「字詞代換」相關的問題。縱使非直接性的單字題，通常題目選項與文中提及的內容也會採用「換句話說」或「換同義字」的方式重新呈現。例如：

lucrative	=	profitable
basic	=	fundamental
outstanding	=	exceptional
friendly	=	affable
creative	=	inventive

針對這類題目，平常除了應多記單字外，更應多查閱「英英」字典，不僅要瞭解一個英文單字的中文對應意思，更要瞭解其用法與同義的英文解釋。更多商務高頻同義字，請參考本書 PART 4 的分類字彙補充。

7. Insert Text（插入句題）

• In which of the positions marked [1], [2], [3], and [4] does the following sentence best belong?

"Thank you for your consideration."

★★★ 解題技巧 ★★★

此類為 2018 年新增的題型，原本也見於 TOEFL iBT（托福）的閱讀考題中，現在也現身到 New TOEIC 考試了。這類題型有何特別之處？讓主考單位將其納入至 New TOEIC？顧名思義，「插入句題」須將一個句子插入到「可與上下文無縫結合」的位置上，假如問題所列句子和空格前後的句子連接後文意不通順，則該處便不是正確位置。

要將句子插入於正確之處，應試者須先具備「上下文」的概念，方可提高答對率。舉例說明，試題是一篇求職信函，題目所問要插入的句子是 "I'm writing to apply for the Sales Manager position."，則大致可推測此「說明寫信目的」的句子最有可能出現在文章前半段。為了節省時間，便可鎖定位置 [1] 或 [2] 從中判斷。又例如在一篇會議紀錄中，要插入的句子是 "To conclude, the company will expand the market in Japan next year."，那麼也可立即判斷，既然是 "To conclude ..." 下結論的句子，其所在位置豈有可能是在會議紀錄的開頭？這樣的機會應該不大，所謂「結論」比較有可能出現於文章的「尾端」才是。因此為了加速作答，便可直接在位置 [3] 或 [4] 之間做選擇。

　　討論了再多的解題策略與技巧，還不如實際地演練題目與檢討。接下來，我們就透過不論在內容或格式上都非常貼近真實考題的兩組模擬試題來應用上述的策略！

Part 2

模擬試題

Test 1

Directions: Part 7 consists of a number of texts such as emails, advertisements, and newspaper articles. After each text or set of texts there are several questions. Choose the best answer to each question and mark the corresponding letter (A), (B), (C), and (D) on your answer sheet.

Questions 147-149 refer to the following email.

To: Kevin Gordon [k.gordon@blankslate.com]

From: Jessie Evans [jessieevans@zapstart.com]

Re: Follow-Up

Date: 13 June, 8:45 am

Dear Mr. Gordon,

I would like to thank you for meeting with us this morning. The initial marketing proposal you presented was generally well-received, but after discussing the matter further with our CFO and sales team, we have decided to make a few changes.

First, we'd like to limit the amount spent on print advertising to 20% of the total. Second, you suggested using 15% of our advertising budget on television and radio ads, but we are convinced it would be more effective to use that money for online advertising instead. Finally, we'd like you to allocate at least 10% of the budget to outdoor advertising. We have previously received very positive responses from our ads on buses and subways, so we were surprised to see that you didn't include them.

Taking these requirements into consideration, could you please resubmit your proposal by the end of next week? As we discussed, the content of all ads should focus on the high quality, ease of use, and reliability of our products rather than the price.

Please let me know if you have any questions or concerns about our requirements, and thank you again for your presentation.

Best regards,

Jessie Evans
Marketing Director, Zap Start Inc.

147. What is the purpose of this email?
(A) To modify a proposal
(B) To reply to a customer
(C) To arrange a meeting
(D) To advertise a service

148. What form of advertising will Zap Start probably NOT use?
(A) Broadcast media
(B) Internet
(C) Newspaper
(D) Transportation

149. According to the email, what can be inferred about Zap Start's products?
(A) They are expensive.
(B) They do not break easily.
(C) They require training to use.
(D) They do not start quickly.

Jessica   10:42 am

Hey Mike, are you free this afternoon?

Mike   10:43 am

Yes, Jessica. My schedule is open for this afternoon. What's up?

Jessica   10:44 am

Good stuff. We need to discuss the budget plan for next year. —[1]—.

Mike   10:45 am

Sure, no problem. I was thinking about it as well. All right, so let me go to your office at 2 pm. —[2]—.

Jessica   10:46 am

2 pm is good with me. And why don't you also invite Joyce from Marketing division to participate? Since we need to integrate marketing activities to our sales plan.

Mike   10:47 am

—[3]—. Yes, I'll let her know later. What else should I prepare in advance then?

Jessica   10:48 am

Well, you can bring your sales plan and budget proposal. I guess that's it. See you this afternoon then. —[4]—.

150. What is the main purpose of this message communication?

   (A) To register for a conference

   (B) To schedule a meeting

   (C) To arrange an interview

   (D) To finalize a business plan

151. In which of the positions marked [1], [2], [3], and [4] does the following sentence best belong?

   "That's a pretty good idea."

   (A) [1]

   (B) [2]

   (C) [3]

   (D) [4]

September 9

To Whom It May Concern:

I am happy to serve as a reference for Cecil Ramirez. Mr. Ramirez worked as a full-time system administrator at Trapeze Software Ltd. for two years. In addition to maintaining our company's servers and website, Mr. Ramirez was also responsible for keeping the roughly 60 computers in the office up and running. He set up new user accounts and taught new employees how to use the company's internal software. We rarely experienced computer problems of any sort, but when there was an issue, Mr. Ramirez usually had it sorted out in hours if not minutes.

I am confident that Mr. Ramirez would be an excellent addition to any IT team. His ability to keep the big picture firmly in mind while capably handling a multitude of details is remarkable. He is a reliable and dedicated worker and a true pleasure to work with. If you have any questions or would like further information, please feel free to contact me personally.

Jessica Delacroix

Jessica Delacroix

Deputy General Manager, Trapeze Software Ltd.

152. What is the purpose of this letter?

    (A) To promote an employee to a higher position

    (B) To explain the system administrator's responsibilities

    (C) To recommend someone for a new job

    (D) To fill a vacancy for a computer specialist

153. What is NOT mentioned as one of Mr. Ramirez's strong points?

    (A) He knows how to write software.

    (B) He has experience training new workers.

    (C) He can maintain computer systems.

    (D) He is a hardworking employee.

Guest Satisfaction Survey

Thank you for taking a moment to complete this satisfaction survey. The Seven Seas Hotel Group will use your feedback to provide you even better service during your future visits.

	Yes	No
• Were you greeted appropriately when you arrived at the hotel?	✔	
• Was the check-in process smooth and efficient?		✔
• Were you escorted to your room by a bellman?	✔	
• Was you room clean and welcoming?	✔	
• Was the check-out process friendly and efficient?	✔	

Which of the following did you use?

Facilities	Services
_____ Business Center	✔ Laundry
_____ Conference Room	✔ Room Service
✔ Fitness Center	_____ Hair Salon
✔ Swimming Pool	✔ Parking

Comments:

The hotel computer had no record of my reservation even though I had received a confirmation email, which I showed to the clerk. This problem was quickly resolved in a professional manner, and I was pleased that he upgraded my room to a suite. Also, I was a little disappointed that I wasn't informed before I arrived that the swimming pool would be closed for maintenance until the final day of my stay. Had I known, I would have postponed my visit. Would it be too much trouble to mention such closures to guests before they arrive? Overall, my stay was pleasant and I look forward to returning again in the summer with my family.

154. What aspect of the hotel was the guest most satisfied with?

(A) The efficiency of the reservation system

(B) The professionalism of the staff

(C) The cleanliness of the room

(D) The renovation of the swimming pool

155. What improvement does the guest suggest?

(A) The hotel's computer system should be replaced.

(B) Reservation confirmations should be sent to all guests.

(C) Room upgrades should be offered to families.

(D) Guests should be informed about facility closures.

Friends of the Wetlands

Janice Noguchi
2593 Seacrest Lane
Port John, FL 03087

April 21

Dear Ms. Noguchi,

Thank you for your renewing your Friends of the Wetlands membership. —[1]—. Your $25 contribution will enable us to continue our missions of environmental research, habitat restoration, and community education. —[2]—.

We would like to take this opportunity to remind you that in addition to paying your membership dues, we encourage all members to assist the Friends of the Wetlands directly. —[3]—. You can help by planting local foliage, leading wetlands tours for students and other community members, or working as a fundraiser. For those interested, we've scheduled an information meeting for 7:30 Friday evening at the visitors center. —[4]—. We look forward to seeing you there.

Sincerely,

Mark Perry

Mark Perry

Director, Friends of the Wetlands

156. Why did Mark Perry write this letter to Ms. Noguchi?

    (A) To request a $25 donation

    (B) To encourage her to join an organization

    (C) To thank her for offering her time

    (D) To ask her to attend an event

157. What is NOT stated as one of the group's activities?

    (A) Marketing natural resources

    (B) Conducting scientific studies

    (C) Restoring the local ecology

    (D) Organizing educational programs

158. In which of the positions marked [1], [2], [3], and [4] does the following sentence best belong?

"Call us today and register."

    (A) [1]

    (B) [2]

    (C) [3]

    (D) [4]

To: All Staff
From: Mitzy Follop
Date: July 29

Re: Changes at the Majestic

I'm happy to announce some exciting new changes in store for us here at the Majestic Theater. We will be closed to the public for renovations from Monday, August 9 to Friday, August 13. By the time we reopen for the Saturday matinee, the balcony in the main theater will have been made available for public seating once again, and the boxoffice will have been equipped with a modern ticketing system. It is important that everyone is aware of the following changes:

1. Because the balcony will no longer be available for storage, all of the cleaning supplies will from now on be kept in the employee break room, which will become even more crowded. I apologize for any inconvenience.

2. The new ticketing system will allow customers to purchase popcorn, drinks, and other items at the same time they purchase their movie tickets. They will be provided with vouchers that they can exchange for their purchase at the snack counter, which should shorten lines. All employees are required to attend the training session for the new ticketing system at 3:30 pm on August 13.

3. Our reopening will coincide with the start of the Daytime Summer Classics Film Festival, which will run from August 14 until the end of the month. As in previous years, festival tickets are half-off the price of tickets sold for regular evening features.

I would like to thank everyone in advance for helping to make this a smooth transition for our valued guests.

Mitzy Follop
General Manager, Majestic Theater

159. Why did Mitzy Follop write this memo?

(A) To announce a new film festival to the public

(B) To inform the staff of recent developments

(C) To attract new customers to the theater

(D) To introduce new employees to the company

160. What benefit of the new ticketing system is mentioned in the memo?

(A) Employees will receive free training.

(B) Customers will receive faster service.

(C) Staff will receive free tickets.

(D) Movie-goers will receive a small discount.

161. According to the memo, which of the following problems might be caused by the renovations?

(A) The theater will be closed until the end of the month.

(B) The balcony will have to be cleaned regularly.

(C) Employees will have less space in the break room.

(D) Customers will receive vouchers instead of tickets.

Friday, July 16

Gerhardt Stacker
3986 Pine Ave.
Hartford, Connecticut 06037

Confidential

Dear Mr. Stacker,

I would like to update you on our local market test of Everyoung Lilac Hand Cream. As you can see from the initial data below, sales are brisk overall for a new product with nothing more than in-store advertising to support it.

Everyoung Lilac Hand Cream Sales: July 1 – July 15

Point of Sale	Store Description	Unit Price	Number Distributed	Number Sold
Blechey	Downtown Flagship	$4.99	150	92
Roxburry	High-end Mall	$4.99	100	77
Airport	Duty-Free Shop	$4.49	50	3
Fairbanks	Supermarket	$3.99	100	21
Ellendale	Discount Drug Store	$3.49	100	26

As we predicted, sales are especially strong at our luxury locations in Blechey and Roxburry, and relatively weak at our low-end locations in Fairbanks and Ellendale. Sales at the airport shop are too low to allow us to draw any useful conclusions at this point.

These preliminary numbers suggest that Everyoung should target less price-sensitive luxury customers in your marketing. In fact, we would like to test the Lilac Hand Cream at two additional locations and price points, $5.99 at Spreeberg and $7.99 at the Galleria. Could you provide us with 400 additional samples by Monday to stock these locations as well as to restock Blechey and Roxburry?

Please give me a call when you get this to confirm whether you can provide the additional samples. The test will run until the end of the month, at which point we will provide you with a detailed sales report and additional recommendations.

Best regards,

Stacey Evans

Stacey Evans, Account Manager
Intercontinental Market Research

162. What is the main purpose of this letter?
   (A) To request sales data on a new product
   (B) To offer a preliminary analysis of a test
   (C) To set up a meeting to discuss a course of action
   (D) To provide samples for further research

163. According to the letter, what can be inferred about the Galleria?
   (A) It is a high-end shop.
   (B) It is located in a mall.
   (C) It is a flagship store.
   (D) It is close to Spreeberg.

164. What does Stacey Evans NOT recommend Gerhardt Stacker do?
   (A) End the test at the duty-free shop
   (B) Target high-end customers
   (C) Send additional samples
   (D) Telephone her immediately

Memorandum

Date: October 2
To: All Teachers and Councelors
From: Gordon Fris
Re: Survey Results

Of the 358 students in the program, 43 have completed the online satisfaction survey so far. The sample size is small, and responses are still coming in, but there are trends in the data that we cannot ignore. Let's discuss them at the staff meeting tomorrow afternoon.

Students who have completed at least two semesters give us high ratings in most areas, especially in teacher quality, student services, and overall satisfaction. Unsurprisingly, we received relatively low ratings for our facilities. In particular, students complained about our small desks, poor lighting, and the generally appalling condition of the classrooms.

New students noted that the hardware and the software available in the computer lab are outdated, but surprisingly they did not suggest that they be upgraded. Several students said that they prefer their own computers to those in the lab, and they hoped teachers could suggest free or low-cost online resources to supplement their lessons.

Viewed together, these responses suggest that we shouldn't spend our development budget on upgrading the computer lab as we had intended, but instead use those funds to improve the physical environment of the school. I believe doing so would also help boost enrollment. We've known for some time that some potential students visiting the campus are not particularly impressed by our facilities.

Because the survey is conducted online, all results are presented in real-time. The numbers today could be substantially different from those tomorrow, so please check the results on the staff website again just before the meeting tomorrow to make sure we're all on the same page.

165. What most likely was the purpose of the survey?

(A) To suggest new classes and services the school could provide

(B) To evaluate the ways potential students are being recruited

(C) To learn what students think about technology in education

(D) To determine how the school's budget should be spent

166. What issue is NOT likely asked about on the survey?

(A) The quality of teaching staff

(B) The condition of the facilities

(C) The usefulness of the technology

(D) The availability of courses

167. What does Gordon Fris imply in the memo?

(A) Survey responses are still being collected.

(B) The survey questions were not chosen well.

(C) It is too soon to draw any conclusions from the data.

(D) The survey results are unlikely to change.

168. What response was NOT expected by Gordon Fris?

(A) Students prefer well-lit classrooms with comfortable desks.

(B) Students would rather have free or low-cost learning resources.

(C) Students are not satisfied with condition of the school.

(D) Students do not want the computer lab to be upgraded.

DISCOVER THE WORLD OF BOOKS
SUMMAR PROGRAM FOR YOUNG READERS

The Philadelphia Public Library is happy to announce our summer program for young readers: Discover the World of Books. The program will begin on Saturday, June 16 and continue until the end of August. Each two-week session of the program will focus on a different nation, region, or city. Our daily Story Time readings will also feature recommended books from or about the area, and they will be available for reading or check-out at a special display case at the entrance of the children's section. Thanks to guidance from The World Library Association and book exchanges with our sister libraries in Mexico City, Rome, Asmara, Bangalore, and Tokyo, original language versions of many of the books will be displayed together with their translations.

Most exciting for young readers are the free Reading Passports that will be distributed to all participants. Young readers who have finished reading a book from or about a particular area can bring it to any children's librarian and receive a stamp representing that area—just like any world traveler! Readers with twenty or more stamps are eligible to enter a drawing to receive a 24-inch diameter globe.

Thanks to special financial assistance from the city council, the program is free of charge. Readers between the ages of 4 and 14 are eligible, and can register starting on June 1 at the main information desk.

169. What is the main purpose of the program?

(A) To inspire young readers to learn a foreign language

(B) To acquire books from various world cities

(C) To encourage children to read about the world

(D) To assist libraries in other countries

170. Who is funding the program?

(A) The World Library Association

(B) The Philadelphia Public library

(C) Sister libraries around the world

(D) The Philadelphia City Council

171. What type of activity is NOT a part of the program?

(A) Daily book readings

(B) International book exchanges

(C) Reading passports

(D) Visits from international authors

Questions 172-175 refer to the following instructions.

Q-Disk 400
More than just a disc drive

Thank you for your purchase. We created Q-Disk to ensure that your most valuable computer files are always safe and accessible whenever you need them, wherever you are. Just pop a Q-Disk in your pocket, and your data goes with you.

Features
- High-Speed Transfer: Small files are moved almost instantly, large files in just seconds.
- Just the Right Size: Q-Disks are light and fit easily into a coat pocket.
- Turn Up the Volume: Q-Disks can hold tens of thousands of songs or hundreds of full-length feature films.
- Stay in Sync: Whenever Q-Disk is connected to your computer, files are automatically updated to the most recent version.
- Secure: Your data can be encrypted on your computer before it is transferred, ensuring that only you have access to your files.

Operation
- After plugging your Q-disk into a power source, connect it to your computer. An icon will appear on the desktop and Q-Disk is ready to use.
- To enable syncing, encryption, and other advanced features, click on the Q-disk icon. A dialog box will appear guiding you through the many configuration options available. Activate those that you need.

Warranty
- All Q-Disk products are guaranteed to be free of manufacturing defects for two years from the time of purchase.
- The warranty is void if the disk is dropped or exposed to water.

Please email support@q-disk.com if you experience any difficulty with your Q-Disk. For bulk orders, call Q-Disk sales support at (716) 984-9398. To receive updates on our latest offerings, visit us online at q-disk.com.

Q-Disk Inc., 2409 Colvin Blvd., Kenmore, NY 14223

172. Why was the Q-Disk 400 invented?

    (A) To store important files

    (B) To transfer files safely

    (C) To make new files accessible

    (D) To recover lost files

173. Which of the following is NOT a feature of the Q-Disk 400?

    (A) Wireless file transfer

    (B) Automatic synchronization

    (C) Large capacity

    (D) Secure encryption

174. What happens when users click on the icon?

    (A) The disc will access the power source.

    (B) The computer will configure automatic syncing.

    (C) The options menu will appear.

    (D) The advanced features will be activated.

175. What should customers do if they have problems using the Q-Disk 400?

    (A) Call the customer service department

    (B) Find an authorized repair center

    (C) Contact the company by email

    (D) Return it to the place of purchase

http://marketwatch.net/

Online Shopping versus Retail Outlets: Game On

By William Harrison for MarketWatch Insider
Posted: May 22 8:39 am

In the past two years, the popularity of online shopping has exploded. Traditional retail companies, joined by thousands of new virtual storefronts, have turned the Internet into a flourishing online marketplace, and in the process made E-commerce one of the fastest growing industries in the world. At the same time, advances in tablet computers and other mobile devices have made it easy for consumers to make online purchases. With just a few touches of a finger, consumers can buy whatever they need wherever they are. How then can retail outlets to survive? Or, to put it another way, should they?

Maybe not. The benefits of online commerce far outweigh those of traditional shopping. Information about the make and model of every product on the market is now always literally at your fingertips. Gone are the days when you spent entire Saturday afternoons traveling to remote specialty stores to compare products. Never again will you have to fend off overbearing store clerks trying to make their daily sales quotas. Instead, you can sit in the comfort of your own home and read impartial product reviews from experts. In addition to saving time and trouble, online shopping also saves you money: the best bargains are always found online. The staffing costs, electricity bills, and other expenses of online businesses are a small fraction of those borne by traditional retailers, and e-commerce retailers don't have to pay rent in expensive retail locations. These savings are passed on to consumers in the form of lower prices and other benefits, such as coupons and free shipping. As more and more customers experience the convenience and low-prices of online shopping, fewer and fewer retail stores will be able to survive.

Dear Mr. Harrison,

Thank you for bringing this discussion to the readers of MarketWatch Insider. You make several valid points, but I am afraid I must disagree with your main claim. E-commerce will continue to grow, but retail outlets will never disappear for the simple reason that they offer numerous benefits unavailable to online shoppers.

- If you purchase online, you have to wait for the item to be delivered to you, and contrary to what you imply in your article, you will likely have to pay for shipping. If you require that the item arrive the next day, the shipping cost will be considerable. If you require a same-day purchase, a regular retail outlet is your only choice.
- Retail outlets offer the opportunity to "try before you buy." A small picture of a chair, swimsuit, or bicycle on your mobile phone isn't going to tell you how well the item fits your body. And if a purchased item doesn't fit, you must pack it up, take it to the post office, and return it to the seller. How convenient is that?
- It is impossible to adequately communicate touch and smell over the Internet. Colors on a computer screen often appear different than they do in real life. If you really want to know what you're spending your money on, you must experience the product first-hand.
- You do a disservice to salespeople by implying that they care more about sales quotas than they do satisfied customers. Most are entirely reputable and use the expertise they have developed in their field to guide customers to the products that best match their needs.

Jeff Clark

176. What is the MarketWatch article mainly about?

(A) The importance of in-store customers for retail outlets

(B) The factors determining the success of retail stores

(C) The benefits of retail shopping and online shopping

(D) The superiority of online shopping to retail shopping

177. What is NOT mentioned in the article as a benefit of online shopping?

(A) Discount coupons

(B) Objective reviews

(C) Mobile devices

(D) Convenient comparisons

178. In the article, the word "overbearing" in paragraph 2, line 6, is closest in meaning to

(A) aggressive

(B) considerate

(C) overpaid

(D) indifferent

179. According to the comment, what is an advantage of shopping at retail stores?

(A) It allows customers to experience what products are really like.

(B) It provides opportunities for experts to provide product reviews.

(C) It helps salespeople reach their sales quotas more quickly.

(D) It enables business owners to charge more for their products.

180. What does Jeff Clark imply in his comment?

(A) He was once a supporter of online shopping.

(B) E-commerce offers fewer benefits than retail shopping.

(C) There are no benefits to shopping online.

(D) Online shopping will inevitably replace retail shopping.

Questions 181-185 refer to the following advertisement and letter.

Sunny's Restaurant "Daily Deals"

A guaranteed good time for all at any of our Southern California locations!

10% off Tuesdays!
On orders more than $10.00.
Not valid with any other offer.

Soup, Salad, & Fruit Bar Just $1
With the purchase of any item from our special "Heart Smart" menu.

Monday through Friday 7:30 – 11am
Saturday & Sunday 7:30 – 2pm

Family Pizza Special
Only $24.99 plus tax

* Large (16-inch) Cheese Pizza
* Spaghetti and Meatballs
* Caeser Salad (serves four)
* Box of Chocolate Chip Cookies

Not valid with any other offer.

Vegetarian-Friendly
Breakfast Bar

AND MORE!

* French Toast
* Belgian Waffles
* omlettes

Glenda Jefferson
2600 6th St., Apt #4
Fair Oaks, CA 90033

July 28

Sunny's Restaurants
Corporate Headquarters
9483 Beltane Rd., Suite 500
Los Angeles, CA 90210

To Whom It May Concern:

Last Tuesday my husband, our three children, my brother, and I ate at the Sunny's Restaurant on Lankershim Blvd. We were eager to try a new restaurant and glad to take advantage of your daily deals coupons printed in the Sunday paper. I'm sorry to say that the moment we stepped through Sunny's doors I knew it was a bad idea. Instead of "a good time for all" it was a "lousy time by all." Let me explain.

It is very difficult to find a decent vegetarian meal in Fair Oaks, so I was especially excited to try Sunny's vegetarian breakfast bar. Imagine my surprise to find that not ONE item at the bar was truly vegetarian. Further, the advertised soup, salad, and fruit bar was not available. It had closed at the early time of 11:30 am! The only item I could eat was the Caesar salad, so I left the restaurant hungry. In addition, our server would not allow us to split up the check. I was going to use the 10% off Tuesday coupon for my brother's sandwich, and my husband was going to pay for the Family Pizza Special. The server kept saying only one coupon was valid per meal, and that the sandwich only cost $7 so my coupon would be invalid anyway.

Your ad doesn't specify what the "guarantee" entails exactly, but I am sure you stand by your offer. I demand a full refund of our meal—$64.25. If I don't receive a check for that amount by August 15, I will be forced to contact the Fair Oaks Chamber of Commerce and post unfavorable reviews on the Internet.

Sincerely,

Glenda Jefferson

Glenda Jefferson

181. What information is mentioned in the advertisement?
    (A) The addresses of the restaurants
    (B) The ending dates of the offers
    (C) The amount of the discounts
    (D) The original prices of the items

182. What can be inferred about the restaurant?
    (A) The salad bar usually costs more than a dollar.
    (B) It does not serve beverages.
    (C) Sunny's is a vegetarian restaurant.
    (D) It only accepts cash payments.

183. Who is the intended reader of the letter?
    (A) A supervisor at the Lankershim Blvd. location
    (B) A dissatisfied customer of the restaurant
    (C) The management of a retail chain
    (D) The Fair Oaks Chamber of Commerce

184. Why does Glenda Jefferson want?
    (A) To return to Sunny's and use the coupons
    (B) To receive compensation for her meal
    (C) To eat at the vegetarian-friendly breakfast bar
    (D) To change how the restaurant operates

185. What is the tone of the letter?
    (A) Furious
    (B) Apologetic
    (C) Ecstatic
    (D) Supportive

Office Manager, Tokyo, Japan

Job Description
➢ Title: Office Manager
➢ Department: Human Resources
➢ Hiring Office: Cloud Software Company, Tokyo, Japan
➢ Travel Requirements: Occasionally

Major responsibilities include
➢ Organizing and coordinating regular offsite and team building events
➢ Assist the HR team and hiring managers by organizing interviews, screening candidates
➢ Assist the accounting team by collecting and scanning invoices, time sheets
➢ Assist with travel arrangements, meeting coordination and other requests
➢ Assist with organizing local trade shows, job fairs, or other events

Requirements
➢ At least 2 years office management, administrative, or related experience
➢ Human resource experience is a plus
➢ Good verbal and written communication skills in English and Japanese
➢ Excellent time management and prioritization skills
➢ Clearly understand and maintain confidentiality with information

To apply, please send your CV to Vivian Jones at vivian.j@cloud-software.com or call 456-3838 X-771.

To: vivian.j@cloud-software.com
From: Jack Lang [jack.l@mail.com]
Date: April 25, 2018
Subject: Office Manager position in Japan

Dear Vivian,

My name is Jack Lang and I'm writing to express my interest in the Office Manager position listed on your company website. I had experience working as HR Specialist at the First-Rate Hotel for one year. While much of my HR experience had been in the hospitality field, I'm still confident that I could apply my HR knowledge in the software industry without any problem.

My previous responsibilities included interviewing applicants, processing promotions and terminations, and conducting training sessions. I also work closely with customer service managers to evaluating the effectiveness of customer service training programs. Such experience has taught me how to communicate with members from different departments at an organization.

In addition, my mother is Japanese and my father is from Taiwan. I received my university education in the US. So I'm fluent in Japanese, Chinese, and English. I believe that my experience and language ability will be great asset to your software company.

Please see the attached resume for additional information on my experience. I am available for further discussion anytime and can be reached via email at jack.l@mail.com or my cell phone, 888-333-4838. Thank you for your consideration. I look forward to speaking with you about this Office Manager position.

Sincerely,

Jack Lang

To: jack.l@mail.com

From: vivian.j@cloud-software.com

Date: May 5, 2018

Subject: Re: Office Manager position in Japan

Dear Mr. Lang:

Thank you for your application for the position of Office Manager at Could-Software in Japan. As you may imagine, we did receive scores of applications. As a matter of fact, we prefer to recruit talents with sufficient experience in the software industry. I am sorry to inform you that you have not been selected for an interview for this position. We encourage you to apply for future openings for which you qualify.

Thank you once again for your interest in Cloud-Software company.

Best regards,

Vivian J.

186. What is the main purpose of the advertisement?

    (A) To recruit a manager

    (B) To announce new policies

    (C) To promote products

    (D) To invite seminar attendees

187. What is NOT true about the job offered?

    (A) It's located in Japan.

    (B) It involves cross-department cooperation.

    (C) It's been vacant for two years.

    (D) Many people are applying for it.

188. What is indicated about Jack Lang?

    (A) He's an experienced software designer.

    (B) He's willing to relocate to the UK.

    (C) He's able to speak several languages.

    (D) He's been rehired by the First-Rate Hotel.

189. Why does Vivian J. send the email?

    (A) To welcome Jack as her new colleague

    (B) To appreciate Jack's contributions

    (C) To encourage Jack to apply for jobs in other branches

    (D) To decline Jack's job application

190. Why is Jack NOT being selected for an interview?

    (A) His English is not fluent enough.

    (B) He lacks sufficient experience in the software industry.

    (C) He has been working in the hotel for too long.

    (D) He doesn't provide effective references.

Hydraulic fracturing, commonly referred to as "fracking," is a technique to make natural gas wells more productive. Water, sand, and chemicals are injected into the ground, so that more natural gas can be pumped to the surface. Energy companies love the extra gas, but the practice has worried thousands of Green Valley residents. They are organizing against the possible leasing of 38,000 acres of the Green National Forest to the gas industry, who plan to install hundreds of fracking wells in the area. If the leasing goes through, the residents claim their quality of life will be threatened and the pristine environment destroyed.

The residents' primary concern is for their health and safety. Fracking has been cited as a source of chemical explosions and water pollution. Studies have shown that disease rates are higher near fracking wells. The residents also claim that because the Green National Forest was declared a public commons the government has a commitment to protect the forest.

Green Valley residents commissioned Public Eyewitness to conduct a survey to summarize residents' opinions on the matter. The results of the environmental organization's poll shows that 87% of citizens would agree to pay higher taxes to fund the research of other sources of energy.

Hydraulic Fracturing in Green Valley

1. How much time do you spend in the Green Valley National Forest?
   A) 1 day a week
   B) 2 days a week
   C) 3 days a week
   D) 4+ days a week

2. What is your primary concern about hydraulic fracturing in Green Valley?
   A) Damage to Habitats
   B) Water Pollution
   C) Accidental Explosions
   D) Disease

3. How receptive would you be to paying a higher sales tax to fund more sustainable energy types, like solar, wind, or geothermal power?
   A) Very unreceptive
   B) Somewhat unreceptive
   C) Somewhat receptive
   D) Very receptive

4. How likely is it that natural gas will replace coal in our domestic market?
   A) Very unlikely
   B) Somewhat unlikely
   C) Somewhat likely
   D) Very likely

Results

1. A) 22%	B) 12%	C) 18%	D) 48%
2. A) 12%	B) 23%	C) 26%	D) 39%
3. A) 5%	B) 4%	C) 4%	D) 87%
4. A) 67%	B) 10%	C) 17%	D) 6%

Poll administered by the Public Eyewitness to 1,000 Green Valley residents by telephone on August 23. Margin of error +/– 3%. Source: Public Eyewitness.

To: Linda Smith [linda.s@environment-tech.com]

From: Jack Wills [jack.w@environment-tech.com]

Subject: Meeting request

Hi Linda,

Please refer to the attached press release and results of the survey conducted in Green Valley. We can see that people are more environmental conscious nowadays than in the past. As we are also planning to launch new environmental friendly products, let's arrange a meeting this week to discuss the issue in details. I'm available this Wednesday morning at 10, and please confirm if this time slot is convenient for you. Prior to the meeting, please contact the organization which conducted the survey and check if they are able to release more detailed information to us.

I'll talk to you further about this.

Jack Wills

191. Why did Green Valley residents organize?

(A) To improve the safety of hydraulic fracturing

(B) To oppose the leasing of public land to the gas industry

(C) To limit government spending on hydraulic fracturing

(D) To discuss ways to increase energy efficiency

192. What is Public Eyewitness?

(A) A local government department

(B) A nature conservation group

(C) A Green Valley citizen's organization

(D) A gas industry advocacy group

193. What topic did Public Eyewitness ask residents about?

(A) Their willingness to move out of the valley

(B) Their use of the public lands

(C) Their views on government policy

(D) Their concerns about local species

194. According to the poll, what issue does the greatest number of Green Valley citizens agree on?

(A) They visit the National Forest at least 4 days a week.

(B) They are concerned about potential diseases.

(C) They are willing to pay higher taxes.

(D) They believe coal will replace natural gas soon.

195. What does Jack ask Linda to do next?

(A) Contact Public Eyewitness for details

(B) Arrange an international conference

(C) Call Green Valley residents for feedback

(D) Send an email to his assistant

Allison Cartwright
1465 Vagabond Road
Fairbanks, AK 99701
(907) 435-8754
allison.cartwright@adp.com

September 24

George Mallory, CEO
World Harvest
1940 L Street NW
Washington DC 20036
(202) 576-9672

Dear Mr. Mallory,

I was very impressed by your keynote presentation at the National Conference for Nonprofit Organizations in February. I was especially pleased to learn that World Harvest engages in projects similar to work I've been involved with for the past ten years at Ageing Affairs. I can only imagine the amount of resumes you are receiving, but I hope you will consider mine carefully. I am very eager to work for World Harvest.

My experience fighting for elderly rights has given me unique experiences and insights that I believe would be of value to your organization. Some highlights of my career include:

• Founded Fairbanks Assistance Program to identify and assist low-income, elderly, and disabled residents
• Conceived and wrote, with State Representative Mark Lang, the first Alaskan statewide law safeguarding tax relief for elderly and disabled residents
• Named Fairbanks Monthly (local newspaper) "Person of the Year" for community service

I also have experience managing large-budget programs, supervising diverse teams of employees and volunteers, and overseeing fundraising events with over 1,200 attendees. Please see my attached resume for details.

I would enjoy an opportunity to talk with you or someone in your organization to see where my skills would be of the greatest benefit to you. I will be in Washington DC again the week of May 15, and could meet with you anytime.

Sincerely,

Allison Cartwright

Allison Cartwright

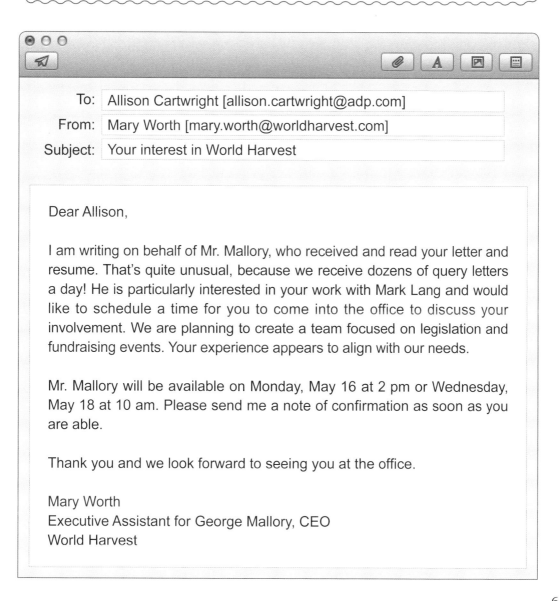

To: Allison Cartwright [allison.cartwright@adp.com]

From: Mary Worth [mary.worth@worldharvest.com]

Subject: Your interest in World Harvest

Dear Allison,

I am writing on behalf of Mr. Mallory, who received and read your letter and resume. That's quite unusual, because we receive dozens of query letters a day! He is particularly interested in your work with Mark Lang and would like to schedule a time for you to come into the office to discuss your involvement. We are planning to create a team focused on legislation and fundraising events. Your experience appears to align with our needs.

Mr. Mallory will be available on Monday, May 16 at 2 pm or Wednesday, May 18 at 10 am. Please send me a note of confirmation as soon as you are able.

Thank you and we look forward to seeing you at the office.

Mary Worth
Executive Assistant for George Mallory, CEO
World Harvest

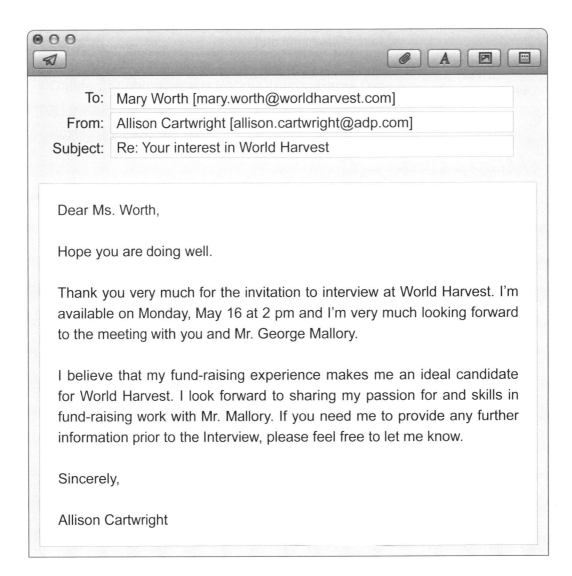

To: Mary Worth [mary.worth@worldharvest.com]

From: Allison Cartwright [allison.cartwright@adp.com]

Subject: Re: Your interest in World Harvest

Dear Ms. Worth,

Hope you are doing well.

Thank you very much for the invitation to interview at World Harvest. I'm available on Monday, May 16 at 2 pm and I'm very much looking forward to the meeting with you and Mr. George Mallory.

I believe that my fund-raising experience makes me an ideal candidate for World Harvest. I look forward to sharing my passion for and skills in fund-raising work with Mr. Mallory. If you need me to provide any further information prior to the Interview, please feel free to let me know.

Sincerely,

Allison Cartwright

196. Why did Allison Cartwright contact George Mallory?
  (A) To thank him for participating in a conference
  (B) To request a donation for her organization
  (C) To inquire about a position with World Harvest
  (D) To discuss fundraising ideas and opportunities

197. In the letter, the word "conceived" in paragraph 3, line 3, is closest in meaning to
  (A) originated
  (B) requested
  (C) drafted
  (D) proved

198. What does Mary Worth's email imply?
  (A) Many people are interested in working at World Harvest.
  (B) World Harvest is not currently hiring new employees.
  (C) Ageing Affairs and World Harvest should work together.
  (D) She is looking for a job in a different industry.

199. Why does George Mallory want to meet with Allison Cartwright?
  (A) She has experience that his organization needs.
  (B) She can recommend Mark Lang for a position.
  (C) She will deliver an important keynote address.
  (D) She is an expert on the rights of the elderly.

200. Where will Allison's interview take place on May 16?
  (A) Fairbanks
  (B) Washington DC
  (C) New York
  (D) Chicago

Part 2

模擬試題

Test 2

Directions: Part 7 consists of a number of texts such as emails, advertisements, and newspaper articles. After each text or set of texts there are several questions. Choose the best answer to each question and mark the corresponding letter (A), (B), (C), and (D) on your answer sheet.

Questions 147-148 refer to the following document.

Anderson Landscaping Company
436 Eastern Blvd.
Clarksville, IN 47129
Telephone: (819) 555-4378
Email: tom@tomandersonlandscaping.com
Web: www.tomandersonlandscaping.com

INVOICE
PAYMENT DUE: 5/16

Customer: Randy Tompkins Realty
Contact: Randy Tompkins
Customer Account #: 1293
Service Description: Front yard landscaping

Date: 04/16
Ph: (819) 387-9723
Payment method: Credit Card

Unit	Unit Cost	Quantity	Total/$
Design/Layout	$1000/150 sq. ft.	N/A	1000.00
Trees	$150	2	300.00
Sod	$3.99 per roll	40	159.60
Planters/Flower Pots	$25 each	5	125.00
Landscape Edging	$12.99	4	51.96
Limestone Stepping Stones	$10.79 per stone	8	86.32
Labor	$40/hour	20	800.00

Sub-total		$2522.88
Returning Customer Discount (4%)		$100.92
Total		$2421.96

Open seven days a week from 8:00 am to 4:00 pm.

147. How many trees did Anderson Landscaping Company buy?

(A) One

(B) Four

(C) Two

(D) Five

148. Why was Randy Tompkins offered a discount?

(A) The total amount was paid one month before the due date.

(B) He agreed to pay for the landscaping with a credit card.

(C) The amount of the invoice exceeded $2,000.

(D) He has done business with Anderson Landscaping before.

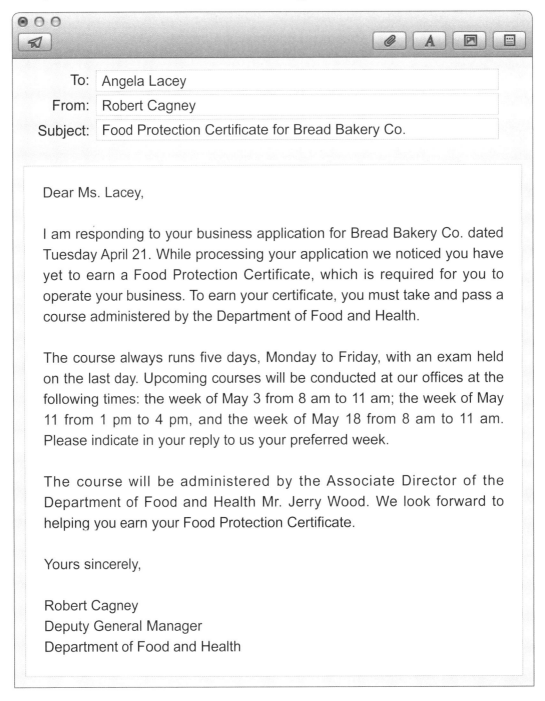

To: Angela Lacey

From: Robert Cagney

Subject: Food Protection Certificate for Bread Bakery Co.

Dear Ms. Lacey,

I am responding to your business application for Bread Bakery Co. dated Tuesday April 21. While processing your application we noticed you have yet to earn a Food Protection Certificate, which is required for you to operate your business. To earn your certificate, you must take and pass a course administered by the Department of Food and Health.

The course always runs five days, Monday to Friday, with an exam held on the last day. Upcoming courses will be conducted at our offices at the following times: the week of May 3 from 8 am to 11 am; the week of May 11 from 1 pm to 4 pm, and the week of May 18 from 8 am to 11 am. Please indicate in your reply to us your preferred week.

The course will be administered by the Associate Director of the Department of Food and Health Mr. Jerry Wood. We look forward to helping you earn your Food Protection Certificate.

Yours sincerely,

Robert Cagney
Deputy General Manager
Department of Food and Health

149. What is the purpose of the email?

 (A) To assign homework to a new student

 (B) To present a certificate to an applicant

 (C) To request that someone take a course

 (C) To ask someone to supply a certificate

150. What does Mr. Cagney want Ms. Lacey to do?

 (A) Schedule a class

 (B) Conduct an exam

 (C) Reapply for a permit

 (D) Contact an associate

Questions 151-152 refer to the following text message chain.

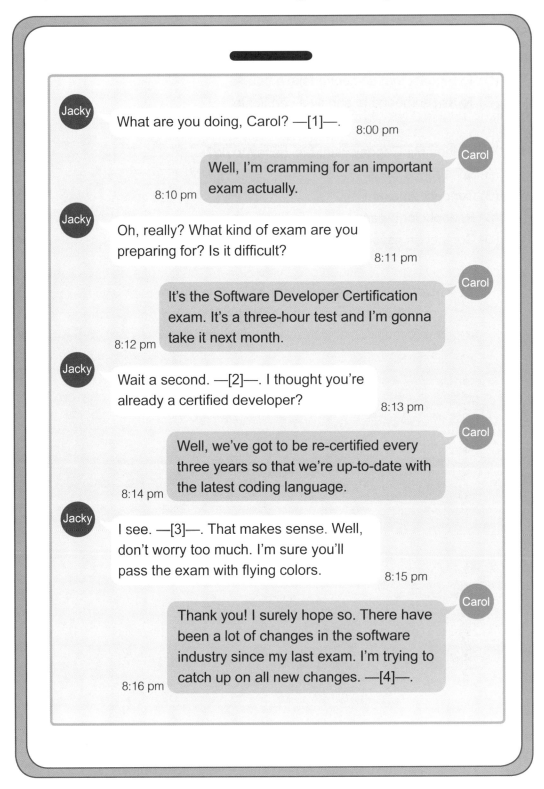

Jacky: What are you doing, Carol? —[1]—. 8:00 pm

Carol: Well, I'm cramming for an important exam actually. 8:10 pm

Jacky: Oh, really? What kind of exam are you preparing for? Is it difficult? 8:11 pm

Carol: It's the Software Developer Certification exam. It's a three-hour test and I'm gonna take it next month. 8:12 pm

Jacky: Wait a second. —[2]—. I thought you're already a certified developer? 8:13 pm

Carol: Well, we've got to be re-certified every three years so that we're up-to-date with the latest coding language. 8:14 pm

Jacky: I see. —[3]—. That makes sense. Well, don't worry too much. I'm sure you'll pass the exam with flying colors. 8:15 pm

Carol: Thank you! I surely hope so. There have been a lot of changes in the software industry since my last exam. I'm trying to catch up on all new changes. —[4]—. 8:16 pm

151. What is the message communication about?

(A) New market trends

(B) The woman's certification exam

(C) A newly launched product

(D) The man's weekend plan

152. In which of the positions marked [1], [2], [3], and [4] does the following sentence best belong?

"I'll do my best."

(A) [1]

(B) [2]

(C) [3]

(D) [4]

National Electric

JAF Station   Account holder: Nancy L. Martin
New York, NY 10116-1702   Account number: 55-5476-8743-0004-2

Billing Summary

Previous charges and payments

Total charges from your last bill $32.29
Payments received. Thank You .... -$32.29 —[1]—.
New electricity charges for the billing period Apr. 06 to May 07

Total amount due $34.07
To avoid a late payment charge of 1.5%, please pay the total amount due by **June 1**

Electricity Charges

These charges are for the electricity you used (supply) and getting that electricity to you
(delivery). Rates are based on a 30-day period. When your billing period is more or less than
30 days, we prorate your bill accordingly. —[2]—.

Electricity used during the Apr. 06 to May 07 billing period (31 days)

We measure your electricity by how many kilowatt hours (kWh) you use.

May 07 actual reading	2815
April 06 actual reading	-2744
Your electricity use	**71 kWh**

❏ **Your supply charges**

Supply 71 kWh @7.2817 c/kWh $5.17
Charge for the electricity supplied to you by National Electric
Total supply charges $5.17

❏ **Your delivery charges**

Basic service charge $19.31
Charge for basic system infrastructure and customer-related services, including customer
accounting, meter reading and meter maintenance. —[3]—.

Delivery 71 kWh @11.4507 c/kWh $8.12
Charge for maintaining the system though which National Electric delivers electricity for you.

Total delivery charges $27.43

❏ **Your sales tax**

Sales tax @4.5000% $1.47
Tax collected on behalf of New York State and/or your locality.

Total electricity charges $34.07

Next meter reading: Wednesday, June 6 —[4]—.

153. What type of document is this?

    (A) Utility bill

    (B) Commercial invoice

    (C) Estimate of charges

    (D) Credit card statement

154. How much is Nancy Martin being charged for delivery?

    (A) $19.31

    (B) $27.43

    (C) $32.29

    (D) $34.07

155. In which of the position marked [1], [2], [3], and [4] does the following sentence best belong?

"Should you have any questions, please send an email to: info@electric.com."

    (A) [1]

    (B) [2]

    (C) [3]

    (D) [4]

Desert Valley Tours
Welcome to Desert Valley – A destination unlike any other!

Located just minutes away from downtown Hagerton, Desert Valley Tours offers a range of hiking and dining options to help you explore and enjoy the beautiful Desert Valley. Departing from the Desert Inn Hotel lobby, you can enjoy scenic views, delightful hiking adventures, or evening elegance. The choice is yours!

Full Day Tour
✳ The Desert Valley Grand Tour is by far our most popular. Enjoy breakfast at the charming Dessert Inn cafe, and then take a mid-day jeep ride and walkabout through the Hagerton Wilderness Area, where a light picnic lunch will be served. Finish the evening with dinner and drinks at the historic Old Horse Saloon in Frankton. The Desert Valley Tour bus will make a stop in downtown Hagerton before returning to the Desert Inn.

Mid-Day Tour
✳ Departing at 11:00 am, the Cactus Peak Day Hike offers beautiful panorama views of Desert Valley as you ramble to the summit of Cactus Peak. Afterwards you'll stop by the historic Old Horse Saloon in historic Frankton for a late buffet lunch, beverages, and live entertainment before returning to downtown Hagerton via Bus 12.

Evening Tours
✳ The Desert Valley Skyline Tour is known for combining gorgeous views with first class convenience. Enjoy the leisurely ride to the top of the mountain on the sleek and comfortable Skyline Tramway. Savor a five-course meal at the luxurious Peak Pit Restaurant and watch the sun set over Desert Valley. The Desert Valley Tour bus will make a stop in downtown Hagerton before returning to the Desert Inn.

✳ For something different, try the Desert Moonlight Hike, offered Monday, Wednesday, and Friday in the spring and summer. Explore Desert Valley and Cactus Peak by night with guide Roger Rick! Tour departs at 5 pm. Flashlights will be provided. Bus 12 will return you to downtown Hagerton.

• Tour Information Hotline: (800) 847-3776
• Tours may be canceled or cut short due to inclement weather.

156. Which tour does NOT include any food or beverages?
    (A) The Desert Valley Grand Tour
    (B) The Cactus Peak Day Hike
    (C) The Desert Valley Skyline Tour
    (D) The Desert Moonlight Hike

157. Why would a tour member take Bus 12?
    (A) To return to downtown Hagerton
    (B) To get to the Old Horse Saloon
    (C) To visit historic Frankton
    (D) To reach the top of Cactus Peak

158. The word "inclement" in the last line is closest in meaning to
    (A) unseasonal
    (B) unpredictable
    (C) humid
    (D) stormy

Retail Sales Up in January Despite Bad Weather
February 6

Last month's snowstorms surprisingly didn't hinder purchasing by consumers, who "are in better shape than feared and have begun the year with a return to more normal buying habits," the Greenwood Times reported. General retail sales rose 4.2% over the previous month according to Retail Analytics Inc.

"It appears that consumers are feeling a little bit more confident about their financial situation and the economy as a whole," said Jordan Smith, president of Retail Analytics Inc. "They're coming out of hibernation."

The Financial Street Journal reported that the International Council of Retail Centers "expects the industry to post a 2.3% same-store sales increase in February. Also, national holidays later this month are likely to help increase sales. So might tax refunds in March." This will be good news for first quarter roundups.

Syngas Services expressed caution, however, noting that despite the "modestly positive results, we remain unconvinced that this is evidence of a sustainable trend." Syngas believes the economy is still fragile and vulnerable to surprise shocks. Unpredictable events such as a sudden increase in oil prices or large-scale changes in the job market could easily affect consumer spending. Furthermore, they claim consumer purchasing has slowed every second quarter for the past four years. "It's unrealistic to believe there will be a turn now."

159. What can be inferred about the January sales increase?

(A) It was not included in Retail Analytics' report.

(B) It was a result of unusual weather.

(C) It was smaller than in previous years.

(D) It was larger than some analysts predicted.

160. What is NOT mentioned as affecting the First Quarter?

(A) Upcoming holidays

(B) Natural disasters

(C) Consumer confidence

(D) Tax refunds

161. Why is Syngas Services concerned?

(A) Higher prices will affect the favorable business climate.

(B) There is no evidence that consumers will continue spending.

(C) Oil and gas prices are expected in to increase in the second quarter.

(D) Most analysts predict the retail industry will suffer a slowdown.

Arts & Crafts Festival

Celebrate Spring! The roses are blooming and the smell of lilacs is in the air. The Lafayette Chamber of Commerce is pleased to announce the 5th Annual Arts & Crafts Festival will take place in downtown Lafayette. On Saturday March 21 and Sunday March 22, the Great Lawn of Lafayette's Public Square will be transformed into an arts and crafts extravaganza!

Twenty local artisans will display their work and offer free arts and crafts programs for both adults and children. Live entertainment will be ongoing throughout the weekend on the Wilburn Stage near the north end of the park. Fine cuisine and beverages will be available at the Food Court located at the south end of the square. For more information on the participating artists, vendors, and schedule of programs please visit www.lafayette.com/artsandcraftsfestival.

Festival hours are 10 am–9 pm. There is no admission charge. Children of all ages are welcome, but no pets are allowed. Please note that parking will be limited. Shuttles from the Shreveport Mall to downtown Lafayette will be available for $2 one way.

We'll see you at Lafayette's Public Square!

162. What does the announcement suggest about the festival?

    (A) It will be held in downtown Lafayette.

    (B) It will be for viewing art only.

    (C) It will be for children only.

    (D) It will be held in the summer.

163. What is Public Square?

    (A) A park

    (B) An auditorium

    (C) A school

    (D) A shopping mall

164. What does the festival prohibit?

    (A) Children

    (B) Pets

    (C) Parking

    (D) Blankets

Mary Cohen
152 Dolores St., Apt 3C
San Francisco, CA 94114

July 28

First Ocean Realty
John Patterson
2500 Divisadero St.
San Francisco, CA 94123

Re: Immediate repairs needed

Dear Mr. Patterson,

I have been living in the apartment at 152 Dolores Street for 14 years. I've been a loyal tenant and paid my rent on time during that entire period. I have also regularly agreed to the yearly increase in rent. However, I am very dissatisfied with how you handle repairs.

Four months ago I sent you notice about several repairs needed in the apartment. This included repairing or replacing windows that do not close and lock properly, fixing the radiator, and replacing the kitchen cabinets.

Exactly one month ago, the superintendent came to my apartment to take a look at the needed repairs. He fixed the radiator and replaced the kitchen cabinets. He told me you handle all window repairs because you deal with the window company directly. I left a phone message for you about this matter but never received a reply.

The last time I called was on July 23, and you told me a window repairman would come to my house the following Tuesday. The repairman did not come.

This problem needs to be addressed immediately. There have been several burglaries in the neighborhood and I do not feel safe in the apartment. I would rather keep this matter out of the courts, but if a window repairman does not come to my apartment by August 2, I will have to seek legal action.

Sincerely,

Mary Cohen

Mary Cohen

165. Why did Mary Cohen write this letter to John Patterson?
    (A) To insist that her windows be repaired
    (B) To report a problem with her radiator
    (C) To ask that the kitchen cabinets be replaced
    (D) To request that her rent be reduced

166. When did Mary Cohen first contact John Patterson?
    (A) Four months ago
    (B) One month ago
    (C) July 23
    (D) July 28

167. What will Mary probably do before August 2?
    (A) Wait for John Patterson to arrange a repair
    (B) Move into a different apartment in the area
    (C) Have the windows replaced at her own expense
    (D) File a legal claim in a court of law

http://www.losfelizsubway.com/lostandfound

Los Feliz Subway Lost and Found

If you have inadvertently left your glasses, umbrella, handbag, or clothing on the subway, we may be able to help you. The Los Feliz Subway Lost and Found Office receives over 4,000 items every year, and we make every effort to reunite each item with its owner.

Please complete the form below, describing your property. If you have lost a high-value item such as a phone or computer, we may ask for additional proof of ownership.

Lost Property Inquiry Form

Describe the Property (color, make, model, material, unique characteristics, etc.)

When and Where Did You Travel?

Date: [ ]   Time: [ ]   From: [ ]   To: [ ]

How Can We Contact You?

Address: [ ]

Email: [ ]   Phone: [ ]

Submit

Claiming Your Property

Items may be picked up at our office at the Alameda St. Station or, for an additional fee, they may be returned to you by mail or courier. Our office is open Monday, Wednesday, and Friday from 2 pm to 10 pm. and Thursday and Saturday from 8 am to 3 pm. If you have not heard from us within three weeks of filing a claim, then unfortunately it means we did not recover your item. Items are held for 30 days and then auctioned off with the proceeds donated to charity.

168. Why would someone use this webpage?

(A) To report an item found on the subway

(B) To inquire about the operation of the subway

(C) To claim an item left behind on the subway

(D) To suggest a service be provided by the subway

169. In what situation would the Lost and Found Office require additional information?

(A) When a lost item has been unclaimed for 30 days

(B) When a lost item is especially valuable

(C) When a lost item has a distinguishing characteristic

(D) When a lost item is delivered to the wrong station

170. When can lost property be picked up?

(A) Monday mornings

(B) Tuesday afternoons

(C) Wednesday evenings

(D) Weekend nights

171. What happens to items that are unclaimed after one month?

(A) They are held until they are picked up.

(B) They are delivered by mail or courier.

(C) They are given to a charity for distribution.

(D) They are sold to the highest bidder.

Tips for Traveling with an Infant on a Plane

1 Try to select a flight that coincides with the infant's normal sleep schedule. A late-afternoon flight would be a good choice if your child regularly naps then. And taking a red eye flight in the early morning hours may not be convenient for you, but it would be worth it if your baby sleeps soundly during the entire flight.

2 Bring a sturdy yet compact stroller. Even if you won't be using it at your final destination, it will come in handy when navigating the airport, especially if you have a layover and have to change planes quickly.

3 Leave plenty of time for surprises before you leave for the airport. If you forget an essential item like a pacifier, extra diapers, or clothing, you will be able to purchase these items before you arrive at the airline check-in counter.

4 Always request the bulkhead seats. It gives you ample floor space for changing diapers and you won't have to worry about your infant kicking the seats in front of you. Window seats preferred because they are slightly darker and offer fewer distractions.

5 Due to changes in cabin air temperature and pressure, it is inevitable that your infant will shed tears. To make your infant comfortable you can remove or add a piece of clothing. To relieve pressure in the ears, walk your infant in the aisle.

6 It is a good idea to bring more items than you think you will need. Be sure to pack extra amounts of all your essential items, including formula, diapers, clothing, toys, and snacks.

172. According to the article, when is the best time for infants to fly?
    (A) During the infant's regular sleeping time
    (B) During the late afternoon
    (C) In the early morning hours
    (D) When it is most convenient for the parents

173. What should you NOT do when traveling with a baby?
    (A) Arrange to be seated next to a window
    (B) Bring a stroller for use in the airport
    (C) Carry extra quantities of items you normally use
    (D) Arrive at the airport just before the check-in time

174. Why should you request a bulkhead seat?
    (A) It is the best place for your infant to nap.
    (B) It is darker and offers fewer distractions.
    (C) It gives parents space for changing diapers.
    (D) It tends to be warmer and more comfortable.

175. The word "inevitable" in point 5, line 1, is closest in meaning to
    (A) avoidable
    (B) certain
    (C) unforeseeable
    (D) unexpected

Measureable Media:
The Next Generation of Internet Marketing Services

If you have a website, Measurable Media can make it better. We use sophisticated software tools to track and measure how visitors engage with your website. We then use this information to increase the number of visitors to your site, the amount of time they spend there, your overall revenue, and—most dramatically—the revenue generated by each purchase.

Measurable Media carefully tests each page of your site by making hundreds of very small changes and then comparing the results. The final product is a webpage optimized for your customers—and your business. We know our methods are effective because we contract with neutral third-party auditors to evaluate our work. If we don't achieve measureable results, you receive our services free of charge. So, if you're wondering how to improve your online marketing efforts, ask yourself these questions:

    Do you know how visitors find your site?
    Do you know how they use it?
    Do you know how to keep users comi ng back?
    Do you know how to encourage them to spend more?

Measurable Media knows, and we're ready to help you serve your customers better.

Comparison of OrganiPure Skin Care Website Metrics
Before and After Measurable Media Overhaul*

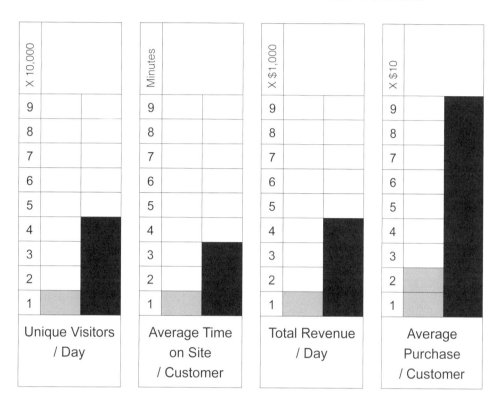

Before Measureable Media Site Overhaul
After Measureable Media Site Overhaul

* All figures verified by Princeton Metrics, an independent research and auditing firm.

176. According to the advertisement, who would benefit most from using Measurable Media Services?

(A) Internet users who visit a large number of websites daily

(B) Individuals who have created personal webpages

(C) Businesses that are interested in creating a homepage

(D) Companies that sell products directly from a website

177. Why does Measurable Media say their results are reliable?

(A) They are achieved with sophisticated software tools.

(B) They are calculated by neutral third parties.

(C) They are independently verified by auditors.

(D) They are guaranteed by a money-back offer.

178. In the advertisement, the word "optimized" in paragraph 2, line 3, is closest in meaning to

(A) enhanced

(B) personalized

(C) popularized

(D) programmed

179. According to the graphs, in what area is Measurable Media most effective?

(A) Doubling the daily number of visitors

(B) Reducing the amount of time visitors spend on the website

(C) Maintaining the revenue generated by the website

(D) Increasing the average amount customers spend

180. What information in NOT shown in the graphs?

(A) The number of visitors to the website

(B) The length of time visitors spend on the website

(C) The total cost per day of running the website

(D) The amount of money visitors spend on the website

To: All Staff
From: Laura Bonn, Principal
Date: May 18
Re: Construction

As many of you already know, Banner Junior High School is scheduled to undergo major renovations in the coming months. Most of the construction will be undertaken during the summer, but due to the extent of work, it will not be completed by the time classes resume in September. To minimize disruption to classes and other school activities, it is important that students, faculty, and staff are aware of the following construction schedule.

Building	Under Construction
South Classroom Building	June 15–September 1
North Classroom Building	July 10–October 12
Library and Media Center	October 20–December 1
Gymnasium	June 1–July 31
Administration Building	September 10–December 10

As you can see, only the South Classroom Building and Gymnasium will be complete by September 15, the first day of school. When school resumes, classes and activities that normally take place in buildings still under construction will unfortunately either be cancelled, postponed, or moved temporarily into the South Classroom Building or the Gymnasium. I will inform all staff of these necessary changes before June 1. I invite teachers affected by the construction to contact me with any questions or particular concerns. I will do my best to accommodate everyone's needs.

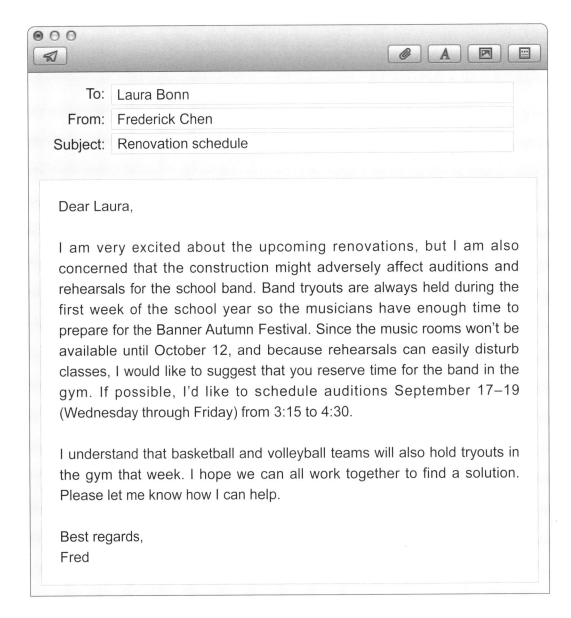

To: Laura Bonn
From: Frederick Chen
Subject: Renovation schedule

Dear Laura,

I am very excited about the upcoming renovations, but I am also concerned that the construction might adversely affect auditions and rehearsals for the school band. Band tryouts are always held during the first week of the school year so the musicians have enough time to prepare for the Banner Autumn Festival. Since the music rooms won't be available until October 12, and because rehearsals can easily disturb classes, I would like to suggest that you reserve time for the band in the gym. If possible, I'd like to schedule auditions September 17–19 (Wednesday through Friday) from 3:15 to 4:30.

I understand that basketball and volleyball teams will also hold tryouts in the gym that week. I hope we can all work together to find a solution. Please let me know how I can help.

Best regards,
Fred

181. Why did Laura Bonn write the memo?
    (A) To inform staff of band auditions
    (B) To announce the opening of a new building
    (C) To seek suggestions about construction
    (D) To ensure staff know about renovations

182. What does Laura Bonn hope to limit?
    (A) The time allowed for construction
    (B) The disruption of classes at Banning Jr. High
    (C) The space required for sporting events
    (D) The number of activities at the school

183. In which building are the music rooms located?
    (A) The South Classroom Building
    (B) The North Classroom Building
    (C) The Library and Media Center
    (D) The Gymnasium

184. What does Frederick Chen recommend?
    (A) Postponing the renovation
    (B) Rescheduling some classes
    (C) Contacting the principal directly
    (D) Moving the location of an activity

185. In the email, the word "adversely" in paragraph 1, line 2, is closest in meaning to
    (A) negatively
    (B) necessarily
    (C) significantly
    (D) surprisingly

Questions 186-190 refer to the following advertisement and emails.

College of Roman

~~ ~~ Put Music in Your Life ~~ ~~

Classical, Contemporary and Jazz
Instrumental and Vocal Ensembles
Lesson for voice and all instruments
Group classes for guitar, piano and voice

Feel the Beat of Music

Dr. Jennifer Adams	Voice Studies	557-483-5838
Mr. George Jefferson	Piano Studies	557-483-5726
Dr. John Lincoln	Drum Studies	557-483-2794
Dr. Adam Coles	Saxophone Studies	557-483-1769
Ms. Jennifer Wolf	General information on music classes	557-483-1769

Visit our official website at www.roman-college.com for more information. To apply, please call Mr. Jack Phil at 557-483-7722 or email: jack.p@roman-college.com

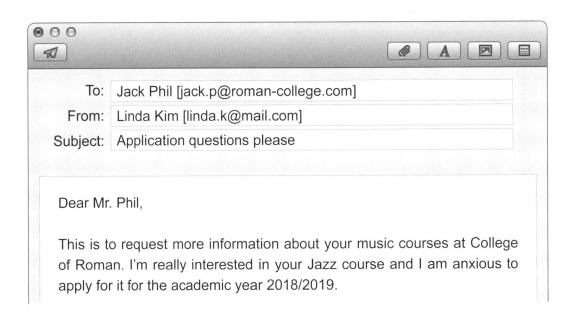

To: Jack Phil [jack.p@roman-college.com]
From: Linda Kim [linda.k@mail.com]
Subject: Application questions please

Dear Mr. Phil,

This is to request more information about your music courses at College of Roman. I'm really interested in your Jazz course and I am anxious to apply for it for the academic year 2018/2019.

First, I would like to inquire about qualifications. I've taken keyboard skills, music and science, and other related courses in a local college in Korea. I would be grateful if you could indicate the academic requirements for an international student like me.

Next, as this will be the first time I'll live away from my hometown in Korea, accommodation is rather important to me. I've decided to rent my own place off-campus, so I wonder if you could please recommend some nearby and affordable apartments for me to choose from.

Thank you in advance for your attention to my requests. I look forward to receiving your response.

Sincerely,

Linda Kim

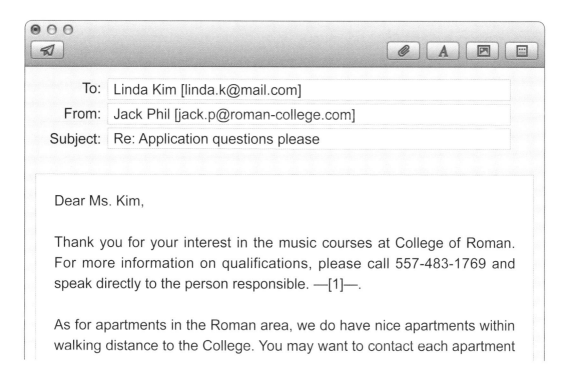

To: Linda Kim [linda.k@mail.com]

From: Jack Phil [jack.p@roman-college.com]

Subject: Re: Application questions please

Dear Ms. Kim,

Thank you for your interest in the music courses at College of Roman. For more information on qualifications, please call 557-483-1769 and speak directly to the person responsible. —[1]—.

As for apartments in the Roman area, we do have nice apartments within walking distance to the College. You may want to contact each apartment office for current pricing and availability. Please note that when renting an apartment off-campus, you as a renter should be responsible for utilities such as electricity. It's the renter's responsibility to contact these apartments for more information on utilities, amenities, fees and refunds. —[2]—.

The Fox Garden
5838 Cedar Drive
Roman City, WA 58379
Telephone: 557-372-4828
Email: info@fox-garden.com
Price range: $200-$400 per month
Size: one / two-bedroom models available, one bath
Distance from the College of Roman: 1 km —[3]—.

The City View Apartments
2525 Spring Road
Roman City, WA 58379
Telephone: 557-367-2827
Email: super@city-view.com
Price range: $250-$500 per month
Size: one / two / three-bedroom models
Distance from College of Roman: 2.5 km

Should you have further questions, please feel free to contact me. —[4]—.

Best regards,

Jack Phil

186. In the advertisement, what does the table list?

  (A) Student names

  (B) Class professors and their numbers

  (C) Tuition fees

  (D) Class schedules

187. What is NOT true about Linda Kim?

  (A) She'd like to attend some music classes.

  (B) She knows how to play keyboards.

  (C) She prefers to live on campus.

  (D) She is a Korean.

188. Who does Jack Phil suggest Linda Kim call for class information?

  (A) John Lincoln

  (B) Jennifer Wolf

  (C) George Jefferson

  (D) Adam Coles

189. Which apartment would Linda Kim probably prefer?

  (A) The City View Apartments

  (B) Roman Houses

  (C) Sunny Palace

  (D) The Fox Garden

190. In which of the position marked [1], [2], [3], and [4] does the following sentence best belong?

  "Here are two apartments that may be better to suit your needs."

  (A) [1]

  (B) [2]

  (C) [3]

  (D) [4]

Wholesome Foods

18732 Becker St., Racine, WI 53401

Marcie Stephenson
Marcie's Downhome Grill
215 Lakeside Dr.
Madison, WI 53701

July 20

Dear Ms. Stephenson,

Today we received your canceled invoice for an order of cheese, crackers, and nuts. I understand that you were not satisfied with your order, but according to the terms of the purchase agreement that you signed, you are still liable for the full amount. Also, because payment was due on July 16, you have incurred a 10% late payment fee. I have added this fee to your original charge of $139.25 and issued a new invoice for $153.18, which I have enclosed. If we do not receive payment by August 5, we will consider you to be in default and will refer the matter to a collection agency.

I would like to remind you that our return policy, which is stated in the purchase agreement, is both clear and generous. It allows you to return by regular mail any purchase for any reason within seven days for a full refund, as long as it is in the original packaging. You received shipment on July 7, nearly two weeks ago, and did not return the purchase.

Your prompt attention to this matter is appreciated.

Regards,

Alice Worley

Alice Worley
Account Manager, Wholesome Foods

Bill to:
Marcie Stephenson
Marcie's Downhome Grill
215 Lakeside Dr.
Madison, WI 53701

INVOICE

Date: June 20
Invoice#: 836382
Customer: Marcie's Downhome Grill

Description	Qty	Unit Price	Price
Cheese	1	$25	$50
Crakers	2	$22.63	$45.26
Nuts	2	$21.99	$43.98
		Sub-total	$139.25
		Late payment fee	$13.93
		Total	$153.18

Dear Alice,

I ordered fresh cheese, whole crackers, and edible nuts. What I received was spoiled cheese, cracker crumbs, and nuts that had spilled out of their plastic containers and all over the box. None of these were safe to eat, and I believe it is quite reasonable to refuse to pay for such products. I am especially displeased that you tried to ask me to pay more for them.

You referenced the purchase agreement I signed, but because you did not provide products that I could use, I do not believe the agreement is binding. I did not return the purchase out of concern for our Wisconsin postal carriers, who no doubt have rules against transporting potentially dangerous packages of spoiled and malodorous food. In any event, I could not return the order in the original packaging because much of the original packaging was not intact when I received it. I suspect that the shipping company is to blame. It is likely that the package was not refrigerated during shipment (hence the spoiled cheese) and not treated gently (hence the crushed crackers and broken nut containers).

I should note that immediately after I realized there was a problem I took several photographs of the package, which I have attached. You can see for yourself what your products looked like when they arrived at my restaurant. You are welcome to use the photos in negotiations with your shipping company, but please do not continue to ask me for payment.

Sincerely,

Marcie Stephenson
Head Chef and Owner, Marcie's Downhome Grill

191. Why did Alice Worley write the letter?

(A) To ask Marcie Stephenson for additional information

(B) To apologize to Marcie Stephenson for poor service

(C) To request payment for an outstanding amount

(D) To inform Marcie Stephenson of a new payment plan

192. What is NOT indicated in the invoice?

(A) Vendor's phone number

(B) Invoice number

(C) Product description

(D) Client's address

193. What reason did Marcie Stephenson NOT give for being dissatisfied with Wholesome Foods?

(A) She was asked to pay an additional fee.

(B) Some products were damaged during shipping.

(C) She received a package of food that had already spoiled.

(D) The shipment arrived nearly two weeks late.

194. What does Marcie Stephenson suggest about the agreement?

(A) It is no longer a valid contract.

(B) She should not have signed it.

(C) It was not signed by both parties.

(D) The payment amount should be negotiable.

195. In the email, the word "malodorous" in paragraph 2, line 5, is closest in meaning to

(A) smelly

(B) spicy

(C) savory

(D) spurious

The Percival Seminars

How Will the New Health Insurance Regulations Affect You?

On January 1, a series of new state laws concerning health insurance will come into effect. These regulations will require significant changes in the ways companies and individuals pay for health insurance, and also how healthcare providers receive payments from insurance companies.

The non-profit Percival Center for Public Health has been offering a monthly seminar at the spacious BGLC Community Room outlining these changes and providing experts to answer questions about the new regulations. Due to the overwhelming popularity of these seminars, we have decided to add an additional monthly seminar during each of the coming three months. The times of all seminars will be announced on percivalcenter.com as soon as they are scheduled. The next seminar is scheduled for:

Time: Wednesday, September 28, 3:30–5:15 pm
Place: The Bruce Grobelaar Leisure Center Community Room

Please note:

Due to the strong demand, it is strongly suggested that those interested in attending make a reservation by visiting our website percivalcenter.com. We will make every effort to accommodate walk-in guests, but seating is limited. Those who have not reserved a space may be turned away at the door.

MEMORANDUM

To: All Human Resources Staff
From: Desmond Croc, HR Director
Subject: Health insurance seminar
Date: September 24

I know that many of you have been fielding questions from our colleagues, who are understandably concerned about how the new health insurance laws will affect them. For those of you who haven't already attended, I strongly recommend making time in your schedule to attend a seminar on the subject offered by the Percival Center for Public Health. The next one is scheduled for just a few days from now, but several additional seminars are planned for the coming months. Check the Percival Center website for times (most have yet to be announced), and also to reserve a seat.

I attended the seminar in August. It was organized by Dr. Janice Ham, one of the authors of the regulations, and I can report that her talk was informative, entertaining, and extraordinarily professional. This is one seminar worth going to. I know that everyone is busy, but the Leisure Center is just a ten-minute taxi ride away, the seminar is free, and the company will reimburse you for transportation to and from the event.

Des

To: Desmond Croc, HR Director

From: Jessica Jones

Subject: Re: Health insurance seminar

Date: September 26

Hello Des,

I did try to register for the seminar online, but I kept receiving a message indicating that the seminar was full and not accepting registration. Also, other schedules have not been announced yet. In the mean time, I suggest that we invite the event organizer to arrange an on-site seminar specifically for our company. This way all our HR team members can learn about the regulation changes within the company without traveling back and forth to the Leisure Center separately. Do you think this is a workable plan? If you do, I'm willing to contact the event coordinator and check if they are able to manage it.

Please advice and thank you.

Jessica

196. In the announcement, what reason is given for the scheduling of additional seminars?
(A) The overwhelming popularity of the new regulations
(B) The relatively small size of the venue
(C) The demand for information about a series of new laws
(D) The extraordinary professionalism of Dr. Ham

197. According to the announcement, what should those interested in attending the seminar do?
(A) Call the Leisure Center to register
(B) Visit the Percival Center to sign up
(C) Make a reservation on a website
(D) Contact the Human Resources department

198. In the memorandum, the word "fielding" in paragraph 1, line 1, is closest in meaning to
(A) posing
(B) receiving
(C) returning
(D) forming

199. What is NOT given in the memo as a reason to attend the seminar?
(A) The information will help HR staff answer their colleagues' questions.
(B) The company will pay the registration fee for the seminar.
(C) The location is convenient for employees of the company.
(D) The quality of the presentations will likely be very high.

200. What does Jessica volunteer to do next?
(A) Get feedback from colleagues
(B) Provide training herself
(C) Call the mayor of the city
(D) Contact Percival Center directly

Part 3

模擬試題解析

Test 1

Questions 147-149 refer to the following email.

To: Kevin Gordon [k.gordon@blankslate.com]
From: Jessie Evans [jessieevans@zapstart.com]
Re: Follow-Up
Date: 13 June, 8:45 am

Dear Mr. Gordon,

I would like to thank you for meeting with us this morning. The initial marketing proposal you presented was generally well-received, but after discussing the matter further with our CFO and sales team, we have decided to make a few changes.

First, we'd like to limit the amount spent on print advertising to 20% of the total. Second, you suggested using 15% of our advertising budget on television and radio ads, but we are convinced it would be more effective to use that money for online advertising instead. Finally, we'd like you to allocate at least 10% of the budget to outdoor advertising. We have previously received very positive responses from our ads on buses and subways, so we were surprised to see that you didn't include them.

Taking these requirements into consideration, could you please resubmit your proposal by the end of next week? As we discussed, the content of all ads should focus on the high quality, ease of use, and reliability of our products rather than the price.

Please let me know if you have any questions or concerns about our requirements, and thank you again for your presentation.

Best regards,

Jessie Evans
Marketing Director, Zap Start Inc.

＊套色字部分請參考「詞彙註解」

【中譯】第 147-149 題請參照下面這封電子郵件。

收件人：Kevin Gordon [k.gordon@blankslate.com]
寄件人：Jessie Evans [jessieevans@zapstart.com]
關於：後續追蹤
日期：6 月 13 日，上午 8:45

親愛的 Gordon 先生：

感謝您今早撥空與我們會面。對於您所提出的初步行銷提案，一般而言大家的接受度都相當高，但是在與本公司的財務長和行銷團隊做了進一步的討論之後，我們決定對提案做一些調整。

首先，我們希望能夠將印刷廣告的預算限制在總成本的 20% 之內。其次，您建議我們將廣告預算的 15% 投入電視與電台的廣告上，但是我們認為將其用於網路廣告上會更加有效。最後，我們希望您能夠至少投入 10% 的資金至戶外廣告上。我們先前在公車與地鐵上所做的廣告反應都非常正面，但是您這次在提案中並沒有這兩者的規劃，我們感到很訝異。

若將以上要求納入考量，您是否可以在下週結束前重新交付一份新的提案？如同我們先前所討論的，所有廣告的內容都應著重在產品的高品質、簡易性與可靠性，而非強調價格。

對於我們的要求，若您有任何進一步的問題或疑慮，請讓我知道。在此再次謝謝您的簡報。

祝好，

Jessie Evans
Zap Start 股份有限公司行銷主管

initial [ɪ`nɪʃəl] (*adj.*) 開始的、最初的

proposal [prə`pozl] (*n.*) 提議、提案

convinced [kən`vɪnst] (*adj.*) 確信的

effective [ɪ`fɛktɪv] (*adj.*) 有效的

allocate [`ælə͵ket] (*v.*) 分配、分派

requirement [rɪ`kwaɪrmənt] (*n.*) 需要、必備條件

content [`kɑntɛnt] (*n.*) 內容

reliability [rɪ͵laɪə`bɪlətɪ] (*n.*) 可信賴度、可靠程度

---

147. What is the purpose of this email?

(A) To modify a proposal

(B) To reply to a customer

(C) To arrange a meeting

(D) To advertise a service

答案 **A**

中譯 此封電郵的主要目的為何？

(A) 修訂一份提案的內容

(B) 回覆一位客戶的來信

(C) 安排一場會議

(D) 宣傳一項服務

解析

此題問 "What is the purpose of this email?"，根據第一段所提到的 "The initial marketing proposal ..., but after discussing the matter further ..., we have decided to make a few changes." 可知，此封電郵的目的在於告知企劃案的內容必須做些許修改。

選項 (A) 提到的 "... modify ... proposal" 正確地使用了 "modify" 此字來替換 "change"，整句的意思也沒改變，為最佳答案。

選項 (B) 的重點是 "... reply ... customer"，但此 email 並不是回覆給客戶的信，故不選。

選項 (C) 的要點是 "... arrange ... meeting"，但根據第一句提到的，雙方才剛結束討論會議，故不選。

選項 (D) 的 "... advertise ... service" 提到「刊登廣告」，也跟 "make a few changes to the marketing proposal" 無關，故不選。

148. What form of advertising will Zap Start probably NOT use?

(A) Broadcast media

(B) Internet

(C) Newspaper

(D) Transportation

答案 A

中譯 下列何種廣告是 Zap Start 公司可能「不會」採用的宣傳方式？

(A) 廣播媒體

(B) 網路

(C) 報紙

(D) 大眾運輸

解析

此題是 "negative factual"（反向細節）的題目，問 "What form of advertising will Zap Start probably NOT use?"，也就是要找到「三個」他們會使用的廣告方式，以便排除掉一個。

根據第二段第二句 "You suggested using 15% ... budget on television and radio ads, but we are convinced ... effective to use that money for online advertising instead." 可以看出，Zap Start 公司並不願意在 "television" 和 "radio" 上登廣告，而是偏好 "online" 做廣告。而 television and radio 可替換成 broadcast media，online 則替換成 Internet，也就是說，Zap Start 公司不選 (A) broadcast media 的廣告方式，而寧願選在 (B) Internet 上登廣告。

另外，根據第二段第一句 "We'd like to limit the amount spent on print advertising to 20% of the total." 可知，Zap Start 也有打算採用 "print advertising"，也就是選項 (C) newspaper 做廣告。最後，根據第二段第四句 "We have previously received very positive responses from our ads on buses and subways." 可知，刊登在 buses 和 subways 上的廣告效果也很好，換言之，他們也將採用 (D) transportation 的方式。選項 (B)、(C)、(D) 等方式都有被採用，而 (A) 是不採用的，故 (A) 為正確答案。

149. **According to the email, what can be inferred about Zap Start's products?**

(A) They are expensive.

(B) They do not break easily.

(C) They require training to use.

(D) They do not start quickly.

答案 B

中譯 根據電子郵件，我們可以得知 Zap Start 的產品大概有哪種特點？

(A) 它們很昂貴。

(B) 它們不容易壞。

(C) 它們需要受訓練才能使用。

(D) 它們沒辦法很快速地被啓用。

解析

此題問的是 "What can be inferred about Zap Start's products?"，因此要找到文中提及該公司產品特性之處。根據第三段第二句 "As we discussed, the content of all ads should focus on the high quality, ease of use, and reliability of our products rather than the price." 可知，該公司產品的特點爲 "high quality"、"ease of use" 和 "reliability" 等三項。

選項 (A) 內重點 "... expensive" 並非上述三個特性之一，故不選。

選項 (B) 的關鍵 "... do not break easily"（不容易壞）與 "reliability" 意思一致，故爲最佳答案。

選項 (C) 提到的 "... require training ..."（需要教育訓練）在文中並未提及，故不選。

選項 (D) 提到 "... do not start quickly"（無法快速啓動）也與上述三個特點不符，故爲錯誤。

📝 重點句型聚焦

此篇的主旨要點 "The initial marketing proposal you presented was generally well-received, but after discussing the matter further with our CFO and sales team, we have decided to make a few changes." 是很適合套用到日常辦公環境上的實用句型。

The initial / original N + was / verb ..., <u>but</u> after ..., we have decided to ...

請看下列例句：

1. The original business plan was accepted, but after consulting with our CEO and VPs for their opinions about this issue, we have decided to modify some details in the plan.

   原本的那份商業計劃可以接受，但是在我們針對此議題徵詢我們執行長和副總們的意見之後，我們決定要將此計劃的一些細節稍做修改。

2. The fundamental theory you mentioned sounded convincing, but after thorough consideration, we have decided to reject this theory.

   你所提出的基本理論聽起來頗具說服力，但是在仔細考慮過後，我們還是決定否決此理論。

Questions 150-151 refer to the following text message chain.

Jessica	10:42 am

Hey Mike, are you free this afternoon?

Mike	10:43 am

Yes, Jessica. My schedule is open for this afternoon. What's up?

Jessica	10:44 am

Good stuff. We need to discuss the budget plan for next year. —[1]—.

Mike	10:45 am

Sure, no problem. I was thinking about it as well. All right, so let me go to your office at 2 pm. —[2]—.

Jessica	10:46 am

2 pm is good with me. And why don't you also invite Joyce from Marketing division to participate? Since we need to integrate marketing activities to our sales plan.

Mike	10:47 am

—[3]—. Yes, I'll let her know later. What else should I prepare in advance then?

Jessica	10:48 am

Well, you can bring your sales plan and budget proposal. I guess that's it. See you this afternoon then. —[4]—.

【中譯】第 150-151 題請參照下面這段手機訊息。

Jessica 上午 **10:42**
嗨，Mike。你今天下午有空嗎？

Mike 上午 **10:43**
是的，Jessica。我下午時間是開放的。怎麼了嗎？

Jessica 上午 **10:44**
那好。我們要討論明年的預算計劃。—[1]—。

Mike 上午 **10:45**
當然，沒問題。我剛好也在想這事，好的，那我下午兩點去妳辦公室吧。—[2]—。

Jessica 上午 **10:46**
下午兩點我可以。你何不也邀請行銷部的 Joyce？因為我們也要整合行銷活動到我們的業務計劃之中呀。

Mike 上午 **10:47**
—[3]—。好的，我等等便告知她。那我還要事先準備什麼嗎？

Jessica 上午 **10:48**
你可以將你的業務計劃和預算提案帶來。我想就是這些吧。那麼就下午見了。—[4]—。

150. **What is the main purpose of this message communication?**

(A) To register for a conference

(B) To schedule a meeting

(C) To arrange an interview

(D) To finalize a business plan

答案 B

中譯 這段手機訊息的主要目的為何？

(A) 為報名研討會

(B) 為約個會議

(C) 為安排面談

(D) 為確認商業計劃

解析

此題問 "What is the main purpose of this message communication?"，因此須鎖定訊息的關鍵點來判斷其所討論之「主題」爲何。根據 Jessica 所提及的 "Are you free this afternoon?" 與 "We need to discuss the budget plan ..." 等可看出，兩人是在約討論預算的「會議時間」較爲合理。

選項 (A) "register for a conference" 意即「報名研討會」，並非溝通訊息之內容，故不選。

選項 (B) 關鍵點是 "schedule a meeting"，即「約會議」，與訊息內容一致。正解爲 (B)。

選項 (C) 提到 "arrange an interview" 說是要「約面談」，但此段訊息與「招募、面談」並無干係，故不選。

選項 (D) 要點爲 "finalize a business plan"（確認商業計劃），但訊息溝通內容其實才剛開始要約討論而已，尚未已確認任何事項，故不適當。

151. **In which of the positions marked [1], [2], [3], and [4] does the following sentence best belong?**

"That's a pretty good idea."

(A) [1]　　　　(B) [2]　　　　(C) [3]　　　　(D) [4]

答案 C

中譯 下面這個句子插入文中標示的 [1]、[2]、[3]、[4] 四處當中的何處最符合文意？

「那是個蠻不錯的主意。」

(A) [1]　　　　　(B) [2]　　　　　(C) [3]　　　　　(D) [4]

解析　★新題型「插入句題」

題目所問的句子是「那是個好主意」的意思，故可判斷其前面應有提到「某個點子、提議」較為合理。選項 [3] 位置前建議 "... why don't you also invite Joyce from Marketing division to participate?"，因此本題選 (C) 為最佳答案。

✍ 重點句型聚焦

此段訊息溝通內的 "We need to discuss the budget plan for next year." 是在職場上經常使用到的句型。但筆者常聽同學誤用為 "discuss about" 或 "discuss with you" 等，但事實上 "discuss" 一字之後須直接接所要討論的「主題」喔！

S + discuss + [討論之主題] / [wh-子句] / [whether 子句]

注意：I discussed with him. 或 We discussed. 這樣的句子皆為錯誤！

請看下列例句：

1. The manager discussed the challenges that our company face today.
   經理討論了現今我們公司面臨到的挑戰。

2. As we discussed, I'll email you the agreement by the end of this week.
   如同我們討論到的，本週內我會將合約以電郵傳給你。

3. My teacher discussed my school performance with my parents.
   我老師跟我父母討論我的課業表現。

4. We need to discuss what actions to take.
   我們要來討論一下該採取什麼行動。

5. They discussed whether to dismiss the team.
   他們討論是否該將團隊解散。

September 9

To Whom It May Concern:

I am happy to serve as a reference for Cecil Ramirez. Mr. Ramirez worked as a full-time system administrator at Trapeze Software Ltd. for two years. In addition to maintaining our company's servers and website, Mr. Ramirez was also responsible for keeping the roughly 60 computers in the office up and running. He set up new user accounts and taught new employees how to use the company's internal software. We rarely experienced computer problems of any sort, but when there was an issue, Mr. Ramirez usually had it sorted out in hours if not minutes.

I am confident that Mr. Ramirez would be an excellent addition to any IT team. His ability to keep the big picture firmly in mind while capably handling a multitude of details is remarkable. He is a reliable and dedicated worker and a true pleasure to work with. If you have any questions or would like further information, please feel free to contact me personally.

Jessica Delacroix

Jessica Delacroix

Deputy General Manager, Trapeze Software Ltd.

＊套色字部分請參考「詞彙註解」

【中譯】第 **152-153** 題請參照下面這封信件。

9 月 9 日

敬啓者：

我很榮幸能夠擔任 Cecil Ramirez 的介紹人。Ramirez 先生在 Trapeze 軟體股份有限公司擔任了兩年的全職系統管理員。除了負責維護本公司的伺服器與網站之外，Ramirez 先生也負責維持辦公室裡約六十台電腦持續運作的工作。他為所有新進人員設定新的使用者帳號，並教導他們如何操作公司的內部作業軟體。我們鮮少遇到電腦出任何狀況，不過當電腦出現問題時，Ramirez 通常可以在數分鐘至幾小時之內就將問題都解決。

我對於 Ramirez 先生在任何 IT 團隊裡都能成為優秀的一員這點感到很有信心。他在能夠掌握大局的同時也可以注意到細微之處的能力是非常讓人讚賞的。他是一位可靠、專注，而且極好相處的員工。如果您有任何疑問，或是想要進一步的資訊，歡迎隨時與我聯繫。

Jessica Delacroix

Jessica Delacroix

Trapeze 軟體股份有限公司副總經理

👉 詞彙註解

administrator [ədˋmɪnəˌstretə] (*n.*) 管理人
maintain [menˋten] (*v.*) 維護、保持
roughly [ˋrʌflɪ] (*adv.*) 粗略地、大概
sort out 整理、理出頭緒

multitude [ˋmʌltəˌtjud] (*n.*) 許多、大量
remarkable [rɪˋmɑrkəbl̩] (*adj.*)
非凡的、卓越的
dedicated [ˋdɛdəˌketɪd] (*adj.*) 專注的

PART 3　TEST 1

123

152. **What is the purpose of this letter?**

(A) To promote an employee to a higher position

(B) To explain the system administrator's responsibilities

(C) To recommend someone for a new job

(D) To fill a vacancy for a computer specialist

答案 **C**

中譯 此封信件的主要目的為何？

(A) 為了將一名員工升遷至更高的職位

(B) 為了說明一名系統管理員的工作與責任

(C) 為了某人的一份新工作做推薦

(D) 為了填補一個電腦技術人員的職缺

解析

在將文章格式類型與開頭所講的要點大略掃瞄過之後，就可以先看第一道題目了。若可以根據第一句所讀到的內容來回答是最好，若無法回答再根據題目的要點去尋找資訊。此題問 "What is the purpose of this letter?"，因此要找出寄出此信件的「目的」為何？信件第一句就提到 "I am happy to serve as a reference for Cecil Ramirez."，由此判斷，此信的目的為「替人做推薦」。

選項 (A) 提及 "... promote an employee ..." 為錯誤，因為此信件用意在「推薦某人」，並非「升遷某人」，故不選。

選項 (B) 的 "... explain ... administrator's responsibilities" 指的是「解釋工作內容」，也跟「推薦某人」無關，並不適當。

選項 (C) 的關鍵點 "... recommend someone ..."（推薦某人），呼應此信內提到的 "serve as a reference" 一事，故正確。

選項 (D) 提到的 "... fill a vacancy ..."（填補空缺）也跟「推薦」無關，故不選。

153. What is NOT mentioned as one of Mr. Ramirez's strong points?

(A) He knows how to write software.

(B) He has experience training new workers.

(C) He can maintain computer systems.

(D) He is a hardworking employee.

答案 **A**

中譯 下列哪項 Ramirez 先生的優勢在文章中「未」被提及？

(A) 他知道如何撰寫軟體程式。

(B) 他有訓練新進員工的經驗。

(C) 他能夠維護電腦系統。

(D) 他是一位勤奮認真的員工。

解析

此類 "negative factual"（反向細節）的問題經常出現，也頗好掌握。既是問四個選項哪個「沒有」被提及，那麼就將焦點放在尋找「三個有被提及」的資訊上，未提及之選項即為正確答案。此題問的是 "What is NOT mentioned as one of Mr. Ramirez's strong points?"，可見得要看出「三個」強項所在。

根據文中資訊："In addition to maintaining our company's servers and website, Mr. Ramirez was also responsible for keeping ... computers ... up and running."，選項 (C) 有被提到。

又看到 "He set up new user accounts and taught new employees how to use the company's internal software."，因此選項 (B) 也是有被提及的。

另，由第二段第三句 "He is a reliable and dedicated worker and a true pleasure to work with." 可知，選項 (D) 的內容亦被提及。

唯獨選項 (A) He knows how to write software.（他知道如何撰寫軟體程式。）的相關資訊並沒有在文中出現，故為正解。

此篇為標準的「推薦函」文章，既然是要幫某員工做推薦去新的公司工作，撰信者當然會提到受推薦人的「正面人格特質」，而不會寫他的負面評價。因此，我們可以就此文章內的這個句子來做個應用。

He is a reliable and dedicated worker and a true pleasure to work with.

除了 reliable（可靠的）和 dedicated（專注的）之外，還有什麼可以形容人格特質的字？以下補充常考的 30 組：

1. enthusiastic 熱心的
2. daring 勇敢的、大膽的
3. diplomatic 圓融的
4. cautious 謹慎的
5. determined 堅定的
6. convincing 令人信服的
7. good-natured 脾氣好的
8. friendly 友善的
9. outspoken 直言的、坦率的
10. calm 鎮定的、沉穩的
11. talkative 愛說話的
12. brilliant 聰穎的
13. intelligent 有智慧的
14. articulate 能言善道的
15. conventional 傳統的、保守的

16. decisive 果斷的、果決的
17. adventurous 喜歡冒險的
18. insightful 有見解的、洞察的
19. out-going 外向的
20. moderate 溫和不偏激的
21. gentle 溫文儒雅的
22. persuasive 令人信服的
23. humble 謙虛的
24. original 創新的、有創見的
25. expressive 富有表情的、善表達的
26. conscientious 認真盡責的
27. dominant 支配的
28. poised 泰然自若的
29. observant 機警的、注意的
30. modest 端莊高雅的、謙遜的

此類形容「人格特質」的形容詞可以多記一些，不但考試時會出現，在真正的辦公環境內更可以拿來活用！

Guest Satisfaction Survey

Thank you for taking a moment to complete this satisfaction survey. The Seven Seas Hotel Group will use your feedback to provide you even better service during your future visits.

	Yes	No
• Were you greeted appropriately when you arrived at the hotel?	✔	
• Was the check-in process smooth and efficient?		✔
• Were you escorted to your room by a bellman?	✔	
• Was you room clean and welcoming?	✔	
• Was the check-out process friendly and efficient?	✔	

Which of the following did you use?

Facilities		Services	
	Business Center	✔	Laundry
	Conference Room	✔	Room Service
✔	Fitness Center		Hair Salon
✔	Swimming Pool	✔	Parking

Comments:

The hotel computer had no record of my reservation even though I had received a confirmation email, which I showed to the clerk. This problem was quickly resolved in a professional manner, and I was pleased that he upgraded my room to a suite. Also, I was a little disappointed that I wasn't informed before I arrived that the swimming pool would be closed for maintenance until the final day of my stay. Had I known, I would have postponed my visit. Would it be too much trouble to mention such closures to guests before they arrive? Overall, my stay was pleasant and I look forward to returning again in the summer with my family.

＊套色字部分請參考「詞彙註解」

PART 3　TEST 1

【中譯】第 154-155 題請參照下面這個表單。

顧客滿意度調查

感謝您抽空填寫這份滿意度調查問卷。Seven Seas 飯店集團將根據您的回饋意見，為您將來再度造訪時提供更完善的服務。

	是	否
• 您抵達飯店時，是否有受到適當的迎接？	✔	
• 辦理登記的流程是否順暢且有效率？		✔
• 是否有服務員帶領您前往您的房間？	✔	
• 您的房間是否乾淨且讓您覺得受到歡迎？	✔	
• 辦理退房的流程是否友善且有效率？	✔	

您使用了下列何種服務？

飯店設施	飯店服務
＿＿ 商務中心	✔ 洗衣房
＿＿ 會議室	✔ 客房服務
✔ 健身中心	＿＿ 美髮廳
✔ 游泳池	✔ 停車場

評語：

飯店電腦竟然沒有我的訂房紀錄，雖然我有收到一封確認電郵，而且也拿給櫃台人員看了。所幸這個問題很快地就以專業的態度被解決了，而我對於服務人員將我的房間等級升級至套房這點也感到很滿意。另外，對於在來之前沒有收到通知說游泳池將關閉以進行維護直到我留宿的最後一天這點，我感到有一點失望。如果我知道的話，我會延後入住的時間。難道在顧客們抵達前告知他們這些事情會很麻煩嗎？整體而言，我的住宿經驗算是好的，而我也期待和我的家人於夏季時再度前來。

詞彙註解

feedback [ˋfidˌbæk] (*n.*) 意見回饋	**resolve** [rıˋzɑlv] (*v.*) 解決
appropriately [əˋproprıˌetlı] (*adv.*) 適當地	**suite** [swit] (*n.*) 套房
escort [ˋɛskɔrt] (*v.*) 陪同、護送	**disappointed** [ˌdısəˋpɔıntıd] (*adj.*) 失望的
bellman [ˋbɛlmən] (*n.*) 飯店內之行李服務員	**maintenance** [ˋmentənəns] (*n.*) 養護、維持
welcoming [ˋwɛlkəmıŋ] (*adj.*) 歡迎的、款待的	**postpone** [postˋpon] (*v.*) 延遲、推延
confirmation [ˌkɑnfəˋmeʃən] (*n.*) 確定、批准	**closure** [ˋkloʒə] (*n.*) 關閉、打烊

154. What aspect of the hotel was the guest most satisfied with?

(A) The efficiency of the reservation system

(B) The professionalism of the staff

(C) The cleanliness of the room

(D) The renovation of the swimming pool

答案 **B**

中譯 這名顧客對於飯店的哪一部分感到最為滿意？

(A) 訂房系統的效率

(B) 員工的專業素養

(C) 房間的整潔程度

(D) 游泳池的整修

解析

在很快地掃瞄了全文，大概瞭解文章的類型（客戶意見調查表）之後，就可以先看題目，以便定位出所需資訊的方向。此題問 "What aspect of the hotel was the guest most satisfied with?"，關鍵就是要找出讓此客戶「感到最滿意」的部分。既然是客戶所提出的意見，那麼就在 "comments" 內找尋。根據第一、二句 "The hotel computer had no record of my reservation .... This problem was quickly resolved in a professional manner, and I was pleased that he upgraded my room ...." 可知，此客戶對服務人員「專業地解決了問題」這點感到滿意。

選項 (A)　提到的 "... efficiency of ... reservation system" 與評語中的 "The hotel computer had no record of my reservation even though I had received a confirmation email ...."「飯店電腦系統有問題」一事不符，故不選。

選項 (B)　的關鍵點 "... professionalism ... staff"「飯店人員的專業」，與文章內容相符，故為最佳答案。

選項 (C) "... cleanliness ... room"「房間的清潔」在文中並未被提及，故不選。

選項 (D) 提到的 "... renovation ... swimming pool" 是此客戶「不滿」之處，而不是感到最滿意的項目，故不可選。

155. What improvement does the guest suggest?

(A) The hotel's computer system should be replaced.

(B) Reservation confirmations should be sent to all guests.

(C) Room upgrades should be offered to families.

(D) Guests should be informed about facility closures.

答案 D

中譯 此名顧客建議做何改善？

(A) 飯店的電腦系統應該要重新更換。

(B) 訂房的確認信應該要寄給所有顧客。

(C) 應該提供房間升級給所有的家庭。

(D) 顧客應該被通知有關設施關閉的訊息。

解析

針對題目所問，該顧客在評論中提到 "I was ... disappointed that I wasn't informed ... that the swimming pool would be closed ... Had I known, I would have postponed my visit. Would it be too much trouble to mention ... to guests ...?"，言下之意他認為若有設施關閉，飯店應該提前跟客戶溝通。

選項 (A) "... system should be replaced." 指「電腦系統的替換」，並不是客戶提到的要點，因此不適當。

選項 (B) 提及 "... confirmations ... sent to all guests." 這是飯店本來就有在做的，而非此客戶的建議，故不正確。

選項 (C) 提到的 "Room upgrades ..."「房間升等」並非此客戶的建議事項，故亦不可選。

選項 (D) 的關鍵 "Guests ... informed about ... closures." 正是此客戶的建議，故為正解。

此文章中有一個假設句型值得來討論：Had I known, I would have postponed my visit.。這句其實就相當於 "If I had know, I would have postponed my visit."，意思是「若我早知道的話，我就會延後我的行程了。」（但事實是，正因先前不知道，所以就沒有延後行程。）

If + S + were / had / would ..., S + V = Were / Had / Should + S ..., S + V

請看下列例句：

1. If I were you, I wouldn't say something like that to the boss.
   = Were I you, I wouldn't say something like that to the boss.
   假如我是你，就不會對老闆說那種話。

2. If Mr. Yang should call, please tell him the meeting has been rescheduled to tomorrow.
   = Should Mr. Yang call, please tell him the meeting has been rescheduled to tomorrow.
   萬一楊先生打電話來，請告訴他會議已被改到明天了。

3. If I had seen her, I might have the chance to close the deal.
   = Had I seen her, I might have the chance to close the deal.
   假如當時我有看到她，我或許有機會可以了結這個案子。

Friends of the Wetlands

Janice Noguchi
2593 Seacrest Lane
Port John, FL 03087

April 21

Dear Ms. Noguchi,

Thank you for your renewing your Friends of the Wetlands membership. —[1]—. Your $25 contribution will enable us to continue our missions of environmental research, habitat restoration, and community education. —[2]—.

We would like to take this opportunity to remind you that in addition to paying your membership dues, we encourage all members to assist the Friends of the Wetlands directly. —[3]—. You can help by planting local foliage, leading wetlands tours for students and other community members, or working as a fundraiser. For those interested, we've scheduled an information meeting for 7:30 Friday evening at the visitors center. —[4]—. We look forward to seeing you there.

Sincerely,

Mark Perry

Mark Perry

Director, Friends of the Wetlands

＊套色字部分請參考「詞彙註解」

濕地之友

Janice Noguchi

Seacrest 路 2593 號

（03087）Florida 州 Port John 區

四月二十一日

親愛的 Noguchi 小姐：

感謝您更新您的「濕地之友」會員資格。—[1]—。您的二十五元捐款將能夠讓我們持續進行環境研究、復原棲息地與社區教育的工作。—[2]—。

我們希望藉由這個機會提醒您，除了支付您的會費之外，我們鼓勵所有會員直接地協助「濕地之友」。—[3]—。您可以藉由在當地種植樹木、帶領學生和其他社區會員參觀濕地或擔任募款者的工作來幫助我們。對於有興趣參加的人，我們於星期五晚上 7:30，在遊客中心安排了一場說明會。—[4]—。我們期望能夠在那看到您。

Mark Perry

濕地之友總監

敬上

PART 3　TEST 1

詞彙註解

wetland [ˋwɛtˌlənd] (n.) 濕地、沼地

renew [rɪˋnju] (v.) 續訂、重新開始

membership [ˋmɛmbəˌʃɪp] (n.) 會員身份

contribution [ˌkɑntrəˋbjuʃən] (n.) 貢獻、捐助

mission [ˋmɪʃən] (n.) 使命、任務

habitat [ˋhæbəˌtæt] (n.) 棲息處

restoration [ˌrɛstəˋreʃən] (n.) 恢復、復原

encourage [ɪnˋkɝɪdʒ] (v.) 鼓勵

foliage [ˋfolɪɪdʒ] (n.) 葉子（總稱）

fundraiser [ˋfʌndˌrezə] (n.) 資金籌募者

156. **Why did Mark Perry write this letter to Ms. Noguchi?**

(A) To request a $25 donation

(B) To encourage her to join an organization

(C) To thank her for offering her time

(D) To ask her to attend an event

答案 **D**

中譯 Mark Perry 為什麼撰寫了這封信給 Noguchi 小姐？

(A) 為了請求二十五元的捐款

(B) 為了鼓勵她加入一個組織

(C) 為了感謝她貢獻時間

(D) 為了邀請她參加一項活動

解析

本題 "Why did Mark Perry write this letter to Ms. Noguchi?" 問的是 Mark Perry 寫信給 Ms. Janice Noguchi 的目的。根據第二段的內容 "We would like to take this opportunity to remind you that ..., we encourage all members to assist the Friends of the Wetlands directly .... we've scheduled an information meeting for 7:30 Friday evening .... We look forward to seeing you there." 可知，Mark 是為了邀請 Janice 去參加週五晚上所舉辦的說明會而寫這封信。

選項 (A) 提到 "... request ... donation"「要求捐款」，但從第一、二句即可知，Janice 已經捐款，故不適當。

選項 (B) 提及 "... encourage ... join an organization"，但根據第一句的內容，Janice 已是會員，且此信亦不是要她再加入其他組織，故不選。

選項 (C) 中的 "... thank her ... time" 指「感謝她所花的時間」，這和「週五的說明會」無關，亦不可選。

選項 (D) 提到的 "... ask ... attend an event" 是邀請 Janice 出席活動，與 "... information meeting for 7:30 Friday evening .... We look forward to seeing you there." 文意相符，故為正解。

157. **What is NOT stated as one of the group's activities?**

(A) Marketing natural resources

(B) Conducting scientific studies

(C) Restoring the local ecology

(D) Organizing educational programs

答案 **A**

中譯 下列何者「非」此組織的活動之一？

(A) 行銷天然資源

(B) 進行科學研究

(C) 復原當地生態

(D) 舉辦教育性質的活動

解析

此題為「反向細節」題，也就是要把文章中提到的資訊找出來，看哪一個是「沒有」被提及的。題目問 "What is NOT stated as one of the group's activities?"，可見得要先找出關於此單位的主要 "activities"（活動）。根據第一段第二句提到的 "... our missions of environmental research, habitat restoration, and community education."，可看出以下配對：

選項 (B) Conducting scientific studies = environmental research，有提及。

選項 (C) Restoring the local ecology = habitat restoration，有提到。

選項 (D) Organizing educational programs = community education，也有提到。

選項 (A) Marketing natural resources 並沒有在文中被提到，故為正確答案。

---

158. In which of the positions marked [1], [2], [3], and [4] does the following sentence best belong?

"Call us today and register."

(A) [1]　　　　(B) [2]　　　　(C) [3]　　　　(D) [4]

答案 **D**

中譯 下面這個句子插入文中標示的 [1]、[2]、[3]、[4] 四處當中的何處最符合文意？

「今天就打電話給我們報名。」

(A) [1]　　　　(B) [2]　　　　(C) [3]　　　　(D) [4]

解析 ★新題型「插入句題」

題目所問句子內提到「報名」，那麼可判斷應與報名「活動」相關較為合理。選項 [4] 位置之前才有提到活動相關訊息，故本題選 (D)。

重點句型聚焦

我們利用本文中之 "You can help by planting local foliage, leading wetlands tours for students and other community members, or working as a fundraiser." 來應用一下「平行結構」的句型。

名詞 + **and** + 名詞	I received a dress and a pair of shoes for my birthday.
形容詞 + **and** + 形容詞	The old man is optimistic and generous.
動詞 + **and** + 動詞	The receptionist opened the door and greeted the guest.
形容詞 + **but** + 形容詞	These shoes are old but comfortable.
動名詞 + **or** + 動名詞	In my spare time, I enjoy reading books or going swimming.
動詞, + 動詞, + **and** + 動詞（三個以上，須以逗點分隔）	Tony would make a good leader because he works effectively with others, has a reputation for integrity, and deals with problems in a professional manner.

請看下列例句：

1. Your job duties include planning sales strategies, implementing programs, and coordinating data.
   你的工作職掌包括規劃業務策略、執行活動和整合資料。

2. A qualified candidate must have a college degree, 3 years of work experience, and excellent communication skills.
   合格的候選人要有大學學歷、三年的工作經驗和良好的溝通能力。

Questions 159-161 refer to the following memo.

To: All Staff
From: Mitzy Follop
Date: July 29

Re: Changes at the Majestic

I'm happy to announce some exciting new changes in store for us here at the Majestic Theater. We will be closed to the public for renovations from Monday, August 9 to Friday, August 13. By the time we reopen for the Saturday matinee, the balcony in the main theater will have been made available for public seating once again, and the boxoffice will have been equipped with a modern ticketing system. It is important that everyone is aware of the following changes:

1. Because the balcony will no longer be available for storage, all of the cleaning supplies will from now on be kept in the employee break room, which will become even more crowded. I apologize for any inconvenience.

2. The new ticketing system will allow customers to purchase popcorn, drinks, and other items at the same time they purchase their movie tickets. They will be provided with vouchers that they can exchange for their purchase at the snack counter, which should shorten lines. All employees are required to attend the training session for the new ticketing system at 3:30 pm on August 13.

3. Our reopening will coincide with the start of the Daytime Summer Classics Film Festival, which will run from August 14 until the end of the month. As in previous years, festival tickets are half-off the price of tickets sold for regular evening features.

I would like to thank everyone in advance for helping to make this a smooth transition for our valued guests.

Mitzy Follop
General Manager, Majestic Theater

＊套色字部分請參考「詞彙註解」

PART 3

TEST 1

【中譯】第 159-161 題請參照下面這份備忘錄。

收件人：全體員工
寄件人：Mitzy Follop
日期：7 月 29 日

關於：Majestic 的各項改變

我很高興宣佈 Majestic 戲院即將產生令人振奮的新改變。我們將從 8 月 9 日星期一至 8 月 13 日星期五期間對外關閉，進行整修。在我們於星期六日場重新開幕時，戲院包廂的座位將再次開放給民眾，而售票亭也將配備現代化的售票系統。以下重要的變革請大家注意配合：

1. 由於包廂已不再作為儲藏室使用，所有清潔用具從現在起都將存放在員工休息室裡，因此那裡會變得稍微擁擠。我為任何可能造成的不便說聲抱歉。

2. 新的售票系統將能讓顧客們於購買電影票的同時也購買爆米花、飲料與其他品項。他們將取得可於零食櫃台兌換餐點的兌換券，這應該能有效地縮短排隊時間。所有員工皆必須在 8 月 13 日下午 3:30 參加新售票系統的訓練課程。

3. 我們的重新開幕活動將和從 8 月 14 日開始至月底結束的 Daytime Summer Classics 電影節同時進行。如同往年，電影節期間的票價是平日晚場票價的一半。

我想預先感謝大家的幫忙，讓我們的貴賓能夠有個順利的轉換體驗。

Mitzy Follop
Majestic 戲院總經理

詞彙註解

announce [ə`naʊns] (v.) 宣佈、發佈	**voucher** [`vaʊtʃə] (n.) 憑單、兌換券
renovation [ˌrɛnə`veʃən] (n.) 更新、恢復活力	**shorten** [`ʃɔrtn̩] (v.) 縮短、減少
matinee [ˌmætən`e] (n.) 日場、日戲	**coincide with** 與……一致
balcony [`bælkənɪ] (n.) 陽台、露台、包廂	**festival** [`fɛstəvl̩] (n.) 節日、喜慶、活動
modern [`mɑdən] (adj.) 現代的、近代的	**regular** [`rɛgjələ] (adj.) 規律的、固定的
storage [`storɪdʒ] (n.) 儲藏、保管	**transition** [træn`zɪʃən] (n.) 轉變、過渡時期

159. Why did Mitzy Follop write this memo?

(A) To announce a new film festival to the public

(B) To inform the staff of recent developments

(C) To attract new customers to the theater

(D) To introduce new employees to the company

答案 B

中譯 Mitzy Follop 為什麼要撰寫這份備忘錄？

(A) 他要向大眾宣佈一個新的電影節。

(B) 他要通知員工最近的發展。

(C) 他要吸引新顧客前來戲院。

(D) 他要向公司同仁介紹新員工。

解析

看到 "Changes at the Majestic" 此標題就可以約略地瞭解本文大概是在講哪方面的事了。第一題問的是 "Why did Mitzy Follop write this memo?"，由文章開頭的第一、二句 "I'm happy to announce some exciting new changes ... at the Majestic Theater. We will be closed to the public for renovations ..." 即可知，這是戲院「關閉整修」的通知。

選項 (A) 提到的 "... announce a new film festival ..." 「宣佈一個新電影節」，與 "renovations"（重新裝修）無關，故不選。

選項 (B) 提到的 "... inform ... recent developments." 「通知最近的發展」與 "announce some new changes" 意思相符，為最佳答案。

選項 (C) 提到的 "... attract new customers ..." 「吸引顧客」與 "new changes" 或 "renovations" 皆無干係，故不適當。

選項 (D) 提到的 "... introduce new employees ..." 「介紹新進員工」也跟 "new changes" 和 "renovations" 無關，故亦不選。

160. **What benefit of the new ticketing system is mentioned in the memo?**

(A) Employees will receive free training.

(B) Customers will receive faster service.

(C) Staff will receive free tickets.

(D) Movie-goers will receive a small discount.

答案 B

中譯 備忘錄裡提到新售票系統的好處為何？

(A) 員工將可以獲得免費訓練。

(B) 顧客們可以得到較迅速的服務。

(C) 員工可以獲得免費電影票。

(D) 看電影的觀眾可以獲得小小的折扣優惠。

解析

題目問 "What benefit of the new ticketing system is mentioned in the memo?"，因此要找出 "ticketing system's benefit"（新購票系統的好處）之相關資訊以回答問題。根據文中注意事項第一、二句 "The new ticketing system will allow customers to purchase ... at the same time they purchase their movie tickets. They will be provided with vouchers ..., which should shorten lines."，新的購票系統可以讓顧客「在買票的同時順便買點心，並節省排隊時間」。

選項 (A)　"Employees ... free training." 「員工免費訓練」於文中並未論及，故不選。

選項 (B)　提到的 "Customers ... faster service." 「給客戶較迅速的服務」與「同一時間可買票和點心，並節省排隊時間」屬同義表達，為最佳答案。

選項 (C)　提到的 "Staff ... receive free tickets." 「員工可以獲得免費票」於文中並未論及，故不選。

選項 (D)　"Movie-goers ... receive ... discount." 「看電影者可獲得折扣」此描述亦未見於文章中，故亦不選。

161. **According to the memo, which of the following problems might be caused by the renovations?**

(A) The theater will be closed until the end of the month.

(B) The balcony will have to be cleaned regularly.

(C) Employees will have less space in the break room.

(D) Customers will receive vouchers instead of tickets.

答案 **C**

中譯 根據備忘錄，下列何者為整修後可能會帶來的問題？

(A) 戲院直到月底之前都會停止營業。

(B) 包廂將要定期清理。

(C) 員工們的休息室空間會變得比較小。

(D) 顧客們將會拿到兌換券而非電影票。

解析

由題目 "Which of the following problems might be caused by the renovations?" 可判斷要找出的是：此 "renovations"（裝修）可能會引發的 "problems"（問題）。根據文中注意事項第一點提到的 "... all of the cleaning supplies will from now on be kept in the employee break room, which will become even more crowded. I apologize for any inconvenience." 可知，問題點在於「因堆放物品的關係，員工休息的空間會變小」。

選項 (A) 提到的 "... theater ... closed ... the end of ... month." 「戲院關閉的時間點」於文中並未出現，故不選。

選項 (B) 提及 "... balcony ... be cleaned regularly." 「包廂要定期清理」，而文中描述的是 "... balcony ... no longer ... for storage"，兩者並不同義，故不選。

選項 (C) "Employees ... have less space ..." 「員工的空間變小」正確地替換了 "crowded" 的意思，是最佳答案。

選項 (D) "Customers ... receive vouchers instead of tickets." 「顧客會拿到兌換券而非電影票」明顯混淆視聽，故不適當。

本篇備忘錄之注意事項第二點第一句的前半段 "The new ticketing system will allow customers to purchase popcorn, drinks, and other items ..." 是相當重要的句型。通常美國人書寫時不會將要表達的東西一一列舉出來，而是先寫出兩個名詞，然後接一個總稱的字含括起來，形成：

名詞 + 名詞 + and +〔形容詞 + 名詞〕

請看下列例句：

1. People like eating sweet food, such as chocolate, cake, and other sugar-based items.
   人們喜歡吃甜食，比如像巧克力、蛋糕和其他含糖的食品。

2. I've been to Hawaii, Florida, and other popular vacation spots.
   我已經去過夏威夷、佛羅里達和其他知名的渡假景點。

3. People are paying more attention to pollution, deforestation, and other environmental damage.
   如今人們更加注意污染、砍伐森林和其他的環境破壞問題。

4. My company is known for making laptops, iPads, and other electronic devices.
   我們公司以生產筆電、平板電腦和其他電子裝置產品出名。

5. Your choices include juice, water, and other soft drinks.
   你的選擇有果汁、水和其他的軟性飲料。

Friday, July 16

Gerhardt Stacker
3986 Pine Ave.
Hartford, Connecticut 06037

Confidential

Dear Mr. Stacker,

I would like to update you on our local market test of Everyoung Lilac Hand Cream. As you can see from the initial data below, sales are brisk overall for a new product with nothing more than in-store advertising to support it.

Everyoung Lilac Hand Cream Sales: July 1 – July 15

Point of Sale	Store Description	Unit Price	Number Distributed	Number Sold
Blechey	Downtown Flagship	$4.99	150	92
Roxburry	High-end Mall	$4.99	100	77
Airport	Duty-Free Shop	$4.49	50	3
Fairbanks	Supermarket	$3.99	100	21
Ellendale	Discount Drug Store	$3.49	100	26

As we predicted, sales are especially strong at our luxury locations in Blechey and Roxburry, and relatively weak at our low-end locations in Fairbanks and Ellendale. Sales at the airport shop are too low to allow us to draw any useful conclusions at this point.

These preliminary numbers suggest that Everyoung should target less price-sensitive luxury customers in your marketing. In fact, we would like to test the Lilac Hand Cream at two additional locations and price points, $5.99 at Spreeberg and $7.99 at the Galleria. Could you provide us with 400 additional samples by Monday to stock these locations as well as to restock Blechey and Roxburry?

Please give me a call when you get this to confirm whether you can provide the additional samples. The test will run until the end of the month, at which point we will provide you with a detailed sales report and additional recommendations.

Best regards,

Stacey Evans

Stacey Evans, Account Manager
Intercontinental Market Research

＊套色字部分請參考「詞彙註解」

【中譯】第 **162-164** 題請參照下面這封信件。

7 月 16 日星期五

Gerhardt Stacker
Pine 大道 3986 號
(06037) Hartford 市 Connecticut 州

機密

親愛的 Stacker 先生：

我要向您報告有關 Everyoung Lilac 護手乳液在本地市場測試的最新結果。如同下列初期數據顯示，整體而言，以一個新產品只靠店內廣告的宣傳，銷售情況相當好。

Everyoung Lilac 護手乳液銷售額：7 月 1 日～ 7 月15日

銷售點	店面描述	單價	配發量	銷售數量
Blechey	市中心旗艦店	$4.99	150	92
Roxburry	高檔購物中心	$4.99	100	77

機場	免稅商店	$4.49	50	3
Fairbanks	超級市場	$3.99	100	21
Ellendale	量販藥局	$3.49	100	26

有如先前我們所估計的，位於精華地點的 Blechey 和 Roxburry 店面銷售量非常高，而位於低檔地點的 Fairbanks 和 Ellendale 店面銷售量則相對較低。由於在機場的銷售額過低，目前我們無法提出任何適用的結論。

這些初步的數據顯示，當您在推廣 Everyoung 時，應該鎖定對價格較不在意的高端顧客。事實上，我們想要在另外兩個地點再以其他兩個價位測試 Lilac 護手乳液：在 Spreeberg 以 5.99 元、在 Galleria 以 7.99 元的價位販售。您是否能夠於星期一前，再提供我們額外 400 份樣品，讓我們可以在這兩個點鋪貨，並在 Blechey 和 Roxburry 進行補貨？

請在您收到這份報告之後，來電與我確認是否能夠提供額外的樣品。這個測試將會持續到月底，屆時我們會提供給您一份詳盡的銷售報告和進一步的建議。

祝好，

Stacey Evans

Stacey Evans
Intercontinental 市場調查公司客戶經理

☞ 詞彙註解

update [ʌpˋdet] (v.) 更新、提供新訊息
brisk [brɪsk] (adj.) 生氣勃勃的、興旺的
predict [prɪˋdɪkt] (v.) 預言、預料
luxury [ˋlʌkʃərɪ] (n.) 豪華、奢侈
relatively [ˋrɛlətɪvlɪ] (adv.) 相對地、比較而言
conclusion [kənˋkluʒən] (n.) 結論

preliminary [prɪˋlɪməˌnɛrɪ] (adj.)
初步的、開端的
target [ˋtɑrgɪt] (v.) 把……作為目標／對象
stock [stɑk] (v.) 進貨、庫存
recommendation [ˌrɛkəmɛnˋdeʃən] (n.)
建議、推薦

145

162. What is the main purpose of this letter?

(A) To request sales data on a new product

(B) To offer a preliminary analysis of a test

(C) To set up a meeting to discuss a course of action

(D) To provide samples for further research

答案 B

中譯 此封信件的主要目的為何？

(A) 要求提供一項新產品的銷售數據

(B) 提供一項測試的初步分析

(C) 安排一場討論行動方案的會議

(D) 提供進一步研究的樣本

解析

掃瞄全信之後可知這是 Stacey Evans 寫給 Mr. Stacker 的信。本題問寫信的目的，應試者應將焦點放在找「主旨」上。根據此信件內第一段 "I would like to update you on our local market test of Everyoung Lilac Hand Cream. As you can see from the initial data below, sales are brisk overall for a new product with nothing more than in-store advertising to support it."，Stacey Evans 透過此信向 Mr. Stacker 報告「Everyong Lilac Hand Cream 的市場測試結果」。

選項 (A) "... request sales data ... new product"「要求某新產品的銷售數據」與主旨不符，故不選。

選項 (B) "... offer ... analysis of ... test"「提供產品測試分析」正是本信主旨，故為最佳答案。

選項 (C) "... set up a meeting ..."「安排一場會議」，與信件內容無關，因此為錯誤。

選項 (D) "... provide samples ... research"「提供研究樣本」亦與主旨不符，故亦不選。

163. According to the letter, what can be inferred about the Galleria?

(A) It is a high-end shop.

(B) It is located in a mall.

(C) It is a flagship store.

(D) It is close to Spreeberg.

中譯 根據這封信件，關於 Galleria 可做何推論？

(A) 它是一間高檔的店面。

(B) 它位於購物中心裡。

(C) 它是一間旗艦店。

(D) 它的位置靠近 Spreeberg。

解析

此題問的是 "What can be inferred about the Galleria?"，必須推論出與 Galleria 相關的訊息。根據文章第三段第一、二句 "These preliminary numbers suggest that Everyoung should target less price-sensitive luxury customers in your marketing. In fact, we would like to test the Lilac Hand Cream at two additional locations and price points, $5.99 at Spreeberg and $7.99 at the Galleria." 可看出，Galleria 是被歸類在 "less price-sensitive luxury customers" 客群的地點。

選項 (A) 的 "a high-end shop" 與 "target less price-sensitive luxury customers" 的意義相符，故為正確答案。

選項 (B) 是說「該店位於購物中心內」，但由文章提供的資訊中並無法看出其地點，故不可選。

選項 (C) 的 "flagship store" 指「旗艦店」，但這點並無法從文章中推論出來，故不選。

選項 (D) 意思是「該店離 Spreeberg 很近」，文章中並沒有提到這一點，故亦不可選。

164. What does Stacey Evans NOT recommend Gerhardt Stacker do?

(A) End the test at the duty-free shop

(B) Target high-end customers

(C) Send additional samples

(D) Telephone her immediately

中譯 Stacey Evans「不」建議 Gerhardt Stacker 做什麼？

(A) 結束免稅商店的測試

(B) 目標鎖定高檔的顧客

(C) 寄更多的樣本過去

(D) 立即與她通電話

解析

此題很明顯是一道問「反向細節」的問題，也就是要找哪個資訊「沒被提及」。根據本文第三、四段中的這些句子 "These preliminary numbers suggest that Everyoung should target less price-sensitive luxury customers in your marketing."、"Could you provide us with 400 additional samples by Monday to stock these locations ...?"、"Please give me a call when you get this to confirm ...." 可看出以下的搭配：

選項 (B)　Target high-end customers = target less price-sensitive luxury customers，有被提到。

選項 (C)　Send additional samples = provide us with 400 additional samples，有被提到。

選項 (D)　Telephone her immediately = give me a call，亦有被提到。

選項 (A)　End the test at the duty-free shop 並沒有在信件中被提及，故為正確答案。

重點句型聚焦

本篇文章內有兩句使用同一句型："As you can see from the initial data below, sales are brisk overall for a new product with nothing more than in-store advertising to support it." 和 "As we predicted, sales are especially strong at our luxury locations in Blechey and Roxburry."。此句型用以表示「正如……」之意。

As you/we/I + know/expect/anticipate/see, S + V

請看下列例句：

1. As you may already know, our team will be dismissed next month.
   如同您可能已經知道的，我們的團隊下個月就要解散了。

2. As we expected, our new products sell like hotcakes.
   如同我們原本預期的，我們的新產品大暢銷。

Questions 165-168 refer to the following memo.

Memorandum

Date: October 2
To: All Teachers and Councelors
From: Gordon Fris
Re: Survey Results

Of the 358 students in the program, 43 have completed the online satisfaction survey so far. The sample size is small, and responses are still coming in, but there are trends in the data that we cannot ignore. Let's discuss them at the staff meeting tomorrow afternoon.

Students who have completed at least two semesters give us high ratings in most areas, especially in teacher quality, student services, and overall satisfaction. Unsurprisingly, we received relatively low ratings for our facilities. In particular, students complained about our small desks, poor lighting, and the generally appalling condition of the classrooms.

New students noted that the hardware and the software available in the computer lab are outdated, but surprisingly they did not suggest that they be upgraded. Several students said that they prefer their own computers to those in the lab, and they hoped teachers could suggest free or low-cost online resources to supplement their lessons.

Viewed together, these responses suggest that we shouldn't spend our development budget on upgrading the computer lab as we had intended, but instead use those funds to improve the physical environment of the school. I believe doing so would also help boost enrollment. We've known for some time that some potential students visiting the campus are not particularly impressed by our facilities.

Because the survey is conducted online, all results are presented in real-time. The numbers today could be substantially different from those tomorrow, so please check the results on the staff website again just before the meeting tomorrow to make sure we're all on the same page.

＊套色字部分請參考「詞彙註解」

【中譯】第 165-168 題請參照下面這份備忘錄。

備忘錄

日期：10 月 2 日
收件人：所有教師與輔導員
寄件人：Gordon Fris
關於：問卷結果

參加計劃的 358 名學生內，目前有 43 名完成了線上滿意度問卷。雖然樣本規模很小，而我們也陸續收到其他的回覆，不過數據裡仍有不容我們忽視的趨勢。我們將在明天下午的員工會議中進行討論。

完成至少兩學期課程的學生在大部分的領域內都給了我們高分，特別是在教師水平、學生服務和整體滿意度上。並不令人意外，我們在學校設施上，得到相對較低的分數。學生特別抱怨桌子太小、照明不良，以及令人詬病的教室狀況。

新學生提到電腦教室提供的硬體和軟體已經太老舊了，但令人驚訝的是，他們並沒有建議需要升級這些設備。多名學生表示他們比較希望使用自己的電腦，他們也希望教師們能夠提供有關免費或低價線上資源的建議以幫助他們學習。

整體看來，這些意見反應顯示，我們不應該如原先構想的將開發預算用在升級電腦教室，反而應該把這些資金運用在提升學校的實體環境上面。我相信這樣做也能夠刺激註冊率。我們早已認知到有些對本校有興趣的學生到校參訪時，對於學校的設備感覺印象並不怎麼好。

由於這份問卷是在線上進行，所以結果都是即時呈現的。今天的數據和明天的有可能大不相同，所以請在明天員工會議之前檢查一下結果，確保大家都擁有同樣的資訊。

詞彙註解

complete [kəm`plit] (v.) 使齊全、使完整

satisfaction [ˌsætɪs`fækʃən] (n.) 滿意度

trend [trɛnd] (n.) 趨勢、潮流

ignore [ɪg`nor] (v.) 忽視、忽略

semester [sə`mɛstə] (n.) 學期

rating [`retɪŋ] (n.) 等級、評價

unsurprisingly [ˌʌnsə`praɪzɪŋlɪ] (adv.)
不足為奇地、不會感到奇怪地

facility [fə`sɪlətɪ] (n.) 設備、設施

appalling [ə`pɔlɪŋ] (adj.) 駭人的、非常低劣的

outdated [ˌaʊt`detɪd] (adj.) 過時的、老舊的

supplement [`sʌpləmənt] (v.) 補充、補增

intend [ɪn`tɛnd] (v.) 想要、打算

physical [`fɪzɪkl] (adj.) 物質的、實體的

boost [bust] (v.) 促進、推動

potential [pə`tɛnʃəl] (adj.) 潛在的、有潛力的

impress [ɪm`prɛs] (v.) 使留下深刻印象、使感動

conduct [kən`dʌkt] (v.) 實施、處理

substantially [səb`stænʃəlɪ] (adv.)
相當程度地、大大地

165. What most likely was the purpose of the survey?

(A) To suggest new classes and services the school could provide

(B) To evaluate the ways potential students are being recruited

(C) To learn what students think about technology in education

(D) To determine how the school's budget should be spent

答案 **D**

中譯 該份問卷最有可能的目的為何？

(A) 建議學校可提供的新課程與服務

(B) 評估招攬學生的各種方法

(C) 瞭解學生對於將科技運用到教育上的看法

(D) 決定學校的預算應該如何使用

解析

題目問 "What most likely was the purpose of the survey?"，應試者應將焦點放在找與此問卷之「目的」相關的資訊上。根據第四段的第一句 "Viewed together, these responses suggest that we shouldn't spend our development budget on upgrading the computer lab as we had intended, but instead use those funds to improve the physical environment of the school."，學校之所以要做這個意見調查，就是要知道學生的需求，以便「將資金的運用放在真正所需的地方」。

選項 (A) 提到 "... suggest new classes and services ..."「建議新課程和服務」，與「資金的運用」無關，故不選。

選項 (B) 提到的 "... evaluate the ways ... students ... recruited" 是說「評估招收新生的方式」，也跟「資金的運用」無關，故不選。

選項 (C) 的 "... learn what students think about technology ..." 提到「瞭解學生對將科技運用到教育上的看法」，和「資金運用」是兩碼子事，亦不適當。

選項 (D) "... determine how the school's budget should be spent"「決定學校預算該如何運用」與文中提到的目的相符，故為最佳答案。

166. What issue is NOT likely asked about on the survey?
(A) The quality of teaching staff
(B) The condition of the facilities
(C) The usefulness of the technology
(D) The availability of courses

答案 D

中譯 下列哪個問題最「不」可能在問卷裡出現？
(A) 教師員工的水平
(B) 學校設施的狀況
(C) 科技的有用程度
(D) 學校有提供什麼課程

解析

第二題問 "What issue is NOT likely asked about on the survey?"，應試者須找出「不會被問及」的議題為何。根據文中第二段內提到的這些資訊："Students who have completed at least two semesters give us high ratings in most areas, especially in teacher quality, student services, and overall satisfaction."，和第三段內提到的 "New students noted that the hardware and the software available in the computer lab are outdated, and they hoped teachers could suggest free or low-cost online resources to supplement their lessons."，可看出以下配對：

選項 (A) The quality of teaching staff = teacher quality，有被提到。

選項 (B) The condition of the facilities = the hardware and the software are outdated，有提及。

選項 (C) The usefulness of the technology = free or low-cost online resources，亦有被提及。

選項 (D) The availability of courses 在文中並沒有被提到，故為正確答案。

167. What does Gordon Fris imply in the memo?

(A) Survey responses are still being collected.

(B) The survey questions were not chosen well.

(C) It is too soon to draw any conclusions from the data.

(D) The survey results are unlikely to change.

答案 A

中譯 Gordon Fris 在備忘錄裡暗示了什麼？

(A) 問卷回覆仍然在收集中。

(B) 問卷問題選擇得不好。

(C) 目前要從資料中做出結論太早了。

(D) 問卷結果不可能改變。

解析

本題屬推論題。根據第一段第一、二句 "Of the 358 students in the program, 43 have completed the online satisfaction survey so far. The sample size is small, and responses are still coming in, but there are trends in the data that we cannot ignore." 可以得知，學生意見「尚未全數交齊，還在陸續送交中。」

選項 (A) "... responses ... still ... collected." 「學生回應還在收集」，與上述兩個句子的內容相符，故為正確答案。

選項 (B) "... questions ... not chosen well." 「問卷題目沒選好」並未出現在文中，故不選。

選項 (C) 提到 "... too soon to draw ... conclusions ...."，但根據第二句的 "... there are trends in the data that we cannot ignore" 可知，雖然資料還沒很多，但仍有重要的資訊在其中，故不選。

選項 (D) "... results are unlikely to change." 是指「結果不可能改變」，但根據最後一段第二句 "The numbers today could be substantially different from those tomorrow ...." 可知，「結果有可能不相同」，故亦不選。

168. What response was NOT expected by Gordon Fris?

(A) Students prefer well-lit classrooms with comfortable desks.

(B) Students would rather have free or low-cost learning resources.

(C) Students are not satisfied with condition of the school.

(D) Students do not want the computer lab to be upgraded.

答案 D

中譯 Gordon Fris 並「未」預期到下列哪一個反應？

(A) 學生比較喜歡有舒適桌子的明亮教室。

(B) 學生比較喜歡免費或低價的學習資源。

(C) 學生對於學校的狀況並不滿意。

(D) 學生並不想要升級電腦教室。

解析

題目問 Gordon Fris「沒有預期」會看到的回應為何。由第三段第一句 "New students noted that the hardware and the software available in the computer lab are outdated, but surprisingly they did not suggest that they be upgraded." 可知，學生雖然認為電腦軟硬體都老舊了，但是他們「並未要求應該將之更新」，而此反應讓 Gordon Fris 感到 "surprised"，換句話說，他原本沒有料到這一點。很明顯地，選項 (D) Students do not want the computer lab to be upgraded. 與文意相符，就是最佳答案。

重點句型聚焦

此文章內的 "Several students said that they prefer their own computers to those in the lab." 這個句子的句型常用來表示對兩樣東西喜好程度之不同，如同中文說的「喜好 A 更甚於 B」。句型如下：

S + prefer + 名詞 A + to + 名詞 B

請看下列例句：

1. I prefer coffee to tea.
   我想喝咖啡甚於喝茶。

2. Some people prefer living in a big city to living in the rural area.
   有些人喜愛住在都市甚於住鄉下地方。

3. Majority of employees prefer having a fix seat to having a hot desk.
   大多數員工喜歡坐固定座位而不想輪用辦公桌。

DISCOVER THE WORLD OF BOOKS
∽∾ SUMMAR PROGRAM FOR YOUNG READERS ∿∽

The Philadelphia Public Library is happy to announce our summer program for young readers: Discover the World of Books. The program will begin on Saturday, June 16 and continue until the end of August. Each two-week session of the program will focus on a different nation, region, or city. Our daily Story Time readings will also feature recommended books from or about the area, and they will be available for reading or check-out at a special display case at the entrance of the children's section. Thanks to guidance from The World Library Association and book exchanges with our sister libraries in Mexico City, Rome, Asmara, Bangalore, and Tokyo, original language versions of many of the books will be displayed together with their translations.

Most exciting for young readers are the free Reading Passports that will be distributed to all participants. Young readers who have finished reading a book from or about a particular area can bring it to any children's librarian and receive a stamp representing that area—just like any world traveler! Readers with twenty or more stamps are eligible to enter a drawing to receive a 24-inch diameter globe.

Thanks to special financial assistance from the city council, the program is free of charge. Readers between the ages of 4 and 14 are eligible, and can register starting on June 1 at the main information desk.

＊套色字部分請參考「詞彙註解」

【中譯】第 **169-171** 題請參照下面這則公告。

發現書本的世界
給小讀者們的暑期計劃

Philadelphia 大眾圖書館很高興宣佈我們為小讀者們所舉辦的暑期活動：發現書本的世界。此計劃將從 6 月 16 日星期六開始，並持續到八月底。本計劃每兩週一個階段，每一階段都將把重點放在一個不同的國家、地區或城市。我們每日故事時間的讀物也會包括有關該地區的建議書籍，它們將會被擺在兒童區入口的一個特別展示櫃中，供讀者閱讀或是借出。非常感謝 The World Library 協會的指導以及與我們位於 Mexico、Rome、Asmara、Bangalore 和 Tokyo 等城市的姊妹圖書館的交流，許多書籍的原文版都將會與它們的翻譯本一同陳列出來。

讓小讀者們感到最興奮的將會是頒發給所有參與者的免費閱讀護照。閱讀完來自或有關一個特別地區的書籍的小讀者們可以將護照拿給任何兒童區的圖書館館員以獲得一個代表該地區的章，就像是一名世界旅行者一樣！擁有超過二十枚蓋章的讀者們就有資格參加抽獎活動，有機會獲得一顆直徑 24 英吋的地球儀。

感謝市議會的特別財務支援，本計劃是完全免費的。四歲至十四歲的讀者們均有資格參加，6 月 1 日起可於服務櫃台報名。

詞彙註解

continue [kənˋtɪnju] (v.) 繼續、持續

session [ˋsɛʃən] (n.) 會議、會期

nation [ˋneʃən] (n.) 國家、國民

region [ˋridʒən] (n.) 地區、區域

available [əˋveləbl] (adj.)
可用的、可利用的、在手邊的

guidance [ˋgaɪdns] (n.) 指導、指引

exchange [ɪksˋtʃendʒ] (n.) 交換、交流

display [dɪˋsple] (v.) 陳列、展出

translation [trænsˋleʃən] (n.) 翻譯

distribute [dɪˋstrɪbjut] (v.) 分配、分發

participant [pɑrˋtɪsəpənt] (n.) 參與人、參加者

particular [pəˋtɪkjələ] (adj.)
特別的、獨有的、特殊的

librarian [laɪˋbrɛrɪən] (n.) 圖書館員

eligible [ˋɛlɪdʒəbl] (adj.) 合格的、符合資格的

drawing [ˋdrɔɪŋ] (n.) 抽獎、抽籤

diameter [daɪˋæmətə] (n.) 直徑

169. What is the main purpose of the program?

(A) To inspire young readers to learn a foreign language

(B) To acquire books from various world cities

(C) To encourage children to read about the world

(D) To assist libraries in other countries

答案 C

中譯 本計劃的主要目的為何？

(A) 啓發小讀者們學習外國語言

(B) 從世界上多個城市獲得書籍

(C) 鼓勵孩童閱讀有關世界的書籍

(D) 協助其他國家的圖書館

解析

約略地掃瞄文章標題和內容後可見端倪，此文章在講的是跟「青少年讀書」相關的活動。根據標題與首句 "Summer program for young readers" 和 "The Philadelphia Public Library is happy to announce our summer program for young readers: Discover the World of Books." 可知，此活動的目的是爲了要「鼓勵孩童閱讀有關世界的書籍」。

選項 (A) 中的 "... learn a foreign language" 提及「學習外語」，與活動內容不符，故不選。

選項 (B) 的 "... acquire books from ... world cities" 提到要「自世界各大都市取得書籍」，並非本公告主旨，故爲錯誤。

選項 (C) 提到的關鍵點 "... encourage children ... read about the world" 與活動標題相符，故爲最佳答案。

選項 (D) "... assist libraries ... other countries" 意指「協助其他國家的圖書館」，亦與此活動無關，故不選。

170. Who is funding the program?

(A) The World Library Association

(B) The Philadelphia Public library

(C) Sister libraries around the world

(D) The Philadelphia City Council

答案 D

誰為本計劃提供資金？

(A) The World Library 協會

(B) Philadelphia 大眾圖書館

(C) 位於世界各地的姊妹圖書館

(D) Philadelphia 市議會

解析

第二題問的是 "Who is funding the program?"，應試者要將焦點放在找「誰 / 哪個單位」贊助此活動的資訊上。根據最後一段第一句 "Thanks to special financial assistance from the city council ..." 可知，提供金錢協助的是該市之市議會。很明顯地，正確答案為 (D)。其他選項雖在文中皆有被提及，但並非贊助單位，故不可選。

171. What type of activity is NOT a part of the program?

    (A) Daily book readings

    (B) International book exchanges

    (C) Reading passports

    (D) Visits from international authors

答案 D

中譯 下列何種活動「非」此計劃的一部分？

(A) 每天閱讀書籍

(B) 國際性的書籍交換

(C) 閱讀護照

(D) 國際作家的參訪

解析

先看到題目問的是 "What type of activity is NOT a part of the program?"，焦點非常明確，就是要找出三個文章當中有提到的 "activity"，以便排除掉一個沒提到的。根據文中的這些資訊："Our daily Story Time readings will also feature recommended books from or about the area ...."、"Thanks to guidance from The World Library Association and book exchanges with our sister libraries ...."、"Most exciting for young readers are the free Reading Passports that will be distributed to all participants." 可知，選項 (A) Daily book readings、(B) International book exchanges、與 (C) Reading passports 都有被提及，因此本題選 (D) Visits from international authors。

✏️ 重點句型聚焦

我們利用此文章中的 "Young readers who have finished reading a book from or about a particular area can bring it to any children's librarian and receive a stamp representing that area!" 這個句子來討論一下關係子句。此句的結構為：

Young readers [who have finished reading a book from or about a particular area] can bring it to any children's librarian and receive a stamp representing that area.

Young readers 為主要子句的主詞，其後的 can bring 是主要動詞，括號內的 who 子句用來修飾其前的 Young readers。

先行詞（主要子句主詞）**+** 關係子句 **[who ...] +** be/V（主要子句動詞）

請看下列例句：

1. The woman is our manager. She is talking to a client.
   = The woman who is talking to a client is our manager.
   那位正在跟客戶講話的女子是我們的經理。

2. Interested candidates can submit a CV and apply for the position. They must have an MBA degree.
   = Interested candidates who have an MBA degree can submit a CV and apply for the position.
   有興趣、具有商管碩士學位的應徵者可以遞交履歷表來申請此職位。

Questions 172-175 refer to the following instructions.

Q-Disk 400
More than just a disc drive

Thank you for your purchase. We created Q-Disk to ensure that your most valuable computer files are always safe and accessible whenever you need them, wherever you are. Just pop a Q-Disk in your pocket, and your data goes with you.

Features
- High-Speed Transfer: Small files are moved almost instantly, large files in just seconds.
- Just the Right Size: Q-Disks are light and fit easily into a coat pocket.
- Turn Up the Volume: Q-Disks can hold tens of thousands of songs or hundreds of full-length feature films.
- Stay in Sync: Whenever Q-Disk is connected to your computer, files are automatically updated to the most recent version.
- Secure: Your data can be encrypted on your computer before it is transferred, ensuring that only you have access to your files.

Operation
- After plugging your Q-disk into a power source, connect it to your computer. An icon will appear on the desktop and Q-Disk is ready to use.
- To enable syncing, encryption, and other advanced features, click on the Q-disk icon. A dialog box will appear guiding you through the many configuration options available. Activate those that you need.

Warranty
- All Q-Disk products are guaranteed to be free of manufacturing defects for two years from the time of purchase.
- The warranty is void if the disk is dropped or exposed to water.

Please email support@q-disk.com if you experience any difficulty with your Q-Disk. For bulk orders, call Q-Disk sales support at (716) 984-9398. To receive updates on our latest offerings, visit us online at q-disk.com.

Q-Disk Inc., 2409 Colvin Blvd., Kenmore, NY 14223

*套色字部分請參考「詞彙註解」

【中譯】第 **172-175** 題請參照下面這篇使用說明。

Q-Disk 400
不僅僅只是個磁碟機

感謝您購買此產品。我們製造 Q-Disk 以確保您最重要的電腦檔案得以安全地保存,而且無論您在何時、何處皆可存取檔案。只需要將 Q-Disk 放到您的口袋裡,您的資料將跟著您一起行動。

特色
- 高速傳輸:小型檔案將以近乎即刻的速度傳輸,大型檔案則只須花費數秒就能完成。
- 剛剛好的大小:Q-Disk 非常輕巧,可以很容易地放在外套口袋中。
- 將音量調高吧:Q-Disk 能夠儲存數千首歌曲,或數百部完整的影片。
- 保持同步:每次將 Q-Disk 連接至電腦時,檔案將會自動更新成最新版本。
- 安全:您的資料能夠在傳輸到 Q-Disk 之前先進行加密,確保只有您才能存取檔案。

操作
- 在為 Q-Disk 插上電源後,將它與電腦連接。桌面會出現一個圖示,代表已經可以開始使用 Q-Disk。
- 如要開啟同步、加密與其他進階功能,請點一下 Q-Disk 圖示。一個對話視窗便會出現,引導您了解各種可以使用的設定選項。您可依所需啟動它們。

保固
- 所有 Q-Disk 產品保證無製造瑕疵,皆享有從購買日期開始為期兩年的保固。
- 如果磁碟掉落或碰觸到液體,保固將會失效。

如果您遇到使用 Q-Disk 的任何問題,請來信至電子郵件信箱 support@q-disk.com。若要大量訂購,請聯絡 Q-Disk 行銷支援部門 (716) 984-9398。若要取得我們最新產品的訊息,請蒞臨我們的網站 q-disk.com。

Q-Disk 公司,(14223) New York 州 Kenmore 村 Colvin 大道 2409 號

PART 3 TEST 1

purchase [`pɜtʃəs] (*n.*) 購買

ensure [ɪn`ʃʊr] (*v.*) 保證、擔保

valuable [`væljuəbl] (*adj.*) 有價值的、有用的

accessible [æk`sɛsəbl] (*adj.*) 易使用的、易得到的

pocket [`pɑkɪt] (*n.*) 口袋

feature [fitʃə] (*n.*) 特色、特性

instantly [`ɪnstəntlɪ] (*adv.*) 立即、馬上

sync [sɪŋk] (*v.*) 同時發生、同步

automatically [͵ɔtə`mætɪklɪ] (*adv.*) 自動地

encrypt [ɛn`krɪpt] (*v.*) 加密

plug [plʌg] (*v.*) 插頭、接電

configuration [kən͵fɪgjə`reʃən] (*n.*) 結構、配置

activate [`æktə͵vet] (*v.*) 啟動、活化

warranty [`wɔrəntɪ] (*n.*) 保固、保證書

defect [dɪ`fɛkt] (*n.*) 缺點、瑕疵

void [vɔɪd] (*adj.*) 空的、無效的

expose [ɪk`spoz] (*v.*) 暴露

bulk [bʌlk] (*n.*) 大量

172. Why was the Q-Disk 400 invented?

(A) To store important files

(B) To transfer files safely

(C) To make new files accessible

(D) To recover lost files

答案 **A**

中譯 開發 Q-Disk 400 產品的目的為何？

(A) 為了儲存重要檔案

(B) 為了安全地傳輸檔案

(C) 為了使新檔案能夠被存取

(D) 為了救回失去的檔案

解析

題目問此裝置的用途為何。根據第一段第二句 "We created Q-Disk to ensure that your most valuable computer files are always safe and accessible whenever you need them, wherever you are." 可知，Q-Disk 400 是用來存檔案的。

選項 (A) 描述與文章內容相符，故正確。

選項 (B) 的 "... transfer files ..." 有可能是 Q-Disk 400 的功能之一，但並非主要的賣點，故不適當。

選項 (C) 提到 "... make new files accessible"，但是該產品並非僅針對「新的」檔案做存取，故不可選。

選項 (D) "... recover lost files"「救回遺失的檔案」並未被提及，故不選。

173. **Which of the following is NOT a feature of the Q-Disk 400?**

(A) Wireless file transfer

(B) Automatic synchronization

(C) Large capacity

(D) Secure encryption

答案 **A**

中譯 下列何者「非」Q-Disk 400 的特色之一？

(A) 無線檔案傳輸

(B) 全自動同步

(C) 龐大的容量

(D) 安全的加密功能

解析

題目問的是 "Which of the following is NOT a feature of the Q-Disk 400?"，因此應試者須找出 Q-Disk 400「沒有被提及」的功能。根據 "Features" 小標題內提到的功能，包括 "High-Speed Transfer"、"Just the Right Size"、"Turn Up the Volume"、"Stay in Sync" 與 "Secure" 等，可看出以下的搭配：

選項 (B) Automatic synchronization = Stay in Sync，有被提到。

選項 (C) Large capacity = Turn Up the Volume，有被提到。

選項 (D) Secure encryption = Secure，亦有被提到。

選項 (A) Wireless file transfer 不等於 High-Speed Transfer，故為正確答案。

174. **What happens when users click on the icon?**

(A) The disc will access the power source.

(B) The computer will configure automatic syncing.

(C) The options menu will appear.

(D) The advanced features will be activated.

答案 **C**

中譯 使用者點擊圖示後，會發生什麼事？

(A) 磁碟機會存取電源。

(B) 電腦會設定自動同步。

(C) 會出現設定選單。

(D) 進階功能會被開啓。

解析

題目問的是 "What happens when users click on the icon?"，應試者應找出 click on the icon 後會發生的事。根據 "Operation" 第二點 "To enable syncing, encryption, and other advanced features, click on the Q-disk icon. A dialog box will appear guiding you through ...." 可知，在 click on the icon 之後，會有「對話視窗」出現。

選項 (A) 提到的 "... disc ... access the power source." 與「對話視窗」無關，故不選。

選項 (B) 提到的 "... configure automatic syncing." 也跟「對話視窗」無關，故不選。

選項 (C) 提及 "... options menu will appear."「會出現設定選單」，故為正確答案。

選項 (D) "... advanced features ... activated."「進階功能被啟動」與文意不符，故不選。

175. What should customers do if they have problems using the Q-Disk 400?

(A) Call the customer service department

(B) Find an authorized repair center

(C) Contact the company by email

(D) Return it to the place of purchase

答案 C

中譯 如果顧客們使用 Q-Disk 400 時遇到問題，應該做什麼？

(A) 聯絡客服部門

(B) 找一間有認證的維修中心

(C) 用電子郵件與該公司聯絡

(D) 到原購買處退貨

解析

針對本題所問，應試者應將焦點放在找「有問題時的處理方式」上。根據最後一段第一句 "Please email support@q-disk.com if you experience any difficulty with your Q-Disk." 可知，若有產品相關的問題須透過 email 詢問。

選項 (A) "Call ... customer service ..." 用「打電話」的方式，不對。

選項 (B) 提到的 "Find ... repair center" 是指找「維修中心」，也不對。

選項 (C) "Contact ... by email"「用 email 的方式聯絡」，為正確答案。

選項 (D) "Return ... place of purchase"「退回原購買處」亦非文章所述，故不選。

✒️ 重點句型聚焦

我們可由本篇中之 "Just pop a Q-Disk in your pocket, and your data goes with you." 來應用包含「祈使句」的句型。這個句型表示前後動作的因果關係，也就是說如果做了前面那個動作，就會有後面動作之結果，就好像中文「若……，就會……」之意。

祈使句 ..., and + S + V

請看下列例句：

1. Work hard, and you will be more likely to be promoted.
   若你認真工作，就比較可能被升遷。

2. Click on the icon, and a dialog box will appear on the screen.
   點一下這個圖像，一個對話視窗就會出現在螢幕上。

PART 3 TEST 1

Questions 176-180 refer to the following article and comment.

http://marketwatch.net/

Online Shopping versus Retail Outlets: Game On
By William Harrison for MarketWatch Insider
Posted: May 22 8:39 am

In the past two years, the popularity of online shopping has exploded. Traditional retail companies, joined by thousands of new virtual storefronts, have turned the Internet into a flourishing online marketplace, and in the process made E-commerce one of the fastest growing industries in the world. At the same time, advances in tablet computers and other mobile devices have made it easy for consumers to make online purchases. With just a few touches of a finger, consumers can buy whatever they need wherever they are. How then can retail outlets to survive? Or, to put it another way, should they?

Maybe not. The benefits of online commerce far outweigh those of traditional shopping. Information about the make and model of every product on the market is now always literally at your fingertips. Gone are the days when you spent entire Saturday afternoons traveling to remote specialty stores to compare products. Never again will you have to fend off overbearing store clerks trying to make their daily sales quotas. Instead, you can sit in the comfort of your own home and read impartial product reviews from experts. In addition to saving time and trouble, online shopping also saves you money: the best bargains are always found online. The staffing costs, electricity bills, and other expenses of online businesses are a small fraction of those borne by traditional retailers, and e-commerce retailers don't have to pay rent in expensive retail locations. These savings are passed on to consumers in the form of lower prices and other benefits, such as coupons and free shipping. As more and more customers experience the convenience and low-prices of online shopping, fewer and fewer retail stores will be able to survive.

Dear Mr. Harrison,

Thank you for bringing this discussion to the readers of MarketWatch Insider. You make several valid points, but I am afraid I must disagree with your main claim. E-commerce will continue to grow, but retail outlets will never disappear for the simple reason that they offer numerous benefits unavailable to online shoppers.

- If you purchase online, you have to wait for the item to be delivered to you, and contrary to what you imply in your article, you will likely have to pay for shipping. If you require that the item arrive the next day, the shipping cost will be considerable. If you require a same-day purchase, a regular retail outlet is your only choice.
- Retail outlets offer the opportunity to "try before you buy." A small picture of a chair, swimsuit, or bicycle on your mobile phone isn't going to tell you how well the item fits your body. And if a purchased item doesn't fit, you must pack it up, take it to the post office, and return it to the seller. How convenient is that?
- It is impossible to adequately communicate touch and smell over the Internet. Colors on a computer screen often appear different than they do in real life. If you really want to know what you're spending your money on, you must experience the product first-hand.
- You do a disservice to salespeople by implying that they care more about sales quotas than they do satisfied customers. Most are entirely reputable and use the expertise they have developed in their field to guide customers to the products that best match their needs.

Jeff Clark

*套色字部分請參考「詞彙註解」

http://marketwatch.net/

網路購物對上零售商店：業務戰準備開打

William Harrison 為 MarketWatch Insider 撰寫

張貼時間：5 月 22 日上午 8:39

過去兩年間，線上購物的普及度出現爆炸性的成長。傳統的零售公司，加上數千家全新的虛擬商店，將網際網路變成了一個生機蓬勃的線上市集，並在過程中讓電子商務成了全世界成長最迅速的產業之一。在此同時，平板電腦與其他行動裝置的進步使得消費者能夠很容易地進行線上購物。只須動動手指，消費者無論在任何地方都能購買任何商品。如此一來，零售商店要如何生存？或者，換一個方式說，他們應該生存嗎？

或許不。網路商務的好處遠遠超過傳統購物方式。有關所有產品的樣式型號可說在彈指之間就能取得。早期人們習慣在星期六下午，到偏遠的專門店尋找並比較商品的日子已經遠去。而你也不必再抵擋那些為了達成每日銷售目標的店員們的糾纏。相反地，你可以在自己家中舒適地坐著，上網閱讀來自專家們對該商品的公正評論。除了省時省力之外，線上購物還可以為你省錢：最好的優惠總是可以在網路上找到。線上公司的員工薪資、電費和其他費用只是傳統商店花費的一小部分，而且電子商務零售商也不需要支付昂貴零售地點的租金。這些省下來的成本都會連帶地以低價和其他好處的方式，如優惠券和免運費等，轉移到消費者的身上。隨著越來越多顧客體驗到線上購物的方便與低價，越來越少零售商店能有辦法存活下去。

親愛的 Harrison 先生：

感謝您為 MarketWatch Insider 的讀者們帶來這個討論主題。您的確提到幾個合理的論點，但是我恐怕無法全然同意您的主要看法。電子商務將會持續成長，但是正因為零售商店仍然可以提供線上購物者無法享有的許多項優勢，所以它們將永遠不會消失。

- 如果你在網站上購物，就必須等待該物品被寄送到你所在的地點，而且與你在文章裡所暗示的相反，大多時候消費者都必須支付運費。如果你要求物品於隔日送達，則運費會相當可觀。如果你想要在當日收到貨品，則一般的零售商店會是你唯一的選擇。
- 零售商店提供「購買前先試用」的機會。在你手機上顯示的椅子、泳衣或腳踏車的小圖片，根本無法讓你得知那項物品是否合用。如果購買的商品不合，你必須將它重新包裝好、帶到郵局，並再次寄回給賣家。這樣會方便嗎？
- 透過網際網路展示的商品，根本無法完整地傳達觸感與味道。電腦螢幕上顯示出來的顏色經常與現實情況有差距。如果你真的想要知道你的錢花在什麼東西上面，你必須第一手體驗那項產品。
- 你暗示了「比起滿足消費者，售貨員更加在乎他們自身的業績」，這一點對他們而言是一種傷害。大部分售貨人員都非常有口碑，他們會利用在自身領域裡所獲得的專業能力，來協助消費者購買最適合他們需求的產品。

Jeff Clark

popularity [ˌpɑpjə`lærətɪ] (*n.*) 普及、流行

explode [ɪk`splod] (*v.*) 爆炸、爆發

virtual [`vɜtʃʊəl] (*adj.*) 虛擬的

storefront [`stor͵frʌnt] (*n.*) 店面

flourishing [`flɜɪʃɪŋ] (*adj.*) 蓬勃的、繁榮的

survive [sə`vaɪv] (*v.*) 存活

outweigh [aʊt`we] (*v.*) 比……重要

literally [`lɪtərəlɪ] (*adv.*) 實在地、不誇張地

fend off 擋開、避開

overbear [`ovə͵bɛr] (*v.*) 壓倒、克服

impartial [ɪm`pɑrʃəl] (*adj.*) 公正、無偏見的

numerous [`njumərəs] (*adj.*) 許多的、眾多的

contrary [`kɑntrɛrɪ] (*adj.*) 相反的、對立的

considerable [kən`sɪdərəbl] (*adj.*) 相當大的、重要的

outlet [`aʊt͵lɛt] (*n.*) 銷路、商店

adequately [`ædəkwɪtlɪ] (*adv.*) 充分地、足夠地

first-hand [`fɜst`hænd] (*adv.*) 第一手地、直接地

disservice [dɪs`sɜvɪs] (*n.*) 傷害行為、幫倒忙行為

imply [ɪm`plaɪ] (*v.*) 暗示、暗喻

reputable [`rɛpjətəbl] (*adj.*) 聲譽好的

expertise [ˌɛkspə`tiz] (*n.*) 專門知識、技術

176. What is the MarketWatch article mainly about?

(A) The importance of in-store customers for retail outlets

(B) The factors determining the success of retail stores

(C) The benefits of retail shopping and online shopping

(D) The superiority of online shopping to retail shopping

答案 **D**

中譯 MarketWatch 這篇文章的主要內容為何？

(A) 來店顧客對於零售商店的重要性

(B) 決定零售商店成功的因素

(C) 商店購物和線上購物的好處

(D) 線上購物凌駕於商店購物的優勢

解析

將兩篇文章大概地掃瞄一下，就可以判斷第一篇是「比較線上購物和傳統商店購物差異」的文章，而第二篇則為讀者投書，表明不同的看法。第一題問的是 "What is the MarketWatch article mainly about?"，即問第一篇文章的「主旨」。依第一段中提到的 "In the past two years, the popularity of online shopping has exploded. Traditional retail companies, joined by thousands of new virtual storefronts, have turned the Internet into a flourishing online marketplace, and in the process made E-commerce one of the fastest growing industries in the world ... How then can retail outlets to survive? Or, to put it another way, should they?" 可知，文中大都在講線上購物的好處。

選項 (A) 提到 "... importance of in-store customers ... retail outlets"「來店顧客對零售商店的重要性」，但沒提到主旨「線上購物」，故不選。

選項 (B) 提到 "... factors ... success of retail stores"「零售商店的成功因素」，也不符合作者一直強調的「線上購物」，故亦不選。

選項 (C) 提到的 "... benefits of retail shopping and online shopping" 指商店購物和線上購物兩種購物型式的優點，但本文一面倒地支持線上購物，故不可選。

選項 (D) "The superiority of online shopping to retail shopping" 為正確答案，因為作者自始至終一直在強調的正是「線上購物」優於「商店購物」。

177. What is NOT mentioned in the article as a benefit of online shopping?

(A) Discount coupons

(B) Objective reviews

(C) Mobile devices

(D) Convenient comparisons

答案 C

中譯 文中「未」提及下列哪一項線上購物的好處？

(A) 折價券

(B) 客觀的評論

(C) 行動裝置

(D) 方便性的比較

解析

本題須找出三個以上在文中被提及之線上購物的好處，以便排除掉一個沒被提到的。根據第二段第三行的 "Gone are the days when you spent entire Saturday afternoons traveling to remote specialty stores to compare products ... Instead, you can sit in the comfort of your own home and read impartial product reviews from experts .... These savings are passed on to consumers in the form of lower prices and other benefits, such as coupons and free shipping."，可看出以下配對：

選項 (A) Discount coupons = coupons，有提到。

選項 (B) Objective reviews = impartial product reviews，有提到。

選項 (D) Convenient comparisons = don't need to travel to remote stores to compare products，有提到。

選項 (C) Mobile devices 非文中提及為線上購物的好處之一，故為正確答案。

178. In the article, the word "overbearing" in paragraph 2, line 6, is closest in meaning to

(A) aggressive

(B) considerate

(C) overpaid

(D) indifferent

答案 A

中譯 文章第二段第六行的 "overbearing" 這個字意思最接近

(A) 有侵略性的

(B) 考慮周到的

(C) 多支付的

(D) 冷漠的

解析

本題為字彙題。"overbearing" 在此處用來形容商店業務員「專橫的、咄咄逼人」的感覺，與選項 (A) aggressive（有侵略的）意思接近，故為最佳答案。選項 (B) considerate（考慮周到的）、選項 (C) overpaid（多支付的）和選項 (D) indifferent（冷淡的）的意思都與 overbearing 相差甚遠，故不選。

179. According to the comment, what is an advantage of shopping at retail stores?

(A) It allows customers to experience what products are really like.

(B) It provides opportunities for experts to provide product reviews.

(C) It helps salespeople reach their sales quotas more quickly.

(D) It enables business owners to charge more for their products.

答案 A

中譯 根據評論，在零售商店購物的優點為何？

(A) 它讓顧客能夠體驗實際的產品。

(B) 它提供專家們給予產品評論的機會。

(C) 它幫助銷售人員更快速地完成他們的銷售目標。

(D) 它讓企業擁有者能夠為產品收取更高的費用。

解析

這題問的是 "According to the comment, what is an advantage of shopping at retail stores?"，必須從第二篇評論文的內容來回答。根據其中第二點和第三點所列出的 "Retail outlets offer the opportunity to 'try before you buy'." 與 "If you really want to know what you're spending your money on, you must experience the product first-hand."，作者強調了「親自試用過再買」的重要性。

選項 (A) 提到的 "... allows customers to experience ... products ...." 與「親自試用過再買」的意思一樣，故為正確答案。

選項 (B) 的 "... provides opportunities ... to provide products reviews." 與作者所強調的不同，故不選。

選項 (C) 的 "... helps salespeople reach ... quotas ... quickly." 也不是作者所強調的傳統商店的優點，故不選。

選項 (D) 的 "... enables business owners ... charge more ..." 提到讓店主可以多收些費用，這也不是作者所強調的傳統商店的好處，故不選。

180. What does Jeff Clark imply in his comment?

(A) He was once a supporter of online shopping.
(B) E-commerce offers fewer benefits than retail shopping.
(C) There are no benefits to shopping online.
(D) Online shopping will inevitably replace retail shopping.

答案 B

中譯 Jeff Clark 在他的評論裡暗示了什麼？

(A) 他曾經是線上購物的支持者。
(B) 電子商務比零售購物提供較少的好處。
(C) 線上購物沒有任何好處。
(D) 線上購物終將取代零售購物。

解析

最後一題須從 Jeff Clark 所表達的意見來判斷其言下之意。由評論首段第三句提到 "E-commerce will continue to grow, but retail outlets will never disappear for the simple reason that they offer numerous benefits unavailable to online shoppers." 可看出，他認為「傳統商店提供的許多好處是線上購物無法比擬的」。

選項 (A) "... was once ... supporter of online shopping." 意指他曾是線上購物的支持者，但文中並無此敘述，故不適當。

選項 (B) 是說，作者認為線上購物的好處比傳統購物來得「少」，故為正確答案。

選項 (C) 提到的 "... no benefits to shopping online." 並非作者的主張，故不可選。

選項 (D) 提及「線上購物終將取代傳統商店」，這完全與作者支持傳統商店的態度 "retail outlets will never disappear" 相反，故亦不可選。

🖊 重點句型聚焦

本題組的第一篇文章內有個值得討論的倒裝句 "Never again will you have to fend off overbearing store clerks trying to make their daily sales quotas."。本句原為 "You will never again have to fend off overbearing store clerks trying to make their daily sales quotas."，也就是，將否定字或有否定意義的片語 (never again) 放在句首時，後面的句子就要倒裝。

| Not/Nor/Neither/Never, Few/Little/Seldom/Less Hardly/Scarcely/Rarely | + 助動詞 + S + 動詞 |

請看下列例句：

1. We had hardly seen our old neighbors since they moved two years ago.
   = Hardly had we seen our old neighbors since they moved two years ago.
   自從我們的老鄰居兩年前搬走之後，我們就鮮少再見過他們了。

2. He not only won the Sales Rep of the Year Award but he also got promoted.
   = Not only did he win the Sales Rep of the Year Award, but he also got promoted.
   他不僅得到「年度最佳業務獎」，還被升遷了。

Sunny's Restaurant "Daily Deals"

A guaranteed good time for all at any of our Southern California locations!

10% off Tuesdays!
On orders more than $10.00.
Not valid with any other offer.

Soup, Salad, & Fruit Bar Just $1
With the purchase of any item from our special "Heart Smart" menu.

Monday through Friday 7:30 – 11am
Saturday & Sunday 7:30 – 2pm

Family Pizza Special
Only $24.99 plus tax

✻ Large (16-inch) Cheese Pizza
✻ Spaghetti and Meatballs
✻ Caeser Salad (serves four)
✻ Box of Chocolate Chip Cookies

Not valid with any other offer.

Vegetarian-Friendly
Breakfast Bar

AND MORE!
✻ French Toast
✻ Belgian Waffles
✻ omlettes

Glenda Jefferson
2600 6th St., Apt #4
Fair Oaks, CA 90033

July 28

Sunny's Restaurants
Corporate Headquarters
9483 Beltane Rd., Suite 500
Los Angeles, CA 90210

To Whom It May Concern:

Last Tuesday my husband, our three children, my brother, and I ate at the Sunny's Restaurant on Lankershim Blvd. We were eager to try a new restaurant and glad to take advantage of your daily deals coupons printed in the Sunday paper. I'm sorry to say that the moment we stepped through Sunny's doors I knew it was a bad idea. Instead of "a good time for all" it was a "lousy time by all." Let me explain.

It is very difficult to find a decent vegetarian meal in Fair Oaks, so I was especially excited to try Sunny's vegetarian breakfast bar. Imagine my surprise to find that not ONE item at the bar was truly vegetarian. Further, the advertised soup, salad, and fruit bar was not available. It had closed at the early time of 11:30 am! The only item I could eat was the Caesar salad, so I left the restaurant hungry. In addition, our server would not allow us to split up the check. I was going to use the 10% off Tuesday coupon for my brother's sandwich, and my husband was going to pay for the Family Pizza Special. The server kept saying only one coupon was valid per meal, and that the sandwich only cost $7 so my coupon would be invalid anyway.

Your ad doesn't specify what the "guarantee" entails exactly, but I am sure you stand by your offer. I demand a full refund of our meal—$64.25. If I don't receive a check for that amount by August 15, I will be forced to contact the Fair Oaks Chamber of Commerce and post unfavorable reviews on the Internet.

Sincerely,

Glenda Jefferson

Glenda Jefferson

Sunny's 餐廳「每日優惠」
我們任何一家位於加州南部的餐廳皆保證給予所有人一個美好時光！

每週二打九折！
適用於超過美金十元的餐點。
無法結合其他優惠。

只要1元，即可享用湯品、沙拉與水果吧
只要您購買任何「對你心臟健康有益」特別菜單中的品項。

星期一至星期五早上 7:30 至 11:00
週末 7:30 至下午 2:00

家庭比薩特餐
只要 **24.99** 元　不含稅

✻ 大起司比薩（16 吋）
✻ 義大利麵佐肉丸
✻ 凱撒沙拉（四人份）
✻ 巧克力碎片餅乾一盒

無法結合其他優惠。

素食早餐吧

還有更多！

✻ 法式土司
✻ 比利時鬆餅
✻ 煎蛋

Glenda Jefferson
第 6 街 2600 號 4 室
(90033) California 州 Fair Oaks 區

7 月 28 日

Sunny's 餐廳
公司總部
Beltane 路 9483 號 500 室
(90210) California 州 Los Angeles 市

敬啓者：

上星期二我和我先生、三個小孩以及我弟弟在 Lankershim 大道的 Sunny's 餐廳用餐。我們很熱切地想嘗試新的餐廳，並很慶幸能夠使用你們印在星期日報紙上的每日優惠券。我必須說，當我們踏進 Sunny's 的大門之後，我就知道這並不是個好主意。與其說是享有一個「給所有人的美好時光」，大家感受到的其實是一個「差勁時光」。請容我解釋原委。

在 Fair Oaks 很難找到一間不錯的素食餐廳，所以我特別想要嘗試 Sunny's 的素食早餐吧。而當我發現整個吧台沒有半樣全素的餐點時，我所感受到的震驚您可想而知。不僅如此，廣告上的湯品、沙拉和水果吧什麼都沒有。原來它早在上午 11:30 就停止供應了！我唯一能夠吃的只有凱撒沙拉，所以離開餐廳時我仍然非常飢餓。除此之外，現場服務生不允許我們分開付帳。我本來想把星期二九折的折價券用在我弟弟的三明治上，而我先生則要另外付家庭比薩特餐的錢。那位服務生一直說每一餐只能使用一張折價券，而且那份三明治價格只有七美元，所以我的折價券也根本無法使用。

您們的廣告內並沒有明確說明貴公司的「保證」包含了什麼，但是我確信您會堅守您們做出的承諾。我要求全額退還我們餐點的費用，一共是 64.25 美元。如果我在 8 月 15 日之前沒有收到該金額的支票，我將被迫聯繫 Fair Oaks 商會，並可能會在網路上發表對貴公司不利的評論。

Glenda Jefferson 上

---

181. What information is mentioned in the advertisement?

(A) The addresses of the restaurants

(B) The ending dates of the offers

(C) The amount of the discounts

(D) The original prices of the items

答案 C

中譯 廣告裡提到什麼訊息？

(A) 餐廳的地址

(B) 優惠的有效日期

(C) 優惠的額度

(D) 餐點的原始價格

解析

看到雙篇的文章與題目，解題方法也一樣，即先將兩篇文章大概掃瞄過一次，瞭解兩篇的要點各是什麼，而關鍵在於識破兩篇文章之間的「關連性」爲何。接著就是直接看題目，根據題目所問去找線索來回答。

此一題組第一篇文章是一家餐廳的折價券廣告，第二篇則是顧客抱怨信。由此兩個要點可以大膽地判斷，這兩篇之間的「關連性」可能就是顧客使用了餐廳折價券，卻不滿意餐廳的服務。第一道題目問 "What information is mentioned in the advertisement?"，只要在廣告中找相關資訊即可，而廣告上最明顯的強調之處爲 "10% off Tuesdays!"「週二打九折！」。

選項 (A) The addresses（地址）、選項 (B) The ending dates of the offers（截止日期）和選項 (D) The original prices of the items（產品原價）等資訊都沒有在廣告中出現，因此不可選。選項 (C) The amount of the discounts 之內容則與 "10% off Tuesdays!" 相符，故爲正確答案。

182. What can be inferred about the restaurant?

(A) The salad bar usually costs more than a dollar.

(B) It does not serve beverages.

(C) Sunny's is a vegetarian restaurant.

(D) It only accepts cash payments.

答案 A

中譯 由文中可以推論出有關該餐廳的什麼事項？

(A) 沙拉吧的平時價格比起一美元還高。

(B) 該餐廳不供應飲料。

(C) Sunny's 是一家素食餐廳。

(D) 該餐廳只接受現金付款。

解析

此題目問 "What can be inferred about the restaurant?"，應試者必須找由餐廳折價券之內容可「推論」出來的要點為何。根據 "Soup, Salad, & Fruit Bar Just $1" 可推測，原價應高於一美元。

選項 (A) The salad bar usually costs more than a dollar. 為最佳答案。選項 (B) It does not serve beverages.（餐廳不提供飲料）、選項 (C) Sunny's is a vegetarian restaurant.（Sunny's 是一家素食餐廳）和選項 (D) It only accepts cash payments.（該餐廳只接受現金付款）都無法自廣告中推斷出來，故皆不可選。

183. Who is the intended reader of the letter?

(A) A supervisor at the Lankershim Blvd. location

(B) A dissatisfied customer of the restaurant

(C) The management of a retail chain

(D) The Fair Oaks Chamber of Commerce

答案 A

中譯 這封信的收件者是誰？

(A) Lankershim 大道分店的主管

(B) 對於該餐廳不滿的一位顧客

(C) 連鎖業者的管理階層

(D) Fair Oaks 商會

解析

第三題問 "Who is the intended reader of the letter?"「這封信的收信者是誰？」。根據信中第一段提到的 "I'm sorry to say that the moment we stepped through Sunny's doors I knew it was a bad idea. Instead of "a good time for all" it was a "lousy time by all." Let me explain." 可看出這是顧客的抱怨信，那麼誰會是處理客訴的人呢？

選項 (A)　提 到 "A supervisor ... Lankershim Blvd. location"，的確，餐廳是位於 Lankershim Blvd. 路上，那麼抱怨信理應是寫給餐廳主管，由主管來處理客訴，故 (A) 為最佳答案。

選項 (B)　提及 "... dissatisfied customer ..."，但是這位不滿意的客戶是寫信人，而不是收信人，故不可選。

選項 (C)　好像對，但是看到其後的 "retail chain"「經銷連鎖店」就知道不對了，因為此篇討論的是「餐廳服務」。

選項 (D)　提到的 "The Fair Oaks Chamber of Commerce" 並非收信人，故不選。

184.　What does Glenda Jefferson want?

　　　　(A) To return to Sunny's and use the coupons

　　　　(B) To receive compensation for her meal

　　　　(C) To eat at the vegetarian-friendly breakfast bar

　　　　(D) To change how the restaurant operates

答案 B

中譯 Glenda Jefferson 要求什麼？

(A) 她要回到 Sunny's 並使用折價券

(B) 獲得補償她餐點的賠償金

(C) 在素食早餐吧吃飯

(D) 改變該餐廳的營運方式

解析

此題目問的是 "What does Glenda Jefferson want?"，可見必須找出寫信人 Glenda Jefferson 向餐廳「要求」的事項為何？由信中第三段第二句 "I demand a full refund of our meal—$64.25." 可知，她要求餐廳「退費」給她。

選項 (A)　"... return ... and use the coupons" 提到再回餐廳使用折價券，但這與「退費」不相符，故不選。

選項 (B)　指「獲得賠償」，即要求退費的意思，故為最佳答案。

181

選項 (C) "... eat at ... breakfast bar" 是說要「吃素食早餐吧」，這也跟「退費」不相符，故不選。

選項 (D) "... change ... restaurant operates" 要求「改變餐廳營運方式」，但這點並未在文中被提及，故亦不選。

185. What is the tone of the letter?

(A) Furious

(B) Apologetic

(C) Ecstatic

(D) Supportive

答案 **A**

中譯 此封信件的語氣為何？

(A) 憤怒的

(B) 充滿歉意的

(C) 欣喜若狂的

(D) 支持的

解析

最後一題問 "What is the tone of the letter?"「此封信的語氣為何？」寫信者在最後一段表示 "If I don't receive a check for that amount by August 15, I will be forced to contact the Fair Oaks Chamber of Commerce and post unfavorable reviews on the Internet."，意即她要跟消費者相關單位聯絡，還要在網路上張貼對餐廳的負評。這種態度與語氣是非常生氣與不滿的，故 (A) Furious（盛怒的）為最佳答案。選項 (B) Apologetic（充滿歉意的）、選項 (C) Ecstatic（欣喜若狂的）和選項 (D) Supportive（支持的）皆與文脈不符。

✍️ 重點句型聚焦

我們以第二篇文章中之此句 "It is very difficult to find a decent vegetarian meal in Fair Oaks." 來做假主詞 It 句型的討論。

It + is/was + 描述事物的形容詞 + (for someone) + to + V

上述例子內真正的主詞是 "to find a decent vegetarian meal in Fair Oaks"。但若是將這串主詞放在句首，會顯得主詞過長："To find a decent vegetarian meal in Fair Oaks is very difficult."；解決的辦法就是將此長主詞移到句尾，句首則以虛主詞 "It" 取代，變成："It is very difficult to find a decent vegetarian meal in Fair Oaks."。

請看下列例句：

1. It is important for all students to learn English well.
   對所有學生而言，學好英文是很重要的。

2. It is necessary for all employees to understand the new reimbursement policy.
   對所有員工而言，瞭解新的請款方式是有必要的。

Office Manager, Tokyo, Japan

Job Description
➢ Title: Office Manager
➢ Department: Human Resources
➢ Hiring Office: Cloud Software Company, Tokyo, Japan
➢ Travel Requirements: Occasionally

Major responsibilities include
➢ Organizing and coordinating regular offsite and team building events
➢ Assist the HR team and hiring managers by organizing interviews, screening candidates
➢ Assist the accounting team by collecting and scanning invoices, time sheets
➢ Assist with travel arrangements, meeting coordination and other requests
➢ Assist with organizing local trade shows, job fairs, or other events

Requirements
➢ At least 2 years office management, administrative, or related experience
➢ Human resource experience is a plus
➢ Good verbal and written communication skills in English and Japanese
➢ Excellent time management and prioritization skills
➢ Clearly understand and maintain confidentiality with information

To apply, please send your CV to Vivian Jones at vivian.j@cloud-software.com or call 456-3838 X-771.

To: vivian.j@cloud-software.com
From: Jack Lang [jack.l@mail.com]
Date: April 25, 2018
Subject: Office Manager position in Japan

Dear Vivian,

My name is Jack Lang and I'm writing to express my interest in the Office Manager position listed on your company website. I had experience working as HR Specialist at the First-Rate Hotel for one year. While much of my HR experience had been in the hospitality field, I'm still confident that I could apply my HR knowledge in the software industry without any problem.

My previous responsibilities included interviewing applicants, processing promotions and terminations, and conducting training sessions. I also work closely with customer service managers to evaluating the effectiveness of customer service training programs. Such experience has taught me how to communicate with members from different departments at an organization.

In addition, my mother is Japanese and my father is from Taiwan. I received my university education in the US. So I'm fluent in Japanese, Chinese, and English. I believe that my experience and language ability will be great asset to your software company.

Please see the attached resume for additional information on my experience. I am available for further discussion anytime and can be reached via email at jack.l@mail.com or my cell phone, 888-333-4838. Thank you for your consideration. I look forward to speaking with you about this Office Manager position.

Sincerely,

Jack Lang

To: jack.l@mail.com
From: vivian.j@cloud-software.com
Date: May 5, 2018
Subject: Re: Office Manager position in Japan

Dear Mr. Lang:

Thank you for your application for the position of Office Manager at Could-Software in Japan. As you may imagine, we did receive scores of applications. As a matter of fact, we prefer to recruit talents with sufficient experience in the software industry. I am sorry to inform you that you have not been selected for an interview for this position. We encourage you to apply for future openings for which you qualify.

Thank you once again for your interest in Cloud-Software company.

Best regards,

Vivian J.

＊色字部分請參考「詞彙註解」

【中譯】第 **186-190** 題請參照下列廣告和電子郵件。

日本東京辦事處經理

職缺描述

➤ 職位：辦事處經理

➤ 部門：人力資源

➤ 招聘辦公室：日本東京雲端軟體公司

➤ 出差要求：偶爾

主要職責包括

➤ 組織和協調定期的團隊合作活動

➤ 協助人資團隊和招募經理安排面試與篩選人選

➤ 協助會計團隊收集和掃描發票與工作時間表

➤ 協助出差行程安排、會議協調和其他要求

➤ 協助規劃當地的貿易展覽、徵才會或其他活動

要求

➤ 至少兩年的辦公室管理、行政或相關經驗

➤ 具備人力資源經驗者優先考慮

➤ 良好的英文和日文口語及書面溝通能力

➤ 擅長於時間管理和設定事務優先順序

➤ 明確地瞭解資訊保密的重要性

意者請將簡歷表寄至：vivian.j@cloud-software.com

或致電：456-3838 X-771。

收件人：vivian.j@cloud-software.com
寄件人：Jack Lang [jack.l@mail.com]
日期：2018 年 4 月 25 日
主旨：日本辦事處經理一職

Vivian 您好：

我的名字叫 Jack Lang，我寫此信是為了表達我對貴公司網站上列出的「辦事處經理」職位的興趣。我有在「一流飯店」擔任人力資源專員的經驗。雖然我的大部分人力資源經驗都在飯店領域，但我仍然有信心將我的人力資源相關知識應用於軟體產業，這對我來說是沒問題的。

我之前的職責包括：面試應徵者，處理升遷和雇用終止事務，以及舉辦訓練課程，並與客戶服務經理密切合作，評估客戶服務訓練計劃的有效性。這樣的經驗讓我學會了在一個組織與不同部門的成員合作的能力。

另外，我的母親是日本人，父親來自台灣。我曾在美國接受了大學教育。所以我能說流利的日文、中文和英文。我相信我的經驗和語言能力對於貴公司而言極具價值。

請參閱附件簡歷以更加瞭解我的經驗。我隨時都可安排進一步的討論，歡迎透過電郵：jack.l@mail.com 或我的手機：888-333-4838 聯繫。謝謝您的考慮。我期待著與您談談此「辦事處經理」職缺之事宜。

Jack Lang 敬上

收件人：jack.l@mail.com
寄件人：vivian.j@cloud-software.com
日期：2018 年 5 月 5 日
回覆：日本辦事處經理一職

親愛的 Lang 先生：

感謝您應徵 Could-Software 公司在日本的「辦事處經理」一職。如您可想像的，我們確實收到了大量的申請函。事實上，我們更傾向於聘用在軟體業界有足夠經驗的人才。我很抱歉要通知您，您沒有被選為來參加此職位面試的候選人。今後若有符合您資格的職位，我們也鼓勵您來應徵。
再次感謝您對 Could-Software 公司的關注。

祝好，

Vivian J.

☞ 詞彙註解

description [dɪˋskrɪpʃən] (*n.*) 描述
occasionally [əˋkeɛənlɪ] (*adv.*) 偶爾
organize [ˋɔrgəˌnaɪz] (*v.*) 規劃
coordinate [koˋɔrdnet] (*v.*) 協調
administrative [ədˋmɪnəˌstretɪv] (*adj.*) 管理的
verbal [ˋvɝbl̩] (*adj.*) 口語的
confidentiality [ˌkɑnfɪˌdɛnʃɪˋælɪtɪ] (*n.*) 機密性
express [ɪkˋsprɛs] (*v.*) 表達
specialist [ˋspɛʃəlɪst] (*n.*) 專員
hospitality [ˌhɑspɪˋtælətɪ] (*n.*) 酒店管理
confident [ˋkɑnfədənt] (*adj.*) 有信心的
previous [ˋprivɪəs] (*adj.*) 之前的
promotion [prəˋmoʃən] (*n.*) 升遷

termination [ˌtɝməˋneʃən] (*n.*) 終止
evaluate [ɪˋvæljuˌet] (*v.*) 評估
effectiveness [əˋfɛktɪvnɪs] (*n.*) 效果
fluent [ˋfluənt] (*adj.*) 流利的
consideration [kənsɪdəˋreʃən] (*n.*) 考慮
imagine [ɪˋmædʒɪn] (*v.*) 想像
scores of 許多
recruit [rɪˋkrut] (*v.*) 招募
talent [ˋtælənt] (*n.*) 有才能者
sufficient [səˋfɪʃənt] (*adj.*) 充足的
inform [ɪnˋfɔrm] (*v.*) 通知
encourage [ɪnˋkɝɪdʒ] (*v.*) 鼓勵
qualify [ˋkwɑləˌfaɪ] (*v.*) 符合資格

186. What is the main purpose of the advertisement?

    (A) To recruit a manager

    (B) To announce new policies

    (C) To promote products

    (D) To invite seminar attendees

答案 A

中譯 廣告文章的主要目的為何？

(A) 為招募經理人

(B) 為公告新政策

(C) 為推廣新產品

(D) 為邀請參加研討會

解析

此題問的是首篇文章的目的為何，根據標題 "Office Manager, Tokyo, Japan" 與 "Job Description" 等關鍵字，便可判斷是「事求人、招聘」廣告。

選項 (A)　關鍵點 "recruit a manager" 的確與標題符合，故為正解。

選項 (B)　提到 "announce policies"「公告新政策」，與首篇內容並不相符，故為錯誤。

選項 (C)　關鍵點 "promote products" 也與「事求人」廣告不相干，故不選。

選項 (D)　提及 "invite attendees"，但此篇廣告與研討會無關，故亦不選。

187. What is NOT true about the job offered?

    (A) It's located in Japan.

    (B) It involves cross-department cooperation.

    (C) It's been vacant for two years.

    (D) Many people are applying for it.

答案 C

中譯 關於此職缺何者為「非」？

(A) 此職缺是在日本。

(B) 此職缺牽涉到跨部門的合作。

(C) 此職缺已開放兩年了。

(D) 很多人都想應徵此職位。

解析

此題問 "What is NOT true about the job offered?"，那麼便應找出「與職缺不相符」的描述以便回答。

選項 (A)　It's located in Japan. 在廣告的標題 "Office Manager, Tokyo, Japan" 中有提到。

選項 (B)　It involves cross-department cooperation. 與此關鍵句 "Assist the accounting team by collecting and scanning invoices, time sheets"「人資專員須協助會計部門事務」之涵義一致，所以是正確敘述。

選項 (C)　It's been vacant for two years. 指「職缺空出兩年了」，此敘述並沒有在文章中出現，故選為答案。

選項 (D)　Many people are applying for it. 提及「很多人想應徵」，而在第三篇文章內，招募方 Vivian 回信道 "As you may imagine, we did receive scores of applications." 呼應了此說法，因此也是正確敘述。

188.　What is indicated about Jack Lang?

    (A) He's an experienced software designer.

    (B) He's willing to relocate to the UK.

    (C) He's able to speak several languages.

    (D) He's been rehired by the First-Rate Hotel.

答案 C

中譯 關於 Jack Lang 描述何者正確？

(A) 他是個有經驗的軟體設計師。

(B) 他願意搬遷到英國。

(C) 他會講數種語言。

(D) 他又再度被「一流飯店」延攬了。

解析

此題 "What is indicated about Jack Lang?" 問的是關於 Jack Lang 之正確描述，那麼便應鎖定文中確實有提及的資訊才可選為答案。

選項 (A)　提及他是「有經驗的軟體開發人」，但根據第二篇文章內的關鍵句 "I had experience working as HR Specialist at the First-Rate Hotel for one year." 可知，他過去的工作經驗是在「飯店產業」，並非軟體產業，故不選。

選項 (B)　說他願意搬去「英國」，但他欲應徵的職缺是在「日本」，不可混淆誤選。

191

選項 (C) He's able to speak several languages. 與第一封電郵中此關鍵句 "So I'm fluent in Japanese, Chinese, and English." 相互呼應，所以是正確答案。

選項 (D) 意指「他要再度回到飯店工作」，但文章中並未有此相關敘述，故不適當。

189. Why does Vivian J. send the email?

(A) To welcome Jack as her new colleague

(B) To appreciate Jack's contributions

(C) To encourage Jack to apply for jobs in other branches

(D) To decline Jack's job application

答案 D

中譯 Vivian J. 為什麼寄這封電郵？

(A) 為歡迎 Jack 當她的新同事

(B) 為感謝 Jack 的貢獻

(C) 為鼓勵 Jack 應徵其他分公司的職缺

(D) 為婉謝 Jack 的工作申請

解析

此題問 Vivian 寄發 email 的目的，直接將焦點放在第三篇文章，Vivian 所寫的電郵內容。由第一段中間的 "I am sorry to inform you that you have not been selected for an interview for this position." 即可知，此電郵意在「告知 Jack 他未被遴選來面談」。

選項 (A) To welcome Jack as her new colleague 之涵義恰好與上述主旨相反。

選項 (B) To appreciate Jack contributions「感謝 Jack 的貢獻」，但文中並未見此相關訊息，故不選。

選項 (C) To encourage Jack to apply for jobs in other branches 關鍵點在於「其他分部的職缺」。Vivian 信中是有鼓勵 Jack 今後再申請沒錯，但通篇並沒提及「其他分公司」之訊息，不可誤選。

選項 (D) To decline Jack's job application 之關鍵為「回絕申請」，確與郵件主旨相符，故選為答案。

190. Why is Jack NOT being selected for an interview?

    (A) His English is not fluent enough.

    (B) He lacks sufficient experience in the software industry.

    (C) He has been working in the hotel for too long.

    (D) He doesn't provide effective references.

答案 **B**

中譯 Jack 為什麼「未」被選上參加面談？

(A) 他英文不夠流利。

(B) 他缺乏在軟體產業的經驗。

(C) 他在飯店工作太久了。

(D) 他沒提供有效的推薦信。

解析

這道題目問 Jack 沒被選上面談的原因。答題線索應在第三篇文章 Vivian 的解釋中。根據第一段第三行 "As a matter of fact, we prefer to recruit talents with sufficient experience in the software industry." 可知，該公司想挑選在「軟體產業」有經驗的人。除此之外，在第二篇文章中 Jack 也提及自己有「一年工作經驗」，但首篇廣告文中即指出要找「有兩年以上工作經驗者」。由上述關鍵點可推測，Jack 是因經驗不足而落選。

選項 (A)   His English is not fluent enough. 指 Jack「英文不好」，並非 Vivian 淘汰他的原因，故不選。

選項 (B)   He lacks sufficient experience in the software industry. 與 Vivian 所表達的意思相符，所以是正確答案。

選項 (C)   提到 Jack「在飯店業工作太久」，這也不是 Vivian 回信中婉拒的理由，故不選。

選項 (D)   說 Jack 的「推薦信不強」，但 Vivian 的電郵中根本未提及此事，故不選。

在第三篇電郵中的此句 "We encourage you to apply for future openings." 之句型：

[someone] encourage [someone] to [do something]

是很常見的鼓勵用語，在日常生活中或工作場合上都非常適合使用。

請看下列例句：

1. My parents always encourage me to pursue my own interests.
   我父母總是鼓勵我要追求我想做的事。

2. Mr. Jones encourages all team members to think out of the box.
   瓊斯先生鼓勵所有同仁要打破成規想法。

Questions 191-195 refer to the following news report, poll, and email.

Hydraulic fracturing, commonly referred to as "fracking," is a technique to make natural gas wells more productive. Water, sand, and chemicals are injected into the ground, so that more natural gas can be pumped to the surface. Energy companies love the extra gas, but the practice has worried thousands of Green Valley residents. They are organizing against the possible leasing of 38,000 acres of the Green National Forest to the gas industry, who plan to install hundreds of fracking wells in the area. If the leasing goes through, the residents claim their quality of life will be threatened and the pristine environment destroyed.

The residents' primary concern is for their health and safety. Fracking has been cited as a source of chemical explosions and water pollution. Studies have shown that disease rates are higher near fracking wells. The residents also claim that because the Green National Forest was declared a public commons the government has a commitment to protect the forest.

Green Valley residents commissioned Public Eyewitness to conduct a survey to summarize residents' opinions on the matter. The results of the environmental organization's poll shows that 87% of citizens would agree to pay higher taxes to fund the research of other sources of energy.

Hydraulic Fracturing in Green Valley

1. How much time do you spend in the Green Valley National Forest?
   A) 1 day a week   C) 3 days a week
   B) 2 days a week   D) 4+ days a week

2. What is your primary concern about hydraulic fracturing in Green Valley?
   A) Damage to Habitats   C) Accidental Explosions
   B) Water Pollution   D) Disease

3. How receptive would you be to paying a higher sales tax to fund more sustainable energy types, like solar, wind, or geothermal power?
   A) Very unreceptive   C) Somewhat receptive
   B) Somewhat unreceptive   D) Very receptive

4. How likely is it that natural gas will replace coal in our domestic market?
   A) Very unlikely   C) Somewhat likely
   B) Somewhat unlikely   D) Very likely

Results

1. A) 22%   B) 12%   C) 18%   D) 48%
2. A) 12%   B) 23%   C) 26%   D) 39%
3. A) 5%   B) 4%   C) 4%   D) 87%
4. A) 67%   B) 10%   C) 17%   D) 6%

Poll administered by the Public Eyewitness to 1,000 Green Valley residents by telephone on August 23. Margin of error +/– 3%. Source: Public Eyewitness.

To:	Linda Smith [linda.s@environment-tech.com]
From:	Jack Wills [jack.w@environment-tech.com]
Subject:	Meeting request

Hi Linda,

Please refer to the attached press release and results of the survey conducted in Green Valley. We can see that people are more environmental conscious nowadays than in the past. As we are also planning to launch new environmental friendly products, let's arrange a meeting this week to discuss the issue in details. I'm available this Wednesday morning at 10, and please confirm if this time slot is convenient for you. Prior to the meeting, please contact the organization which conducted the survey and check if they are able to release more detailed information to us.

I'll talk to you further about this.

Jack Wills

PART 3 TEST 1

＊套色字部分請參考「詞彙註解」

水力壓裂，一般稱之為「壓裂」，是一種提升天然氣井生產率的技術。將水、沙與化學物質注入地層內，使得天然氣能夠被抽至地層表面。能源公司能取得更多的瓦斯當然值得高興，但是這項技術讓數千名 Green Valley 居民感到憂心。他們正結合起來反對將 Green 國家森林 38,000 畝的土地租借給天然氣產業，該產業計劃在該地區裝設數百座壓裂井。如果租借通過了的話，居民們表示他們的生活品質將會遭到威脅，而且天然環境也會遭受破壞。

居民們的主要憂慮是他們自身的健康與安全。壓裂技術已被指出會導致化學爆炸和水汙染。研究顯示壓裂井附近的染病率比其他地方還來得高。居民同時也表示，由於 Green 國家森林已宣佈為公有地，政府有保護該森林之義務。

Green Valley 的居民聘請了 Public Eyewitness 來進行一項調查，以統計居民對於這件事的看法。該環境組織的調查結果顯示，87% 的居民表達了願意支付更高稅金來資助替代能源研究的意願。

在 **Green Valley** 進行水力壓裂

1. 您花費多少時間待在 Green Valley 國家林區內？

   A) 每週 1 天　　　　　　C) 每週 3 天

   B) 每週 2 天　　　　　　D) 每週超過 4 天

2. 對於在 Green Valley 進行水力壓裂，您主要的顧慮為何？

   A) 對生態的破壞　　　　C) 意外爆炸

   B) 水汙染　　　　　　　D) 疾病

3. 您對於支付較高的營業稅來資助尋找更能永續發展的替代能源，如太陽能、風力或地熱發電的意願為何？

   A) 非常無法接受　　　　C) 稍微可以接受

   B) 稍微無法接受　　　　D) 非常願意接受

4. 您對於天然氣在我們的家用市場上取代煤炭之可能性的看法為何？

   A) 非常不可能　　　　　C) 有點可能

   B) 有點不可能　　　　　D) 非常可能

結果

1. A) 22%　　B) 12%　　C) 18%　　D) 48%

2. A) 12%　　B) 23%　　C) 26%　　D) 39%

3. A) 5%　　B) 4%　　C) 4%　　D) 87%

4. A) 67%　　B) 10%　　C) 17%　　D) 6%

由 Public Eyewitness 於八月二十三日針對一千名 Green Valley 居民進行電話訪談。誤差值 +/– 3%。來源：Public Eyewitness。

收件人：	Linda Smith [linda.s@environment-tech.com]
寄件人：	Jack Wills [jack.w@environment-tech.com]
主　旨：	會議邀請

嗨，Linda：

請參考附件的新聞和在 Green Vally 所做的問卷調查結果。我們可以看到人們現在比以往更有環保意識了。剛好我們也計劃要推出新的環保產品，我們本週內來約個會議討論一下細節吧。我本週三早上十點有空，請確認此時間妳是否方便？在開會之前，請跟做問卷調查的廠商聯絡，並詢問他們是否可以將更多細節告知我們。

我會再與妳詳談。

Jack Wills

☛ 詞彙註解

hydraulic [haɪˋdrɔlɪk] (*adj.*) 水力學的、水壓的

fracture [ˋfræktʃə] (*n.*) 斷層、裂面

productive [prəˋdʌktɪv] (*adj.*) 生產的、多產的

inject [ɪnˋdʒɛkt] (*v.*) 注射、注入

lease [lis] (*v.*) 出租

install [ɪnˋstɔl] (*v.*) 安裝、裝設

claim [klem] (*v.*) 聲稱、主張、斷言

threatened [ˋθrɛtn̩d] (*adj.*) 受到威脅的

pristine [ˋprɪstin] (*adj.*) 原始的、清新的

destroyed [dɪˋstrɔɪd] (*adj.*) 受到破壞的

explosion [ɪkˋsploʒən] (*n.*) 爆炸

declare [dɪˋklɛr] (*v.*) 宣告、聲明

commons [ˋkɑmənz] (*n.*) 公有地

commission [kəˋmɪʃən] (*v.*) 委託、委任

summarize [ˋsʌməˌraɪz] (*v.*) 總結、概括

accidental [ˌæksəˋdɛntl̩] (*adj.*) 意外的

receptive [rɪˋsɛptɪv] (*adj.*) 善於接受的、能接納的

sustainable [səˋstenəbl̩] (*adj.*) 能維持的、能承受的

geothermal [ˌdʒioˋθɜml̩] (*adj.*) 地熱的

coal [kol] (*n.*) 煤

poll [pol] (*n.*) 民調

margin [ˋmɑrdʒɪn] (*n.*) 邊緣、餘地

press release 新聞稿

conscious [ˋkɑnʃəs] (*adj.*) 有知覺的

launch [lɔntʃ] (*v.*) 發表

prior to 在⋯⋯之前

191. Why did Green Valley residents organize?

(A) To improve the safety of hydraulic fracturing

(B) To oppose the leasing of public land to the gas industry

(C) To limit government spending on hydraulic fracturing

(D) To discuss ways to increase energy efficiency

答案 B

中譯 Green Valley 的居民為何結合起來？

(A) 以提升水力壓裂的安全性

(B) 以反對將公共土地租借給天然氣產業

(C) 以限制政府花費在水力壓裂技術上的金額

(D) 以討論能夠提升能源效能的方法

解析

本題組的第一篇文章是一則新聞報導，第二篇是一份問卷調查，最後則是一封電郵。此題問 "Why did Green Valley residents organize?"，須找出 Green Velley 居民集結的原因。根據第一篇第一段中提到的 "Energy companies love the extra gas, but the practicc has worried thousands of Green Valley residents. They are organizing against the possible leasing of 38,000 acres of the Green National Forest to the gas industry, who plan to install hundreds of fracking wells in the area." 可知，居民之所以集結是為了要「抗議在他們居住地裝設數百座壓裂井」之故。

選項 (A) 提及 "... improve ... safety of ..." 是說為了「增加安全性」，這與「為了要抗議」不符，故不選。

選項 (B) 提到的是 "... oppose ... leasing of public land ... gas industry"，的確，居民結合起來為了抗議土地給天然氣產業做使用，故為最佳答案。

選項 (C) "... limit government spending ..."「限制政府花費」，這一點並沒有在文中被提及，故不選。

選項 (D) 中的 "... discuss ... increase energy efficiency" 指目的「討論提高能源效能」，也與文章敘述不符，故亦不選。

192. What is Public Eyewitness?

(A) A local government department

(B) A nature conservation group

(C) A Green Valley citizen's organization

(D) A gas industry advocacy group

答案 **B**

中譯 Public Eyewitness 是什麼？

(A) 一個當地的政府部門

(B) 一個自然保育團體

(C) 一個 Green Valley 居民的組織

(D) 一個天然氣產業的擁護團體

解析

由第一篇文章最後一段提到的 "Green Valley residents commissioned Public Eyewitness to conduct a survey to summarize residents' opinions on the matter. The results of the environmental organization's poll shows that ..." 即可知，Public Eyewitness 是一個「環保組織」。

選項 (A) 的 "... government department" 指「政府部門」，不選。

選項 (B) 的 "... nature conservation group" 指「自然保育團體」，與 "environmental organization"（環保單位）同義，故為最佳答案。

選項 (C) 提到的 "... citizen's organization" 是指當地的「居民組織」，不可選。

選項 (D) "... gas industry advocacy group" 是指「天然氣產業的擁護團體」亦不可選。

193. What topic did Public Eyewitness ask residents about?

(A) Their willingness to move out of the valley

(B) Their use of the public lands

(C) Their views on government policy

(D) Their concerns about local species

答案 **B**

中譯 Public Eyewitness 詢問居民的問題以什麼為主題？

(A) 搬離山谷區的意願

(B) 他們對於公有土地的使用

(C) 他們對於政府政策的看法

(D) 他們對於當地物種感到的憂心

解析

由題目 "What topic did Public Eyewitness ask residents about?" 可知，要看出 Public Eyewitness 問了居民哪方面的問題。根據問卷中出現的四個問題判斷，問卷的主題環繞在公有地的使用。

選項 (A)　"... willingness to move out ..." 指居民「遷出的意願」，並沒有在問卷中被提及，故不選。

選項 (B)　"... use of the public lands"「公有土地的使用」即問卷之主題，故為最佳答案。

選項 (C)　"... views on government policy"「對政府政策的看法」，在問卷並未提到，故不選。

選項 (D)　"... concerns about local species"「對於當地物種的憂心」也沒被提到，故亦不選。

194. According to the poll, what issue does the greatest number of Green Valley citizens agree on?

(A) They visit the National Forest at least 4 days a week.

(B) They are concerned about potential diseases.

(C) They are willing to pay higher taxes.

(D) They believe coal will replace natural gas soon.

答案 C

中譯 根據調查，Green Valley 最多數的居民同意的議題為何？

(A) 他們每週至少有四天會去國家林區。

(B) 他們很擔心可能的疾病。

(C) 他們願意支付較高的稅金。

(D) 他們相信煤炭將會取代天然氣。

本題問的是最多數居民都同意什麼事。根據第一篇報導的最後一段第二句 "The results of the environmental organization's poll shows that 87% of citizens would agree to pay higher taxes to fund the research of other sources of energy.",以及第二篇問卷第三題所問出的結果可得知,居民「願意多繳稅來資助替代能源的研發」。

選項 (A) 提到的 "... visist ... National Forest ... 4 days a week",是說居民一週去 National Forest 至少四次,而這並不是最多數居民同意的事,故不選。

選項 (B) 提到的 "... concerned ... potential diseases." 只佔 39%,也不是最多數居民同意的一點,故不選。

選項 (C) 是說「居民願意支付較高的稅金」,的確,居民覺得「付多點稅來支持替代能源的研發」這一點沒問題,故為最佳答案。

選項 (D) "... believe coal will replace natural gas ...."「相信煤將會取代天然氣」並非事實,問卷中第四題所呈現的結果是有 67% 的居民認為天然氣「非常不可能取代煤」,故不可選。

195. What does Jack ask Linda to do next?

(A) Contact Public Eyewitness for details
(B) Arrange an international conference
(C) Call Green Valley residents for feedback
(D) Send an email to his assistant

答案 A

中譯 Jack 要求 Linda 接下來做什麼?
(A) 與 Public Eyewitness 聯絡問詳細資訊
(B) 安排一場國際會議
(C) 打電話給 Green Valley 居民問意見
(D) 寄電郵給他的助理

解析

最後一題問的是 What does Jack ask Linda to do next?,那麼便應鎖定「Jack 請 Linda 做的事」之相關資訊。根據第三篇 Jack 所寫的電郵中之此關鍵句 "Prior to the meeting, please contact the organization which conducted the survey and check if they are able to release more detailed information to us.",他要 Linda 去跟「問卷調查公司」聯絡。接著再掃瞄至第二篇文章可知,「問卷調查公司」的名稱爲 Public Eyewitness。

選項 (A) Contact Public Eyewitness for details 正確描述 Jack 於電郵中所要求之事，故為正解。

選項 (B) 內的關鍵點 "international conference" 並沒有在文章中出現，故不選。

選項 (C) 提到 "Call residents for feedback"，意思變成要 Linda 自己去做調查了，明顯錯誤。

選項 (D) 說寄電郵給他助理，而這點在文中完全沒被提及，故不選。

📝 重點句型聚焦

我們藉由本組文章第一篇內的 "Water, sand, and chemicals are injected into the ground, so that more natural gas can be pumped to the surface." 這個句子來討論使用連接詞 so that 的句型。

S + V + so that + S + 助動詞 + 原形動詞
= S + V + in order that + S + 助動詞 + 原形動詞

此句型表示藉由前面的動作來達成後半句內的未來的目的，如同中文的「以便……」或「以求……」之意。

請看下列例句：

1. I work hard so that I may become a millionaire one day.
   我努力工作以求有一天可能成為百萬富翁。

2. All team members try their best to contribute good ideas so that the problem can be resolved soon.
   所有的團體成員都盡力貢獻好點子，以求該問題能儘速解決。

Allison Cartwright
1465 Vagabond Road
Fairbanks, AK 99701
(907) 435-8754
allison.cartwright@adp.com

September 24

George Mallory, CEO
World Harvest
1940 L Street NW
Washington DC 20036
(202) 576-9672

Dear Mr. Mallory,

I was very impressed by your keynote presentation at the National Conference for Nonprofit Organizations in February. I was especially pleased to learn that World Harvest engages in projects similar to work I've been involved with for the past ten years at Ageing Affairs. I can only imagine the amount of resumes you are receiving, but I hope you will consider mine carefully. I am very eager to work for World Harvest.

My experience fighting for elderly rights has given me unique experiences and insights that I believe would be of value to your organization. Some highlights of my career include:

- Founded Fairbanks Assistance Program to identify and assist low-income, elderly, and disabled residents
- Conceived and wrote, with State Representative Mark Lang, the first Alaskan statewide law safeguarding tax relief for elderly and disabled residents
- Named Fairbanks Monthly (local newspaper) "Person of the Year" for community service

I also have experience managing large-budget programs, supervising diverse teams of employees and volunteers, and overseeing fundraising events with over 1,200 attendees. Please see my attached resume for details.

I would enjoy an opportunity to talk with you or someone in your organization to see where my skills would be of the greatest benefit to you. I will be in Washington DC again the week of May 15, and could meet with you anytime.

Sincerely,

Allison Cartwright

Allison Cartwrigh

To:	Allison Cartwright [allison.cartwright@adp.com]
From:	Mary Worth [mary.worth@worldharvest.com]
Subject:	Your interest in World Harvest

Dear Allison,

I am writing on behalf of Mr. Mallory, who received and read your letter and resume. That's quite unusual, because we receive dozens of query letters a day! He is particularly interested in your work with Mark Lang and would like to schedule a time for you to come into the office to discuss your involvement. We are planning to create a team focused on legislation and fundraising events. Your experience appears to align with our needs.

Mr. Mallory will be available on Monday, May 16 at 2 pm or Wednesday, May 18 at 10 am. Please send me a note of confirmation as soon as you are able.

Thank you and we look forward to seeing you at the office.

Mary Worth
Executive Assistant for George Mallory, CEO
World Harvest

To:	Mary Worth [mary.worth@worldharvest.com]
From:	Allison Cartwright [allison.cartwright@adp.com]
Subject:	Re: Your interest in World Harvest

Dear Ms. Worth,

Hope you are doing well.

Thank you very much for the invitation to interview at World Harvest. I'm available on Monday, May 16 at 2 pm and I'm very much looking forward to the meeting with you and Mr. George Mallory.

I believe that my fund-raising experience makes me an ideal candidate for World Harvest. I look forward to sharing my passion for and skills in fund-raising work with Mr. Mallory. If you need me to provide any further information prior to the Interview, please feel free to let me know.

Sincerely,

Allison Cartwright

＊套色字部分請參考「詞彙註解」

Allison Cartwright

Vagabond 路 1465 號

(99701) Alaska 州 Fairbanks 市

(907) 435-8754

allison.cartwright@adp.com

9 月 24 日

George Mallory

World Harvest 執行長

L 街 NW 1940 號

(20036) Washington DC

(202) 576-9672

親愛的 Mallory 先生：

我對您於二月在 Nonprofit Organizations 全國研討會上所發表的主題演講印象非常深刻。我特別高興地得知 World Harvest 正在進行和我過去十年間在 Ageing Affairs 所參與的工作非常相似的計劃。我想像您一定收到為數不少的履歷，但是我希望您可以仔細地考慮我提出的申請。我非常熱切地想要在 World Harvest 工作。

過去為年長族群爭取權益的經驗給予了我獨特的經歷與洞察力，對貴公司而言，我相信我將會很有價值。我事業生涯的重點包括：

• 成立 Fairbanks 協助計劃，以確認並協助低收入、年長的及有行動障礙的居民。
• 構思並與州眾議員 Mark Lang 共同撰寫 Alaska 州首都保障年長和殘障居民稅金減免的法令。
• 因參與社區服務而獲得 Fairbanks 月刊（當地報紙）頒發「年度風雲人物」獎項。

我同時也擁有負責大規模預算計劃、管理多重團隊員工和志工，以及主辦超過一千兩百名參與者的募款活動之經驗。請參閱附件的履歷表以便獲得更多的資訊。

我很希望有和您或貴機構裡其他成員面談的機會，並討論如何運用我的能力來為貴機構獲得最大的利益。我將會於 5 月 15 日再次前往 Washington DC，並可以在任何時間與您會面。

Allison Cartwright
敬上

收件人：	Allison Cartwright [allison.cartwright@adp.com]
寄件人：	Mary Worth [mary.worth@worldharvest.com]
主　旨：	您對 World Harvest 的興趣

親愛的 Allison 您好：

我謹代表 Mallory 先生撰寫這封 email，他已經收到並閱讀過您的信件和履歷。他會這樣做相當不尋常，因為我們一天會收到數十封詢問信件！他對於您與 Mark Lang 合作的工作特別感到興趣，並想要與您安排一個時間請您到我們辦公室來討論一下您當初的參與情況。我們正計劃要組一個專注於立法和募款活動的小組。您的經驗看起來與我們所需相符。

Mallory 先生將於 5 月 16 日星期一下午 2 點或 5 月 18 日星期三早上 10 點有空。請您儘快與我確認。

謝謝您，我們期待在辦公室見到您。

Mary Worth
George Mallory 執行長特別助理
World Harvest

收件人：	Mary Worth [mary.worth@worldharvest.com]
寄件人：	Allison Cartwright [allison.cartwright@adp.com]
主　旨：	關於：您對 World Harvest 的興趣

親愛的 Worth 小姐：

您好。

非常感謝您邀請我到 World Harvest 公司面談。我五月十六日週一的下午兩點有空，很期待前往與您和 George Mallory 先生會面。

我相信我在募款方面的經驗足以讓我成為 World Harvest 公司理想的職位候選人。我期待將我對辦募款活動的熱情與能力與您和 Mallory 先生分享。若您需要我在面談之前再提供任何資料，請隨時告知我。

Allison Cartwright
敬上

📌 詞彙註解

keynote [ˋkiˌnot] (n.) 演說主旨、要點演說

engage [ɪnˋgedʒ] (v.) 參與、從事

involve [ɪnˋvɑlv] (v.) 使牽涉、使忙於

imagine [ɪˋmædʒɪn] (v.) 想像、猜想

eager [ˋigə] (adj.) 熱心的、急切的

unique [juˋnik] (adj.) 獨一無二的、獨特的

insight [ˋɪnˌsaɪt] (n.) 洞察力、眼光

highlight [ˋhaɪˌlaɪt] (n.) 突顯、最突出的部分

identify [aɪˋdɛntəˌfaɪ] (v.) 識別、鑑定、確認

conceive [kənˋsiv] (v.) 設想、構思

safeguard [ˋsefˌgɑrd] (v.) 保護、防衛

diverse [daɪˋvɜs] (adj.) 不同的、多變化的

on behalf of 代表

query [ˋkwɪrɪ] (n.) 詢問、質問

involvement [ɪnˋvɑlvmənt] (n.) 參與

legislation [ˌlɛdʒɪsˋleʃən] (n.) 制定法律、立法

align with 使結盟、使互相合作

look forward to 期望、盼望

invitation [ˌɪnvəˋteʃən] (n.) 邀請函

interview [ˋɪntəˌvju] (v.) 面談

ideal [aɪˋdiəl] (adj.) 理想的

candidate [ˋkændədet] (n.) 候選人

passion [ˋpæʃən] (n.) 熱情

further [ˋfɜðə] (adj.) 進一步的

196. Why did Allison Cartwright contact George Mallory?

(A) To thank him for participating in a conference

(B) To request a donation for her organization

(C) To inquire about a position with World Harvest

(D) To discuss fundraising ideas and opportunities

答案 C

中譯 為什麼 Allison Cartwright 會和 George Mallory 聯絡？

(A) 為了感謝他參加一場研討會

(B) 為了要求捐款給她的公司

(C) 為了詢問有關在 World Harvest 的一個職缺

(D) 為了討論募款的點子與機會

解析

先將三篇文章大致掃瞄一遍，以便瞭解各篇的大意與文章之間的關連性。第一篇是 Allison Cartwright 寫給 George Mallory 的信，並根據首段的內容 "I was very impressed by your keynote presentation ... I was especially pleased to learn that World Harvest engages in projects similar to work I've been involved with ..., but I hope you will consider mine carefully. I am very eager to work for World Harvest." 可知，此信的目的是 Allison 請 World Harvest 公司考慮她的職位申請。

選項 (A) "... thank him ... participating ... conference" 提及「感謝他參加研討會」，與信件主旨風馬牛不相干，故不選。

選項 (B) "... request ... donation ..." 說要請他「捐款」，文中完全沒提到，不選。

選項 (C) 與 Allison 欲請 World Harvest 考慮她的職位申請相符，故為最佳答案。

選項 (D) 的 "... discuss fundraising ideas and opportunities" 表示要「討論募款的點子與機會」，而文中未提到這一點，故不選。

197. In the letter, the word "conceived" in paragraph 3, line 3, is closest in meaning to

(A) originated

(B) requested

(C) drafted

(D) proved

答案 A

中譯 信件第三段第三行的 "conceived" 這個字意思最接近

(A) 創作出

(B) 要求

(C) 起草

(D) 證明

解析

本題為字彙題。"conceived" 指「構想出、設想、想像出」，與 originated「創作出」的意思最接近，故 (A) 為最佳答案。選項 (B) drafted（起草）、選項 (C) requested（要求）、選項 (D) proved（證明）都不相符，故不選。

198. What does Mary Worth's email imply?

(A) Many people are interested in working at World Harvest.

(B) World Harvest is not currently hiring new employees.

(C) Ageing Affairs and World Harvest should work together.

(D) She is looking for a job in a different industry.

答案 A

中譯 Mary Worth 的電子郵件暗示了什麼？

(A) 許多人都有興趣在 World Harvest 工作。

(B) World Harvest 目前並沒有在招募新員工。

(C) Ageing Affairs 和 World Harvest 應該合作。

(D) 她正在找尋另一個產業的工作。

此題問的是 "What does Mary Worth's email imply?",則應於第二篇文章內搜尋線索,來判斷其言下之意。由第一段第二句 "That's quite unusual, because we receive dozens of query letters a day!" 可知,Mary Worth 提及「World Harvest 一天所收到的應徵信函不計其數」,意指很多人想進 World Harvest 公司工作。

選項 (A) 與 Mary Worth 所要表達的意思相符,故為正解。

選項 (B) "... is not ... hiring new employees." 說該公司現在「沒有在徵人」,但由 Allison 的信中看不出這一點,故不選。

選項 (C) "Ageing Affaire and World Harvest ... work together." 認為兩間公司應該合作,這也不是 Allison 的看法,故不選。

選項 (D) "... looking for a job in different industry." 提到她「在找另一個產業的工作」,這點在郵件中也沒被提到,故不選。

199. Why does George Mallory want to meet with Allison Cartwright?

(A) She has experience that his organization needs.
(B) She can recommend Mark Lang for a position.
(C) She will deliver an important keynote address.
(D) She is an expert on the rights of the elderly.

答案 **A**

中譯 為什麼 George Mallory 想要與 Allison Cartwright 會面?

(A) 她擁有他的機構所需要的經驗。
(B) 她能夠推薦 Mark Lang 擔任一個職位。
(C) 她會發表一個重要的主題演說。
(D) 她是年長族群權益的專家。

解析

由題目 "Why does George Mallory want to meet with Allison Cartwright?" 可知必須從第二篇 email 的內容來判斷 George Mallory 的目的。根據首段第一、二句的描述 "I am writing on behalf of Mr. Mallory, who received and read your letter and resume. He is particularly interested in your work with Mark Lang and would like to schedule a time for you to come into the office to discuss your involvement.",Mr. Mallory 對 Allison 先前與 Mark Lang 合作的經驗有興趣,所以才想約她見面。

選項 (A) "She has experience that his organization needs." 為正確答案，因為，George Mallory 顯然認為 Allison 的經驗對他的機構有幫助才會約她來面談。

選項 (B) "... recommend Mark Lang for a position." 提及她 (Allison) 能「推薦 Mark Lang 擔任一個職位」，但文中並未提及此事，故不選。

選項 (C) 的 "... deliver ... keynote address." 是說她將要「發表主題演說」，這一點也沒在文中被提及，故不可選。

選項 (D) 提到的 "... an expert on the rights of the elderly." 亦非 Mr. Mallory 欲聯絡 Allison 的原因，故不可選。

200. Where will Allison's interview take place on May 16?

(A) Fairbanks

(B) Washington DC

(C) New York

(D) Chicago

答案 B

中譯 Allison 在五月十六日會前往何處面談？

(A) Fairbanks

(B) Washington DC

(C) New York

(D) Chicago

解析

此題問的是 Allison 將要面談的地點，根據第三篇文章可得知，Allison 接受五月十六日的面談了，她會前往 World Harvest 公司；再連結到首篇文章內容，World Harvest 公司位於 Washington DC，故可判斷 Allison 的面談將在 Washington DC 進行較為合理，所以選項 (B) 是正確答案。

✏️ **重點句型聚焦**

第一篇信件文章中 "I was especially pleased to learn that World Harvest engages in projects similar to work I've been involved with for the past ten years at Ageing Affairs." 的這句話以 "I was especially pleased to learn ..." 開頭，是使用率相當高的句型，如同中文的「我很樂意得知、我很高興聽到……」之意。此句型和其他幾個類似短句常用來作為介紹好消息的起始句：

			learn	that ...
	happy		announce	
I am	glad	to		
	pleased		inform	you that ...
			advice	

請看下列例句：

1. I am more than happy to assist you in completing that business report.
   我非常樂意協助你完成那份商業報告。

2. I am pleased to inform you that you have been successful in your application for the Sales Assistant position.
   我很高興要通知您，您順利被錄取擔任業務助理一職。

Part 3

模擬試題解析

Test 2

Questions 147-148 refer to the following document.

Anderson Landscaping Company
436 Eastern Blvd.
Clarksville, IN 47129
Telephone: (819) 555-4378
Email: tom@tomandersonlandscaping.com
Web: www.tomandersonlandscaping.com

INVOICE
PAYMENT DUE: 5/16

Customer: Randy Tompkins Realty

Contact: Randy Tompkins

Customer Account #: 1293

Service Description: Front yard landscaping

Date: 04/16

Ph: (819) 387-9723

Payment method: Credit Card

Unit	Unit Cost	Quantity	Total/$
Design/Layout	$1000/150 sq. ft.	N/A	1000.00
Trees	$150	2	300.00
Sod	$3.99 per roll	40	159.60
Planters/Flower Pots	$25 each	5	125.00
Landscape Edging	$12.99	4	51.96
Limestone Stepping Stones	$10.79 per stone	8	86.32
Labor	$40/hour	20	800.00
Sub-total			$2522.88
Returning Customer Discount (4%)			$100.92
Total			$2421.96

Open seven days a week from 8:00 am to 4:00 pm.

＊套色字部分請參考「詞彙註解」

【中譯】第 **147-148** 題請參照下面這份文件。

Anderson 景觀設計公司

Eastern 大道 436 號

(47129) Indiana 州 Clarksville 鎮

電話：(819) 555-4378

電子郵件：tom@tomandersonlandscaping.com

網址：www.tomandersonlandscaping.com

發票

付款期限：5 月 16 日

客戶姓名：Randy Tompkins Realty
聯絡人：Randy Tompkins
客戶帳戶編號：1293
服務內容：前院景觀美化

日期：4 月 16 日
電話：(819) 387-9723
付款方式：信用卡

單位	單位報價	數量	總金額
設計 / 面積	1000 元 / 150 平方英呎	不適用	1000.00
樹木	150 元	2	300.00
草皮	每綑 3.99 元	40	159.60
盆栽 / 花盆	每個 25 元	5	125.00
造景邊飾	12.99 元	4	51.96
石灰岩腳踏石	每塊 10.79 元	8	86.32
工資	40 元 / 每小時	20	800.00

小計	$2522.88
老客戶優惠 (4%)	$100.92
總計	$2421.96

營業時間：週一至週日上午 8 點到下午 4 點

landscape [ˋlændˌskep] (*n.*) 風景、景色　　**layout** [ˋleˌaʊt] (*n.*) 安排、設計、布局

invoice [ˋɪnvɔɪs] (*n.*) 發票、請款單　　**limestone** [ˋlaɪmˌston] (*n.*) 石灰岩

payment [ˋpemənt] (*n.*) 支付、付款　　**labor** [ˋlebɚ] (*n.*) 勞動、勞工、勞方

147. How many trees did Anderson Landscaping Company buy?

　　　(A) One

　　　(B) Four

　　　(C) Two

　　　(D) Five

答案 **C**

中譯 Anderson 景觀設計公司購買了幾棵樹？

(A) 一棵

(B) 四棵

(C) 兩棵

(D) 五棵

解析

題目問 "How many trees did Anderson Landscaping Company buy?"，很簡單，只要去找他們所購買的樹的「數量」即可。看到關鍵點 "Trees" 的 "Quantity" 處是 "2"，因此 (C) Two 為正確答案。

148. Why was Randy Tompkins offered a discount?

(A) The total amount was paid one month before the due date.

(B) He agreed to pay for the landscaping with a credit card.

(C) The amount of the invoice exceeded $2,000.

(D) He has done business with Anderson Landscaping before.

答案 D

中譯 為什麼 Randy Tompkins 可得到優惠？

(A) 總金額在付款期限前一個月就付清。

(B) 他同意用信用卡付景觀美化的費用。

(C) 帳單總金額超過了 2,000 元。

(D) 他以前和 Anderson 景觀設計公司做過生意。

解析

此題問的是 "Why was Randy Tompkins offered a discount?"，必須找出 Randy 可獲得折扣的「原因」為何。由 "Returning Customer Discount (4%)" 可以很明確地看出，會打折是因為他是「舊客戶」的關係。

選項 (A) 提到的 "... total ... paid ... before the due date." 是說因為他「提早一個月付款」的關係，與 "Returning Customer" 無關，故不選。

選項 (B) 提到的 "... pay ... with a credit card." 是說因為他使用「信用卡付款」的關係，這也與 "Returning Customer" 無關，故不選。

選項 (C) 表示因為「金額超過兩千」的緣故，也不對。

選項 (D) "He has done business with ... before." 指「他之前就與該公司做過生意」，也就是說他是「舊客戶」，因此為最佳答案。

To:	Angela Lacey
From:	Robert Cagney
Subject:	Food Protection Certificate for Bread Bakery Co.

Dear Ms. Lacey,

I am responding to your business application for Bread Bakery Co. dated Tuesday April 21. While processing your application we noticed you have yet to earn a Food Protection Certificate, which is required for you to operate your business. To earn your certificate, you must take and pass a course administered by the Department of Food and Health.

The course always runs five days, Monday to Friday, with an exam held on the last day. Upcoming courses will be conducted at our offices at the following times: the week of May 3 from 8 am to 11 am; the week of May 11 from 1 pm to 4 pm, and the week of May 18 from 8 am to 11 am. Please indicate in your reply to us your preferred week.

The course will be administered by the Associate Director of the Department of Food and Health Mr. Jerry Wood. We look forward to helping you earn your Food Protection Certificate.

Yours sincerely,

Roberl Cagney
Deputy General Manager
Department of Food and Health

＊套色字部分請參考「詞彙註解」

【中譯】第 **149-150** 題請參照下面這封電子郵件。

收件人：	Angela Lacey
寄件人：	Robert Cagney
主　旨：	Bread Bakery 公司之食品安全認證

親愛的 Lacey 小姐：

我寫此信件是為了回覆您於 4 月 21 日星期二為 Bread Bakery 公司所提出的申請。我們在處理您的申請案件時，發現貴公司仍未取得食品安全認證，而貴公司若要開張營業，此項認證是必要的。貴公司若要取得這項認證，就必須接受並通過由食品衛生局所主辦的課程。

本課程需時五日，從星期一至星期五，而測驗將在最後一天舉行。往後幾個星期的課程都將在我們辦公室進行，時間如下：5 月 3 日那個禮拜，早上 8 點至 11 點；5 月 11 日那個禮拜，下午 1 點至 4 點；以及 5 月 18 日那個禮拜，早上 8 點至 11 點。請回覆並告知我們最適合您的時段。

該課程將由食品衛生局副總監 Jerry Wood 先生負責指導。我們期待能協助您取得食品安全認證。

Robert Cagney
食品衛生局副總經理
謹上

📖 **詞彙註解**

respond [rɪ`spɑnd] (v.) 反應、回答　　**course** [kors] (n.) 課程、科目

process [`prɑsɛs] (v.) 進行、處理　　**conduct** [kən`dʌkt] (v.) 實施、處理

certificate [sə`tɪfəkɪt] (n.) 證書、執照　　**indicate** [`ɪndə‚ket] (v.) 指出、表明

149. What is the purpose of the email?

(A) To assign homework to a new student

(B) To present a certificate to an applicant

(C) To request that someone take a course

(C) To ask someone to supply a certificate

答案 C

中譯 此封信件的目的為何？

(A) 派發作業給一名新學生

(B) 頒發證書給一名申請人

(C) 要求某人參加一個課程

(D) 要求某人繳交一張證書

解析

在掃瞄文章之後，可得知這是一封跟 "business application for Bread Bakery" 相關的 email。第一題問其「目的」，由第一段第三句 "To earn your certificate, you must take and pass a course administered by the Department of Food and Health." 可知，若要申請執照，必須去「上課和考試」。

選項 (A) 中的 "... assign homework to ... student" 是說「給學生出作業」，這與主題內容完全無關，故不選。

選項 (B) 提到的 "... present a certificate ..." 是說要「頒發執照」，亦為錯誤。

選項 (C) 提及 "... request ... take a course"，的確，此信之目的是要請 Ms. Lacey 去上課並通過考試，故為正解。

選項 (D) "... ask ... supply a certificate"「要求繳交證書」也與首段內容無關，故不選。

150. What does Mr. Cagney want Ms. Lacey to do?

(A) Schedule a class

(B) Conduct an exam

(C) Reapply for a permit

(D) Contact an associate

答案 A

中譯 Cagney 先生要求 Lacey 小姐做什麼？

(A) 預訂課程時間

(B) 舉辦一場測驗

(C) 重新申請許可

(D) 聯繫一位同事

解析

第二題問的是 "What does Mr. Cagney want Ms. Lacey to do?"，應試者應將焦點放在 Ms. Lacey 被要求「採取什麼行動」上。根據第二段的內容 "Upcoming courses will be conducted at our offices at the following times ... Please indicate in your reply to us your preferred week."，Robert Cagney 在 email 內提出了數個上課的時間選項並請 Ms. Lacey「回覆她何時方便上課」。

選項 (A) 內的關鍵點為 "Schedule ... class"，的確，Robert Cagney 是要 Ms. Lacey 安排一個上課時間，故為最佳答案。

選項 (B) "Conduct ... exam" 是說要 Ms. Lacey「舉辦一場測驗」，這點並沒有在 email 內被提及，故不選。

選項 (C) "Reapply ... permit" 是說要 Ms. Lacey「重新申請許可」，這也沒有在 email 內被提及，故不選。

選項 (D) "Contact ... associate" 是說要請她「聯繫一位同事」，這也不是 Robert 提出的建議，故亦不選。

📝 重點句型聚焦

我們可以由 "To earn your certificate, you must take and pass a course administered by the Department of Food and Health." 這個句子來討論一下包含 "in order to"「為了要……」的句型。

In order to + 原形 V, S + V ...
= To + 原形 V, S + V ...
= S + V ... + in order to / to + 原形 V

因此，本文中的句子也可以用以下方式呈現：

- In order to earn your certificate, you must take and pass a course ....
- You must take and pass a course to earn your certificate ....

請看下列例句：

1. (In order) to earn some money for my school expenses, I need to get a part-time job.
   = I need to get a part-time job to earn some money for my school expenses.
   為了賺錢來支付學費，我需要找個兼職工作。

2. (In order) to get some fresh air in the meeting room, the secretary opened the window.
   = The secretary opened the window to get some fresh air in the meeting room.
   為了讓會議室空氣流通，秘書將窗戶打開。

3. (In order) to finish this project in time, I need to pull an all-nighter again.
   = I need to pull an all-nighter again in order to finish this project in time.
   為了準時將此案子做完，我又得通宵工作了。

Questions 151-152 refer to the following text message chain.

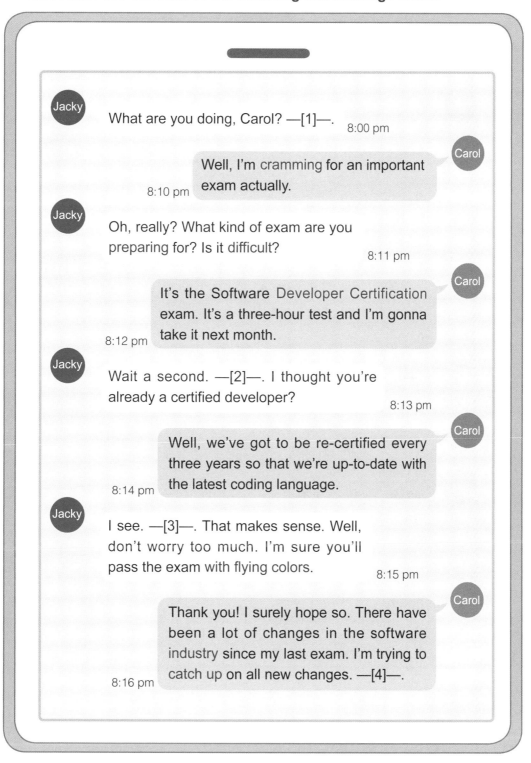

Jacky
What are you doing, Carol? —[1]—.
8:00 pm

Carol
Well, I'm cramming for an important exam actually.
8:10 pm

Jacky
Oh, really? What kind of exam are you preparing for? Is it difficult?
8:11 pm

Carol
It's the Software Developer Certification exam. It's a three-hour test and I'm gonna take it next month.
8:12 pm

Jacky
Wait a second. —[2]—. I thought you're already a certified developer?
8:13 pm

Carol
Well, we've got to be re-certified every three years so that we're up-to-date with the latest coding language.
8:14 pm

Jacky
I see. —[3]—. That makes sense. Well, don't worry too much. I'm sure you'll pass the exam with flying colors.
8:15 pm

Carol
Thank you! I surely hope so. There have been a lot of changes in the software industry since my last exam. I'm trying to catch up on all new changes. —[4]—.
8:16 pm

* 套色字部分請參考「詞彙註解」

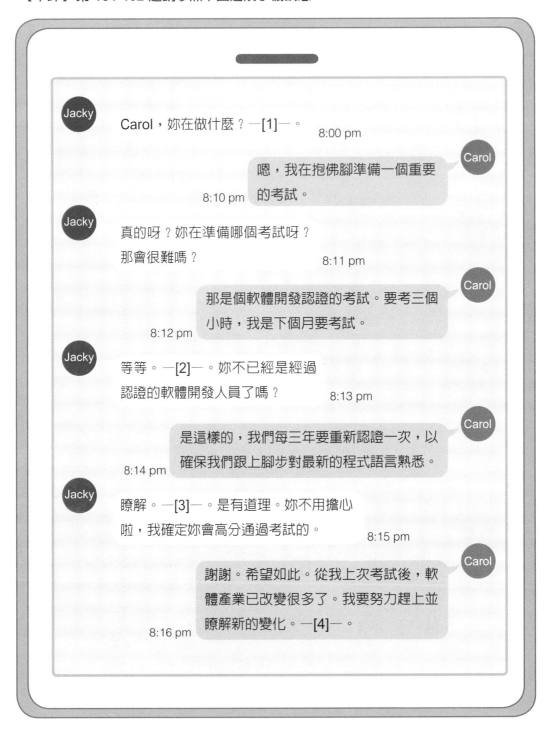

Jacky
Carol，妳在做什麼？—[1]—。
8:00 pm

Carol
嗯，我在抱佛腳準備一個重要的考試。
8:10 pm

Jacky
真的呀？妳在準備哪個考試呀？那會很難嗎？
8:11 pm

Carol
那是個軟體開發認證的考試。要考三個小時，我是下個月要考試。
8:12 pm

Jacky
等等。—[2]—。妳不已經是經過認證的軟體開發人員了嗎？
8:13 pm

Carol
是這樣的，我們每三年要重新認證一次，以確保我們跟上腳步對最新的程式語言熟悉。
8:14 pm

Jacky
瞭解。—[3]—。是有道理。妳不用擔心啦，我確定妳會高分通過考試的。
8:15 pm

Carol
謝謝。希望如此。從我上次考試後，軟體產業已改變很多了。我要努力趕上並瞭解新的變化。—[4]—。
8:16 pm

cram [kræm] (*v.*) 硬背、猛塞

prepare [prɪˋpɛr] (*v.*) 準備

difficult [ˋdɪfəˌkəlt] (*adj.*) 困難的

developer [dɪˋvɛləpə] (*n.*) 開發人員

certification [ˌsɝtɪfəˋkeʃən] (*n.*) 認證

with flying colors 成功地、出色地

industry [ˋɪndəstrɪ] (*n.*) 產業

catch up 趕上

151. What is the message communication about?

(A) New market trends

(B) The woman's certification exam

(C) A newly launched product

(D) The man's weekend plan

答案 B

中譯 此訊息溝通主要是關於何事？

(A) 新市場趨勢

(B) 女子的認證考試

(C) 一個新上市的產品

(D) 男子的週末計劃

解析

本題問的是這段訊息主要在講什麼。由女子說的此關鍵句 "It's the Software Developer Certification exam. It's a three-hour test and I'm gonna take it next month." 可知，兩人在討論女子要考程式開發員一事，故選項 (B) 為最佳答案。

152. In which of the positions marked [1], [2], [3], and [4] does the following sentence best belong?

"I'll do my best."

(A) [1]　　　　(B) [2]　　　　(C) [3]　　　　(D) [4]

答案 D

中譯 下面這個句子插入文中標示的 [1]、[2]、[3]、[4] 四處當中的何處最符合文意？

「我會盡力的。」

(A) [1]　　　　(B) [2]　　　　(C) [3]　　　　(D) [4]

PART 3 TEST 2

解析 ★ 新題型「插入句題」

題目要插入的句子意指「會盡一己之力」，由此便可判斷其應接在「某個明確目標」之後較為合理，而選項 [4] 位置前女子說 "I'm trying to catch up on all new changes."，其後再接 "I'll do my best."，就文意上是通順的，故本題選 (D)。

📝 重點句型聚焦

本篇文章內 I'm sure you'll pass the exam with flying colors. 此句中的片語 "with flying colors" 指「顯著成功」。可以想像一下，在某比賽之後，贏的那方將旗幟舉起使其隨風飄揚的情境，因此便衍生出「表現得很出色」之意了。

請看下列例句：

1. My daughter passed the algebra test with flying colors.
   我女兒高分通過代數考試。

2. Tom came home with flying colors after the competition.
   湯姆在比賽之後凱旋歸來。

Questions 153-155 refer to the following document.

National Electric

JAF Station
New York, NY 10116-1702

Account holder: Nancy L. Martin
Account number: 55-5476-8743-0004-2

Billing Summary

Previous charges and payments

Total charges from your last bill $32.29
Payments received. Thank You .... -$32.29 —[1]—.

New electricity charges for the billing period Apr. 06 to May 07

Total amount due $34.07

To avoid a late payment charge of 1.5%, please pay the total amount due by **June 1**

Electricity Charges

These charges are for the electricity you used (supply) and getting that electricity to you
(delivery). Rates are based on a 30-day period. When your billing period is more or less than
30 days, we prorate your bill accordingly. —[2]—.

Electricity used during the Apr. 06 to May 07 billing period (31 days)

We measure your electricity by how many kilowatt hours (kWh) you use.

May 07 actual reading	2815
April 06 actual reading	-2744
Your electricity use	**71 kWh**

❏ Your supply charges

Supply 71 kWh @7.2817 c/kWh $5.17
Charge for the electricity supplied to you by National Electric

Total supply charges $5.17

❏ Your delivery charges

Basic service charge $19.31

Charge for basic system infrastructure and customer-related services, including customer
accounting, meter reading and meter maintenance. —[3]—.

Delivery 71 kWh @11.4507 c/kWh $8.12

Charge for maintaining the system though which National Electric delivers electricity for you.

Total delivery charges $27.43

❏ Your sales tax

Sales tax @4.5000% $1.47

Tax collected on behalf of New York State and/or your locality.

Total electricity charges $34.07

Next meter reading: Wednesday, June 6 —[4]—.

National Electric

JAF 站

(10116-1702) New York 州 New York 市

帳戶姓名：Nancy L. Martin

帳戶號碼：55-5476-8743-0004-2

計費總覽

前期金額與繳款紀錄

您上次的繳款金額 $32.29

款項已收到 謝謝您 .... -$32.29 —[1]—。

本期電費金額 計費期間自 4 月 6 日至 5 月 7 日

應付總額 $34.07

請於 **6 月 1 日** 前繳清費用，以免支付 1.5% 的滯納金。

電力費用

此費用係根據您實際使用的電力（供電）和將電力傳輸至您的地址（輸電）計算。費用的計算方式以每 30 天為一個單位。如果您的計費日數多或少於 30 天，我們將會視天數調整您的帳單。—[2]—。

4 月 6 日至 5 月 7 日計費期間（**31天**）所使用的電量

我們根據您每小時使用電力的千瓦量 (kWh) 來測量您的使用量。

5 月 7 日讀錶實際值為   <u>2815</u>

4 月 6 日讀錶實際值為   -2744

本月電力使用量為   **71 kWh**

❏ **本月供電費用**

供應 71 kWh @7.2817 c/kWh $5.17

供應電力的 National Electric 之費用

供應總金額 $5.17

❏ **本月輸電費用**

基本服務收費 $19.31

基礎系統架構和客戶相關服務之費用，包括客戶計價、電錶讀取與電錶維護。—[3]—。

輸送 71 kWh @11.4507 c/kWh $8.12

National Electric 用以輸送電力之系統設施的維護費用

輸送總金額 $27.43

❏ **本月營業稅**

營業稅 @4.5000% $1.47

由紐約州政府和／或當地政府所收取的稅金

電力費用總金額 $34.07

下次讀錶日期：6 月 6 日星期三 —[4]—。

prorate [proˋret] (*v.*) 按比例分配   **infrastructure** [ˋɪnfrəˌstrʌktʃə] (*n.*) 基礎建設

measure [ˋmɛʒə] (*v.*) 量測、量   **maintenance** [ˋmentənəs] (*n.*) 維護、維修

153. What type of document is this?

(A) Utility bill

(B) Commercial invoice

(C) Estimate of charges

(D) Credit card statement

答案 **A**

中譯 這是一份什麼類型的文件？

(A) 公共事業帳單

(B) 商務發票

(C) 費用估價單

(D) 信用卡帳單

解析

大約掃瞄一下此表格就可以很清楚地看出這是一張 "Billing Summary"（收費明細表），也就是「帳單」。接下來看題目 "What type of document is this?" 問此表單是「什麼」文件。由兩個關鍵字 "Electric" 和 "Billing Summary" 便可確定是一張「電費帳單」。選項 (A) Utility bill 正確，"utility" 即指水、電、瓦斯等「公共事業」，故選為正確答案。

154. How much is Nancy Martin being charged for delivery?

(A) \$19.31   (B) \$27.43   (C) \$32.29   (D) \$34.07

答案 **B**

中譯 Nancy Martin 必須支付多少輸電費用？

(A) 19.31 元   (B) 27.43 元   (C) 32.29 元   (D) 34.07 元

解析

第二題問 "How much is Nancy Martin being charged for delivery?"，應試者只要將焦點放在找尋 "delivery" 的費用上即可。由表格內之 "Total delivery charges" 項可知，費用是 "\$27.43"，故 (B) 為正確答案。

155. **In which of the position marked [1], [2], [3], and [4] does the following sentence best belong?**

"Should you have any questions, please send an email to: info@electric.com."

(A) [1]　　　　　(B) [2]　　　　　(C) [3]　　　　　(D) [4]

答案 D

中譯 下面這個句子插入文中標示的 [1]、[2]、[3]、[4] 四處當中的何處最符合文意？
「若您有任何問題，請寄電郵至：info@electric.com 信箱。」
(A) [1]　　　　　(B) [2]　　　　　(C) [3]　　　　　(D) [4]

解析 ★ 新題型「插入句題」
由題目所問的句子提到「有問題的話，可以聯絡的方式」，便可判斷該句應出現在帳單的後半部較為合理，而非在開頭或中間之處，因此選 (D) 最適當。

📝 **重點句型聚焦**

我們藉此篇內的 "When your billing period is more or less than 30 days, we prorate your bill accordingly." 這個句子來討論一下使用從屬連接詞 when 的句型：

When S + V ..., S + V ...　＝　S + V ..., when S + V ...

請看下列例句：

1. When our clients come tomorrow, we can propose this solution to them.
   當客戶明天來的時候，我們可以跟他們提出這一個解決方案。

2. When your order exceeds US$20K, we will provide you with a 10% off discount.
   當您的訂單金額超過兩萬美元時，我們會提供給您九折的優惠。

Questions 156-158 refer to the following announcement.

Desert Valley Tours
Welcome to Desert Valley — A destination unlike any other!

Located just minutes away from downtown Hagerton, Desert Valley Tours offers a range of hiking and dining options to help you explore and enjoy the beautiful Desert Valley. Departing from the Desert Inn Hotel lobby, you can enjoy scenic views, delightful hiking adventures, or evening elegance. The choice is yours!

Full Day Tour
✳ The Desert Valley Grand Tour is by far our most popular. Enjoy breakfast at the charming Dessert Inn cafe, and then take a mid-day jeep ride and walkabout through the Hagerton Wilderness Area, where a light picnic lunch will be served. Finish the evening with dinner and drinks at the historic Old Horse Saloon in Frankton. The Desert Valley Tour bus will make a stop in downtown Hagerton before returning to the Desert Inn.

Mid-Day Tour
✳ Departing at 11:00 am, the Cactus Peak Day Hike offers beautiful panorama views of Desert Valley as you ramble to the summit of Cactus Peak. Afterwards you'll stop by the historic Old Horse Saloon in historic Frankton for a late buffet lunch, beverages, and live entertainment before returning to downtown Hagerton via Bus 12.

Evening Tours
✳ The Desert Valley Skyline Tour is known for combining gorgeous views with first class convenience. Enjoy the leisurely ride to the top of the mountain on the sleek and comfortable Skyline Tramway. Savor a five-course meal at the luxurious Peak Pit Restaurant and watch the sun set over Desert Valley. The Desert Valley Tour bus will make a stop in downtown Hagerton before returning to the Desert Inn.

✳ For something different, try the Desert Moonlight Hike, offered Monday, Wednesday, and Friday in the spring and summer. Explore Desert Valley and Cactus Peak by night with guide Roger Rick! Tour departs at 5 pm. Flashlights will be provided. Bus 12 will return you to downtown Hagerton.

• Tour Information Hotline: (800) 847-3776
• Tours may be canceled or cut short due to inclement weather.

✳套色字部分請參考「詞彙註解」

【中譯】第 156-158 題請參照下面這則公告。

Desert Valley 之旅

歡迎來到 Desert Valley —— 無與倫比的觀光勝地！

Desert Valley 離 Hagerton 市中心只有幾分鐘的路程，它提供了一系列健行活動和各類餐飲，幫助您探索並享受沙漠谷地之美。從 Desert Inn 飯店大廳出發，您可以享受風景名勝、愉快的健行冒險，或美麗的晚間景致。一切任君選擇！

全日遊

✻ Desert Valley 豪華之旅是最受歡迎的。您可以在充滿魅力的 Desert Inn 咖啡廳享用早餐，然後搭中午的吉普車行程，並在 Hagerton 自然保留區徒步健行，在那裡我們將會提供簡單的野餐作為午餐。之後可以在位於 Frankton 歷史悠久的 Old Horse Saloon 享用晚餐與飲料來為當天晚上劃下句點。Desert Valley 之旅的遊覽車將會在回到 Desert Inn 飯店之前，在 Hagerton 市中心稍作停靠。

半日遊

✻ 於早上 11 點出發，Cactus Peak 日間健行之旅能夠在您遊走於 Cactus Peak 的山峰時，讓您欣賞到 Desert Valley 美麗的全景。接著，您將可以前往歷史悠久位於古老 Frankton 的 Old Horse Saloon 享用自助餐式的午晚餐、喝飲料，並觀賞現場表演，之後再搭乘 12 號公車回到 Hagerton 市中心。

晚間遊

✻ Desert Valley 天際線之旅以結合美麗的景色與無比的便利性聞名。您可以享受搭乘豪華舒適的 Skyline 電車前往山頂的悠閒旅程。在山頂的豪華 Peak Pit 餐廳享用五道菜餚的餐點，並欣賞 Desert Valley 的日落。Desert Valley 之旅的遊覽車將會在回到 Desert Inn 飯店之前，於 Hagerton 市中心稍作停靠。

✻ 若要來一點不同的，可以嘗試沙漠夜光健行之旅，於春季與夏季每週一、三、五提供。您可以和導遊 Roger Rick 一起探索夜間的 Desert Valley 與 Cactus Peak！行程將於下午 5 點出發。我們會提供手電筒。12 號公車將會載您回到 Hagerton 市中心。

• 行程資訊熱線：(800) 847-3776
• 行程可能會因為氣候不佳而取消或縮短。

詞彙註解

explore [ɪk`splor] (*v.*) 探索	**afterwards** [`æftəwədz] (*adv.*) 以後、後來
delightful [dɪ`laɪtfəl] (*adj.*) 令人愉快的	**gorgeous** [`gɔrdʒəs] (*adj.*)
elegance [`ɛləgəns] (*n.*) 典雅、雅緻	燦爛的、華麗的、豪華的
charming [`tʃɑrmɪŋ] (*adj.*) 迷人的、可愛的	**leisurely** [`liʒəlɪ] (*adv.*) 從容不迫地、悠閒地
walkabout [`wɔkə‚baʊt] (*n.*) 徒步旅行	**sleek** [slik] (*adj.*) 光滑的、圓滑的
historic [hɪs`tɔrɪk] (*adj.*) 具歷史意義的	**savor** [`sevə] (*v.*) 品嚐
panorama [‚pænə`ræmə] (*n.*) 全景、全貌	**inclement** [ɪn`klɛmənt] (*adj.*)
ramble [`ræmbl̩] (*v.*) 漫步、閒逛	天氣險惡的、氣候嚴酷的

156. Which tour does NOT include any food or beverages?

(A) The Desert Valley Grand Tour

(B) The Cactus Peak Day Hike

(C) The Desert Valley Skyline Tour

(D) The Desert Moonlight Hike

答案 **D**

中譯 哪一個行程「不」包含任何食物或飲料？

(A) Desert Valley 豪華之旅

(B) Cactus Peak 日間健行之旅

(C) Desert Valley 天際線之旅

(D) 沙漠夜光健行之旅

解析

很快地將文章大略地掃瞄過一次，看到標題 "Desert Valley Tours" 便知這是與旅行團相關的文章，再看到三個標題 (Full Day, Mid-Day, Evening) 就可以預測至少會有三個不同時間點的旅遊活動。本題問 "Which tour does NOT include any food or beverages?"，則應聚焦於「沒有」提供餐點或飲料的是哪個團？第一個 "Full Day Tour" 提供 "a light picnic lunch"，第二個 "Mid-Day Tour" 提供 "a late buffet lunch"，第三個 "Evening Tour" 提供 "a five-course meal"，而最後一段的 "The Dessert Moonlight Hike" 並沒有說會提供任何餐飲，故選項 (D) 為正解。

157. **Why would a tour member take Bus 12?**

    (A) To return to downtown Hagerton

    (B) To get to the Old Horse Saloon

    (C) To visit historic Frankton

    (D) To reach the top of Cactus Peak

答案 A

中譯 參加行程的成員為何會需要搭 12 號公車？

(A) 以回到 Hagerton 市中心

(B) 以前往 Old Horse Saloon

(C) 以造訪歷史悠久的 Frankton

(D) 以抵達 Cactus Peak 的頂端

解析

第二題問 "Why would a tour member take Bus 12?"，只要鎖定找搭十二號公車的「目的」就能回答了。根據 Mid-Day Tour 介紹的第二句 "Afterwards you'll stop by the historic Old Horse Saloon in historic Frankton for a late buffet lunch, beverages, and live entertainment before returning to downtown Hagerton via Bus 12."，以及最後一段最後一句 "Bus 12 will return you to downtown Hagarton." 皆可知，搭十二號公車是可以回到 "downtown Hagerton" 的，故 (A) To return to downtown Hagerton 為正確答案。選項 (B)、(C) 和 (D) 之內容都跟 "Bus 12" 無關，故不選。

158. **The word "inclement" in the last line is closest in meaning to**

    (A) unseasonal

    (B) unpredictable

    (C) humid

    (D) stormy

答案 D

中譯 最後一行中的 "inclement" 這個字意思最接近

(A) 不合季節的

(B) 無法預料的

(C) 潮濕的

(D) 暴風雨的

最後一題問 "inclement" 這個字的意思最接近哪個字。"inclement" 是「天氣惡劣的」之意，與 stormy（暴風雨的）的涵義最類似，故選項 (D) 為最佳答案。

✎ 重點句型聚焦

文中 "The Desert Valley Skyline Tour is known for combining gorgeous views with first class convenience." 這句話裡的 "known for" 是「因……而著名」之意。

請看下列例句：

1. Our company is known for its excellent customer service and technical support.
   我們公司因優良的客戶服務與技術支援而著名。

2. That restaurant is known for its mouthwatering desserts.
   那家餐廳因令人垂涎的甜點而著名。

Questions 159-161 refer to the following article.

Retail Sales Up in January Despite Bad Weather
February 6

Last month's snowstorms surprisingly didn't hinder purchasing by consumers, who "are in better shape than feared and have begun the year with a return to more normal buying habits," the Greenwood Times reported. General retail sales rose 4.2% over the previous month according to Retail Analytics Inc.

"It appears that consumers are feeling a little bit more confident about their financial situation and the economy as a whole," said Jordan Smith, president of Retail Analytics Inc. "They're coming out of hibernation."

The Financial Street Journal reported that the International Council of Retail Centers "expects the industry to post a 2.3% same-store sales increase in February. Also, national holidays later this month are likely to help increase sales. So might tax refunds in March." This will be good news for first quarter roundups.

Syngas Services expressed caution, however, noting that despite the "modestly positive results, we remain unconvinced that this is evidence of a sustainable trend." Syngas believes the economy is still fragile and vulnerable to surprise shocks. Unpredictable events such as a sudden increase in oil prices or large-scale changes in the job market could easily affect consumer spending. Furthermore, they claim consumer purchasing has slowed every second quarter for the past four years. "It's unrealistic to believe there will be a turn now."

＊套色字部分請參考「詞彙註解」

【中譯】第 **159-161** 題請參照下面這篇文章。

縱使一月份氣候不佳,營業額仍然有所起色
2 月 6 日

根據 Greenwood 時報的報導,上個月的暴風雪令人訝異地並沒有影響消費者們的購物意願,他們「比原先擔心的好,一開春就回歸到接近平時的正常購物習慣。」根據 Retail Analytics 公司的調查,本月的一般零售比上個月提升了 4.2%。

「消費者們顯然對於自身的財務和社會整體的經濟狀況稍微感到比較有信心,」Retail Analytics 公司的總裁 Jordan Smith 表示,「他們正在從冬眠中甦醒。」

Financial Street 期刊報導說,國際零售中心諮議會「預期產業在二月份的同店面銷售額將提升 2.3%。同時,本月稍後的全國假期將很有可能幫助提升銷售量。三月份的退稅,同樣也可能會有幫助。」這對於第一季財報是很好的消息。

但是 Syngas Services 則較為謹慎,表示縱使呈現出「適度的正面結果,但我們仍然不確定這是否能視為一個長久趨勢的證據。」Syngas 認為經濟仍然處於脆弱的狀況,並無法承受突如其來的衝擊。若出現油價突然上漲或工作市場的大規模改變之類的突發情況,皆可能很容易地影響到消費者的消費行為。他們更近一步指出消費者的消費行為在過去四年都於第二季時趨緩。「相信現在會出現改變的想法是非常不實際的。」

● 詞彙註解

despite [dɪˋspaɪt] (*prep.*) 儘管、任憑
hinder [ˋhɪndə] (*v.*) 妨礙、阻礙
fear [fɪr] (*v.*) 擔心、畏懼
appear [əˋpɪr] (*v.*) 顯露、出現
hibernation [͵haɪbəˋneʃən] (*n.*) 冬眠、過冬
be likely to 可能
roundup [ˋraʊnd͵ʌp] (*n.*) 綜述、綜合報導

caution [ˋkɔʃən] (*n.*) 告誡、謹慎
modestly [ˋmɑdɪstlɪ] (*adv.*) 適度地
fragile [ˋfrædʒəl] (*adj.*) 脆弱的、虛弱的
vulnerable [ˋvʌlnərəbl] (*adj.*) 易受傷的
unpredictable [͵ʌnprɪˋdɪktəbl] (*adj.*)
不可預測的、無法預期的
unrealistic [͵ʌnrɪəˋlɪstɪk] (*adj.*) 不切實際的

159. What can be inferred about the January sales increase?

(A) It was not included in Retail Analytics' report.

(B) It was a result of unusual weather.

(C) It was smaller than in previous years.

(D) It was larger than some analysts predicted.

答案 D

中譯 從一月銷售額提升的結果可以推論出什麼？

(A) 它並沒有被包括在 Retail Analytics 的報告中。

(B) 它是不尋常的氣候所導致的結果。

(C) 它比起往年要少。

(D) 它比一些分析師所預估的要多。

解析

由題目 "What can be inferred about the January sales increase?" 可知，應試者必須找尋與「一月業績上升」相關的資訊來回答。由首段提到的 "Last month's snowstorms surprisingly didn't hinder purchasing by consumers .... General retail sales rose 4.2% over the previous month according to Retail Analytics Inc." 來推斷，一般零售業績的上升超乎預期。

選項 (A) "... not included in ... report." 指「未有包含在分析報告內」，這與首段所提到的內容搭不上關係，故不選。

選項 (B) "... a result of unusual weather." 指「不尋常氣候所導致的結果」，這跟首句中的「未受暴風雪的影響」的意思相悖，故不選。

選項 (C) 中的 "... smaller than ... previous years." 是說「比往年少」，亦與首段的內容相反，故不選。

選項 (D) 提到 "... larger than ... predicted."，的確，業績上升是比原來分析師預測的還要好，故為最佳答案。

160. What is NOT mentioned as affecting the First Quarter?

(A) Upcoming holidays

(B) Natural disasters

(C) Consumer confidence

(D) Tax refunds

答案 B

(A) 即將到來的假期

(B) 天然災害

(C) 消費者信心

(D) 退稅

解析

本題問哪一項「不是」影響第一季結果的因素，應試者須找出三個有被提到的影響因素，以便排除掉一個沒被提到的。根據第二段第一句 "It appears that consumers are feeling a little bit more confident about their financial situation and the economy as a whole ...."，以及第三段第二、三句 "Also, national holidays later this month are likely to help increase sales. So might tax refunds in March."，可歸納出以下配對：

選項 (A) Upcoming holidays = national holidays later this month，有被提到。

選項 (C) Consumer confidence = consumers are feeling more confident，有被提到。

選項 (D) Tax refunds = tax refunds in March，也有被提到。

選項 (B) Natural disasters 並沒有被提及是原因之一，故為正確答案。

161. Why is Syngas Services concerned?

(A) Higher prices will affect the favorable business climate.

(B) There is no evidence that consumers will continue spending.

(C) Oil and gas prices are expected in to increase in the second quarter.

(D) Most analysts predict the retail industry will suffer a slowdown.

答案 B

中譯 為什麼 Syngas Services 感到憂心？

(A) 更高的價位將會影響到有利的商業環境。

(B) 沒有確切證據顯示消費者會持續花費。

(C) 油與瓦斯的價格預計將在第二季調漲。

(D) 大多數分析師都預測零售業會衰退。

解析

最後一題問的是 "Why is Syngas Services concerned?"，必須找出 Syngas 所「擔憂的事」為何。由最後一段第一句 "Syngas Services expressed caution, however, noting that despite the 'modestly positive results, we remain unconvinced that this is evidence of a sustainable trend.'" 可知，Syngas 心存疑慮是因爲「沒有足夠證據顯示消費者會持續發揮同等的購買力」。

選項 (A)　"Higher prices ... affect ...." 提到高售價的影響，但這與上述要點無關，故不選。

選項 (B)　中的 "... no evidence ... consumers will continue spending." 與上述要點所提到的一致，故爲最佳答案。

選項 (C)　"Oil and gas prices ... increase ..." 提到油和瓦斯的價格，但這跟 Syngas 的疑慮無關，故不選。

選項 (D)　中的 "... analysts predict the retail ... suffer a slowdown." 是說「分析師預測零售業會衰退」，這一點與事實並不相符，故亦不選。

📝 重點句型聚焦

文中的 It appears that consumers are feeling a little bit more confident about their financial situation. 其實相當於 Consumers appear to feel a little bit more confident about their financial situation.。也就是：

It seems / appears + that + S + V
= S + seem(s) / appear(s) + to + 原形動詞

此句型常用來表示「不是很精確的看法」，有如中文的「似乎……」。

請看下列例句：

1. It appears that the customer likes our proposal.
   = The customer appears to like our proposal.
   那個客戶似乎很喜歡我們的提議案。

2. It seems that Tim won many cases before.
   = Tim seems to have won many cases before.
   提姆以前似乎贏得過很多案子。
   P.S. 本句使用 to + have + p.p. 來表示過去。

Questions 162-164 refer to the following announcement.

Arts & Crafts Festival

Celebrate Spring! The roses are blooming and the smell of lilacs is in the air. The Lafayette Chamber of Commerce is pleased to announce the 5th Annual Arts & Crafts Festival will take place in downtown Lafayette. On Saturday March 21 and Sunday March 22, the Great Lawn of Lafayette's Public Square will be transformed into an arts and crafts extravaganza!

Twenty local artisans will display their work and offer free arts and crafts programs for both adults and children. Live entertainment will be ongoing throughout the weekend on the Wilburn Stage near the north end of the park. Fine cuisine and beverages will be available at the Food Court located at the south end of the square. For more information on the participating artists, vendors, and schedule of programs please visit www.lafayette.com/artsandcraftsfestival.

Festival hours are 10 am–9 pm. There is no admission charge. Children of all ages are welcome, but no pets are allowed. Please note that parking will be limited. Shuttles from the Shreveport Mall to downtown Lafayette will be available for $2 one way.

We'll see you at Lafayette's Public Square!

＊套色字部分請參考「詞彙註解」

【中譯】第 **162-164** 題請參照下面這則公告。

藝術與手工藝品節

歡慶春天！玫瑰花正在綻放著，紫丁香的香氣瀰漫在空中。Lafayette 商會非常高興地宣佈，第五屆年度藝術與手工藝品節將在 Lafayette 市中心舉行。3 月 21 日星期六與 3 月 22 日星期日 Lafayette 大眾廣場的大草坪將會變成藝術與手工藝品的盛大展覽場！

二十位本地的藝術家將展出他們的作品，並為大人與小孩提供免費的藝術與手工藝課程。現場的娛樂表演將會在公園北區的 Wilburn 表演台上持續整個週末。而廣場南區的小吃區將會提供各種美食與飲料。欲瞭解參與藝術家、攤位賣家與演出排程表之相關詳細資訊，請上 www.lafayette.com/artsandcraftsfestival 網站。

慶祝活動由早上 10 點進行至晚上 9 點。無須購買任何門票。任何年紀的孩童皆歡迎蒞臨，但請勿攜帶寵物進場。請注意，車位有限。來賓可搭乘由 Shreveport 購物中心至 Lafayette 市中心的接駁車，票價為單程 2 美元。

我們期待在 Lafayette 大眾廣場見到您！

👉 詞彙註解

bloom [blum] (*v.*) 開花、茂盛

lilac [ˋlaɪlək] (*n.*) 紫丁香

transform [trænsˋfɔrm] (*v.*) 轉化、改變

extravaganza [ɪkˌstrævəˋgænzə] (*n.*) 有狂氣的作品、盛典

artisan [ˋɑrtəzn̩] (*n.*) 工匠、技工

cuisine [kwɪˋzin] (*n.*) 烹飪、菜餚

vendor [ˋvɛndɚ] (*n.*) 小販

admission [ədˋmɪʃən] (*n.*) 許可、入場（費）

shuttle [ˋʃʌtl̩] (*n.*) 接駁車

162. **What does the announcement suggest about the festival?**

    (A) It will be held in downtown Lafayette.

    (B) It will be for viewing art only.

    (C) It will be for children only.

    (D) It will be held in the summer.

答案 A

中譯 此公告提到了哪項有關節慶的訊息？

(A) 節慶將會在 Lafayette 市中心舉行。

(B) 節慶將只包含藝術欣賞。

(C) 節慶將只為孩童舉辦。

(D) 節慶將會在夏季舉行。

解析

看到標題 "Arts and Crafts Festival" 就知道此文有關藝文展的活動。第一題問 "What does the announcement suggest about the festival?"，根據首段最後一句所提到的 "... the Great Lawn of Lafayette's Public Square will be transformed into an arts and crafts extravaganza!"，以及尾段最後一句 "Shuttles from the Shreveport Mall to downtown Lafayette will be available for $2 one way." 可推斷，此活動將於市中心的 Lafayette's Public Square 舉辦。

選項 (A) 中的 "... held in downtown Lafayette." 與段落內的資訊相符，故為最佳答案。

選項 (B) 提到的是 "... for viewing art only."，但文中除了提到看藝術品外，還有其他如 "free arts and crafts programs for both adults and children" 等活動，故不選。

選項 (C) "... for children only." 指此為兒童專屬活動，但根據公告內容，大人也可以參加，故不適當。

選項 (D) 說 "... held in the summer."，但文中提到的日期是 3/21 和 3/22，而三月並非夏天，故亦不選。

163. What is Public Square?

(A) A park

(B) An auditorium

(C) A school

(D) A shopping mall

答案 A

中譯 大眾廣場是什麼？

(A) 一座公園

(B) 一個禮堂

(C) 一所學校

(D) 一個購物中心

解析

此題問 Public Square 是什麼。由第二段第二句 "Live entertainment will be ongoing throughout the weekend on the Wilburn Stage near the north end of the park." 可知，它是一個公園，故選項 (A) 為正解。

164. What does the festival prohibit?

(A) Children

(B) Pets

(C) Parking

(D) Blankets

答案 B

中譯 節慶現場禁止什麼？

(A) 孩童

(B) 寵物

(C) 停車

(D) 毛毯

解析

此題問 "What does the festival prohibit?"，應試者必須找出「活動中不被允許」的資訊來回答問題。由第三段第二句所提到的 "Children of all ages are welcome, but no pets are allowed." 可知，寵物是不可以入場的，故 (B) Pets 為最佳答案。

本文中之：

- Twenty local artisans will display their work and offer free arts and crafts programs ....
- Live entertainment will be ongoing throughout the weekend ....
- Fine cuisine and beverages will be available at the Food Court ....

等句都是最基本的未來式句型。

S + will + ...（+ 未來的時間副詞）

請看下列例句：

1. Some sales representatives will fly to Japan for a conference tomorrow morning.
   一些業務人員明天早上將飛往日本參加一個會議。

2. The plane to Hong Kong will depart in 20 minutes.
   前往香港的班機將於二十分鐘後起飛。

Mary Cohen
152 Dolores St., Apt 3C
San Francisco, CA 94114

July 28

First Ocean Realty
John Patterson
2500 Divisadero St.
San Francisco, CA 94123

Re: Immediate repairs needed

Dear Mr. Patterson,

I have been living in the apartment at 152 Dolores Street for 14 years. I've been a loyal tenant and paid my rent on time during that entire period. I have also regularly agreed to the yearly increase in rent. However, I am very dissatisfied with how you handle repairs.

Four months ago I sent you notice about several repairs needed in the apartment. This included repairing or replacing windows that do not close and lock properly, fixing the radiator, and replacing the kitchen cabinets.

Exactly one month ago, the superintendent came to my apartment to take a look at the needed repairs. He fixed the radiator and replaced the kitchen cabinets. He told me you handle all window repairs because you deal with the window company directly. I left a phone message for you about this matter but never received a reply.

The last time I called was on July 23, and you told me a window repairman would come to my house the following Tuesday. The repairman did not come.

This problem needs to be addressed immediately. There have been several burglaries in the neighborhood and I do not feel safe in the apartment. I would rather keep this matter out of the courts, but if a window repairman does not come to my apartment by August 2, I will have to seek legal action.

Sincerely,

Mary Cohen

Mary Cohen

【中譯】第 165-167 題請參照下面這封信件。

Mary Cohen
Dolores 街 152 號之 3C
(94114) California 州 San Francisco 市

7 月 28 日

First Ocean 房地產
John Patterson
Divisadero 街 2500 號
(94123) California 州 San Francisco 市

關於：須即刻處理的修理事項

親愛的 Patterson 先生：

我已住在 Dolores 街 152 號的公寓十四年了。我一直是位忠實的房客，在整段期間內皆按時繳交房租。我同時也接受了每年調漲的房租金額。不過，我對於你們進行維修的方式感到非常不滿意。

四個月前，我寄給了您一封信，提到公寓裡有多處需要維修，其中包括修理或更換無法正常關閉或鎖上的窗戶、修理暖器以及更換廚房的櫥櫃。

在整整一個月前，公寓管理人來我的公寓檢查需要修理的物件。他修理了暖器，並更換了廚房櫥櫃。他告知我您是負責修理所有窗戶的人，因為您能夠直接與窗戶公司接洽。我留了一則有關這件事情的電話留言給您，但是一直沒有收到您的回覆。

上一次我打電話的日期是 7 月 23 日，您那時告訴我在接下來的星期四會有一名窗戶維修工來處理。那位維修工並沒有來。

這個問題需要即刻處理。這個社區已經發生了多起竊案，而我住在公寓裡感到並不安全。我很希望這件事情能夠不上法院就得以解決，但是如果維修窗戶的工人沒有在 8 月 2 日之前來我的公寓的話，我將會尋求法律途徑解決。

Mary Cohen

Mary Cohen
敬上

---

165. Why did Mary Cohen write this letter to John Patterson?

    (A) To insist that her windows be repaired

    (B) To report a problem with her radiator

    (C) To ask that the kitchen cabinets be replaced

    (D) To request that her rent be reduced

答案 **A**

中譯 Mary Cohen 為什麼要寫這封信給 John Patterson ？

(A) 為了堅持她的窗戶必須修理好

(B) 為了報告她的暖器出了問題

(C) 為了要求更換廚房櫥櫃

(D) 為了要求降低她的房租

解析

此題 "Why did Mary Cohen write this letter to John Patterson?" 問房客 Mary Cohen 寫此信的「目的」為何。根據第一段的資訊 "I have been living in the apartment .... I've been a loyal tenant and paid my rent on time .... However, I am very dissatisfied with how you handle repairs." 可看出她不滿的態度，而不滿的起因為第四段提到的 "... you told me a window repairman would come ... The repairman did not come."，也就是說，她在意的是「窗戶遲遲未修好」這件事，而這正是她寫此信的原因。

選項 (A)　提到的 "... insist ... windows be repaired" 與上述「修窗戶」的事件一致，故為正解。

選項 (B)　提到 "... report a problem with ... radiator"，但根據文章，暖器的問題已解決，故不選。

選項 (C)　提到 "... ask ... kitchen cabinets be replaced"，但一樣地，根據信件內容，廚房櫥櫃的問題也已經解決了，故不選。

選項 (D)　"... rent be reduced" 指 Mary 要求「降房租」，但信中並沒有提到此事，故亦不選。

166. When did Mary Cohen first contact John Patterson?

    (A) Four months ago

    (B) One month ago

    (C) July 23

    (D) July 28

答案 A

中譯 Mary Cohen 何時首次與 John Patterson 聯絡？

(A) 4 個月前

(B) 1 個月前

(C) 7 月 23 日

(D) 7 月 28 日

解析

本題問的是 "When did Mary Cohen first contact John Patterson?"，可見要找出 Mary 最早跟 John 聯絡的「時間點」。由第二段第一句 "Four months ago I sent you notice about several repairs needed in the apartment." 可看出，Mary 早在四個月前就開始跟房東 John 反應問題了。很明確地 (A) Four months ago 為正確答案。

167. What will Mary probably do before August 2?

(A) Wait for John Patterson to arrange a repair

(B) Move into a different apartment in the area

(C) Have the windows replaced at her own expense

(D) File a legal claim in a court of law

答案 A

中譯 Mary 在 8 月 2 日前可能會做什麼？

(A) 等待 John Patterson 安排維修

(B) 搬到當地其他的公寓

(C) 自己花錢更換窗戶

(D) 到法院提告

解析

最後一題問 "What will Mary probably do before August 2?"，應試者必須找出 "August 2" 之前 Mary 會採取什麼「行動」。由尾段第三句 "I would rather keep this matter out of the courts, but if a window repairman does not come to my apartment by August 2, I will have to seek legal action." 可知，若 8 月 2 日窗戶還沒修好的話，Mary 就要訴諸法律了；換言之，在 8 月 2 日之前她會等房東派人來修窗戶。

選項 (A) 提到 "Wait for ... arrange a repair."，的確，8 月 2 日是最後期限，但在那之前 Mary 還是會等房東派人來，故為最佳答案。

選項 (B) "Move into ... different apartment ...." 提到要「搬家」，這跟信件內容無關，故不選。

選項 (C) "... windows replaced at her own expense." 提到她要「自己花錢更換窗戶」，但信中並未提及此事，故不選。

選項 (D) 說要「訴諸法律」，但這是在 8 月 2 日之後的事，故不適當。

☑ 重點句型聚焦

我們藉以下這個句子來討論一下「現在完成進行式」。

- I have been living in the apartment at 152 Dolores Street for 14 years.

S + has / have + been + p.p. + for + 一段時間

此時態用以表示某個動作自「過去」到「目前」已「持續了一段時間」且「還在進行」。

請看下列例句：

1. I have been waiting here for the manager for an hour.
   我在此等候經理已經一個小時了。

2. He has been thinking about changing his career recently.
   他最近一直在考慮轉換工作跑道。

3. You have been working for three straight hours. Why don't you take a break?
   你已經連續工作了三小時。何不休息一下？

4. It has been raining all day.
   雨已經下了一整天。

5. I have been working at this company for more than three years.
   我在這間公司上班已經超過三年的時間了。

http://www.losfelizsubway.com/lostandfound

Los Feliz Subway Lost and Found

If you have inadvertently left your glasses, umbrella, handbag, or clothing on the subway, we may be able to help you. The Los Feliz Subway Lost and Found Office receives over 4,000 items every year, and we make every effort to reunite each item with its owner.

Please complete the form below, describing your property. If you have lost a high-value item such as a phone or computer, we may ask for additional proof of ownership.

Lost Property Inquiry Form

Describe the Property (color, make, model, material, unique characteristics, etc.)

When and Where Did You Travel?

Date: [   ]   Time: [   ]   From: [   ]   To: [   ]

How Can We Contact You?

Address: [   ]

Email: [   ]   Phone: [   ]

Submit

Claiming Your Property

Items may be picked up at our office at the Alameda St. Station or, for an additional fee, they may be returned to you by mail or courier. Our office is open Monday, Wednesday, and Friday from 2 pm to 10 pm and Thursday and Saturday from 8 am to 3 pm. If you have not heard from us within three weeks of filing a claim, then unfortunately it means we did not recover your item. Items are held for 30 days and then auctioned off with the proceeds donated to charity.

＊套色字部分請參考「詞彙註解」

【中譯】第 **168-171** 題請參照下面這個網頁。

---

http://www.losfelizsubway.com/lostandfound

Los Feliz 地鐵失物招領

若您不小心將您的眼鏡、雨傘、提包或衣物等物品留在車上了的話，我們可以協助您找回失物。Los Feliz 地鐵失物招領中心每年拾獲超過四千件物品，我們也盡我們所能地物歸原主。

請詳填下表，並描述您遺失物品的特徵。若您所遺失的物品價值較高，比如像手機、電腦等，我們可能會要求您出示證明。

失物協尋表

遺失物描述（顏色、樣式、型號、質料、特殊性能等）

乘車的時間與地點

日期：☐　　時間：☐　　上車站：☐　　下車站：☐

如何與您聯絡？

地址：☐

電郵：☐　　電話：☐

送出

領取遺失物

您可親洽我們位於 Alameda St. Station 的辦公室領取，或支付額外費用，我們可以郵寄或快遞的方式歸還給您。我們辦公室開放的時間為週一、週三和週五的下午兩點到晚上十點，週四和週六的早上八點到下午三點。若您在送出協尋要求後的三週內未收到回覆，那麼很不幸地這意味我們沒有找回您的物品。我們保留遺失物三十天，之後會將物品拍賣掉並將所得捐給慈善單位。

inadvertently [ˌɪnədˋvɝtn̩tlɪ] (*adv.*)
不慎地、非故意地

reunite [ˌrijuˋnaɪt] (*v.*) 使重聚、再結合

property [ˋprɑpətɪ] (*n.*) 資產、所有物

claim [klem] (*v.*) 要求、聲稱

auction [ˋɔkʃən] (*n.* / *v.*) 拍賣

donate [ˋdonet] (*v.*) 捐贈、捐出

charity [ˋtʃærətɪ] (*n.*) 慈善單位

---

168. Why would someone use this webpage?

    (A) To report an item found on the subway

    (B) To inquire about the operation of the subway

    (C) To claim an item left behind on the subway

    (D) To suggest a service be provided by the subway

答案 **C**

中譯 人們為什麼會使用到此網頁？

(A) 為了提報在地鐵內找到的物品

(B) 為了詢問有關地鐵的運作

(C) 為了認領在地鐵上遺失的物品

(D) 為了建議地鐵單位提供一項服務

解析

看到標題內的關鍵字 "lost and found" 和中間的表格，大概就可以猜出這是「找失物填的表格」。題目 "Why would someone use this webpage?" 問上網填此表格的「目的、原因」為何，答案當然是「為了找回失物」了。

選項 (A)　的 "... report ... item found ..." 是說要「回報所撿到的物品」，這與表格標題不符，故不選。

選項 (B)　的 "... inquire ... operation of the subway" 是說要「詢問地鐵的運作」，亦與表格標題不符，故不選。

選項 (C)　"... claim ... item left behind ..." 指「認領遺失的物品」，顯然為正確答案。

選項 (D)　提及 "... suggest a service ..."「建議一項服務」，與表格標題不相干，故不選。

169. **In what situation would the Lost and Found Office require additional information?**

(A) When a lost item has been unclaimed for 30 days

(B) When a lost item is especially valuable

(C) When a lost item has a distinguishing characteristic

(D) When a lost item is delivered to the wrong station

答案 B

中譯 失物招領中心在什麼狀況之下會要求提供額外資訊？

(A) 當失物過了三十天都無人招領時

(B) 當失物具有特別價值時

(C) 當失物具有明顯的獨特性時

(D) 當失物被送往錯誤的車站時

解析

本題問 "In what situation would the Lost and Found Office require additional information?"，則應找出該協尋失物的單位要求額外資訊的「時機、情況」。根據第二段第二句 "If you have lost a high-value item such as a phone or computer, we may ask for additional proof of ownership." 可知，如果遺失「較貴重的物品」時，會被要求多提供一些資料。

選項 (A) 的 "... item ... unclaimed for 30 days" 是說「失物超過三十天沒人認領」時，與文中描述不符，故不選。

選項 (B) 提到的 "... item ... especially valuable" 是指「失物具特別價值」，也就是「貴重物品」的意思，故為正解。

選項 (C) 提到的 "... item ... distinguishing characteristic" 是說「失物具有獨特性」，這點並未記載於網頁上，故不選。

選項 (D) "... item ... delivered to the wrong station" 指「失物被送錯車站」，這點並沒有在文中被提及，故亦不選。

170. When can lost property be picked up?

    (A) Monday mornings

    (B) Tuesday afternoons

    (C) Wednesday evenings

    (D) Weekend nights

答案 C

中譯 在什麼時間可以去領取失物？

(A) 週一早上

(B) 週二下午

(C) 週三晚上

(D) 週末晚上

解析

回答此題須留意文中提及可領取失物「時間」之處。由表格下方 Claiming Your Property 中的第二句 "Our office is open Monday, Wednesday, and Friday from 2 pm to 10 pm and Thursday and Saturday from 8 am to 3 pm" 可知，四個選項內只有 (C) Wednesday evenings 符合 "Wednesday from 2 pm to 10 pm" 的時間點，故為最佳答案。

171. What happens to items that are unclaimed after one month?

    (A) They are held until they are picked up.

    (B) They are delivered by mail or courier.

    (C) They are given to a charity for distribution.

    (D) They are sold to the highest bidder.

答案 D

中譯 超過一個月還沒有被領取的失物會被做何處置？

(A) 它們會被保留直到有人來領取為止。

(B) 它們會被郵寄或快遞出去。

(C) 它們會被捐到慈善機構以便分發出去。

(D) 它們會賣給出價最高的人。

解析

此題問的是 "What happens to items that are unclaimed after one month?"，焦點應放在找「一個月後沒人招領的失物會怎麼樣？」的資訊上。根據 Claiming Your Property 中的最後一句 "Items are held for 30 days and then auctioned off with the proceeds donated to charity." 可知，過了三十天後，物品會被拍賣，然後再將拍賣的收益捐給慈善機構。

選項 (A)　提及 "... held until ... picked up." 「會保留到有人認領為止」，這與文中描述不符，故不選。

選項 (B)　提到的 "... delivered by mail ...." 是說「會被郵件寄出」，這也與文中描述的不符，故不選。

選項 (C)　"... given to a charity ...." 指「捐給慈善單位」，但文中是說會「先拍賣，再將所得捐出」，不可誤選。

選項 (D)　"... sold to the highest bidder." 指「賣給出價最高的人」，也就是「拍賣」的意思，故為最佳答案。

重點句型聚焦

藉由文中的 "Items may be picked up at our office at the Alameda St. Station." 這個句子我們來複習一下被動式：

主詞（原受詞）+ be + p.p.（+ by 受詞〔原主詞〕）

比方說 "The secretary opens the window." 這句的被動式即為 "The window is opened by the secretary."。

請看下列例句：

1. He was elected mayor of the city.
   他被選為本市市長。

2. The project is supported by the government.
   此計劃是由政府支助。

Tips for Traveling with an Infant on a Plane

1 Try to select a flight that coincides with the infant's normal sleep schedule. A late-afternoon flight would be a good choice if your child regularly naps then. And taking a red eye flight in the early morning hours may not be convenient for you, but it would be worth it if your baby sleeps soundly during the entire flight.

2 Bring a sturdy yet compact stroller. Even if you won't be using it at your final destination, it will come in handy when navigating the airport, especially if you have a layover and have to change planes quickly.

3 Leave plenty of time for surprises before you leave for the airport. If you forget an essential item like a pacifier, extra diapers, or clothing, you will be able to purchase these items before you arrive at the airline check-in counter.

4 Always request the bulkhead seats. It gives you ample floor space for changing diapers and you won't have to worry about your infant kicking the seats in front of you. Window seats preferred because they are slightly darker and offer fewer distractions.

5 Due to changes in cabin air temperature and pressure, it is inevitable that your infant will shed tears. To make your infant comfortable you can remove or add a piece of clothing. To relieve pressure in the ears, walk your infant in the aisle.

6 It is a good idea to bring more items than you think you will need. Be sure to pack extra amounts of all your essential items, including formula, diapers, clothing, toys, and snacks.

＊套色字部分請參考「詞彙註解」

帶嬰兒搭飛機的小秘訣

1 試著選擇一個與嬰兒正常睡眠時間相符的班機。如果您的孩子規律性地會睡午覺,則午後的班次會是一個好選擇。而雖然搭乘夜班飛機對您可能不是很方便,但是若您的寶寶在整趟航程都熟睡著,那就會值得了。

2 準備一輛堅固又便於攜帶的嬰兒車。就算您在目的地不會用到它,但是當您在機場內行動時,嬰兒車會非常有用,特別是當您需要中途停留並得迅速地轉機時。

3 出發到機場前預留足夠的時間以防各種突發狀況。如果您忘記了必要物品,像是奶嘴、尿布或衣物時,您就可以在前往航空公司的報到櫃台前去添購這些東西。

4 務必要求坐在靠艙壁的最前端座位。那將能夠給您足夠的換尿布空間,而且您不需要擔心您的寶寶會踢到前方的座位。靠窗的座位通常比較合適,因為那裡燈光較為暗一點,相對地干擾因素會比較少些。

5 由於機艙內溫度與壓力的變化,您的寶寶一定會哭鬧。如果要讓您的寶寶感到舒適一點,您可以為他／她添加或移除衣物。如果要緩和耳內的壓力,您可以抱他／她在走道上走動一下。

6 攜帶比您預想的還要多的東西會是一個好主意。必要物品,包括了奶粉、尿布、衣物、玩具與零食等,一定要帶額外的量。

詞彙註解

infant [`ɪnfənt] (n.) 嬰兒	**layover** [`le͵ovə] (n.) 中途停留
nap [næp] (v.) 打盹、午睡	**pacifier** [`pæsə͵faɪə] (n.) 平定者、奶嘴
red eye flight 午夜班機	**bulkhead** [`bʌlk͵hɛd] (n.) 艙壁、隔板
soundly [`saundlɪ] (adv.) 酣然地、安穩地	**ample** [`æmpl] (adj.) 大量的、充裕的
sturdy [`stɜdɪ] (adj.) 堅固的、結實的	**pressure** [`prɛʃə] (n.) 壓力
compact [kəm`pækt] (adj.) 小巧的、簡潔的	**inevitable** [ɪn`ɛvətəbl] (adj.) 不可避免的
stroller [strolə] (n.) 嬰兒車	**shed** [ʃɛd] (v.) 流出
navigate [`nævə͵get] (v.)	**pack** [pæk] (v.) 打包、包裹
導航、駕駛（船、飛機等）	**formula** [`fɔrmjələ] (n.) 常規、配方、嬰兒奶粉

172. According to the article, when is the best time for infants to fly?

(A) During the infant's regular sleeping time

(B) During the late afternoon

(C) In the early morning hours

(D) When it is most convenient for the parents

答案 **A**

中譯 根據文章，什麼時候是帶嬰兒搭飛機的最佳時間？

(A) 嬰兒正常睡眠的時候

(B) 接近傍晚的時候

(C) 一大早的時候

(D) 父母最方便的時候

解析

題目問 "When is the best time for infants to fly?"，則應將焦點放在找出最適合嬰兒搭機的「時間」上。由第一點第一句 "Try to select a flight that coincides with the infant's normal sleep schedule." 可知，「與嬰兒正常睡眠時段相符」的時間乃最佳時間。

選項 (A) "During ... infant's regular sleeping time" 與文中的重點相符，故為最佳答案。

選項 (B) "... late afternoon" 提到的是「接近傍晚」的時間，並不正確。

選項 (C) "... early morning"「一大早」亦為錯誤。

選項 (D) "... convenient for ... parents" 指「父母方便」的時間，但文章中並未見此敘述，故亦不選。

173. What should you NOT do when traveling with a baby?

(A) Arrange to be seated next to a window

(B) Bring a stroller for use in the airport

(C) Carry extra quantities of items you normally use

(D) Arrive at the airport just before the check-in time

答案 D

中譯 帶嬰兒一起飛行時,「不」應該做什麼?

(A) 安排坐在靠窗的位置

(B) 攜帶一輛嬰兒車在機場內使用

(C) 攜帶比正常使用數量更多的物品

(D) 在報到時限的前一刻才抵達機場

解析

第二題問的是 "What should you NOT do when traveling with a baby?",必須要找出三個帶嬰兒搭機應做的事,以便排除掉一個「沒有」被提到的。根據 "Bring a sturdy yet compact stroller."、"Window seats preferred because they are slightly darker and offer fewer distractions." 和 "It is a good idea to bring more items than you think you will need. Be sure to pack extra amounts of all your essential items ....",可以得到以下配對:

選項 (A) Arrange to be seated next to a window = Window seats preferred,有被提到。

選項 (B) Bring a stroller for use in the airport = Bring a sturdy yet compact stroller,也有被提及。

選項 (C) Carry extra quantities of items you normally use = Be sure to pack extra amounts of essential items,也有被提到。

選項 (D) Arrive at the airport just before the check-in time 與文中的 "Leave plenty of time for surprises before you leave for the airport." 相悖,為正確答案。

174. Why should you request a bulkhead seat?

(A) It is the best place for your infant to nap.

(B) It is darker and offers fewer distractions.

(C) It gives parents space for changing diapers.

(D) It tends to be warmer and more comfortable.

答案 C

中譯 為什麼應要求坐在靠艙壁的座位？

(A) 那裡是讓嬰兒小睡最好的地方。

(B) 那裡比較暗，干擾因素比較少。

(C) 那裡讓父母有空間為嬰兒換尿布。

(D) 那裡通常比較溫暖舒適。

解析

這題問的是 "Why should you request a bulkhead seat?"，應試者應將焦點放在找出要求坐靠艙壁座位的「原因」。根據第四點提到的 "Always request the bulkhead seats. It gives you ample floor space for changing diapers ...." 可知，如此一來父母會有「較大的空間」幫小孩換尿布。

選項 (A) 提到 "... for ... infant to nap."，說是可以讓嬰兒睡午覺，這與文中描述的句子不符，故不選。

選項 (B) 提到 "... darker ... fewer distractions."，根據同一點最後一句，是坐 "window seats" 的好處才對，不可誤選。

選項 (C) "... gives ... space for changing diapers." 與文中的關鍵句一致，故為最佳答案。

選項 (D) "... warmer ... more comfortable."「較溫暖和舒適」，這一點並未記載於文中，故不選。

175. The word "inevitable" in point 5, line 1, is closest in meaning to

(A) avoidable

(B) certain

(C) unforeseeable

(D) unexpected

答案 B

中譯 第五點第一行的 "inevitable" 這個字意思最接近

(A) 可避免的

(B) 確定的

(C) 無法預見的

(D) 出乎意料的

最後一題問 "inevitable" 這個單字的涵義與哪個字最接近。"inevitable" 是「不可避免的」亦即「必然」之意，與 certain（確定的）意思最相近。正解爲選項 (B)。

重點句型聚焦

我們藉文章第 5 點 "Due to changes in cabin air temperature and pressure, it is inevitable that your infant will shed tears." 這句話來討論表示「因果關係」的句型：

Due to / Because of + 名詞受詞, S + V ....
= Because S + V, S + V ....

換句話說，原句可改寫成：Because air temperature and pressure in cabin change, it is inevitable that you infant will shed tears.。注意，due to 與 because of 爲「片語介系詞」，而 because 爲「從屬連接詞」。

請看下列例句：

1. Due to the heavy traffic, we were late to the meeting.
   = Because the traffic was heavy, we were late to the meeting.
   因為塞車，我們開會遲到。

2. Due to Tina's assistance, I was able to hand in the research paper in time.
   = Because Tina assisted me, I was able to hand in the research paper in time.
   由於蒂娜的協助，我才有辦法將研究報告準時交出去。

Measureable Media:
The Next Generation of Internet Marketing Services

If you have a website, Measurable Media can make it better. We use sophisticated software tools to track and measure how visitors engage with your website. We then use this information to increase the number of visitors to your site, the amount of time they spend there, your overall revenue, and—most dramatically—the revenue generated by each purchase.

Measurable Media carefully tests each page of your site by making hundreds of very small changes and then comparing the results. The final product is a webpage optimized for your customers—and your business. We know our methods are effective because we contract with neutral third-party auditors to evaluate our work. If we don't achieve measureable results, you receive our services free of charge. So, if you're wondering how to improve your online marketing efforts, ask yourself these questions:

Do you know how visitors find your site?
Do you know how they use it?
Do you know how to keep users comi ng back?
Do you know how to encourage them to spend more?

Measurable Media knows, and we're ready to help you serve your customers better.

Comparison of OrganiPure Skin Care Website Metrics Before and After Measurable Media Overhaul*

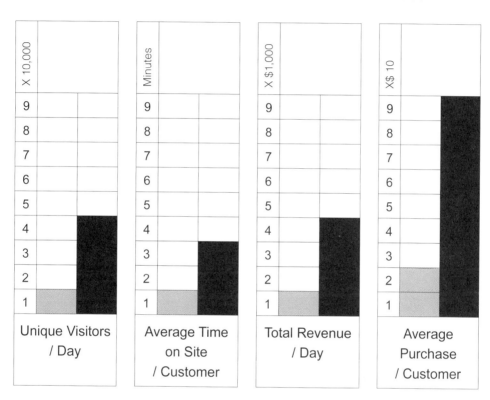

Before Measureable Media Site Overhaul
After Measureable Media Site Overhaul

* All figures verified by Princeton Metrics, an independent research and auditing firm.

＊套色字部分請參考「詞彙註解」

【中譯】第 **176-180** 題請參照下列廣告和圖表。

Measureable Media：
新一代的網路行銷服務

如果您擁有一個網站，Measurable Media 能夠將它變得更好。我們使用精密的工具軟體來追蹤判斷使用者如何接觸到您的網站。然後我們進一步使用此資訊來增加造訪該網站的人數、他們停留在網站上的時間、您整體的收益，而最顯著的是增加每筆消費的收益。

Measurable Media 藉由進行數百項極細微的修改並比較結果，來仔細地測試您網站上的每一個頁面。而最終的產品就是一個對於您的客戶與生意而言最優質的網站。我們知道這些方法有效因為我們與中立的第三方審核員簽約來評估我們的成品。如果我們無法達到明顯的成果，我們會將服務費用退還給您。所以，如果您正在思考如何增進您的線上行銷效果，請問問自己以下的問題：

　　您知道使用者如何找到您的網站嗎？
　　您知道他們是如何使用您的網站嗎？
　　您知道如何讓使用者持續回到您的網站嗎？
　　您知道要如何說服他們做更多的消費嗎？

Measurable Media 知道，而且我們已經準備好協助您更加完善地服務您的客戶。

OrganiPure 肌膚保養品網站數據在
Measurable Media 對網站執行重整之前後比較*

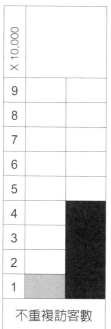

X 10,000

| 9 |
| 8 |
| 7 |
| 6 |
| 5 |
| 4 |
| 3 |
| 2 |
| 1 |

不重複訪客數
／日

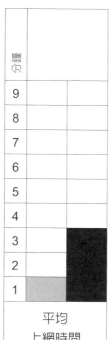

分鐘

| 9 |
| 8 |
| 7 |
| 6 |
| 5 |
| 4 |
| 3 |
| 2 |
| 1 |

平均
上網時間
／客戶

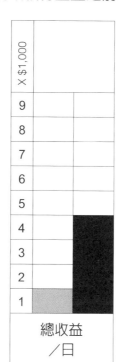

X $1,000

| 9 |
| 8 |
| 7 |
| 6 |
| 5 |
| 4 |
| 3 |
| 2 |
| 1 |

總收益
／日

X $10

| 9 |
| 8 |
| 7 |
| 6 |
| 5 |
| 4 |
| 3 |
| 2 |
| 1 |

平均消費
／客戶

	Measurable Media 對網站執行重整之前
	Measurable Media 對網站執行重整之後

*所有數據皆經由獨立研究與審查公司 Princeton Metrics 認證。

☞ 詞彙註解

sophisticated [sə`fɪstɪˌketɪd] (*adj.*)
精緻的、高度精細的

engage [ɪn`gedʒ] (*v.*) 接合、從事、參加

dramatically [drə`mætɪkḷɪ] (*adv.*)
戲劇化地、引人注目地

generate [`dʒɛnəˌret] (*v.*) 產生、造成、引起

optimize [`ɑptəˌmaɪz] (*v.*) 使完美、優化

neutral [`njutrəl] (*adj.*) 中立的

auditor [`ɔdɪtə] (*n.*) 審查員

wonder [`wʌndə] (*v.*) 想知道、瞭解

overhaul [ˌovə`hɔl] (*v.*)
大修、徹底改革、追趕上

176. **According to the advertisement, who would benefit most from using Measurable Media Services?**

(A) Internet users who visit a large number of websites daily

(B) Individuals who have created personal webpages

(C) Businesses that are interested in creating a homepage

(D) Companies that sell products directly from a website

答案 **D**

中譯 根據廣告，誰能夠從使用 Measurable Media 的服務獲得最大的利益？

(A) 每天造訪大量網站的網路使用者

(B) 已經架設個人網頁的人

(C) 有興趣建立網頁的公司

(D) 直接在網站上販售商品的公司

解析

本題問此公司所服務的「客戶對象」為何。根據首段內容提到的 "We use sophisticated software tools to track and measure how visitors engage with your website. We then use this information to increase the number of visitors to your site ..." 可知，此公司要協助的客戶是「有架設網站的企業客戶」。

選項 (A) "Internet users ..." 不對，因為文中提到的是要幫「有網頁的公司」做網頁優化，而非為「瀏覽網頁的人」，故不選。

選項 (B) "Individuals ... created personal webpages"「架設個人網頁的人」也跟廣告內容不相符，故不選。

選項 (C) 亦不適當。Measurable Media 並不是要幫公司「做網頁」，而是針對現有的網頁做優化，小心不要誤選。

選項 (D) "Companies that sell products directly from a website" 正確，因為只有「利用網站做生意」的公司才會需要瞭解網路流量等資訊，故可選為最佳答案。

177. Why does Measurable Media say their results are reliable?

(A) They are achieved with sophisticated software tools.

(B) They are calculated by neutral third parties.

(C) They are independently verified by auditors.

(D) They are guaranteed by a money-back offer.

答案 C

中譯 Measurable Media 為什麼說他們的成效數據是可靠的？

(A) 他們利用精密的工具軟體達到這些成果。

(B) 這些數據是由中立的第三方所計算出來的。

(C) 這些數據經過審查員獨立的查證。

(D) 這些數據有退款方案為保證。

解析

這題問的是 "What does Measurable Media say their results are reliable?"，應試者應將焦點放在找出 Measurable Media 公司提到測試結果準確是根據「什麼條件」。由第二段第三句 "We know our methods are effective because we contract with neutral third-party auditors to evaluate our work." 可知，這是因為有「公正中立的第三方審查人員」在評斷。

選項 (A) 的 "... achieved ... sophisticated ... tools." 是說靠「精密的軟體工具」，這點跟上述的關鍵句內容不符，故不選。

選項 (B) "... calculated by neutral third parties." 「由第三方計算出來」不對，因為第三方做的是「查驗」而非「計算」，故不選。

選項 (C) 提及 "... independently verified by auditors"，的確，數據是由公正的第三方 "auditors" 來查證，故為最佳答案。

選項 (D) "... guaranteed ... money-back offer." 提到有「退款保證」，但這跟題目所問無關，故不選。

178. **In the advertisement, the word "optimized" in paragraph 2, line 3, is closest in meaning to**

(A) enhanced

(B) personalized

(C) popularized

(D) programmed

答案 A

中譯 廣告第二段第三行的 "optimized" 這個字意思最接近

(A) 強化的

(B) 個人化的

(C) 普及化的

(D) 程式化的

解析

此題問的是 "optimized" 的意思最接近哪個字。"optimized" 是「最佳化、優化」之意，與 enhanced（強化的）的涵義最類似，故選項 (A) 為正解。

179. **According to the graphs, in what area is Measurable Media most effective?**

(A) Doubling the daily number of visitors

(B) Reducing the amount of time visitors spend on the website

(C) Maintaining the revenue generated by the website

(D) Increasing the average amount customers spend

答案 D

中譯 根據圖表，Measurable Media 在哪一個領域最為有效？

(A) 增加一倍的每日造訪者人數

(B) 減少造訪者停留在網站上的時間

(C) 維持網站所產生的營收

(D) 增加客戶消費的平均額度

解析

此題問 "According to the graphs, in what area is Measurable Media most effective?"，應試者須將焦點放在找出 Measurable Media 做得最好的項目。最後一個柱狀圖黑色部分明顯比其他高出許多，也就是經過 Measurable Media 做網站優化之後，客戶在

網上購物的平均金額提高了許多。選項 (D) Increasing the average amount customers spend 表達的正是這個意思，故爲最佳答案。

180. What information is NOT shown in the graphs?

(A) The number of visitors to the website
(B) The length of time visitors spend on the website
(C) The total cost per day of running the website
(D) The amount of money visitors spend on the website

答案 C

中譯 下列哪一項資訊「未」出現在圖表中？

(A) 每日造訪該網站的人數
(B) 造訪者花費在該網站上的時間長度
(C) 經營該網站的每日花費
(D) 造訪者花費在該網站上的金額

解析

最後一題問的是 "What information is NOT shown in the graphs?"，也就是得去找圖表中三個有提及的項目，再排除掉一個「沒被提到」的資訊。

選項 (A)　The number of visitors to the website = Unique Visitors / Day，有出現。

選項 (B)　The length of time visitors spend on the website = Average Time on Site / Customer，有出現。

選項 (D)　The amount of money visitors spend on the website = Average Purchase / Customer，也有出現。

選項 (C)　The total cost per day of running the website 則沒出現，故爲正確答案。

📝 重點句型聚焦

第一篇文章中連續出現了數個問句：“Do you know how visitors find your site?”、“Do you know how they use it?” 等。“Do you know ...?” 是「你知道⋯⋯嗎？」之意，在此讓我們討論幾個客氣的問句句型：

- **Would you mind V-ing? = Do you mind V-ing?**（你介意⋯⋯嗎？）
- **Will you + 原形 V ...? = Would you + 原形 V ...?**（你願意⋯⋯嗎？）
- **Can I / Could I / May I + 原形 V ...?**（我可以⋯⋯嗎？）

請看下列例句：

1. Would you mind opening the window for me?

   = Do you mind opening the windows for me?

   你介意幫我開個窗戶嗎？

2. Will you go over these files with me please?

   = Would you go over these files with me please?

   = Can you go over these files with me please?

   = Could you go over these files with me please?

   你願意跟我一起看一下這些檔案嗎？

3. Can I borrow your stapler for a second?

   = Could I borrow your stapler for a second?

   = May I borrow your stapler for a second?

   可以借你的訂書機用一下嗎？

Questions 181-185 refer to the following memo and email.

To: All Staff
From: Laura Bonn, Principal
Date: May 18
Re: Construction

As many of you already know, Banner Junior High School is scheduled to undergo major renovations in the coming months. Most of the construction will be undertaken during the summer, but due to the extent of work, it will not be completed by the time classes resume in September. To minimize disruption to classes and other school activities, it is important that students, faculty, and staff are aware of the following construction schedule.

Building	Under Construction
South Classroom Building	June 15–September 1
North Classroom Building	July 10–October 12
Library and Media Center	October 20–December 1
Gymnasium	June 1–July 31
Administration Building	September 10–December 10

As you can see, only the South Classroom Building and Gymnasium will be complete by September 15, the first day of school. When school resumes, classes and activities that normally take place in buildings still under construction will unfortunately either be cancelled, postponed, or moved temporarily into the South Classroom Building or the Gymnasium. I will inform all staff of these necessary changes before June 1. I invite teachers affected by the construction to contact me with any questions or particular concerns. I will do my best to accommodate everyone's needs.

To:	Laura Bonn
From:	Frederick Chen
Subject:	Renovation schedule

Dear Laura,

I am very excited about the upcoming renovations, but I am also concerned that the construction might adversely affect auditions and rehearsals for the school band. Band tryouts are always held during the first week of the school year so the musicians have enough time to prepare for the Banner Autumn Festival. Since the music rooms won't be available until October 12, and because rehearsals can easily disturb classes, I would like to suggest that you reserve time for the band in the gym. If possible, I'd like to schedule auditions September 17–19 (Wednesday through Friday) from 3:15 to 4:30.

I understand that basketball and volleyball teams will also hold tryouts in the gym that week. I hope we can all work together to find a solution. Please let me know how I can help.

Best regards,
Fred

＊套色字部分請參考「詞彙註解」

【中譯】第 181-185 題請參照下列備忘錄和電子郵件。

收件人：全體員工

寄件人：Laura Bonn 校長

日期：5 月 18 日

關於：整修工程

誠如各位可能已經得知的，Banner 國中在接下來幾個月計劃要進行大規模的整修工程。大部分的工程會於暑假中進行，但是由於工程規模龐大，將無法在九月學期開始之前完成。為了將此工程對上課和其他學校活動的干擾降至最低，所有學生、教師和員工必須知道以下的施工時間表。

建築	施工期間
南教學大樓	6 月 15 日～9 月 1 日
北教學大樓	7 月 10 日～10 月 12 日
圖書館和媒體中心	10 月 20 日～12 月 1 日
體育館	6 月 1 日～7 月 31 日
行政大樓	9 月 10 日～12 月 10 日

如各位所見，在 9 月 15 日開學的第一天只會有南教學大樓和體育館完成施工。當學期再度開始時，平時於施工大樓內舉行的課程和活動很遺憾地將會被取消、延期，或暫時移至南教學大樓或體育館。我會在 6 月 1 日前向所有教職員告知必要的改變。課程受到施工影響的教師若有任何問題或特別的考量都可以和我聯絡。我將會盡我所能滿足所有人的需求。

收件人：	Laura Bonn
寄件人：	Frederick Chen
主　旨：	翻新工程時間表

親愛的 Laura：

我對於即將進行的更新工程感到非常興奮，但是同時也擔心這些工程會嚴重影響學校樂團的面試和排練。樂團選拔一直都是在新學年的第一週舉行，以便讓所有樂手都能夠有充分的時間為 Banner 秋季慶典做準備。由於音樂教室在 10 月 1 日之前都無法使用，而且因為樂團排演很容易影響其他班級上課，所以我建議您為樂團保留使用體育館的時間。如果可以的話，我希望能夠將面試安排在 9 月 17 日至 19 日（星期三至星期五）從 3:15 至 4:30。

我知道籃球隊和排球隊同時也會在當週舉辦選拔。我希望我們大家可以協力找出一個解決的方案。請讓我知道我如何可以幫得上忙。

Fred
敬上

☞ 詞彙註解

principal [ˋprɪnsəpl] (n.) 校長
undergo [ˌʌndɚˋgo] (v.) 經歷、承受
renovation [ˌrɛnəˋveʃən] (n.) 更新、整修
extent [ɪkˋstɛnt] (n.) 程度、範圍
resume [rɪˋzjum] (v.) 重新開始
minimize [ˋmɪnəˌmaɪz] (v.) 最小化、減至最小程度
disruption [dɪsˋrʌpʃən] (n.) 打擾、中斷、瓦解

temporarily [ˋtɛmpəˌrɛrəlɪ] (adv.) 暫時地、臨時地
particular [pɚˋtɪkjələ] (adj.) 特別的、特有的
accommodate [əˋkɑməˌdet] (v.)
把……考慮進去、滿足……的需要
audition [ɔˋdɪʃən] (n. / v.) 試唱、試演
rehearsal [rɪˋhɜsl] (n.) 排演、預演
tryout [ˋtraɪˌaut] (n.) 選拔、試用

181. Why did Laura Bonn write the memo?

(A) To inform staff of band auditions

(B) To announce the opening of a new building

(C) To seek suggestions about construction

(D) To ensure staff know about renovations

答案 D

中譯 Laura Bonn 為什麼撰寫這份備忘錄？

(A) 為了通知教職員有關樂團面試的消息

(B) 為了宣佈一棟新大樓的開幕

(C) 為了尋求有關施工工程的建議

(D)為了確保教職員都知道有關更新工程的事

解析

大概地掃瞄一下兩篇文章，得知第一篇是 Laura Bonn 校長宣達校舍整修消息的備忘錄，而第二篇則是有老師反應擔心樂團練習會受影響。本題 "Why did Laura Bonn write the memo?" 問備忘錄的「主旨」為何。根據首句 "As many of you already know, Banner Junior High School is scheduled to undergo major renovations in the coming months." 即可知，「校長在跟教職員宣佈校舍整修的相關事宜」。

選項 (A) "... inform ... band auditions" 是說要通知有關「樂團面試」的事，與主旨不符，故不選。

選項 (B) 的 "... announce ... opening ... new building" 表示要宣佈「新大樓的啟用」，這點並沒有在備忘錄中被提及，故不選。

選項 (C) 的 "... seek suggestions ... construction" 指「尋求施工工程之建議」，也與文章內容不相干，故不選。

選項 (D) 提到 "... ensure staff know about renovations"「確保教職員知道更新工程之事」，的確，此備忘錄的目的是要告知大家整修的事，故為最佳答案。

182. What does Laura Bonn hope to limit?

(A) The time allowed for construction

(B) The disruption of classes at Banning Jr. High

(C) The space required for sporting events

(D) The number of activities at the school

答案 B

中譯 Laura Bonn 希望能夠降低什麼？

(A) 施工的時間

(B) 對 Banning 國中上課的干擾

(C) 體育活動所需的空間

(D) 學校活動的數量

解析

此題 "What does Laura Bonn hope to limit?" 問的是 Laura Bonn 想儘量避免的事為何。由第一段第三句 "To minimize disruption to classes and other school activities, it is important that students, faculty, and staff are aware of the following construction schedule." 可知，校長希望可以將「干擾減低到最小」。

選項 (A) 提到的 "... time allowed for construction" 指「工程施工時間」，這一點在文中並沒提到，故不選。

選項 (B) 提到 "... disruption of classes ..."「上課的干擾」，的確，這正是校長 Laura Bonn 希望做到的，故為最佳答案。

選項 (C) 的 "... space ... for sporting events" 是說要減少「體育活動的空間」，這與文中所提不符，故不選。

選項 (D) 的 "... number of activities ..." 是說要減少「學校活動的數量」，這也與文中提到的不符，故亦不選。

183. In which building are the music rooms located?

(A) The South Classroom Building

(B) The North Classroom Building

(C) The Library and Media Center

(D) The Gymnasium

答案 B

中譯 音樂教室位於哪一棟建築？

(A) 南教學大樓

(B) 北教學大樓

(C) 圖書館和媒體中心

(D) 體育館

解析

本題問 "In which building are the music rooms located?",要找出音樂教室位於「哪一棟樓」。根據第二篇 Frederick Chen 所寫的信第一段第三句的 "Since the music rooms won't be available until October 12 ....",再對照備忘錄中的表格即可知,音樂教室就在 "The North Classroom Building",故 (B) 為正確答案。其他選項的樓名和整修的時間都與 Chen 信中提到的「10 月 12 日」不相符,故皆不選。

184. What does Frederick Chen recommend?

      (A) Postponing the renovation

      (B) Rescheduling some classes

      (C) Contacting the principal directly

      (D) Moving the location of an activity

答案 D

中譯 Frederick Chen 建議什麼?

(A) 延後更新工程

(B) 重新安排某些課程的時間

(C) 直接聯絡校長

(D) 移動某活動的地點

解析

此題問的是 "What does Frederick Chen recommend?",必須找出 Chen 所「建議的事項」。根據信件第一段第三句 "Since the music rooms won't be available until October 12, and because rehearsals can easily disturb classes, I would like to suggest that you reserve time for the band in the gym." 可知,Chen 建議將樂團練習移到體育館去。

選項 (A)   "Postponing ... renovation"「延後更新工程」,但是文中並沒有提到這一點,故不選。

選項 (B)   "Rescheduling ... classes"「重新安排課程時間」也沒有在文中被提及,故不選。

選項 (C)   的 "Contacting ... principal ..." 指「跟校長聯絡」,這也不是 Chen 的建議事項,故亦不選。

選項 (D)   提到 "Moving ... location of ... activity"「移動活動地點」,的確,Chen 是建議將「樂團練習移到體育館」,故為最佳答案。

185. In the email, the word "adversely" in paragraph 1, line 2, is closest in meaning to

(A) negatively

(B) necessarily

(C) significantly

(D) surprisingly

答案 A

中譯 電子郵件第一段第二行的 "adversely" 這個字意思最接近

(A) 負面地

(B) 必要地

(C) 顯著地

(D) 令人驚訝地

解析

本題問 "adversely" 的意思最接近哪個字。"adversely" 是「不利地」之意，與 negatively （負面地）的涵義最類似，故選項 (A) 為最佳答案。

📝 重點句型聚焦

我們藉由 "I would like to suggest that you reserve time for the band in the gym." 這個句子來討論一下省略助動詞 should 的句型：

S + 建議、要求、規定、命令、堅持、必須 + that + S + (should) + 原形 V

主詞之後若接表示「建議、要求」等意的動詞或表「必須、必要」之意的形容詞時，其後的 that 子句中通常將 "should" 省略，也就是使用原形動詞。

以下列出常用於此句型的字詞：

- 建議：suggest, propose, recommend, urge, advise
- 要求：ask, demand, desire, require, request
- 規定：rule, regulate
- 命令：order, command
- 堅持：insist
- 必須：necessary (adj.), essential (adj.), urgent (adj.)

請看下列例句：

1. The boss suggested that we (should) propose a solution to this problem by this Friday.

   老闆建議我們在本週五之前要對此問題提出解決方案。

2. Since the manager won't be back until 2 pm, his assistant suggests that the meeting (should) be postponed.

   因為經理要到下午兩點之後才會回來，他的助理建議將會議延後。

3. It is essential that you (should) know what your goals are.

   知道你自己的目標是什麼是絕對必要的。

College of Roman

⤳ ⤳ Put Music in Your Life ⤳ ⤳

Classical, Contemporary and Jazz
Instrumental and Vocal Ensembles
Lesson for voice and all instruments
Group classes for guitar, piano and voice

Feel the Beat of Music

Dr. Jennifer Adams	Voice Studies	557-483-5838
Mr. George Jefferson	Piano Studies	557-483-5726
Dr. John Lincoln	Drum Studies	557-483-2794
Dr. Adam Coles	Saxophone Studies	557-483-1769
Ms. Jennifer Wolf	General information on music classes	557-483-1769

Visit our official website at www.roman-college.com for more information. To apply, please call Mr. Jack Phil at 557-483-7722 or email: jack.p@roman-college.com

To:	Jack Phil [jack.p@roman-college.com]
From:	Linda Kim [linda.k@mail.com]
Subject:	Application questions please

Dear Mr. Phil,

This is to request more information about your music courses at College of Roman. I'm really interested in your Jazz course and I am anxious to apply for it for the academic year 2018/2019.

First, I would like to inquire about qualifications. I've taken keyboard skills, music and science, and other related courses in a local college in Korea. I would be grateful if you could indicate the academic requirements for an international student like me.

Next, as this will be the first time I'll live away from my hometown in Korea, accommodation is rather important to me. I've decided to rent my own place off-campus, so I wonder if you could please recommend some nearby and affordable apartments for me to choose from.

Thank you in advance for your attention to my requests. I look forward to receiving your response.

Sincerely,

Linda Kim

To:	Linda Kim [linda.k@mail.com]
From:	Jack Phil [jack.p@roman-college.com]
Subject:	Re: Application questions please

Dear Ms. Kim,

Thank you for your interest in the music courses at College of Roman. For more information on qualifications, please call 557-483-1769 and speak directly to the person responsible. —[1]—.

As for apartments in the Roman area, we do have nice apartments within walking distance to the College. You may want to contact each apartment office for current pricing and availability. Please note that when renting an apartment off-campus, you as a renter should be responsible for utilities such as electricity. It's the renter's responsibility to contact these apartments for more information on utilities, amenities, fees and refunds. —[2]—.

The Fox Garden
5838 Cedar Drive
Roman City, WA 58379
Telephone: 557-372-4828
Email: info@fox-garden.com
Price range: $200-$400 per month
Size: one / two-bedroom models available, one bath
Distance from the College of Roman: 1 km —[3]—.

The City View Apartments
2525 Spring Road
Roman City, WA 58379
Telephone: 557-367-2827
Email: super@city-view.com
Price range: $250-$500 per month
Size: one / two / three-bedroom models
Distance from College of Roman: 2.5 km

Should you have further questions, please feel free to contact me. —[4]—.

Best regards,

Jack Phil

*套色字部分請參考「詞彙註解」

【中譯】第 186-190 題請參照下列廣告和電子郵件。

羅 門 學 院

〜〜 〜〜 把音樂置入你的生活中 〜〜 〜〜

古典、當代和爵士樂

器樂合奏和聲樂合唱

聲樂和所有樂器課程

吉他、鋼琴和聲樂團體班

感受音樂的節奏

Jennifer Adams 博士	聲樂課程	557-483-5838
George Jefferson 先生	鋼琴課程	557-483-5726
John Lincoln 博士	鼓樂課程	557-483-2794
Adam Coles 博士	薩克斯風課程	557-483-1769
Jennifer Wolf 小姐	音樂課程之一般資訊	557-483-1769

取得更多相關資訊，請造訪我們的官方網站：www.roman-college.com。如欲申請上課，請致電 Jack Phil 先生 557-483-7722，或寄電子郵件到：jack.p@roman-college.com

收件人：	Jack Phil [jack.p@roman-college.com]
寄件人：	Linda Kim [linda.k@mail.com]
主 旨：	申請上課相關問題

親愛的 Phil 先生您好：

我想進一步瞭解更多關於羅門學院音樂課程的訊息。我對貴校開的爵士課很感興趣，我非常想申請 2018/2019 學年度的課程。

首先，我想詢問有關入學的資格。我在韓國當地的一所大學學習了鍵盤技巧、音樂和科學，以及其他相關課程。希望您能告知我針對國際學生的學術要求，不勝感激。

再者，因為這將是我第一次離開韓國家鄉，住宿對我來說是相當重要的。我已經決定在校外租屋，所以我想知道您能否推薦一些接近學校又價格合理的公寓供我選擇？

感謝您的協助。期待收到您的回覆。

Linda Kim
敬上

收件人：	Linda Kim [linda.k@mail.com]
寄件人：	Jack Phil [jack.p@roman-college.com]
主　旨：	回覆：申請上課相關問題

Kim 小姐您好，

感謝您對羅門大學音樂課程的興趣。有關申請資格的更多資訊，請致電 557-483-1769 並直接與負責人聯繫。─[1]─。

至於在羅門地區的公寓，我們確實有很不錯的公寓且僅須步行就可抵達學校。您可能需要自行聯繫各公寓的辦公室，以瞭解目前的租金和是否有空房。請注意，在校外租屋時，承租人應自行負擔水電費用。承租人有責任自行聯繫這些公寓負責人，以取得更多關於水電費、設施、租金和退款的資訊。─[2]─。

福克斯花園
Cedar 路 5838 號

(58379) Washington 州 Roman 市

電話：557-372-4828

電子郵件：info@fox-garden.com

價格範圍：每月 $200 - $400

大小：一／兩間臥室、一間浴室的屋型

距離羅門學院：1 公里—[3]—。

城市景觀公寓

Spring 路 2525 號

(58379) Washington 州 Roman 市

電話：557-367-2827

電子郵件：super@city-view.com

價格範圍：每月 $250 - $500

大小：一／二／三房型式

距離羅門學院：2.5 公里

如果您還有其他問題，請隨時與我聯繫。—[4]—。

祝好，

Jack Phil

詞彙註解

classical [ˈklæsɪkl̩] (*adj.*) 古典的

contemporary [kənˈtɛmpəˌrɛrɪ] (*adj.*) 當代的

instrumental [ˌɪnstrəˈmɛntl̩] (*adj.*) 樂器的

vocal [ˈvokl̩] (*adj.*) 嗓音的

ensemble [ɑnˈsɑmbl̩] (*n.*) 歌舞團、劇團

anxious [ˈæŋkʃəs] (*adj.*) 急切的

academic [ˌækəˈdɛmɪk] (*adj.*) 學校的、大學的

qualification [ˌkwɑləfəˈkeʃən] (*n.*) 資格

grateful [ˈgretfəl] (*adj.*) 感謝的

indicate [ˈɪndəˌket] (*v.*) 指出、說明

accommodation [əˌkɑməˈdeʃən] (*n.*) 住宿

affordable [əˈfɔrdəbl̩] (*adj.*) 負擔得起的

attention [əˈtɛnʃən] (*n.*) 注意力

response [rɪˈspɑns] (*n.*) 回應

amenity [əˈmɛnətɪ] (*n.*) 設備、設施

refund [ˈriˌfʌnd] (*n.*) 退款

186. **In the advertisement, what does the table list?**

    (A) Student names

    (B) Class professors and their numbers

    (C) Tuition fees

    (D) Class schedules

答案 B

中譯 廣告中的表格所列出的是什麼訊息？

(A) 學生名字

(B) 課程教授和電話

(C) 學費金額

(D) 課程時間

解析

第一題問首篇文章內的表格所列何事？根據表格內容可看出，是教授的名字與電話號碼。

選項 (A)　為「學生姓名」，但表格內列的稱謂是 "Dr."，並非學生。

選項 (B)　表格所列的確是教授名與電話號碼沒錯，所以是正確答案。

選項 (C)　為「學費」，但這些數字是電話號碼，並非學費金額，故不選。

選項 (D)　為「課程時間」，但這些數字也並非日期，故不選。

187. **What is NOT true about Linda Kim?**

    (A) She'd like to attend some music classes.

    (B) She knows how to play keyboards.

    (C) She prefers to live on campus.

    (D) She is a Korean.

答案 C

中譯 關於 Linda Kim 何者為「非」？

(A) 她想要上一些音樂課程。

(B) 她會彈鍵盤。

(C) 她想要住校。

(D) 她是韓國人。

此題 "What is NOT true about Linda Kim?" 問的是關於 Linda Kim 的「錯誤」描述。由第二篇文章中可看出 Linda Kim 想上音樂課程,且在韓國已上過鍵盤技巧課,以及得知她來自韓國,而她想詢問「在校外租屋」的資訊。

選項 (A) She'd like to attend some music classes. 在文中有提到,與 "I'm really interested in your Jazz course." 一句相符。

選項 (B) She knows how to play keyboards. 有提到,與 "I've taken keyboard skills ... in Korea." 相符。

選項 (C) She prefers to live on campus. 與文中此句 "I've decided to rent my own place off-campus ..." 意思相左,故選為答案。

選項 (D) She is a Korean. 在文中有被提及,與此句 "I'll live away from my hometown in Korea ..." 意思相符。

188. Who does Jack Phil suggest Linda Kim call for class information?

(A) John Lincoln

(B) Jennifer Wolf

(C) George Jefferson

(D) Adam Coles

【答案】 **B**

【中譯】 Jack Phil 建議 Linda Kim 打電話給誰以詢問課程資訊?

(A) John Lincoln

(B) Jennifer Wolf

(C) George Jefferson

(D) Adam Coles

【解析】

此題問的是 Jack 建議 Linda 要問課程訊息的話,應致電給誰?根據第三封電子郵件內的此關鍵句 "For more information on qualifications, please call 557-483-1769 and speak directly to the person responsible.",再對照首篇文章中的表格內容,便可得知應直接聯繫負責人 Jennifer Wolf,故選項 (B) 為正解。

189. Which apartment would Linda Kim probably prefer?

(A) The City View Apartments

(B) Roman Houses

(C) Sunny Palace

(D) The Fox Garden

答案 D

中譯 Linda Kim 可能會比較想租哪間公寓？

(A) 城市景觀公寓

(B) 羅門住宅

(C) 陽光皇宮

(D) 福克斯花園

解析

本題問 Linda 可能比較想要租哪間公寓？根據 Linda 的需求 "I wonder if you could please recommend some nearby and affordable apartments for me to choose from."，她是想要「離學校近、便宜一點」的租屋，再對照第三篇文章 Jack 的回信內所列出的兩個租屋資訊可看出，離學校比較近、價格又比較低的應是 "The Fox Garden" 才對，故選 (D) 為最佳答案。

190. In which of the position marked [1], [2], [3], and [4] does the following sentence best belong?

"Here are two apartments that may be better to suit your needs."

(A) [1]   (B) [2]   (C) [3]   (D) [4]

答案 B

中譯 下面這個句子插入文中標示的 [1]、[2]、[3]、[4] 四處當中的何處最符合文意？

「此為兩個可能比較符合你需求的公寓資訊。」

(A) [1]   (B) [2]   (C) [3]   (D) [4]

解析 ★ 新題型「插入句題」

本題須將 "Here are two apartments that may be better to suit your needs." 安插於文中最通順的位置。此句提及「兩個符合你需求的選擇」，由此便可判斷其後應接續列出「該二選項」的細部內容較為合理，故本題選 (B)。

☑ 重點句型聚焦

在第二篇文章內有一個禮貌性要求的句型，非常值得學起來於日常生活中使用："I would be grateful if you could indicate the academic requirements for an international student like me."。此句型便是：

I would be grateful if you could [do something].

用以表示「麻煩你幫我〔做某事〕，真的非常感謝」之意。

請看下列例句：

1. I would be grateful if you could complete this questionnaire for me.
   若你可以幫我填此問卷，我真的非常感激。

2. I would be grateful if you could review my presentation and give me some feedback.
   若你可以幫我看一下簡報並給我意見，我會很感謝。

Wholesome Foods

18732 Becker St., Racine, WI 53401

Marcie Stephenson
Marcie's Downhome Grill
215 Lakeside Dr.
Madison, WI 53701

July 20

Dear Ms. Stephenson,

Today we received your canceled invoice for an order of cheese, crackers, and nuts. I understand that you were not satisfied with your order, but according to the terms of the purchase agreement that you signed, you are still liable for the full amount. Also, because payment was due on July 16, you have incurred a 10% late payment fee. I have added this fee to your original charge of $139.25 and issued a new invoice for $153.18, which I have enclosed. If we do not receive payment by August 5, we will consider you to be in default and will refer the matter to a collection agency.

I would like to remind you that our return policy, which is stated in the purchase agreement, is both clear and generous. It allows you to return by regular mail any purchase for any reason within seven days for a full refund, as long as it is in the original packaging. You received shipment on July 7, nearly two weeks ago, and did not return the purchase.

Your prompt attention to this matter is appreciated.

Regards,

Alice Worley

Alice Worley
Account Manager, Wholesome Foods

Bill to:
Marcie Stephenson
Marcie's Downhome Grill
215 Lakeside Dr.
Madison, WI 53701

INVOICE

Date: June 20
Invoice#: 836382
Customer: Marcie's Downhome Grill

Description	Qty	Unit Price	Price
Cheese	1	$25	$50
Crakers	2	$22.63	$45.26
Nuts	2	$21.99	$43.98
		Sub-total	$139.25
		Late payment fee	$13.93
		Total	$153.18

To:	Alice Worley [aw@wholesomefoods.com]
From:	Marcie Stephenson [chef@DownhomeGrill.com]
Subject:	Canceled Invoice
Attachment:	𝒫 cheese.jpg (1.2MB); 𝒫 crackers.jpg (599KB); 𝒫 nuts.jpg (616KB)

Dear Alice,

I ordered fresh cheese, whole crackers, and edible nuts. What I received was spoiled cheese, cracker crumbs, and nuts that had spilled out of their plastic containers and all over the box. None of these were safe to eat, and I believe it is quite reasonable to refuse to pay for such products. I am especially displeased that you tried to ask me to pay more for them.

You referenced the purchase agreement I signed, but because you did not provide products that I could use, I do not believe the agreement is binding. I did not return the purchase out of concern for our Wisconsin postal carriers, who no doubt have rules against transporting potentially dangerous packages of spoiled and malodorous food. In any event, I could not return the order in the original packaging because much of the original packaging was not intact when I received it. I suspect that the shipping company is to blame. It is likely that the package was not refrigerated during shipment (hence the spoiled cheese) and not treated gently (hence the crushed crackers and broken nut containers).

I should note that immediately after I realized there was a problem I took several photographs of the package, which I have attached. You can see for yourself what your products looked like when they arrived at my restaurant. You are welcome to use the photos in negotiations with your shipping company, but please do not continue to ask me for payment.

Sincerely,

Marcie Stephenson
Head Chef and Owner, Marcie's Downhome Grill

＊套色字部分請參考「詞彙註解」

【中譯】第 191-195 題請參照下列信件、文件和電子郵件。

Wholesome 食品

(53401) Wisconsin 州 Racine 市 Becker 街 18732 號

Marcie Stephenson
Marcie's 家常燒烤
Lakeside 路 215 號
(53701) Wisconsin 州 Madison 市

7 月 20 日

親愛的 Stephenson 小姐：

我們於今日收到您欲取消乳酪、蘇打餅與堅果訂單的帳單。我瞭解您對於您訂的東西感到不滿意，但是根據您簽下的購買同意書裡的條款，您仍然必須支付全額的款項。同時，由於該筆款項的支付期限為 7 月 16 日，您將需要額外支付 10% 的滯納金。我已經將此筆金額加入原始金額的 139.25 美元之中，並重新開出了一張金額 153.18 美元的帳單附於本信內。如果我們於 8 月 5 日前仍然沒有收到款項的話，我們將認定您不履行合約，並將尋找討債公司協助解決。

請容我再次提醒您，本公司載明於購買同意書裡的退貨政策是非常清楚且合理的。依退貨規定您在購買日之後的七天之內，只要以原始包裝將購買之商品以郵寄方式退回本公司，就可以獲得全額的退款。您於 7 月 7 日，幾乎是兩個禮拜之前，收到貨品，但是您並沒有將貨品退回本公司。

如果您能儘快處理這件事，我們將非常感激。

祝好，

Alice Worley

Alice Worley
Wholesome 食品公司客戶經理

帳單寄至：

Marcie Stephenson

Marcie's 家常燒烤

Lakeside 路 215 號

（53701）Wisconsin 州 Madison 市

發 票

日期：6 月 20 日

發票號碼：836382

客戶：Marcie's 家常燒烤

產品描述	數量	單價	價格
起司	1	$25	$50
蘇打餅	2	$22.63	$45.26
堅果	2	$21.99	$43.98
		小計	$139.25
		滯納金	$13.93
		總計	$153.18

收件人：	Alice Worley [aw@wholesomefoods.com]
寄件人：	Marcie Stephenson [chef@DownhomeGrill.com]
主　旨：	取消的帳單
附　件：	𝒪cheese.jpg (1.2MB); 𝒪crackers.jpg (599KB); 𝒪nuts.jpg (616KB)

親愛的 Alice：

我當初訂購的是新鮮的乳酪、完整的蘇打餅與可食用的堅果，而我實際收到的卻是壞掉的乳酪、蘇打餅碎屑和從塑膠容器中灑落在箱子四處的堅果。這些沒有一個是可以安全食用的，而我認為拒絕支付這些產品的費用是非常合理的。你居然想要求我為這些產品支付更多款項，我覺得非常地不高興。

你提到了我簽下的購買同意書，但是因為你們並沒有提供我能夠使用的產品，所以我不認為那份同意書具有效力。我之所以沒有將產品退回，是因為我擔心 Wisconsin 州的郵差們，他們一定都必須遵守不得運輸內含腐壞惡臭食物之具有危險性包裹的相關規定。不管怎麼說，由於原始包裹送達時已經非常不完整，我根本無法將它以原始包裝寄送回去。我覺得或許貨運公司應該負責。有可能該包裹在運送途中根本沒有經冷藏（因此乳酪才會壞掉），也沒有被輕輕地搬運（因此蘇打餅才會碎掉，而堅果也都從包裝裡掉了出來）。

我應該提一下，在我一發現有問題時，我就拍了幾張包裹的照片，而我已經把這些照片附在本郵件裡。你可以自己看看你們的產品抵達我的餐館時是什麼樣貌。歡迎你在與貨運公司協商時使用那些照片，但是請別再繼續要求我支付款項。

Marcie Stephenson
Marcie's 家常燒烤主廚兼店主
謹上

wholesome [`holsəm] (*adj.*) 有益健康的、合乎衛生的	**crumb** [krʌm] (*n.*) 碎屑
cracker [`krækə] (*n.*) 薄脆的蘇打餅	**spill** [spɪl] (*v.*) 溢出
liable [`laɪəbl] (*adj.*) 有義務的	**refuse** [rɪ`fjuz] (*v.*) 拒絕
incur [ɪn`kɜ] (*v.*) 招致、引來	**displeased** [dɪs`plizd] (*adj.*) 不高興的
default [dɪ`fɔlt] (*n.*) 拖欠、違約	**reference** [`rɛfərəns] (*v.*) 提及、涉及
collection agency 討債公司	**binding** [`baɪndɪŋ] (*adj.*) 有約束力的
description [dɪ`skrɪpʃən] (*n.*) 描述	**malodorous** [mæl`odərəs] (*adj.*) 有惡臭的
Qty = quantity [`kwɑntətɪ] (*n.*) 數量	**suspect** [sə`spɛkt] (*v.*) 懷疑、覺得可疑
spoil [spɔɪl] (*v.*) (食物) 腐敗、變壞	**blame** [blem] (*v.*) 指責、為過失負責
	refrigerated [rɪ`frɪdʒəˌretɪd] (*adj.*) 冷藏的

191. Why did Alice Worley write the letter?

(A) To ask Marcie Stephenson for additional information

(B) To apologize to Marcie Stephenson for poor service

(C) To request payment for an outstanding amount

(D) To inform Marcie Stephenson of a new payment plan

答案 **C**

中譯 Alice Worley 為什麼撰寫這封信？

(A) 為了要求 Marcie Stephenson 提供進一步的資訊

(B) 為不良的服務向 Marcie Stephenson 表達歉意

(C) 為了要求支付一筆未付清的款項

(D) 為了通知 Marcie Stephenson 有一種新的付款方式

解析

先將三篇文章大致掃瞄一遍，得知第一篇是一張催客戶繳款的信，第二篇是一份請款單，第三篇則是客戶抱怨產品差，因此不願付款的電子郵件。本題問 "Why did Alice Worley write the letter?"，應試者必須找出第一篇信件的「目的」為何。根據第一段中提到的 "... according to the terms of the purchase agreement that you signed, you are still liable for the full amount. Also, because payment was due on July 16, you have incurred a 10% late payment fee." 可知，撰寫該信是為了請客戶付款。

選項 (A) "... ask ... for ... information"「要求更多資訊」，但是這與「付款」無關，故不選。

選項 (B) 中的 "... apologize ... for poor service" 是說要「為服務不周道歉」，這也跟「付款」無關，故不選。

選項 (C) 指「要求客戶付款」，正確無誤。

選項 (D) 指「告知有新的付款方式」，這一點並未在文中提及，故不選。

192. What is NOT indicated in the invoice?

(A) Vendor's phone number

(B) Invoice number

(C) Product description

(D) Client's address

答案 A

中譯 發票內「未」標出什麼項目？

(A) 供應商的電話號碼

(B) 發票號碼

(C) 產品描述

(D) 客戶地址

解析

此題問的是在發票內未包括的資訊，掃瞄一下整張發票之後可以看出，選項 (B) Invoice number、選項 (C) Product description，以及選項 (D) Client's address 都有記載於其中，唯有選項 (A) Vendor's phone number 沒被寫出，故選 (A) 為答案。

193. What reason did Marcie Stephenson NOT give for being dissatisfied with Wholesome Foods?

(A) She was asked to pay an additional fee.

(B) Some products were damaged during shipping.

(C) She received a package of food that had already spoiled.

(D) The shipment arrived nearly two weeks late.

答案 D

下列何者「非」Marcie Stephenson 提到不滿意 Wholesome Foods 的原因？

(A) 她被要求支付額外的款項。

(B) 有些產品在運送過程中受到損壞。

(C) 她收到了已經腐壞掉的食物的包裹。

(D) 貨品幾乎慢了兩週才寄達。

解析

此題問的是 "What reason did Marcie Stephenson NOT give for being dissatisfied with Wholesome Foods?"，應試者必須找出三個 Marcie 對產品感到不滿意的原因，以便排除掉一個選項。根據以下這些內容 "I am especially displeased that you tried to ask me to pay more for them."、"... potentially dangerous packages of spoiled and malodorous food."，以及 "... much of the original packaging was not intact when I received it."，可得出以下配對：

選項 (A)　She was asked to pay an additional fee. = I am especially displeased that you tried to ask me to pay more for them.，有提到，故不選。

選項 (B)　Some products were damaged during shipping. = the original packaging was not intact，有提到，故不選。

選項 (C)　She received a package of food that had already spoiled. = spoiled and malodorous food，也有提到，故不選。

選項 (D)　The shipment arrived nearly two weeks late. 「貨品幾乎慢了兩週才寄達」，這一點非事實，亦非 Marcie Stephenson 不滿的原因，故為正確答案。

194.　What does Marcie Stephenson suggest about the agreement?

　　(A) It is no longer a valid contract.

　　(B) She should not have signed it.

　　(C) It was not signed by both parties.

　　(D) The payment amount should be negotiable.

答案 A

中譯 下列何者為 Marcie Stephenson 對同意書的看法？

(A) 它不再是個具效力的合約。

(B) 她當時不應該簽下它。

(C) 同意書並沒有經過雙方簽署。

(D) 款項金額應該是可以協商的。

本題問 "What does Marcie Stephenson suggest about the agreement?"，則應聚焦於 Marcie 提及關於「合約」的相關資訊以便作答。由第二段第一句 "You referenced the purchase agreement I signed, but because you did not provide products that I could use, I do not believe the agreement is binding." 可知，她認為合約是沒有效力的。

選項 (A)	提到 "... no longer a valid contract.",的確，Marcie 認為合約不再具有效力，故為最佳答案。
選項 (B)	"... should not have signed it." 意指她「當時不該簽同意書」，文章中並未見此表述，故不選。
選項 (C)	"... was not signed by both parties." 說同意書「雙方都沒簽」，但這點從文中無法判斷，故不可選。
選項 (D)	"The payment amount should be negotiable." 「款項金額應該是可以協商的」，這一點文中並未提到，故不選。

195. In the email, the word "malodorous" in paragraph 2, line 5, is closest in meaning to

(A) smelly
(B) spicy
(C) savory
(D) spurious

答案 A

中譯 電子郵件第二段第五行的 "malodorous" 這個字意思最接近

(A) 發臭的
(B) 辣的
(C) 美味的
(D) 偽造的

解析

本題問 "malodorous" 的意思最接近哪個字。"malodorous" 是「有惡臭的」之意，與 smelly（發臭的）的涵義最類似，故選項 (A) 為最佳答案。

我們可以藉由電子郵件中的 "It is likely that the package was not refrigerated during shipment and not treated gently." 這個句子來認識一下用來表達「某事有可能會發生」的句型：

It is likely + that + S + V

請看下列例句：

1. It is likely that the conference will be called off this year.
   今年的會議有可能會被取消。

2. It is very likely that Mr. James will be promoted soon.
   詹姆士先生非常可能快被升官了。

The Percival Seminars

How Will the New Health Insurance Regulations Affect You?

On January 1, a series of new state laws concerning health insurance will come into effect. These regulations will require significant changes in the ways companies and individuals pay for health insurance, and also how healthcare providers receive payments from insurance companies.

The non-profit Percival Center for Public Health has been offering a monthly seminar at the spacious BGLC Community Room outlining these changes and providing experts to answer questions about the new regulations. Due to the overwhelming popularity of these seminars, we have decided to add an additional monthly seminar during each of the coming three months. The times of all seminars will be announced on percivalcenter.com as soon as they are scheduled. The next seminar is scheduled for:

Time: Wednesday, September 28, 3:30–5:15 pm
Place: The Bruce Grobelaar Leisure Center Community Room

Please note:

Due to the strong demand, it is strongly suggested that those interested in attending make a reservation by visiting our website percivalcenter.com. We will make every effort to accommodate walk-in guests, but seating is limited. Those who have not reserved a space may be turned away at the door.

MEMORANDUM

To:	All Human Resources Staff
From:	Desmond Croc, HR Director
Subject:	Health insurance seminar
Date:	September 24

I know that many of you have been fielding questions from our colleagues, who are understandably concerned about how the new health insurance laws will affect them. For those of you who haven't already attended, I strongly recommend making time in your schedule to attend a seminar on the subject offered by the Percival Center for Public Health. The next one is scheduled for just a few days from now, but several additional seminars are planned for the coming months. Check the Percival Center website for times (most have yet to be announced), and also to reserve a seat.

I attended the seminar in August. It was organized by Dr. Janice Ham, one of the authors of the regulations, and I can report that her talk was informative, entertaining, and extraordinarily professional. This is one seminar worth going to. I know that everyone is busy, but the Leisure Center is just a ten-minute taxi ride away, the seminar is free, and the company will reimburse you for transportation to and from the event.

Des

To:	Desmond Croc, HR Director
From:	Jessica Jones
Subject:	Re: Health insurance seminar
Date:	September 26

Hello Des,

I did try to register for the seminar online, but I kept receiving a message indicating that the seminar was full and not accepting registration. Also, other schedules have not been announced yet. In the mean time, I suggest that we invite the event organizer to arrange an on-site seminar specifically for our company. This way all our HR team members can learn about the regulation changes within the company without traveling back and forth to the Leisure Center separately. Do you think this is a workable plan? If you do, I'm willing to contact the event coordinator and check if they are able to manage it.

Please advice and thank you.

Jessica

＊套色字部分請參考「詞彙註解」

Percival 研討會

新的健康保險條例將對您產生什麼影響？

1 月 1 日起，一系列於本州有關健康保險的新法律將會生效。這些條例將會很顯著地改變企業與個人支付健康保險費的方式，同時也會改變醫療提供者自保險公司收取款項的方式。

非營利的 Percival 大眾健康中心一直以來每個月都會在寬敞的 BGLC 社區聯誼廳舉辦一次概述這些改變的說明會，並邀請專家們來回答有關新條例的問題。由於這些說明會大受歡迎，我們決定在接下來三個月裡，每個月加開一場額外的說明會。各場說明會的時間都將於確定之後，在 percivalcenter.com 上發佈。下一場說明會的安排如下：

時間：9 月 28 日星期三，下午 3:30 至 5:15
地點：Bruce Grobelaar 活動中心社區聯誼廳

請注意：

由於參與人數眾多，強烈建議有興趣的參與者先上我們的網站 percivalcenter.com 進行預約。我們會嘗試儘量容納所有無預約的參與者，但是座位有限。沒有預約座位者將可能無法被允許入場。

備 忘 錄

收件人：	所有人力資源部門員工
寄件人：	人力資源主管 Desmond Croc
主　旨：	健康保險說明會
日　期：	9 月 24 日

我知道各位有許多人都接獲了同事們的詢問，他們對於新的健康保險法律會如何影響到他們感到關心是理所當然的。還沒有參加過 Percival 大眾健康中心所舉辦的說明會的人，我強烈建議你們抽空參加。下一次的說明會就在幾天之後，但是還有幾場說明會將會於接下來幾個月舉辦。請上 Percival 中心的網站查看時間（大部分都還沒公告），也請先預約座位。

我參加了 8 月的那場說明會。那是由新條例起草者之一的 Janice Ham 醫生所主辦的，我可以告訴各位她的演講內容非常充實、有趣，而且極度專業。這是一個值得參與的說明會。我知道大家都很忙碌，但是到活動中心搭乘計程車只需要 10 分鐘，說明會是免費的，而公司將會核銷你來回交通費用。

Des

收件人：	人力資源主管 Desmond Croc
寄件人：	Jessica Jones
主　旨：	回覆：健康保險說明會
日　期：	9 月 26 日

嗨，Des：

我數度嘗試在線上報名研討會，但是我不斷收到一個訊息，表示研討會已經額滿，不再接受註冊。另外，其他研討會的時間表也尚未公佈。在此同時，我建議我們邀請活動主辦單位專門為我們公司安排一場說明會。透過這種方式，公司所有的人力資源團隊成員都可以一起瞭解規章制度的改變，而無須個別地前往活動中心聽研討會了。您認為這是一個可行的建議嗎？如果您覺得可以，我願意聯絡活動單位，並詢問他們是否能夠幫我們辦一場說明會。

請指教，謝謝。

Jessica

詞彙註解

regulation [ˌrɛgjəˋleʃən] (n.) 規定、條款

significant [sɪgˋnɪfəkənt] (adj.) 意味深長的、重大的

outline [ˋaʊtˌlaɪn] (v.) 概述、大概描繪出

overwhelming [ˌovɚˋhwɛlmɪŋ] (adj.) 壓倒性的、勢不可擋的

announce [əˋnaʊns] (v.) 宣佈、公告

reservation [ˌrɛzɚˋveʃən] (n.) 預約

field [fild] (v.) 接、回答

informative [ɪnˋfɔrmətɪv] (adj.) 提供大量資訊的

extraordinarily [ɪkˋstrɔrdnˌɛrɪlɪ] (adv.) 格外地

reimburse [ˌriɪmˋbɝs] (v.) 核銷、補償

register [ˋrɛdʒɪstɚ] (v.) 註冊

receive [rɪˋsiv] (v.) 接收

specifically [spɪˋsɪfɪk]ɪ] (adv.) 特定地

separately [ˋsɛpərɪtlɪ] (adv.) 分別地、分開地

workable [ˋwɝkəb]] (adj.) 可行的

coordinator [koˋɔrdnˌetɚ] (n.) 協調者

196. In the announcement, what reason is given for the scheduling of additional seminars?

(A) The overwhelming popularity of the new regulations

(B) The relatively small size of the venue

(C) The demand for information about a series of new laws

(D) The extraordinary professionalism of Dr. Ham

答案 C

中譯 公告中所提到的說明會需要加開場次的理由為何？

(A) 新條例極高的受歡迎程度

(B) 相對而言較小的場地

(C) 對於一系列新法規的資訊之需求

(D) Ham 醫生所具備的超高專業水準

解析

此題問 "In the announcement, what reason is given for the scheduling of additional seminars?"，可見要去找的是「研討會加開場次的原因」。由第二段第二句 "Due to the overwhelming popularity of these seminars, we have decided to add an additional monthly seminar during each of the coming three months." 可知，理由是因為「研討會很熱門，太多人想去參加」。

選項 (A) "... overwhelming popularity ... new regulations" 提到的是「新法規非常熱門」，但這並非吸引人的原因，人們之所以要參加說明會，是因為「想瞭解新法規內容」，而不是因為「喜歡新法規本身」，故不選。

選項 (B) 的 "... relatively small size of the venue" 是說因為「場地太小」的關係，而文中並未提到這一點，只說座位有限但人數過多，故不可選。

選項 (C) 提到 "... demand for information ... of new laws"，的確，人們是因為「想瞭解新法規內容」所以才會去參加說明會，故為最佳答案。

選項 (D) 的 "... extraordinary professionalism of Dr. Ham" 是說因為「Dr. Ham 極度專業」，但這也不是文中的重點，故不選。

PART 3 TEST 2

197. **According to the announcement, what should those interested in attending the seminar do?**

(A) Call the Leisure Center to register

(B) Visit the Percival Center to sign up

(C) Make a reservation on a website

(D) Contact the Human Resources department

答案 **C**

中譯 根據公告，有興趣參與說明會的人應該做什麼？

(A) 打電話到活動中心報名

(B) 前往 Percival 中心報名

(C) 在網站上辦理預約

(D) 聯絡人力資源部門

解析

題目問 "What should those interested in attending the seminar do?"，要找的資訊是「有興趣參加的人必須採取的行動」。由最後一段第一句 "Due to the strong demand, it is strongly suggested that those interested in attending make a reservation by visiting our website percivalcenter.com." 可知，有意者必須在「線上報名」，故 (C) Make a reservation on a website 為最佳答案。其他選項提到的「打電話」、「前去報名」、「跟人資部門聯絡」都不對，故不選。

198. **In the memorandum, the word "fielding" in paragraph 1, line 1, is closest in meaning to**

(A) posing   (C) returning

(B) receiving   (D) forming

答案 **B**

中譯 備忘錄第一段第一行的 "fielding" 這個字意思最接近

(A) 造成   (C) 返回

(B) 接收   (D) 形成

解析

此題問的是 "fielding" 的意思最接近哪個字。"field" 在此文中是動詞，有「接受問題、巧妙回答問題」之意，與 receiving（收到、接收）的涵義最類似，故選項 (B) 為最佳答案。

199. **What is NOT given in the memo as a reason to attend the seminar?**

(A) The information will help HR staff answer their colleagues' questions.

(B) The company will pay the registration fee for the seminar.

(C) The location is convenient for employees of the company.

(D) The quality of the presentations will likely be very high.

答案 B

中譯 下列何者「非」備忘錄中提到必須參加說明會的理由？

(A) 得到的資訊將可以幫助人力資源員工回答他們同事的問題。

(B) 公司會支付說明會的報名費用。

(C) 說明會的地點對於公司員工而言很方便。

(D) 說明會演講的水平極可能相當高。

解析

題目問 "What is NOT given as a reason to attend the seminar?"，必須找出三個有提到的參加研討會之理由，然後排除掉「沒提到」的那一個。根據第一段第一句 "I know that many of you have been fielding questions from our colleagues, who are understandably concerned about how the new health insurance laws will affect them."，以及第二段中提到的 "... I can report that her talk was informative, entertaining, and extraordinarily professional. This is one seminar worth going to ... the Leisure Center is just a ten-minute taxi ride away, the seminar is free ...."，可歸納出以下配對：

選項 (A)　The information will help HR staff answer their colleagues' questions. 有提到，因為 HR Director 會要求大家去聽，就是因為希望大家瞭解了之後，可以回答相關問題。

選項 (C)　The location is convenient = ten-minute taxi ride away，有提到。

選項 (D)　The quality of the presentations will likely be very high. = informative and professional，也有提到。

選項 (B)　The company will pay the registration fee for the seminar. 是說「公司會支付說明會的報名費用」，但是事實上此研討會是免費的 "the seminar is free"，故為正確答案。

200. What does Jessica volunteer to do next?

(A) Get feedback from colleagues

(B) Provide training herself

(C) Call the mayor of the city

(D) Contact Percival Center directly

答案 D

中譯 Jessica 接下來自願做什麼事？

(A) 跟同事收集意見

(B) 由她自己提供訓練

(C) 打電話給市長

(D) 直接與 Percival 中心聯絡

解析

針對題目所問，應鎖定 Jessica 提及「她可以採取的行動」的相關資訊以回答問題。根據第三篇文章內的關鍵句 "Do you think this is a workable plan? If you do, I'm willing to contact the event coordinator and check if they are able to manage it."，Jessica 願意去跟說明會的主辦單位聯絡，而再推回到第二篇文章內容可得知，主辦單位是 Percival Center，故選項 (D) 為正解。

選項 (A) 提及「問同事的意見回饋」，這跟聯繫 Percival Center 毫無干係，故不選。

選項 (B) 說要「自己提供訓練」，Jessica 根本沒有這麼說，明顯錯誤。

選項 (C) 指「打電話給市長」，此敘述也沒有在文中出現，亦為錯誤。

選項 (D) 為 Contact Percival Center directly「直接跟主辦單位、也就是 Percival Center 聯絡」，確實符合文意，故為正解。

📝 重點句型聚焦

我們藉由第二篇備忘錄中的 "This is one seminar worth going to." 這個句子來討論一下使用 worth 的句型：

> **S + be + worth + V-ing**
> **= S + be + worthy + to be + p.p.**
> **= It is worth one's while + to + 原形 V**

因此，原句 This is one seminar worth going to. 也可以改寫成：

This is one seminar worthy to be attended.
= It is worth your while to attend this seminar.

請看下列例句：

1. That new management book is worth reading.
   = That new management book is worthy to be read.
   = It is worth your while to read that new management book.
   那本新的管理書很值得一讀。

2. New York is a city worth visiting.
   = New York is a city worthy to be visited.
   = It is worth your while to visit New York.
   紐約是值得一遊的都市。

Part 4

實用商務字彙補給

（同義字 600 組）

第一類：會議英文

編號	單字		中譯	同義字
1	agenda [əˋdʒɛndə]	n.	議程	schedule; program; plan
2	meeting minutes	n.	會議紀錄	summary; record; notes
3	adjourn [əˋdʒɝn]	v.	結束、延期、休會	discontinue; postpone; suspend
4	chair [tʃɛr]	n.	主席	director; monitor
5	arrange [əˋrendʒ]	v.	安排、計劃	blueprint; construct; establish
6	absent [ˋæbsn̩t]	adj.	未出席的	away; not present
7	participant [pɑrˋtɪsəpənt]	n.	參與者	associate; colleague; contributor
8	unanimous [juˋnænəməs]	adj.	一致同意的	accordant
9	kick off	ph.	開始、啟始	start
10	ground rule	n.	基本規則	basic principle
11	atmosphere [ˋætməsˌfɪr]	n.	氣氛、氛圍	ambience; surroundings; setting
12	refreshment [rɪˋfrɛʃmənt]	n.	茶點、提神便餐	snack; food and drink
13	diplomacy [dɪˋploməsɪ]	n.	交際手段、圓滑	tact; graciousness; tactfulness
14	brainstorm [ˋbrenˌstɔrm]	v.	集思廣益	ponder
15	domination [ˌdɑməˋneʃən]	n.	控制、支配	authority; control; rule
16	circulate [ˋsɝkjəˌlet]	v.	傳遞、周旋、循環	go around; distribute; spread
17	essential [ɪˋsɛnʃəl]	adj.	必要、精華的	necessary; vital; required

編號	單字		中譯	同義字
18	nominate [`nɑmə͵net]	v.	任命、指派	appoint; assign; designate
19	proposal [prə`pozl̩]	n.	建議、提案	suggestion; proposition; plan
20	target [`tɑrgɪt]	n.	目標	object; goal; aim
21	realistic [rɪə`lɪstɪk]	adj.	實際可行的	reasonable; practical; rational
22	efficiency [ɪ`fɪʃənsɪ]	n.	效率、效能	productivity; performance; capability
23	comment [`kɑmɛnt]	n.	註解、評論	remark; note
24	flexibility [͵flɛksə`bɪlətɪ]	n.	彈性、靈活性	compliance; resilience
25	understate [͵ʌndə`stet]	v.	保守地說、少報	downplay; minimize
26	absolutely [`æbsə͵lutlɪ]	adv.	絕對、完全地	completely; entirely
27	reformulate [ri`fɔrmjə͵let]	v.	重新表述	alter; revise
28	motivate [`motə͵vet]	v.	刺激、激發	inspire; provoke; actuate
29	clarify [`klærə͵faɪ]	v.	闡明、澄清	explain; make clear; simplify
30	relevant [`rɛləvənt]	adj.	有關、切題的	applicable; suitable; connected
31	exploit [`ɛksplɔɪt]	n.	功績、成就	achievement; feat; deed
32	elaborate [ɪ`læbərɪt]	adj.	精巧、複雜的	complicated; sophisticated
33	consensus [kən`sɛnsəs]	n.	一致	unity; concord; harmony
34	confirm [kən`fɝm]	v.	確認、證實	prove; verify

編號	單字		中譯	同義字
35	reject [rɪ`dʒɛkt]	v.	拒絕、抵制	exclude; eliminate; decline
36	contribution [ˌkɑntrə`bjuʃən]	n.	貢獻	donation; offering
37	declare [dɪ`klɛr]	v.	宣告、聲明	state; announce; affirm
38	summarize [`sʌməˌraɪz]	v.	概括、總結	outline; abstract; sum up
39	constructive [kən`strʌktɪv]	adj.	有建設性的	productive; practical
40	implement [`ɪmpləmənt]	v.	履行、實施	fulfill; actualize; carry out
41	fruitful [`frutfəl]	adj.	成果豐碩的	successful; profitable
42	pointless [`pɔɪntlɪs]	adj.	無要領的	meaningless; unnecessary
43	productive [prə`dʌktɪv]	adj.	多產的	prolific; fruitful; yielding
44	stimulating [`stɪmjəˌletɪŋ]	adj.	激勵的	inspiring; invigorating
45	manpower [`mænˌpauə]	n.	人力資源	personnel; staff
46	anticipate [æn`tɪsəˌpet]	v.	預期、期望	expect; hope for
47	confront [kən`frʌnt]	v.	面臨、遭遇	face; encounter
48	overcome [ˌovə`kʌm]	v.	戰勝、克服	conquer; overpower; defeat
49	contingency [kən`tɪndʒənsɪ]	n.	偶發事件	uncertainty; likelihood
50	ultimate [`ʌltəmɪt]	adj.	極致、最終的	conclusive; final; terminal; eventual

第二類：社交英文

編號	單字		中譯	同義字
1	**journey** [ˋdʒɝnɪ]	*n.*	行程、旅行	expedition; outing; voyage
2	**manage** [ˋmænɪdʒ]	*v.*	管理、經營	direct; operate; regulate
3	**scorching** [ˋskɔrtʃɪŋ]	*adj.*	極熱的	sweltering; burning; fiery
4	**consultant** [kənˋsʌltənt]	*n.*	諮詢者、顧問	advisor; mentor
5	**specialize** [ˋspɛʃəl͵aɪz]	*v.*	專攻、專門	pursue; train for
6	**freelance** [ˋfriˋlæns]	*v.*	當自由作家	selling work or services by the hour, day, etc.
7	**stressful** [ˋstrɛsfəl]	*adj.*	壓力重的	full of tension
8	**custom** [ˋkʌstəm]	*n.*	習俗、慣例	tradition; manner; habit
9	**creative** [krɪˋetɪv]	*adj.*	有創意的	inventive; innovative; imaginative
10	**spare** [spɛr]	*adj.*	多的、額外的	extra; surplus; remainder
11	**performance** [pɚˋfɔrməns]	*n.*	表現、成果	presentation; show; production
12	**shallow** [ˋʃælo]	*adj.*	淺的、膚淺的	superficial
13	**excursion** [ɪkˋskɝʒən]	*n.*	遠足、旅行	journey; tour; trip
14	**monument** [ˋmɑnjəmənt]	*n.*	遺址、遺跡	memorial
15	**rural** [ˋrʊrəl]	*adj.*	鄉村、田園的	rustic; countrified
16	**cosmopolitan** [͵kɑzməˋpɑlətn̩]	*adj.*	世界、國際的	universal; global; international
17	**dynamic** [daɪˋnæmɪk]	*adj.*	活力、動態的	active; lively; spirited

編號	單字		中譯	同義字
18	marvelous [`mɑrvələs]	adj.	非凡、極棒的	extraordinary; fabulous; surprising
19	picturesque [ˌpɪktʃəˋrɛsk]	adj.	圖畫般的	artistic; colorful
20	diversification [daɪˌvɜsəfəˋkeʃən]	n.	多樣化	assortment; diversity
21	investment [ɪnˋvɛstmənt]	n.	投入、投資	contribution; venture
22	recession [rɪˋsɛʃən]	n.	衰退、退回	downturn; slump
23	benchmark [`bɛntʃˌmɑrk]	n.	基準點、水準	standard; measure; gauge
24	regulate [`rɛgjəˌlet]	v.	管理、控制	administer; supervise
25	outsource [`autˌsɔrs]	v.	服務委外	contract out
26	fluke [fluk]	n.	僥倖	stroke of luck
27	restructure [riˋstrʌktʃə]	v.	改組、調整	to change or restore the structure
28	allergic [əˋlɜdʒɪk]	adj.	過敏的	sensitive
29	invitation [ˌɪnvəˋteʃən]	n.	邀請、引誘	solicitation; enticement
30	confiscate [`kɑnfɪsˌket]	v.	沒收、充公	seize; take
31	decline [dɪˋklaɪn]	v.	下跌、婉拒	weaken; descent; reject
32	delighted [dɪˋlaɪtɪd]	adj.	快樂、高興的	glad; pleased; happy
33	overdressed [ˌovəˋdrɛst]	adj.	過度打扮的	to dress with too much display
34	vegetarian [ˌvɛdʒəˋtɛrɪən]	n.	素食者	a person who doesn't eat meat

編號	單字		中譯	同義字
35	**pleasure** [ˋplɛʒɚ]	*n.*	樂趣、愉快	enjoyment; satisfaction; gladness
36	**appreciate** [əˋpriʃɪˏet]	*v.*	欣賞、感激	value; admire; be grateful for
37	**animation** [ˏænəˋmeʃən]	*n.*	生氣、活潑	vitality; excitement; passion
38	**expression** [ɪkˋsprɛʃən]	*n.*	措詞、表達	verbalization; articulation
39	**gesture** [ˋdʒɛstʃɚ]	*n./v.*	（做）手勢	signal; motion
40	**hierarchy** [ˋhaɪəˏrɑrkɪ]	*n.*	等級制度	scale
41	**hospitality** [ˏhɑspɪˋtælətɪ]	*n.*	好客、招待	generosity; entertainment; reception
42	**punctuality** [ˏpʌŋktʃʊˋælətɪ]	*n.*	守時、規矩	promptness
43	**stereotype** [ˋstɛrɪəˏtaɪp]	*n.*	陳規、刻板	cilché; formula
44	**consider** [kənˋsɪdɚ]	*v.*	考慮、細想	ponder; deliberate; think carefully
45	**interpret** [ɪnˋtɝprɪt]	*v.*	說明、詮釋	explain; analyze
46	**appropriate** [əˋproprɪˏet]	*adj.*	恰當、適當的	suitable; fitting; proper
47	**explicit** [ɪkˋsplɪsɪt]	*adj.*	明確、清楚的	distinct; definite
48	**genuine** [ˋdʒɛnjʊɪn]	*adj.*	真的、非偽的	authentic; true; legitimate
49	**presence** [ˋprɛzn̩s]	*n.*	出席、眼前	attendance; existence; appearance
50	**proximity** [prɑkˋsɪmətɪ]	*n.*	接近、鄰近	closeness; nearness

第三類：談判英文

編號	單字		中譯	同義字
1	conflict ['kɑnflɪkt]	v.	分歧、衝突	disagree; clash
2	expectation [ˌɛkspɛk'teʃən]	n.	預期、期望	anticipation; prospect; expectancy
3	position [pə'zɪʃən]	n.	立場、態度	standing; place
4	priority [praɪ'ɔrətɪ]	n.	優先權	primacy; preference
5	procedure [prə'sidʒə]	n.	步驟、常規	practice; process
6	statement ['stetmənt]	n.	陳述、說明	proclamation; declaration
7	strategy ['strætədʒɪ]	n.	戰略、策略	tactics; planning; manipulation
8	bargain ['bɑrgɪn]	v.	討價還價	haggle; negotiate
9	rehearse [rɪ'hɜs]	v.	排練、演習	practice; drill
10	mutual ['mjutʃuəl]	adj.	相互、彼此的	common; reciprocal
11	commission [kə'mɪʃən]	n.	佣金、委任	cut; fee; delegation; entrusting
12	counterpart ['kaʊntə,pɑrt]	n.	互補、配對人 / 物	complement; equivalent
13	exclusive [ɪk'sklusɪv]	adj.	獨有、排外的	unshared; privileged
14	opponent [ə'ponənt]	n.	對手、反對者	enemy; competitor; rival
15	tactic ['tæktɪk]	n.	策略、手法	plan; scheme; method
16	compromise ['kɑmprə,maɪz]	v.	妥協、讓步	settle; yield
17	dispute [dɪ'spjut]	v.	爭論不休	argue; quarrel

編號	單字		中譯	同義字
18	articulate [ɑr`tɪkjəlɪt]	adj.	口才好的	expressive; enunciated
19	competent [`kɑmpətənt]	adj.	有能力的	capable; qualified
20	persuasive [pɚ`swesɪv]	adj.	有說服力的	convincing
21	preliminary [prɪ`lɪmə͵nɛrɪ]	adj.	初步、開端的	inaugural; beginning
22	rational [`ræʃənl̩]	adj.	理性、明理的	reasonable; logical; level-headed
23	aim [em]	n.	目的、目標	purpose; objective; goal
24	feedback [`fid͵bæk]	n.	意見、反應	evaluation; reaction
25	accordingly [ə`kɔrdɪŋlɪ]	adv.	相應地、於是	correspondingly; consequently; thus
26	argument [`ɑrgjəmənt]	n.	爭吵、論點	quarrel; contention
27	consideration [kənsɪdə`reʃən]	n.	考慮	deliberation
28	paraphrase [`pærə͵frez]	v.	改述、解釋	restate; explain
29	sympathetic [͵sɪmpə`θɛtɪk]	adj.	有同情心的	compassionate
30	scenario [sɪ`nɛrɪ͵o]	n.	情境、局面	outline; scheme; plot
31	alternative [ɔl`tɝnətɪv]	n.	選擇、二擇一	choice; option; substitute
32	authority [ə`θɔrətɪ]	n.	權力、職權	dominion; authorization; control
33	guarantee [͵gærən`ti]	v.	保證、擔保	promise; warrant; assure
34	reiterate [ri`ɪtə͵ret]	v.	重申、反覆講	repeat; review; retell

編號	單字		中譯	同義字
35	**commitment** [kə`mɪtmənt]	*n.*	承諾、保證	promise; engagement
36	**intonation** [ˌɪnto`neʃən]	*n.*	語調、聲調	pitch; tone
37	**mediator** [`midɪˌetə]	*n.*	調停者	go-between; intermediary
38	**reassure** [ˌriə`ʃʊr]	*v.*	使放心、保證	comfort; guarantee
39	**demanding** [dɪ`mændɪŋ]	*adj.*	要求高的	difficult; challenging
40	**potential** [pə`tɛnʃəl]	*adj.*	潛在、可能的	promising; possible; conceivable
41	**progress** [`prɑgrɛs]	*n.*	前進、進展	breakthrough; improvement
42	**accurate** [`ækjərɪt]	*adj.*	準確、精準的	precise; correct
43	**outstanding** [`aʊt`stændɪŋ]	*adj.*	突出、顯著的	prominent; distinguished; famous
44	**valid** [`vælɪd]	*adj.*	有效、合法的	effective; sound; proven
45	**objective** [əb`dʒɛktɪv]	*n.*	目的、目標	motive; target
46	**interrupt** [ˌɪntə`rʌpt]	*v.*	打斷、阻礙	stop; intrude; interfere with
47	**reasonable** [`rizņəbļ]	*adj*	通情達理的、公道的	rational; sensible; fair; just
48	**improvise** [`ɪmprəvaɪz]	*v.*	臨時做、即興表演	make up; invent; performance without preparation
49	**stalemate** [`stelˌmet]	*n.*	僵持狀態、困境	deadlock; impasse
50	**precise** [prɪ`saɪs]	*adj.*	精準、確切的	exact; accurate; correct

第四類：求職・面試英文

編號	單字		中譯	同義字
1	**strengthen** [`strɛŋθən]	v.	增強、加強	reinforce; fortify
2	**interview** [`ɪntə‚vju]	n.	會見、訪談	meeting; conversation
3	**candidate** [`kændədet]	n.	候選人、應徵者	nominee; applicant
4	**application** [‚æplə`keʃən]	n.	申請、應用	putting to use
5	**reference** [`rɛfərəns]	n.	提及、推薦	mention; endorsement; testimonial
6	**curriculum vitae (CV)**	n.	個人簡歷	resume
7	**prospective** [prə`spɛktɪv]	adj.	預期、未來的	expected; eventual; future
8	**executive** [ɪg`zɛkjʊtɪv]	adj.	執行、實施的	directing; managing; administrative
9	**affiliate** [ə`fɪlɪ‚et]	v.	使有關連	associate; unite; connect
10	**division** [də`vɪʒən]	n.	區域、部門	section; segment; department
11	**personnel** [‚pɜsn̩`ɛl]	n.	員工、人事科	staff; manpower; human resources
12	**subsidiary** [səb`sɪdɪ‚ɛrɪ]	n.	子公司	affiliate; division; branch
13	**enterprise** [`ɛntə‚praɪz]	n.	企業、公司	business; venture; company
14	**periodical** [‚pɪrɪ`ɑdɪkl̩]	n.	定期刊物	magazine; journal
15	**talent** [`tælənt]	n.	天資、有才能者	aptitude; capability; genius
16	**poach** [potʃ]	v.	侵佔、偷補	steal; encroach
17	**responsive** [rɪspɑnsɪv]	adj.	反應、應答的	reactive; sharp

編號	單字		中譯	同義字
18	confidence [`kɑnfədəns]	n.	信心、把握	faith; assurance; self-reliance
19	qualification [ˌkwɑləfə`keʃən]	n.	資格、能力	competence; suitability; ability
20	accomplishment [ə`kɑmplɪʃmənt]	n.	成就、實現	fulfillment; realization; acquirement
21	competition [ˌkɑmpə`tɪʃən]	n.	競爭、角逐	contest; tournament; match
22	confirm [kən`fɝm]	v.	確認、證實	certify; verify; establish
23	workplace [`wɝkˌples]	n.	工作場所	a person's place of employment
24	remuneration [rɪˌmjunə`reʃən]	n.	酬金、報償	salary; wage; payment
25	overqualified [`ovɚ`kwɑləˌfaɪd]	adj	條件超過標準的	have more education, training or experience than is required
26	eclectic [ɛk`lɛktɪk]	adj.	折衷的、不拘一派的	selective; mixed; assorted
27	adaptive [ə`dæptɪv]	adj.	適合、適應的	flexible
28	cooperative [ko`ɑpəˌretɪv]	adj.	合作的	supportive; collaborative
29	weakness [`wiknɪs]	n.	弱點、缺點	fragility; fault; imperfection
30	responsibility [rɪˌspɑnsə`bɪlətɪ]	n.	責任、任務	accountability; duty; liability
31	job description	n.	職務說明	an abstract of a job analysis
32	evaluation [ɪˌvæljʊ`eʃən]	n.	評價、估算	assessment; estimate
33	obvious [`ɑbvɪəs]	adj.	明顯、顯著的	apparent; explicit; distinct
34	ethic [`ɛθɪk]	n.	倫理、道德標準	moral principle

編號	單字		中譯	同義字
35	ambiguous [æm`bɪgjʊəs]	adj.	含糊不清的	vague; equivocal
36	acceptable [ək`sɛptəbḷ]	adj.	可以接受的	admissible; worthy
37	outcome [`aʊt͵kʌm]	n.	結果、後果	result; conclusion; consequence
38	personality [͵pɝsṇ`æləti]	n.	人格、性格	individuality; characteristic
39	merit [`mɛrɪt]	n.	長處、優點	virtue; excellence; value
40	attitude [`ætətjud]	n.	態度、看法	manner; position; standpoint
41	legitimate [lɪ`dʒɪtəmɪt]	adj.	合法、正當的	lawful; legal
42	criterion [kraɪ`tɪrɪən]	n.	標準、尺度	measure; standard; yardstick
43	desirable [dɪ`zaɪrəbḷ]	adj.	值得擁有的	advisable; worthwhile
44	retirement [rɪ`taɪrmənt]	n.	退休、退職	removal from service
45	pension [`pɛnʃən]	n.	養老、退休金	annuity; retirement payment
46	discrimination [dɪ͵skrɪmə`neʃən]	n.	歧視、不公平待遇	prejudice; bias; differential treatment
47	persuade [pɚ`swed]	v.	勸服、說服	convince; induce
48	deadline [`dɛd͵laɪn]	n.	最後期限	limit; cut-off date
49	antagonist [æn`tægənɪst]	n.	對手、敵手	opponent; contestant; competitor
50	recruit [rɪ`krut]	v.	招聘、徵募	enlist; draft; enroll

第五類：簡報英文

編號	單字		中譯	同義字
1	anticipate [æn`tɪsə,pet]	v.	預先考慮	expect; foresee
2	represent [,rɛprɪ`zɛnt]	v.	表現、呈現	demonstrate; display
3	agreeable [ə`griəbl]	adj.	欣然贊同的	acceptable; harmonious; compatible
4	complexity [kəm`plɛksətɪ]	n.	複雜性	convolution; complicacy
5	equipment [ɪ`kwɪpmənt]	n.	設備、裝置	apparatus; rig; gear
6	formality [fɔr`mælətɪ]	n.	禮節、正式	etiquette; propriety
7	handout [`hændaʊt]	n.	傳單、印刷品	flyer; a copy of information
8	impact [`ɪmpækt]	n.	影響、作用	influence; effect
9	introduction [,ɪntrə`dʌkʃən]	n.	介紹、引見	initiation; presentation
10	involvement [ɪn`vɑlvmənt]	n.	牽連、關係	engagement; relationship; association
11	structure [`strʌktʃə]	n.	結構、組織	configuration; construction
12	visual aid	n.	視覺輔助工具	materials as films, slides, photographs, etc.
13	adjust [ə`dʒʌst]	v.	調節、校準	modify; adapt
14	engage [ɪn`gedʒ]	v.	使從事、吸引	involve; engross
15	distract [dɪ`strækt]	v.	使分心	divert; draw away
16	convention [kən`vɛnʃən]	n.	會議、集會	meeting; conference; powwow
17	teamwork [`tim`wɝk]	n.	協力、配合	partnership; synergy; union

編號	單字		中譯	同義字
18	analyze [`ænḷ͵aɪz]	v.	分析、解析	diagnose; investigate; scrutinize
19	examine [ɪg`zæmɪn]	v.	檢查、診察	inspect; investigate
20	split [splɪt]	v.	劈開、分擔	separate; divide; partition
21	thought [θɔt]	n.	思維、見解	thinking; consideration; idea
22	brief [brif]	adj.	簡略、簡潔的	concise; short
23	clarify [`klærə͵faɪ]	v.	闡明、澄清	explain; make clear
24	sequence [`sikwəns]	n.	順序、一連串	succession; series; progression
25	repetition [͵rɛpɪ`tɪʃən]	n.	重複、反覆	duplication; recurrence; recitation
26	solution [sə`luʃən]	n.	解答、解決	answer; outcome; explanation
27	brilliant [`brɪljənt]	adj.	傑出、優秀的	intelligent; smart
28	remarkable [rɪ`markəbḷ]	adj.	非凡、卓越的	unusual; noteworthy; exceptional
29	rapport [ræ`por]	n.	和諧一致	agreement; empathy
30	ignore [ɪg`nor]	v.	不理、忽視	disregard; overlook; neglect
31	diplomatic [͵dɪplə`mætɪk]	adj.	得體、圓滑的	tactful; smooth; gracious
32	rhetorical [rɪ`tɔrɪkḷ]	adj.	華麗、誇張的	exaggerated; pretentious
33	diagram [`daɪə͵græm]	n.	圖表、圖示	drawing; chart
34	transparency [træns`pɛrənsɪ]	n.	幻燈片	slide

編號	單字		中譯	同義字
35	**compatible** [kəm`pætəb!]	adj.	相容、兼用的	harmonious; congenial
36	**deterioration** [dɪ͵tɪrɪə`reʃən]	n.	惡化、退化	downfall; decline; lapse
37	**fluctuation** [͵flʌktʃʊ`eʃən]	n.	波動、變動	variation; change
38	**significant** [sɪg`nɪfəkənt]	adj.	有意義的	vital; critical; essential
39	**enormous** [ɪ`nɔrməs]	adj.	巨大、龐大的	immense; giant; vast
40	**superior** [sə`pɪrɪə]	adj.	較高的、上級的	better; higher; greater
41	**exaggerate** [ɪg`zædʒə͵ret]	v.	誇大、誇張	overstate; enlarge; magnify
42	**overstate** [`ovə`stet]	v.	將……講得誇張	amplify; enlarge
43	**utilize** [`jut!͵aɪz]	v.	利用	use; apply; employ
44	**criticism** [`krɪtə͵sɪzəm]	n.	批評、苛求	critique; censure
45	**hedge** [hɛdʒ]	n.	界限、圍牆	boundary; limit; borderline
46	**confidential** [͵kɑnfə`dɛnʃəl]	adj.	祕密、機密的	secret; privatc
47	**audience** [`ɔdɪəns]	n.	聽眾、觀眾	spectators; listeners; viewers
48	**handle** [`hænd!]	v.	處理、操作	manage; operate; manipulate
49	**interaction** [͵ɪntə`rækʃən]	n.	互動	communication; synergy
50	**sufficient** [sə`fɪʃənt]	adj.	足夠、充足的	enough; adequate; ample

第六類：書信英文

編號	單字		中譯	同義字
1	**abbreviation** [əˌbrivɪˋeʃən]	n.	縮寫、節略	brief; abstract; shortening; abridgement
2	**content** [ˋkɑntɛnt]	n.	內容、要旨	text; matter; meaning
3	**letterhead** [ˋlɛtəˌhɛd]	n.	印有信頭之信紙	stationery with a printed heading
4	**jargon** [ˋdʒɑrgən]	n.	行話、廣告詞	vocabulary; lexicon
5	**phrase** [frez]	n.	片語、詞組	word group; expression
6	**punctuation** [ˌpʌŋktʃuˋeʃən]	n.	標點符號	punctuation marks
7	**reinforce** [ˌriɪnˋfɔrs]	v.	強化、增援	intensify; strengthen; fortify
8	**courteous** [ˋkɝtjəs]	adj.	恭謙、有禮的	polite; well-mannered; gracious
9	**specific** [spɪˋsɪfɪk]	adj.	特殊、特定的	definite; particular
10	**chronology** [krəˋnɑlədʒɪ]	n.	年表	sequence of past events
11	**incident** [ˋɪnsədn̩t]	n.	事件、插曲	happening; event; occurrence
12	**pyramid** [ˋpɪrəmɪd]	v.	使步步高升	to increase gradually
13	**activate** [ˋæktəˌvet]	n.	使活化	trigger; motivate; arouse
14	**instructional** [ɪnˋstrʌkʃən!]	n.	教學用的	used for teaching or for imparting information
15	**layout** [ˋleˌaut]	n.	安排、佈局	outline; organization; blueprint
16	**salutation** [ˌsæljəˋteʃən]	n.	招呼、致意	greeting; hello
17	**signature** [ˋsɪgnətʃə]	n.	簽名、畫押	autograph; mark

編號	單字		中譯	同義字
18	consistent [kənˋsɪstənt]	adj.	始終如一的	coherent; consonant; clinging
19	justified [ˋdʒʌstəfaɪd]	adj.	有正當理由的	to show to be just or right
20	correspondence [ˌkɔrəˋspɑndəns]	n.	通信、聯繫	mail; intercourse
21	apologize [əˋpɑləˌdʒaɪz]	v.	道歉	express regret; beg pardon; make apology
22	enclose [ɪnˋkloz]	v.	封入	include; insert
23	hesitate [ˋhɛzəˌtet]	v.	猶豫、躊躇	pause; falter; waver
24	grateful [ˋgretfəl]	adj.	感謝、感激的	thankful; appreciative; obliged
25	confirmation [ˌkɑnfɚˋmeʃən]	n.	確定、批准	affirmation; verification; assent
26	assess [əˋsɛs]	v.	評估	estimate; evaluate; appraise
27	overdue [ˋovɚˋdju]	adj.	過期的	delayed; belated
28	format [ˋfɔrmæt]	n.	編排、格式	form; structure
29	reprimand [ˋrɛprəˌmænd]	v./n.	訓斥	criticize; admonish
30	highlight [ˋhaɪˌlaɪt]	n.	最突出重要部分	feature; focus
31	indentation [ˌɪndɛnˋteʃən]	n.	首行縮排	the setting back from the margin, as the first line of a paragraph
32	investigation [ɪnˌvɛstəˋgeʃən]	n.	研究、調查	analysis; research
33	integrate [ˋɪntəˌgret]	v.	使整合、結合	combine; merge; coordinate
34	alphabetical [ˌælfəˋbɛtɪkl]	adj.	按字母順序的	in the order of the letters of the alphabet

編號	單字		中譯	同義字
35	ample [ˋæmpl]	adj.	大量、充裕的	abundant; sufficient; plenty
36	replacement [rɪˋplesmənt]	n.	取代（者）、更替（者）	substitution; substitute
37	crux [krʌks]	n.	要點、關鍵點	essence; core; purport
38	partial [ˋpɑrʃəl]	adj.	部分、局部的	fractional; fragmentary
39	respectively [rɪˋspɛktɪvlɪ]	adv.	各自、分別地	in precisely the order given
40	ellipsis [ɪˋlɪpsɪs]	n.	省略部分	the omission from a sentence
41	subordinate [səˋbɔrdnɪt]	adj.	次要的	secondary; inferior
42	variation [ˌvɛrɪˋeʃən]	n.	變化、變動	change; modification; fluctuation
43	abuse [əˋbjuz]	v.	濫用	misuse; maltreat
44	retrieve [rɪˋtriv]	v.	取回、收回	get back; recoup; recover
45	tilt [tɪlt]	v.	使傾斜	slope; incline
46	offensive [əˋfɛnsɪv]	adj.	唐突、冒犯的	rude; insulting; insolent
47	distinction [dɪˋstɪŋkʃən]	n.	區別、差別	differentiation; discrimination
48	duplicate [ˋdjupləkɪt]	adj.	完全一樣、複製的	equivalent; counterpart
49	typography [taɪˋpɑgrəfɪ]	n.	排版、印刷	the process of printing with type
50	recipient [rɪˋsɪpɪənt]	n.	接收者、受領者	receiver; beneficiary

第七類：商旅英文

編號	單字		中譯	同義字
1	**diary** [ˋdaɪərɪ]	n.	日記	journal; log
2	**complain** [kəmˋplen]	v.	抱怨、埋怨、不滿	criticize; grumble; whine
3	**workshop** [ˋwɜkˏʃɑp]	n.	實習、專題討論	seminar; session
4	**invitation** [ˏɪnvəˋteʃən]	n.	邀請、引誘	attraction; solicitation; temptation
5	**domestic** [dəˋmɛstɪk]	adj.	家庭、國內的	internal; within the country
6	**upgrade** [ˋʌpˋgred]	v.	升級、提升	advance; enhance
7	**directory** [dəˋrɛktərɪ]	n.	指南、手冊	index; register
8	**cancel** [ˋkænsl̩]	v.	刪去、劃掉、取消	erase; delete; obliterate
9	**attract** [əˋtrækt]	v.	吸引、引起注意	charm; allure; draw; pull
10	**register** [ˋrɛdʒɪstə]	n.	登記、註冊	enroll
11	**warning** [ˋwɔrnɪŋ]	n.	警告、前兆	advice; sign; alarm
12	**shipment** [ˋʃɪpmənt]	n.	裝運、裝載貨物	transport; freight; cargo; load
13	**carrier** [ˋkærɪə]	n.	搬運人、運送人	transporter; conveyor; messenger
14	**signature** [ˋsɪgnətʃə]	n.	簽名、簽署、畫押	antograph; symbol; mark
15	**preparation** [ˏprɛpəˋreʃən]	n.	準備、預備	arrangement; plan
16	**lobby** [ˋlɑbɪ]	n.	大廳、門廊	entrance; foyer; hall
17	**tenant** [ˋtɛnənt]	n.	房客、住戶	dweller; occupant; resident

編號	單字		中譯	同義字
18	foreign [`fɔrɪn]	adj.	外國、陌生的	alien; outlandish
19	reasonable [`rizŋəbl]	adj.	通情達理的	sensible; logical; rational
20	individual [ˌɪndə`vɪdʒuəl]	adj.	個人、個別的	single; separate; personal
21	beverage [`bɛvərɪdʒ]	n.	飲料	drink
22	depart [dɪ`pɑrt]	v.	啟程、出發、離去	leave; exit; set out
23	destination [ˌdɛstə`neʃən]	n.	目的地、終點	end; goal; objective
24	entertainment [ˌɛntə`tenmənt]	n.	娛樂、消遣	amusement; fun; recreation
25	approach [ə`protʃ]	v.	接近、靠近	advance; come near
26	relaxation [ˌrilæks`eʃən]	n.	鬆緩、放鬆	rest; repose; relief
27	leisure [`liʒə]	n.	閒暇、空暇時間	free time; spare time
28	convenience [kən`vinjəns]	n.	方便、合宜	expedience; handiness
29	insurance [ɪn`ʃurəns]	n.	安全保障、保險	surety; security; guaranty
30	eye-catcher [`aɪˌkætʃə]	n.	引人注目的人／物	center of attention
31	word-of-mouth [`wɝdəv`mauθ]	n.	口耳相傳	oral communication
32	survey [sə`ve]	n.	調查	study; review; investigation
33	baggage [`bægɪdʒ]	n.	行李	luggage; suitcases
34	oversea [`ovə`si]	adj.	海外、國外的	foreign

編號	單字		中譯	同義字
35	retirement [rɪ`taɪrmənt]	n.	退休、隱退	retreat; withdrawal
36	participate [pɑr`tɪsə‚pet]	v.	參與、參加	engage; take part; engage in
37	etiquette [`ɛtɪkɛt]	n.	禮節、禮儀	rules of behavior; courtesy
38	episode [`ɛpə‚sod]	n.	一段節目、情節	occurrence; happening; scene
39	loyalty [`lɔɪəltɪ]	n.	忠誠、忠貞	faithfulness; fidelity
40	complimentary [‚kɑmplə`mɛntərɪ]	adj.	恭維、免費的	praiseful; free; gratis
41	footprint [`fʊt‚prɪnt]	n.	腳印、足跡	imprint; track
42	continent [`kɑntənənt]	n.	大陸	mainland
43	worthwhile [`wɝθ`hwaɪl]	adj.	值得的	worthy; valuable; rewarding
44	perfectionism [pɚ`fɛkʃənɪzm̩]	n.	完美主義	flawlessness
45	downshift [`daʊnʃɪft]	n.	減速生活	simple living
46	attire [ə`taɪr]	v.	穿衣、裝飾、打扮	dress; array; adorn
47	postpone [post`pon]	v.	使延期、延緩	delay; defer; suspend
48	deluxe [dɪ`lʌks]	adj.	豪華、高級的	luxurious; superior
49	elegance [`ɛləgəns]	n.	優雅、雅緻	class; delicacy; gracefulness
50	renowned [rɪ`naʊnd]	adj.	出名、聲譽的	famous; notable; well-known

第八類：財經英文

編號	單字		中譯	同義字
1	greenback [ˋgrin͵bæk]	n.	美鈔	a note of US currency
2	dividend [ˋdɪvə͵dɛnd]	n.	股利、股息	bonus; allotment; interest
3	usury [ˋjuʒʊrɪ]	n.	高利貸	an exorbitant rate of interest
4	insolvent [ɪnˋsɑlvənt]	adj.	無力償還的	unable to meet debts
5	deficit [ˋdɛfɪsɪt]	n.	赤字、不足額	shortfall; shortage; deficiency
6	balance [ˋbæləns]	n.	結餘	remainder
7	expense [ɪkˋspɛns]	n.	花費、開支	expenditure; outlay
8	revenue [ˋrɛvə͵nju]	n.	收入、營收	return; earnings; proceeds; income
9	budget [ˋbʌdʒɪt]	n.	預算	financial plan; allocation; apportion
10	collect [kəˋlɛkt]	v.	採集、收集、募集	gather; accumulate; assemble
11	property [ˋprɑpətɪ]	n.	財產、資產	possessions; ownership; resources; estate
12	allocate [ˋælə͵ket]	v.	分派、分配	designate; assign; distribute
13	estimate [ˋɛstə͵met]	v.	估計、估量、評價	judge; calculate; evaluate
14	term [tɝm]	n.	條件	condition
15	audit [ˋɔdɪt]	v.	審核、查帳	examine; review; check
16	resources [rɪˋsorsiz]	n.	資源、財力	property; goods; possessions; wealth
17	withhold [wɪðˋhold]	v.	抑制、阻擋	suppress; refrain; hold back; keep back

編號	單字		中譯	同義字
18	**forecast** [`for͵kæst]	*v.*	預測、預報	predict; foretell; foresee
19	**inspect** [ɪn`spɛkt]	*v.*	檢查、審查	examine; observe; study
20	**license** [`laɪsn̩s]	*n.*	許可、特許	permission; allowance; consent
21	**annually** [`ænjʊəlɪ]	*adv.*	每年一次	yearly; every year
22	**shareholder** [`ʃɛr͵holdə]	*n.*	股東	shareowner
23	**fiscal** [`fɪskl̩]	*adj.*	財政／會計的	financial; monetary; budgetary
24	**refund** [rɪ`fʌnd]	*n.*	償還、退款	compensation; repayment; reimbursement
25	**mortgage** [`mɔrgɪdʒ]	*n.*	抵押	title; deed
26	**outlook** [`aʊt͵lʊk]	*n.*	前景、展望	prospect; expectation; opportunity
27	**statement** [`stetmənt]	*n.*	陳述、財務報告	declaration; balance sheet
28	**inventory** [`ɪnvən͵torɪ]	*n.*	存貨清單、目錄	stock; supply; list
29	**transaction** [træn`zækʃən]	*n.*	交易、辦理	business dealing; operation
30	**provision** [prə`vɪʒən]	*n.*	供給、儲備	supplying; arrangement; preparation
31	**emerging** [ɪ`mɝdʒɪŋ]	*adj.*	新興的	rising; developing
32	**margin** [`mɑrdʒɪn]	*n.*	邊緣、利潤	edge; gross profit
33	**unemployment** [͵ʌnɪm`plɔɪmənt]	*n.*	失業、失業人數	the state of being unemployed
34	**marketplace** [`mɑrkɪt͵ples]	*n.*	商業中心、市場	mart

編號	單字		中譯	同義字
35	belongings [bə`lɔŋɪŋz]	n.	財產	possessions; holdings; personal property
36	assessment [ə`sɛsmənt]	n.	評價、估計	judgment; estimate; evaluation
37	canteen [kæn`tin]	n.	販賣部、福利社	a general store
38	excel [ɪk`sɛl]	v.	勝過、優於他人	surpass; exceed; be better
39	lease [lis]	v.	租賃、租約	rent; hire; charter
40	auction [`ɔkʃən]	n.	拍賣	bargain; sale
41	capital [`kæpətl]	n.	資金	investment funds
42	ledger [`lɛdʒə]	n.	底帳、分戶總帳	account book
43	patent [`pætṇt]	n.	專利（權）	certificate of invention; inventor's exclusive rights
44	ratio [`reʃo]	n.	比例、比率	proportion; rate
45	subcontract [sʌb`kɑntrækt]	v.	轉包	farm out
46	turnover [`tɜn,ovə]	n.	營業額、人員更換率	the rate at which items are sold; the change of employees
47	analysis [ə`næləsɪs]	n.	分析、解析	examination; discussion
48	executive [ɪg`zɛkjʊtɪv]	adj.	經營管理的	directing; managing; administrative
49	proprietary [prə`praɪə,tɛrɪ]	adj.	業主的	belonging or control as property
50	credit [`krɛdɪt]	n.	信用、信賴	trust; faith

第九類：業務‧行銷英文

編號	單字		中譯	同義字
1	relationship [rɪˋleʃənˏʃɪp]	n.	關係、關連	affiliation; association; correlation
2	image [ˋɪmɪdʒ]	n.	圖象、形象	representation; effigy; icon
3	luncheon [ˋlʌntʃən]	n.	午宴、正式午餐	formal lunch
4	optimistic [ˏɑptəˋmɪstɪk]	adj.	樂觀的	promising; positive
5	project [ˋprɑdʒɛkt]	n.	方案、規劃	undertaking; plan; scheme
6	budget [ˋbʌdʒɪt]	n.	預算	allocation; apportion
7	notice [ˋnotɪs]	n.	公告、通知	notification; announcement
8	worksheet [ˋwɝkˏʃit]	n.	工作表單、底稿	plan of a project
9	ambition [æmˋbɪʃən]	n.	抱負、野心	aspiration; initiative
10	promise [ˋprɑmɪs]	n.	承諾、諾言	pledge; vow
11	expertise [ˏɛkspɚˋtiz]	n.	專門知識、技術	skill; knowledge
12	mentor [ˋmɛntɚ]	n.	良師益友	advisor; teacher; coach
13	client [ˋklaɪənt]	n.	顧客、客戶	customer; patron
14	reputation [ˏrɛpjəˋteʃən]	n.	聲望、名聲	repute; distinction; character
15	promotion [prəˋmoʃən]	n.	推廣、升遷	advertising; advancement
16	innovative [ˋɪnoˏvetɪv]	adj.	創新的	original; inventive; creative
17	publicity [pʌbˋlɪsətɪ]	n.	宣傳	advertising; promulgation; propaganda

編號	單字		中譯	同義字
18	media [`midɪə]	n.	媒體	means of communication
19	approachable [ə`protʃəbl]	adj.	易接近的	reachable; attainable; affable
20	campaign [kæm`pen]	n.	活動	activity; drive
21	straightforward [ˌstret`fɔrwəd]	adj.	簡單明瞭的	uncomplicated; unambiguous
22	lucrative [`lukrətɪv]	adj.	有利可圖的	profitable; fruitful
23	uncertainty [ʌn`sɝtn̩tɪ]	n.	不確定、不可靠	doubt; skepticism
24	seasoned [`siznd]	adj.	經過磨練的	experienced; professional; qualified
25	compensation [ˌkɑmpən`seʃən]	n.	補償金、薪資	settlement; remuneration; restitution; payment
26	propaganda [ˌprɑpə`gændə]	n.	宣傳活動	advertising; promotion
27	leading-edge [`lidɪŋ`ɛdʒ]	adj.	高科技的	cutting-edge; state-of-the-art
28	credibility [ˌkrɛdə`bɪlətɪ]	n.	可信度、真實性	believability; trustworthiness; plausibility; probability
29	bustling [`bʌslɪŋ]	adj.	熙來攘往的	busy; exciting; thriving
30	endeavor [ɪn`dɛvə]	n.	盡力、努力	effort; striving
31	privilege [`prɪvl̩ɪdʒ]	n.	特權、殊榮	entitlement; prerogative
32	subsidize [`sʌbsəˌdaɪz]	v.	補助、津貼	finance; sponsor; fund
33	proactive [pro`æktɪv]	adj.	主動積極的	spirited; zealous
34	penetrate [`pɛnəˌtret]	v.	滲透、滲入、打進	drill; go through; insert

編號	單字		中譯	同義字
35	**acquaintance** [əˋkwentəns]	*n.*	熟識、理解	familiarity; awareness; understanding
36	**accountability** [ə͵kauntəˋbɪlətɪ]	*n.*	有責任、有義務	responsibility; liability
37	**segment** [ˋsɛgmənt]	*n.*	部分、區塊	division; section; part
38	**benchmark** [ˋbɛntʃ͵mɑrk]	*n.*	水準點、基準	criterion; standard; measure
39	**regulatory** [ˋrɛgjələ͵torɪ]	*adj.*	管理、控制的	administrative; managing
40	**retain** [rɪˋten]	*v.*	保留、維持	keep; hold; maintain
41	**workaholic** [͵wɜkəˋhɔlɪk]	*n.*	工作狂	workhorse
42	**subordinate** [səˋbɔrdŋɪt]	*adj.*	下級、從屬的	lower; secondary
43	**originality** [ə͵rɪdʒəˋnælətɪ]	*n.*	創造力、獨創性	ingenuity; creativity
44	**counterfeit** [ˋkauntə͵fɪt]	*adj.*	假冒、虛偽的	copied; imitative; fake
45	**miscellaneous** [͵mɪsɪˋlenjəs]	*adj.*	各種、雜項的	varied; diversified; mixed
46	**vanity** [ˋvænətɪ]	*n.*	自負、虛榮心	egotism; pride; conceit; self-worship
47	**earmark** [ˋɪr͵mɑrk]	*n.*	特徵、標記	distinction; attribute; feature; trait; trademark
48	**acquisition** [͵ækwəˋzɪʃən]	*n.*	獲得、取得	procurement; takeover; obtainment
49	**radical** [ˋrædɪkl̩]	*adj.*	根本、基本的	basic; fundamental; revolutionary; progressive
50	**mandatory** [ˋmændə͵torɪ]	*adj.*	命令、強制的	imperative; obligatory; compulsory; required

第十類：工程・研發英文

編號	單字		中譯	同義字
1	production [prə`dʌkʃən]	n.	產量、產品生產	generation; output; yield
2	yield [jild]	v.	出產	output; produce; generate
3	outsource [`aut,sɔrs]	v.	外包、委外服務	to subcontract work to another co.
4	reform [,rɪ`fɔrm]	v.	改革	revolutionize; convert
5	compile [kəm`paɪl]	v.	編輯、收集	gather; collect; assemble
6	progress [`prɑgrɛs]	n.	進步、進行	development; breakthrough
7	spectrum [`spɛktrəm]	n.	光譜、系列、幅度	hue cycle; series; array; range
8	dimension [dɪ`mɛnʃən]	n.	尺寸、範圍	measurement; size; extent
9	tedious [`tidɪəs]	adj.	乏味、厭煩的	dull; dreary; boring; dry
10	lasting [`læstɪŋ]	adj.	永久性的	persistent; permanent
11	burden [`bɝdn̩]	n.	負荷、義務	load; charge; task
12	standardize [`stændəd,aɪz]	v.	標準化、使統一	systematize
13	constitute [`kɑnstə,tjut]	v.	構成、組成、設立	organize; form; establish
14	discard [dɪs`kɑrd]	v.	放棄	desert; abandon
15	diagnose [`daɪəgnoz]	v.	診斷、分析	interpret; analyze; deduce
16	examine [ɪg`zæmɪn]	v.	檢查、細查、分析	inspect; study; scrutinize
17	rectify [`rɛktə,faɪ]	v.	矯正、調節	correct; adjust; remedy; regulate

編號	單字		中譯	同義字
18	supply [sə`plaɪ]	v.	供應、提供	furnish; provide
19	ingredient [ɪn`gridɪənt]	n.	組成部分、要素	part; element
20	criticism [`krɪtə͵sɪzəm]	n.	批評、評論	censure; critique; review; comment
21	prerequisite [͵pri`rɛkwəzɪt]	n.	事物、必要條件	requirement; necessity
22	diversify [daɪ`vɜsə͵faɪ]	v.	使多樣化	vary; variegate
23	integral [`ɪntəgrəl]	adj.	整體所必須的	constituent; constitutional
24	alternative [ɔl`tɜnətɪv]	n.	選擇、替代	choice; option; substitute; replacement
25	systematically [͵sɪstə`mætɪkl̩ɪ]	adv.	有組織系統地	consistently; methodically
26	accomplishment [ə`kɑmplɪʃmənt]	n.	完成、實現	fulfillment; realization; success
27	energize [`ɛnə͵dʒaɪz]	v.	供給能量、激勵	strengthen; stimulate
28	dilute [daɪ`lut]	v.	稀釋、使薄弱	weaken; thin
29	collaboration [kə͵læbə`reʃən]	n.	合作、共謀	cooperation; conjunction; complicity
30	cautiously [`kɔʃəslɪ]	adv.	小心謹慎地	carefully; warily
31	divide [də`vaɪd]	v.	使分開、劃分	separate; portion; partition
32	complexity [kəm`plɛksətɪ]	n.	複雜性	complication; intricacy
33	discrepancy [dɪ`skrɛpənsɪ]	n.	不一致、差異	inconsistency; variance; difference
34	authorize [`ɔθə͵raɪz]	v.	授權給、允許	empower; entitle; approve

編號	單字		中譯	同義字
35	**coordinator** [koˋɔrdṇˌetɚ]	*n.*	協調者	organizer
36	**successive** [səkˋsɛsɪv]	*adj.*	連續、系列的	consecutive; serial; in a row
37	**determination** [dɪˌt3məˋneʃən]	*n.*	決定、判定	decision; solution; adjudication
38	**methodology** [ˌmɛθədˋɑlədʒɪ]	*n.*	方法論、教學法	approach; procedure; way
39	**guarantee** [ˌgærənˋti]	*v.*	保證	promise; pledge; assure
40	**burnout** [ˋb3nˌaut]	*n.*	燃料燒盡	exhaustion
41	**attachment** [əˋtætʃmənt]	*n.*	附屬物、連接物	addition; connection; extension
42	**detect** [dɪˋtɛkt]	*v.*	發現、察覺、查出	discover; uncover; locate; spot
43	**intangible** [ɪnˋtændʒəbl̩]	*adj.*	無形的	untouchable; unsubstantial
44	**substantially** [səbˋstænʃəlɪ]	*adv.*	本質、實質上	essentially; virtually
45	**narrow** [ˋnæro]	*adj.*	狹窄、受限的	slim; slender; close; tight
46	**experiment** [ɪkˋspɛrəmənt]	*v.*	試驗、證明	try; test; prove; verify
47	**volume** [ˋvɑljəm]	*n.*	體積、容積	amount; quantity; capacity
48	**duration** [djuˋreʃən]	*n.*	期間	time; period; term
49	**secure** [sɪˋkjʊr]	*v.*	弄到、獲得	get; obtain; acquire
50	**produce** [prəˋdjus]	*v.*	生產、創造、製作	make; generate; create

第十一類：新聞英文

編號	單字		中譯	同義字
1	**recession** [rɪ`sɛʃən]	*n.*	不景氣、衰退	decline; slump
2	**overpopulated** [ˌovə`pɑpjəˌletɪd]	*adj.*	人口過多的	swarming
3	**devastating** [`dɛvəsˌtetɪŋ]	*adj.*	破壞性極大的	disastrous; destructive
4	**chaotic** [ke`ɑtɪk]	*adj.*	混亂的	confused; disordered; disorganized
5	**aftermath** [`æftəˌmæθ]	*n.*	後果、餘波	consequence; fallout
6	**tremendous** [trɪ`mɛndəs]	*adj.*	頗大的、棒的	enormous; immense
7	**revolutionize** [ˌrɛvə`luʃənˌaɪz]	*v.*	改革、徹底改造	change; reform; transform
8	**paparazzi** [ˌpɑpə`rɑtsi]	*n.*	狗仔隊（義文）	cameraperson; celebrity photographer
9	**manipulate** [mə`nɪpjəˌlet]	*v.*	操作、操控	control; operate; tamper with
10	**overwhelming** [ˌovə`hwɛlmɪŋ]	*adj.*	壓倒性的	staggering; stunning
11	**meltdown** [`mɛltˌdaʊn]	*n.*	崩潰、瓦解	downfall; devastation
12	**slash** [slæʃ]	*v.*	猛砍、大幅刪減	chop; hack; slice
13	**inflation** [ɪn`fleʃən]	*n.*	通貨膨脹	an economic process in which prices increase so that money become less valuable
14	**sustainable** [sə`stenəbl̩]	*adj.*	能承受、維持的	endurable; defensible
15	**devastation** [ˌdɛvəs`teʃən]	*n.*	荒廢、摧殘	havoc; destruction
16	**misconduct** [mɪs`kɑndʌkt]	*n.*	不規矩、不端	delinquency; criminality

編號	單字		中譯	同義字
17	**collapse** [kə`læps]	v.	倒塌、崩潰	fail; crash; topple
18	**transparency** [træns`pɛrənsɪ]	n.	透明度、透明	clarity
19	**liberty** [`lɪbətɪ]	n.	自由、自由權	freedom; independence
20	**demographic** [ˌdimə`græfɪk]	adj.	人口統計學的	relating to population
21	**redeem** [rɪ`dim]	v.	履行、救贖	fulfill; rescue; recover
22	**dominate** [`dɑmə͵net]	v.	支配、統治、控制	control; rule; command
23	**disband** [dɪs`bænd]	v.	解散	separate; scatter; disperse
24	**autonomy** [ɔ`tɑnəmɪ]	n.	自治、自治權	self-government; independence
25	**theory** [`θiərɪ]	n.	理論、推測	hypothesis; proposed explanation
26	**bureaucracy** [bju`rɑkrəsɪ]	n.	官僚政治	officialdom; government
27	**depreciation** [dɪ͵priʃɪ`eʃən]	n.	價值減低、折舊	decrease in value; lowering in estimation
28	**prosper** [`prɑspə]	v.	昌盛、繁榮、興隆	flourish; thrive; advance; succeed
29	**philosophy** [fə`lɑsəfɪ]	n.	哲學、原理	conception; viewpoint; ideology
30	**guideline** [`gaɪd͵laɪn]	n.	指標、指導方向	instruction; guidance
31	**rebel** [rɪ`bɛl]	adj.	反抗的	revolutionary; rebellious
32	**recovery** [rɪ`kʌvərɪ]	n.	復原、恢復	recuperation; restoration
33	**spokesman** [`spoksmən]	n.	發言人、代表者	mouthpiece; representative; delegate; mediator

編號	單字		中譯	同義字
34	merchant [`mɝtʃənt]	_n._	商人、店主	dealer; vendor; shopkeeper
35	counteract [ˌkaʊntəˋækt]	_v._	對抗、起反作用	oppose; act against
36	harmony [`hɑrmənɪ]	_n._	和協、融洽	consistency; concord
37	deadlock [`dɛdˌlɑk]	_n./v._	僵局、使停頓	impasse; stalemate; standstill
38	ceiling [`silɪŋ]	_n._	最高限額	top limit
39	stability [stəˋbɪlətɪ]	_n._	安定、穩定性	steadiness; durability; reliability
40	restore [rɪˋstor]	_v._	恢復、重建、復原	recover; reestablish; rehabilitate
41	exploratory [ɪkˋsplorəˌtorɪ]	_adj._	探險的	explorative
42	isolate [`aɪsḷˌet]	_v._	使隔離、孤立	separate; segregate; disconnect
43	downturn [`daʊntɝn]	_v._	下跌、沉滯	decline; plunge; slump
44	battle [`bætḷ]	_n._	戰鬥、戰役	combat; clash; encounter
45	contemporary [kənˋtɛmpəˌrɛrɪ]	_adj._	現代的	modern; current; concurrent; up-to-date
46	protest [`protɛst]	_n._	抗議、反對	demonstration; objection
47	refugee [ˌrɛfjuˋdʒi]	_n._	流亡者、難民	outcast; exile; fugitive
48	immigrant [`ɪməgrənt]	_n._	移民、僑民	new comer; migrant
49	union [`junjən]	_n._	同盟、工會	confederation; consolidation
50	democracy [dɪˋmɑkrəsɪ]	_n._	民主政治	government by the people; equality; political

第十二類：商用片語・慣用語

編號	片語・慣用語	中譯	解釋
1	**at a loss**	虧本	sell something and lose money
2	**ballpark figure**	約略數字	a rough estimate
3	**banker's hours**	短工時	short work hours
4	**bean counter**	會計師	accountant
5	**bigwig** [ˋbɪgˏwɪg]	大老闆	an important and powerful person
6	**bottom line**	總合	the total
7	**break even**	打平	have expenses equal to profits
8	**buy off**	收買	use a gift or money to divert someone
9	**carry the day**	大獲全勝	win completely
10	**close the books**	關帳	end a bookkeeping period
11	**cold call**	陌生拜訪	a call to potential customer
12	**cook the books**	作假帳	to falsify
13	**cut corners**	節省成本	economize
14	**double check**	再次確認	check something again to confirm
15	**fair play**	公平競爭	equal and right action to someone
16	**gain ground**	有進步、有進展	make progress
17	**work graveyard**	上大夜班	to work the late-night shift

編號	片語 · 慣用語	中譯	解釋
18	hard sell	強迫推銷	sell something by being aggressive
19	in black and white	白紙黑字寫下	in writing
20	in short supply	不足	not enough
21	in the black	（公司）有賺錢	making money
22	in the red	（公司）負債	losing money
23	keep books	記帳	keep records of money gained / spent
24	kickback	回扣	money paid illegally for favorable treatment
25	mean business	正經的	be serious
26	on the block	出清拍賣	for sale
27	hot goods	贓物	stolen goods
28	sell like hotcakes	熱賣、熱銷	sell very quickly
29	sell out	賣完、售罄	sell all of a product
30	take a nosedive	急速下滑	decrease sharply in value
31	put out feelers	試探	test the water
32	call on the carpet	訓斥、責罵	to reprimand a person
33	bring home the bacon	賺錢、維生	to make money
34	deadwood [ˋdɛdˏwʊd]	冗員	a useless employee

編號	片語·慣用語	中譯	解釋
35	don't make waves	勿惹麻煩	don't cause any problems
36	grease monkey	修車工人	mechanic
37	between jobs	待業中	to be unemployed
38	knock off early	早退	to leave work early
39	work like a dog	勤奮工作	to work extremely hard
40	know the ropes	熟知內情	to know the procedures in a company
41	breadwinner [ˈbrɛdˌwɪnə]	經濟支柱	money-maker
42	wear several hats	(公司內) 身兼數職	to have several responsibilities
43	skirt the issue	顧左右而言他	to avoid the topic
44	slack off	偷懶	to decrease one's productivity
45	wheel and deal	談判	to negotiate
46	see eye to eye	同意	to agree
47	call a meeting to order	會議開始	to begin a formal meeting
48	work around the clock	不眠不休地工作	to work all day and night
49	bad-mouth someone	說某人壞話	to say negative things about someone
50	rule of thumb	基本原則	a general guideline

ANSWER SHEET

TEST 1 (PART 7)

No.						No.						No.				
147	Ⓐ	Ⓑ	Ⓒ	Ⓓ		165	Ⓐ	Ⓑ	Ⓒ	Ⓓ		183	Ⓐ	Ⓑ	Ⓒ	Ⓓ
148	Ⓐ	Ⓑ	Ⓒ	Ⓓ		166	Ⓐ	Ⓑ	Ⓒ	Ⓓ		184	Ⓐ	Ⓑ	Ⓒ	Ⓓ
149	Ⓐ	Ⓑ	Ⓒ	Ⓓ		167	Ⓐ	Ⓑ	Ⓒ	Ⓓ		185	Ⓐ	Ⓑ	Ⓒ	Ⓓ
150	Ⓐ	Ⓑ	Ⓒ	Ⓓ		168	Ⓐ	Ⓑ	Ⓒ	Ⓓ		186	Ⓐ	Ⓑ	Ⓒ	Ⓓ
151	Ⓐ	Ⓑ	Ⓒ	Ⓓ		169	Ⓐ	Ⓑ	Ⓒ	Ⓓ		187	Ⓐ	Ⓑ	Ⓒ	Ⓓ
152	Ⓐ	Ⓑ	Ⓒ	Ⓓ		170	Ⓐ	Ⓑ	Ⓒ	Ⓓ		188	Ⓐ	Ⓑ	Ⓒ	Ⓓ
153	Ⓐ	Ⓑ	Ⓒ	Ⓓ		171	Ⓐ	Ⓑ	Ⓒ	Ⓓ		189	Ⓐ	Ⓑ	Ⓒ	Ⓓ
154	Ⓐ	Ⓑ	Ⓒ	Ⓓ		172	Ⓐ	Ⓑ	Ⓒ	Ⓓ		190	Ⓐ	Ⓑ	Ⓒ	Ⓓ
155	Ⓐ	Ⓑ	Ⓒ	Ⓓ		173	Ⓐ	Ⓑ	Ⓒ	Ⓓ		191	Ⓐ	Ⓑ	Ⓒ	Ⓓ
156	Ⓐ	Ⓑ	Ⓒ	Ⓓ		174	Ⓐ	Ⓑ	Ⓒ	Ⓓ		192	Ⓐ	Ⓑ	Ⓒ	Ⓓ
157	Ⓐ	Ⓑ	Ⓒ	Ⓓ		175	Ⓐ	Ⓑ	Ⓒ	Ⓓ		193	Ⓐ	Ⓑ	Ⓒ	Ⓓ
158	Ⓐ	Ⓑ	Ⓒ	Ⓓ		176	Ⓐ	Ⓑ	Ⓒ	Ⓓ		194	Ⓐ	Ⓑ	Ⓒ	Ⓓ
159	Ⓐ	Ⓑ	Ⓒ	Ⓓ		177	Ⓐ	Ⓑ	Ⓒ	Ⓓ		195	Ⓐ	Ⓑ	Ⓒ	Ⓓ
160	Ⓐ	Ⓑ	Ⓒ	Ⓓ		178	Ⓐ	Ⓑ	Ⓒ	Ⓓ		196	Ⓐ	Ⓑ	Ⓒ	Ⓓ
161	Ⓐ	Ⓑ	Ⓒ	Ⓓ		179	Ⓐ	Ⓑ	Ⓒ	Ⓓ		197	Ⓐ	Ⓑ	Ⓒ	Ⓓ
162	Ⓐ	Ⓑ	Ⓒ	Ⓓ		180	Ⓐ	Ⓑ	Ⓒ	Ⓓ		198	Ⓐ	Ⓑ	Ⓒ	Ⓓ
163	Ⓐ	Ⓑ	Ⓒ	Ⓓ		181	Ⓐ	Ⓑ	Ⓒ	Ⓓ		199	Ⓐ	Ⓑ	Ⓒ	Ⓓ
164	Ⓐ	Ⓑ	Ⓒ	Ⓓ		182	Ⓐ	Ⓑ	Ⓒ	Ⓓ		200	Ⓐ	Ⓑ	Ⓒ	Ⓓ

TEST 2 (PART 7)

No.						No.						No.				
147	Ⓐ	Ⓑ	Ⓒ	Ⓓ		165	Ⓐ	Ⓑ	Ⓒ	Ⓓ		183	Ⓐ	Ⓑ	Ⓒ	Ⓓ
148	Ⓐ	Ⓑ	Ⓒ	Ⓓ		166	Ⓐ	Ⓑ	Ⓒ	Ⓓ		184	Ⓐ	Ⓑ	Ⓒ	Ⓓ
149	Ⓐ	Ⓑ	Ⓒ	Ⓓ		167	Ⓐ	Ⓑ	Ⓒ	Ⓓ		185	Ⓐ	Ⓑ	Ⓒ	Ⓓ
150	Ⓐ	Ⓑ	Ⓒ	Ⓓ		168	Ⓐ	Ⓑ	Ⓒ	Ⓓ		186	Ⓐ	Ⓑ	Ⓒ	Ⓓ
151	Ⓐ	Ⓑ	Ⓒ	Ⓓ		169	Ⓐ	Ⓑ	Ⓒ	Ⓓ		187	Ⓐ	Ⓑ	Ⓒ	Ⓓ
152	Ⓐ	Ⓑ	Ⓒ	Ⓓ		170	Ⓐ	Ⓑ	Ⓒ	Ⓓ		188	Ⓐ	Ⓑ	Ⓒ	Ⓓ
153	Ⓐ	Ⓑ	Ⓒ	Ⓓ		171	Ⓐ	Ⓑ	Ⓒ	Ⓓ		189	Ⓐ	Ⓑ	Ⓒ	Ⓓ
154	Ⓐ	Ⓑ	Ⓒ	Ⓓ		172	Ⓐ	Ⓑ	Ⓒ	Ⓓ		190	Ⓐ	Ⓑ	Ⓒ	Ⓓ
155	Ⓐ	Ⓑ	Ⓒ	Ⓓ		173	Ⓐ	Ⓑ	Ⓒ	Ⓓ		191	Ⓐ	Ⓑ	Ⓒ	Ⓓ
156	Ⓐ	Ⓑ	Ⓒ	Ⓓ		174	Ⓐ	Ⓑ	Ⓒ	Ⓓ		192	Ⓐ	Ⓑ	Ⓒ	Ⓓ
157	Ⓐ	Ⓑ	Ⓒ	Ⓓ		175	Ⓐ	Ⓑ	Ⓒ	Ⓓ		193	Ⓐ	Ⓑ	Ⓒ	Ⓓ
158	Ⓐ	Ⓑ	Ⓒ	Ⓓ		176	Ⓐ	Ⓑ	Ⓒ	Ⓓ		194	Ⓐ	Ⓑ	Ⓒ	Ⓓ
159	Ⓐ	Ⓑ	Ⓒ	Ⓓ		177	Ⓐ	Ⓑ	Ⓒ	Ⓓ		195	Ⓐ	Ⓑ	Ⓒ	Ⓓ
160	Ⓐ	Ⓑ	Ⓒ	Ⓓ		178	Ⓐ	Ⓑ	Ⓒ	Ⓓ		196	Ⓐ	Ⓑ	Ⓒ	Ⓓ
161	Ⓐ	Ⓑ	Ⓒ	Ⓓ		179	Ⓐ	Ⓑ	Ⓒ	Ⓓ		197	Ⓐ	Ⓑ	Ⓒ	Ⓓ
162	Ⓐ	Ⓑ	Ⓒ	Ⓓ		180	Ⓐ	Ⓑ	Ⓒ	Ⓓ		198	Ⓐ	Ⓑ	Ⓒ	Ⓓ
163	Ⓐ	Ⓑ	Ⓒ	Ⓓ		181	Ⓐ	Ⓑ	Ⓒ	Ⓓ		199	Ⓐ	Ⓑ	Ⓒ	Ⓓ
164	Ⓐ	Ⓑ	Ⓒ	Ⓓ		182	Ⓐ	Ⓑ	Ⓒ	Ⓓ		200	Ⓐ	Ⓑ	Ⓒ	Ⓓ

NOTES

國家圖書館出版品預行編目資料

新多益大師指引：閱讀滿分關鍵 / 文喬, David Katz 作. --
二版. -- 臺北市：貝塔，2018.06
面；　公分
ISBN 978-986-94176-9-3（平裝）
1. 多益測驗

805.1895   107006866

新多益大師指引：閱讀滿分關鍵

作　　者 / 文喬、David Katz
執行編輯 / 游玉旻

出　　版 / 貝塔出版有限公司
地　　址 / 100 台北市館前路 12 號 11 樓
電　　話 / (02) 2314-2525
傳　　真 / (02) 2312-3535
客服專線 / (02) 2314-3535
客服信箱 / btservice@betamedia.com.tw
郵撥帳號 / 19493777
郵撥戶名 / 貝塔出版有限公司

總 經 銷 / 時報文化出版企業股份有限公司
地　　址 / 桃園市龜山區萬壽路二段 351 號
電　　話 / (02) 2306-6842

出版日期 / 2018 年 6 月二版一刷
定　　價 / 420 元
I S B N / 978-986-94176-9-3

貝塔網址：www.betamedia.com.tw

喚醒你的英文語感！

對折後釘好，直接寄回即可！

100 台北市中正區館前路12號11樓

 貝塔語言出版 收
Beta Multimedia Publishing

寄件者住址 ☐ ☐ ☐

貝塔語言出版
Beta Multimedia Publishing

讀者服務專線（02）2314-3535　讀者服務傳真（02）2312-3535
客戶服務信箱　btservice@betamedia.com.tw

www.betamedia.com.tw

謝謝您購買本書！！

貝塔語言擁有最優良之英文學習書籍，為提供您最佳的英語學習資訊，您可填妥此表後寄回（免貼郵票）將可不定期收到本公司最新發行書訊及活動訊息！

姓名：＿＿＿＿＿＿＿＿＿＿　性別：□男 □女　生日：＿＿＿年＿＿月＿＿日

電話：(公)＿＿＿＿＿＿＿(宅)＿＿＿＿＿＿＿(手機)＿＿＿＿＿＿＿

電子信箱：＿＿＿＿＿＿＿＿＿＿＿＿＿＿＿＿＿

學歷：□高中職含以下　□專科　□大學　□研究所含以上

職業：□金融　□服務　□傳播　□製造　□資訊　□軍公教　□出版
　　　□自由　□教育　□學生　□其他

職級：□企業負責人　□高階主管　□中階主管　□職員　□專業人士

1.您購買的書籍是？＿＿＿＿＿＿＿＿＿＿＿＿＿

2.您從何處得知本產品？(可複選)
　　　□書店 □網路 □書展 □校園活動 □廣告信函 □他人推薦 □新聞報導 □其他

3.您覺得本產品價格：
　　　□偏高 □合理 □偏低

4.請問目前您每週花了多少時間學英語？
　　　□ 不到十分鐘 □ 十分鐘以上，但不到半小時 □ 半小時以上，但不到一小時
　　　□ 一小時以上，但不到兩小時 □ 兩個小時以上 □ 不一定

5.通常在選擇語言學習書時，哪些因素是您會考慮的？
　　　□ 封面 □ 內容、實用性 □ 品牌 □ 媒體、朋友推薦 □ 價格□ 其他＿＿＿＿

6.市面上您最需要的語言書種類為？
　　　□ 聽力 □ 閱讀 □ 文法 □ 口說 □ 寫作 □ 其他＿＿＿＿＿

7.通常您會透過何種方式選購語言學習書籍？
　　　□ 書店門市 □ 網路書店 □ 郵購 □ 直接找出版社 □ 學校或公司團購
　　　□ 其他＿＿＿＿＿

8.給我們的建議：＿＿＿＿＿＿＿＿＿＿＿＿＿＿＿
＿＿＿＿＿＿＿＿＿＿＿＿＿＿＿＿＿＿＿＿＿

喚醒你的英文語感！

Get a Feel for English !